JOURNEY OF COURAGE

The Three Cord Series

Book Two

JOURNEY OF COURAGE

This novel transcends genres.
It's a historical family saga.
It's a fast moving adventure.
It's a love story, not fluffy or erotic.
It's a story of life and death, that
takes place in a harsh environment.

A Novel By
Shirley Downing

To order additional copies of this book, contact:
Xlibris Corporation
1-888-795-4274
www.Xlibris.com
Orders@Xlibris.com
46132

This book is dedicated to my three grandsons

Nicholas,
Alexander, and
Jacob

A Fictionalized family saga

Journey of Courage is a companion novel to:
Oceans of Change.
It's based on true-life experiences that have been fictionalized.
My novel does have elements of autobiography.
Whatever the proportion of fact or fiction, it's always the truth.

'To forget ones ancestors
is to be a tree
without roots.'

A Chinese Proverb

'How will our children know who they are,
If they don't know where they come from?'

Grapes of Wrath

BOOK TWO

Journey of Courage

The family saga continues with Hope and Abraham. They move this ongoing adventure to Northern Rhodesia. As part of the spearhead into this country, they face many challenges including the uprising of the Mau Mau. The story continues with their daughter Colleen, her life brings us into the present. This saga is packed with social and moral energy. As in the Russian and Scottish beginning of this family saga, the three cords are woven around these strong characters.

CHAPTER 1

Scotland—1986

Twenty four year old Maureen was sitting at her mother's bedside. She had pulled the drab green hospital curtains wide open so the sun could shine in. Her mother-hated windows covered. Two months ago, her mother had brain surgery to remove a tumor, and never regained consciousness.

In the months since the surgery her hair had grown back, and although Colleen was only forty-five, her red curls had been replaced by silver ones. The doctors could not say why Colleen remained in this comatose state. The surgery was successful, and tests show there was no re-growth.

Maureen shifted her body to accommodate her twins. They were active this morning; her belly was constantly changing shape as they kicked, searching for more space.

Dr. Ferguson smiled as he entered the room. "Maureen, I'm glad you are still here, I wanted to talk to you about your mother. Don't look so alarmed nothing has changed. In fact, that's the problem—nothing is changing. We are baffled as to why she remains in this state. Medically there is no reason for it."

"Is there anything we, I, can do to . . . to . . . bring her out of this sleep?"

"Not really, as you can see she does not even need life support. She could wake tomorrow, next week, or even next year. It's almost as though she is hiding in her mind. She will wake when she is ready. We have done all we can, now it is a waiting game."

Maureen stood to ease her back pain. "What do you suggest?" Her voice broke as she looked at Dr. Ferguson.

"We need to move her to a nursing home. They will take care of her daily needs, but I will still be monitoring her progress. There is another matter, Maureen; does your mother have a living will?"

"I don't know, she never spoke of one. She is too young . . . she never . . . wait, I could care for her!"

"Maureen, in time maybe you could care for her, but not now. Your twins are due next month; you will have your hands full. The nursing home is best for now. I suggest that you and your brother go through her papers and see if she has a living will."

After the doctor had left, Maureen sat staring out the window. She was scared and felt so alone. Would her mother wake in time for the birth of her children? They had spoken of it often and made so many plans together. The nursery was not finished, the blankets they were knitting were only half done. Her husband, Adam, would be flying in for the event, but she wanted her mother.

The view from the window was breathtaking. The Scottish hillside was slowly being covered in mist, and she heard bagpipes in the distance. "Come on Mom, wake up."

That evening Maureen called her brother Jacob. He was five years her junior, and studying at the Scottish University. His hero's were William Wallace and Robert the Bruce. Jacob had thrown himself into the research of clans and castles. Since his great grandmother had come from Scotland, it made the history even more interesting.

"Jacob, come spend the weekend with me at Mom's house. I have to go through some of her papers looking for a living will, and would rather not do it by myself. I promise to make your favorite American meal, and since it is supposed to snow, we could spread out by the fireplace.

"Sounds good to me Reeny." He had always shortened her name to Reeny.

When Jacob arrived Friday evening, they caught up on each other's news. He kidded Maureen about her expanding waistline, and she kidded him about his expanding girlfriend collection.

"So, Reeny, how is Mom? On the way here I stopped at the hospital, she looks the same. But, if you are looking for a living will . . . ?"

"Dr. Ferguson said it was just a matter of precaution. Since there is nothing medically wrong, Mom needed a different type of care, a nursing home. Since the twins are due in a few weeks, he did not think I could manage it."

Jacob sniffed the air, "Hamburgers and French fries, you know Reeny, I believe what I miss the most from America is the food. That reminds me, when is Adam flying in from America for the birth?"

"He's due in two weeks, but he won't be flying in from America. His last business trip was to France, so he will have a short flight."

The first few boxes they went through on Saturday morning had normal tax information, banking documents, and the legal papers on the three homes Colleen owned, this one in Scotland, and two in South Africa. The one in Blouberg, just outside of Cape Town, was an exact replica of the Scottish home. The second house in SA was just outside of Johannesburg; this one was called the 'Haven'.

Among these legal papers was Colleen's will. She had left Jacob the property in Scotland, Maureen inherited the home in Cape Town, and someone named Mike was to inherit the Johannesburg house.

"Who is Mike?" They voiced together.

"The only Mike I know," said Jacob, "Is our uncle in SA, but why would Mom leave him something and not her other siblings?"

Jacob opened another box, while Maureen made coffee. Returning to the fireplace with two steaming mugs, she saw a strange look on his face. "Reeny, look at all these notebooks. They are numbered one through thirty. You know how Mom always told us about the Russian and Scottish sides of our family, well it looks as though she wrote everything down."

Maureen picked up one of the books. "Do you think we could read them?"

"Sure, it's not like it was a personal diary. This is a record of family history, our history, Mom's history."

Picking up the book marked one, Jacob added, "Looks as though these ten books are about the Russian side, starting with a boy named Nicholas. The books marked eleven through twenty, is the Scottish record. Look Reeny, a Maureen, I bet that is who you are named after."

Maureen picked up the remaining books—the last few were blank. "These must be about Mom and her life. Oh! This feels so weird. It's like going back in time and getting a look at her as a little girl, and a young woman. I know Mom loves us, she has woven her life around us, but don't you sometimes feel that she is in a dream world?"

Jacob nodded and said, "Yeah, and then there is that strange thing, she does not like to be touched. I've seen her recoil, as though it hurts."

Maureen's voice was so soft; Jacob had to lean in to hear her. "Jacob, I think someone, or something hurt her. The doctor said it is as though she is hiding and that's why she won't wake up."

As Jacob stoked the fire he said, "Then Reeny, I think for sure we must read these notebooks. They may hold the answer, and if we know the answer we could say or do the right thing to bring her out of that deep sleep."

"You may be right Jacob, but let's get the setting in correct order and read the Russian and Scottish side first." This took them the rest of the day. They were amazed at the history of their ancestors and vowed to keep the record alive for future generations.

In the morning they rushed though breakfast, and brought in enough wood for the day. "Jacob, let's visit Mom before we start reading, I have this overwhelming need to see her." Colleen's two children stood on either side of her bed; Maureen was brushing her hair. "She looks so peaceful Jacob, what are we going to discover about our mother? What has hurt her so badly that she feels happier or maybe safer remaining sleeping?"

They took turns reading the last few journals, then sat in silence looking at one another in shock and disbelief. "Well! That answers a lot of questions to say the least!" said Jacob. "Reeny, stop crying, you are working yourself up into a state. Come, let's go for a walk."

Although the sun was shining it was cold and windy. Maureen pulled her scarf over the bottom half of her face and her knitted hat over her ears. Her coat flapped around her legs, but she pushed forward, almost angrily. After a brisk walk they headed home, but then climbed the hill behind their house. Maureen sank to her knees next to the three graves, which up till now had meant nothing to her, but her mother had a habit of sitting there every morning. She started crying again. "Sorry Jacob, it must be the baby hormone thing. I never realized just how close Mom and Shawn were; he was like a second father to her. They went thought so much together, so much pain, I can see why she loves it in the quiet recess of her mind.

Jacob lowered himself next to Maureen. "Reeny, our father . . . !"

"No, Jacob . . . no, don't even go there, it's too hard to accept. I'm cold; let's go back to the house." Jacob had to help her up, and they fell back into the snow. They laughed as they struggled to get back on their feet.

As they hung up their coats the phone rang. It was an overseas call. Adam was arriving tonight, could they come to the airport. Maureen breathed a sigh of relief; the last few hours she'd been having suspicious twinges. Her babies were on their way.

"Shawn and Laura, are you sure, Maureen?" Adam was a little disappointed that after their birth she'd wanted to change the names they had chosen for the twins.

"Please Adam, they were born in Scotland, we have a Scottish background, I always want them to remember. If my mother does not recover, I plan on finishing the writings of her journal. The story needs to continue. Now at this time, it just seems right to give them these names. Someday you should read the story of Shawn and Laura that are buried on the hill behind this house"

"You know I cannot say no to anything you want, Maureen. It's fine with me. Just remember, they are part American, they need to know that too. Promise that I get to name the next two."

"Sure, if they're born in America!" She grinned.

"Where else would they be born?" Adam looked puzzled.

"Who knows, maybe here, maybe Russia, maybe even Africa? Remember, I am to inherit a beautiful piece of property in Africa and Jacob wants to do research in Russia."

Adam sighed. His wife was so attached to her mother and brother—this was going to be a problem. For now, while his work took him traveling around the world, he would let it go. But as soon as he was based back in America, this situation would have to change.

On the way home from the hospital, Maureen insisted they stop to see her mother in the nursing home, "Adam, help me sit her up." Maureen propped pillows around Colleen, then nestled a baby in each of her arms. "Mom, this is Laura and Shawn, my twins . . . your grandchildren."

"Maureen, don't, you know she's . . ."

"Stop," said Maureen. "She has to wake up. I'm not ready to lose my mother and she has to know these babies." Shawn wiggled a little, as Maureen reached over to make sure he was safe, she noticed Colleen move her fingers so he wouldn't roll. "Look at that Adam, look, she's holding the babies!"

Every day Maureen would visit her mother. The nurse would help her position Colleen into a sitting position. Then Maureen would put the babies in Colleen's arms, and sitting back she'd start talking about anything and everything. She kept an eye on Colleen's hands and arms; they were now holding the babies. About two weeks after Maureen started doing this, Shawn was really fussy, she took him out of Colleen's arms; maybe a little nursing was what he wanted. Settling into a chair she started nursing her son. Maureen looked up to check on her daughter and got the surprise of her life. Her mother's eyes were open; she was watching her nurse Shawn. Maureen stared for a few minutes, getting up slowly so as not to startle her mother, she sat on the edge of the bed. "Mom?" Colleen smiled at Maureen, and then looked down at the baby in her arms. "Oh Mom . . . you're back!" Maureen's eyes brimmed with unshed tears. She leaned over and while kissing her mother's cheek, pushed the button for a nurse.

Colleen was transferred back to the hospital. The doctors needed to check on her recovery. The main problem was Colleen had forgotten everything—her whole life. However, the doctors said that with help and reminders her memory would come back slowly. Her speech was also a little halted, but in time that would even out. In addition, Colleen had trouble with one of her legs, but with therapy this would improve, maybe not completely, but using a cane, she'd be walking again.

For the next two weeks, Colleen made rapid improvement. Maureen would take her first for walks in a wheelchair, then driving across the countryside that her mother loved so much. At last Colleen was able to leave the hospital.

Her bags packed, ready to go home, Colleen held back. "Maureen, I'm afraid. You say you're my daughter, and these are my grandchildren. That I also have a son here in Scotland, and a home I was left by someone in Africa. I don't remember any of it. What if I never remember?"

"You will Mom, because Jacob and I are going to help you remember. First, let's go home, that may even trigger some memories. Jacob is due tomorrow for the long weekend. Between us we're going to re-cap your whole life and even your ancestry if you like."

Colleen was very quiet during the ride home, but Maureen chatted as they drove; pointing out stores they loved to visit, hills they had climbed, and even their favorite lake where they would picnic. After Maureen ushered Colleen into the house, and carried in the babies and luggage, she said. "Mom, I'm going to put the babies down for their nap, and then I'll make us some tea. Will you put the kettle on?"

When Maureen entered the kitchen, she saw her mother moving the canisters around, the way they used to be. Good sign she thought, at least ingrained habits were still there. For now tea was forgotten as Colleen walked through the house asking questions. The mantle above the fireplace was full of family pictures. Colleen picked up one with her, Maureen and Jacob.

"So this is my son, Jacob. Where is my husband?"

"In America." Maureen had decided to answer truthfully any questions her mother asked even if painful. "You are divorced, but have remained friends."

Colleen looked at her daughter with raised eyebrows. "And where is your husband?"

"His business takes him traveling around the world, but he flies in every now and then. He left right before you woke, so he won't be back for a few months."

"Is Jacob married?"

Maureen laughed, "No, but he's having fun dating these Scottish lassies—nothing serious yet." Picking up another picture, Colleen raised her eyebrows again. "Your mother and father, they live in South Africa, and this is a picture of your three brothers and sister." Maureen watched her mother carefully to see if her expression changed when looking at Mike, but it did not. One by one they went through the pictures, Maureen explaining and Colleen just nodding.

While Maureen saw to the babies after their nap, Colleen wandered through the garden and up the hill behind the house. When she returned, she asked Maureen, "There are three graves up on the hill, a mother Laura, a baby with my name Colleen, and a father Shawn. The mother and baby died the same time, but the father many years later. What can you tell me about them? Did you name your twins after them?"

"Mom, let's take the babies for a walk and I'll tell you about them." As they walked Maureen condensed the story for her mother. "Laura and the baby Colleen were killed in a house fire, while Shawn was out in the fields. He buried them on that hill and rebuilt the house, this one that we're living in. Not being able to get over his loss, he moved to Africa. He made a fortune there, built a replica of this Scottish home in Blouberg, Cape Town. He met your mom and dad when you were very young, and because your name was the same as his daughter, you and he had a special bond. When he died he left you his two homes, and a fair amount of money. You brought his ashes back here to bury next to his wife and baby."

"How sad," said Colleen, after a pause, "Are you saying I lived in Africa?"

"Oh yes, not only were you born there, as were your parents, but you had a very interesting life."

Jacob arrived early the next morning. Colleen was sitting on the hill next to the graves trying to remember. Jacob and Maureen watched through the kitchen window for a while. As Jacob opened the kitchen door he looked back at his sister. "What do I say to her?"

"Just be yourself, talk as though she does remember you." Maureen smiled "You should be glad she doesn't remember all the mischief you got into." Jacob sighed as he climbed the hill, he was nervous. His mother stood up and slowly walked towards him. They stood looking at one another for a while, then habit took over and Jacob grabbed her in a bear hug.

"Welcome back Mom, you look great, even with white hair, and a cane." Colleen smiled up at him and grabbed his earlobe.

"Watch it my boy, this cane can be used for more than walking."

Jacob grew serious, "Mom, do you know what you just did? You grabbed my earlobe you always did that. Are you remembering?"

"No, I'm doing things out of habit. Dr. Ferguson says that's a good sign. Come, sit with me awhile Jacob, and help me catch up on what you are doing."

While Jacob and Colleen talked, Maureen took care of the babies and some household chores, knowing they would be busy with the journals later.

During brunch Colleen asked, "So, how are you going to help me re-cap my memory?"

Maureen grinned at her mother, "Easy, you wrote very detailed journals, not only about your life . . . . but . . . even your ancestors. From the early 1800's when they arrived from Russia and Scotland."

"I did!" Colleen exclaimed.

"Yes, you traced the family history in great detail. The question is, do you want to hear the story of your family from the 1800's to now, or your life first, and work backwards."

Colleen thought awhile. "I need to know who I am, who my parents are and what brought me to this point of my life. Once comfortable with that we can go back in history, if I haven't remembered."

Jacob went into the storage room and brought out the journals. He handed book number twenty-one to Maureen. It was the one beginning with Colleen's parents meeting.

"This is the setting Mom, the Russian, Nicholas had a grandson named Abraham, Maureen the Scot, had a granddaughter name Hope. Abraham and Hope married, these are your parents."

As Colleen settled into the couch with a cup of tea she nodded and said, "With you so far."

"You wrote very detailed accounts—it's like reading a novel, and you are the author."

Maureen opened the journal and started to read . . .

CHAPTER 2

South Africa—1939

Abraham was early enough this Saturday morning that he managed to get a parking spot opposite the store window she would be arranging. He loved to watch this woman work. For one thing, she wore trousers when working; he had never seen a woman in trousers before. Abraham understood that she needed to wear them; she climbed ladders, bent over and worked in tight corners. The thing that first caught his eye about two months ago was that she had flaming red, curly hair; cut to shoulder length which she wore loose, so it was like a halo around her head. She wore make up, her lips were as red as her hair. This woman was different from any woman he knew, with their sensible colored clothing, long hair drawn back and no make up. Hope, he'd enquired about her name; even that was different, it was like a rainbow on a dreary day. There she was walking up the street. Today he was going to speak to her, he had plucked up enough courage and was going to introduce himself and ask her out.

Hope had gotten a ride into town today. She was excited about her idea for the store window, each Saturday morning she came in early to change it, something new and enticing for the weekend shoppers. She looked forward to seeing her shy admirer. For about two months now he had parked near her window. First, they just smiled at one another, and then they progressed to a wave. Last week he said, 'Hello', although she could hardly hear it through the glass window. He was tall, had dark curly hair and very expressive eyes, good looking in a rugged sort of way. She could picture him at the family farm, on horseback. Yes, he was already here; she saw his car and the outline of him sitting waiting. Her thoughts were on the young man, the window dressing she had planned, and today was her mothers wedding day. Her mother, Shannon, was finally marrying a man she had loved for many years.

Hope heard a scraping sound to her right. As she turned her head, she got a glimpse of three burly black men before she was knocked down and dragged into the back lane. One man had her pinned to the ground; his hand was over her mouth to stop her from screaming. His face was so close to her face that she could smell his foul breath as he spoke.

"You are the daughter, and sister of the two men that raped and killed Samuel's daughter. Samuel took revenge for his daughter, but what about our daughters, you must pay that price."

Since Hope was wearing her trousers, it was easy for her to move. She brought her knee up and jammed it into his groin. He let out a screech of pain and fell backwards clutching himself. Hope was on her feet with her knife out, and ready. She always carried a flick knife—a trick she learned from her mother. The three men had not expected a fight from her. While one was rolling in pain on the ground, the other two looked at the scene, dumbfounded for a minute. Hope took advantage of this split second and slipped an elastic band around her hair. She was ready—now the two standing men charged her. She managed to swing her knife and cut the arm of one attacker before she was thrown to the ground. She saw stars as her head hit the steel garbage can. As she struggled to stand up, she saw a fourth person running towards them, it was her admirer.

Abraham had looked away for a split second. When he looked up again she was gone. Where did she go? She was not near the store yet so could not have decided to use the back entrance. He got out of his car and slowly walked toward where he had last seen her. He heard a muffled cry and started to run. Turning into the back lane, with a glance he took in the scene. One man was on the ground clutching his groin, Abraham smiled to himself; she'd kicked him. He saw her knife drawn facing the other two—what a woman!! She swung her knife; the African swung his fist. She'd cut him but he'd hit her so hard she flew backwards.

Abraham roared with anger, and ran towards the two standing Africans, jumped high in the air, and used both feet to kick one of the attackers in the head. As he landed, he twisted himself around and double punched the third man. By now, the first African was staggering to his feet; but he was still bent over. Abraham kicked him, his head shot back, blood flying and then he lay motionless. The other two had recovered and were facing Abraham. Out of the corner of his eye, he saw Hope standing up. She took aim and threw her knife, hitting one of them, square in his back. The surprised look on his face matched Abraham's surprise; this woman is a fighter! The third attacker and Abraham were struggling with one another; the African pulled the knife out of his friend's back and faced Abraham. Abraham used his famous kicks and sent the knife flying, and then using his fists, he boxed. In no time, he had the third attacker knocked out. The two surviving Africans lay sprawled in the back lane, the third was dead from the knife Hope had thrown. Before they could wake, Abraham removed their shirts, rolled them on their stomachs; he then bent their arms behind their backs and bent their legs upwards. This way he could tie their hands and feet together with their shirts. They could not move, other than to roll over.

Now he turned to Hope. "Hope, are you OK? Your head is bleeding." He reached her and started dabbing at her wound.

"It's only a cut and a bump." Hope took his hands in her hands. "But look at your hands, the skin is off the knuckles. I've never seen anyone box and kick like that. You know my name . . . ." Hope would have continued her chatter, but she fainted.

Abraham did not want to leave her laying there with the two Africans while he went for help. So he picked her up and carried her out of the back lane. By now, more people were milling around. The police were summoned and took care of Hope's attackers. The store manager had Hope lie down for a while, but told her to take the day off. The cut in Hope's head looked as though it needed stitches. Abraham volunteered to drive her to the hospital. Hope was still very woozy so did not argue. She had six stitches put in her head and a cold pack put on the huge lump. The doctor checked Abraham's hands and suggested keeping an ice pack on them, so they wouldn't swell.

Abraham turned to her and said "Hope, my name is Abraham and I'm going to drive you home. Where do you live?" Hope gave him Nathaniel's address since that is where everyone would be for the wedding later this afternoon. As they drove, Hope's head cleared and she felt a little better, the car's window was open, so the wind helped clear her head. She was not concerned that it blew her curls into a wild mess.

"Abraham, thank you for coming to my rescue, it is a good job you were early today."

Abraham gave a little cough and said, "I had plucked up enough courage to speak to you, I was going to ask you to go out with me. I came early to go over my little speech. Little did I realize I was going to rescue you, although you put up a pretty good fight. Do you know who those Africans were or even why the attacked you?" Abraham kept looking sideways at her as he drove. He could not believe the last few hours, and that she was in the car with him.

"My father and brother were men that abused girls and women; even my mother was terribly abused by my father. My father and brother attacked many young, sometimes very young African girls. The father of their latest victim took revenge and killed them in the mines; it was made to look like an accident. These men today, were fathers of girls that had been abused by my father and brother. They were looking for revenge."

Abraham was quiet as he took in this information. As they drove into the driveway, he said, "Whoo! Look at this place." Nathaniel's home always had that effect on people seeing it for the first time. There was a long circular driveway with immaculate lawns and flowers. The house was a long rambling brick ranch with red bougainvillea draped over walls, and climbing into trees. The view from the house was breathtaking; it looked out over the mountains that today had a mist floating around it.

"This is Dr. Nathaniel's home, the man my mother is marrying this afternoon. I gave you this address because the family will already be here. Next week we will be moving our possessions from town."

Shannon had been banished from the house, and the back garden overlooking the valley of hills. This is where the wedding was going to take place and chairs were being set up. Flowers and other decorations were being worked on, and the kitchen was bustling with hired cooks. Yesterday some of her family and friends arrived for the wedding. Now she and Kelly, her cousin, were sitting on the garden swing in the front yard having a quiet cup of tea. Just then, a strange car pulled up and a young man got out, both his hands were bandaged. He ran around and opened the passenger door for Hope; her clothes were blood stained. Shannon ran to the car. "Hope, Hope, what happened?" Shannon put her arm around her daughter's waist.

"Mom, this is Abraham. This morning he saved my life. Look at his hands; they got hurt fighting off three Africans that had attacked me." Shannon took Abraham's bandaged hands in hers.

"Abraham, thank you, thank you." Abraham was embarrassed at all this fuss. However, he was also taken aback at Shannon's red-scarred hands that held his. They had obviously been burned. By now Shannon had shepherded them into the house, got them settled on the couch and ordered some tea. Everyone gathered around to hear the story.

"This is bad," said Nathaniel. "What's to stop them from coming after Hope again?" Being a doctor, Nathaniel had a telephone. He called the police and asked what was going to happen to the two surviving Africans.

"Meneer Van Jaarsvelt, you won't ever have to worry about those two *Kaffiers* again." The police were right. They were never seen or heard from again. Nathaniel did not ask for any details.

After lunch, which Abraham enjoyed with them, Shannon insisted that Hope lie down for a while and rest her head. Abraham stood up to leave, but Shannon said, "No, please Abraham, don't go. In fact, I would like you to stay for the wedding." Abraham hesitated. They did not know him and this was a small family wedding.

Hope walked up to him, putting her hands on his bandaged ones, she said, "Please, you did say you were going to ask me out, maybe this could be the—out."

Hope grinned at him and raised one of her eyebrows. Abraham agreed to stay for the wedding; his eyes followed Shannon and Hope as they disappeared down the hallway. This was turning out to be a very interesting day. He knew then and there that he was going to marry Hope.

Abraham went to move his car out of the way. As he parked in the side yard, he had another breathing attack. Damn, he had hoped moving from Natal to the Transvaal would help. Abraham was bent over double, hanging on the car for support. His breathing was coming in gasps, his eyes felt as though they would pop, his heart was pounding and torrents of sweat were dripping from his face. Someone grabbed his arms and raised them above his head; this opened up his breathing passages. After a few minutes he felt better, well enough to talk. "Thank you," he gasped.

Standing before him was a beautiful blond woman, maybe in her early thirties. "I'm Anetta, a friend of the family, and a doctor. I just arrived yesterday for the wedding. Have you always had asthma?"

"No, the first time I started having trouble was when we moved from the Transvaal to Natal. I was about 11 or 12 years old then. Gradually it got worse until even just walking in the sugar fields brought on attacks. A doctor advised me to move away from the coast with its humidity. So I moved up here to our Transvaal farm, the Four Corners, but anything to do with farming, tilling soil, harvesting the mealies and wheat, seems to bring on an attack."

"So how do you manage?" Being a doctor, Anetta was interested in how Abraham coped. While at medical school in Cape Town, she had actually written a paper on asthma. Over tea, and then lunch, Anetta had noticed little signs; she suspected he had asthma.

"Well, I moved from the farm to Johannesburg, and applied for a job with the mines, as a blacksmith. At first that seemed like the answer, but soon the attacks returned."

"Do you go underground, Abraham?"

"Yes."

"That's it; you need to remain on the surface. In farming, certain plants and pollens trigger an attack. Underground there are certain fumes that will also trigger an attack. Maybe you can get a transfer to the surface."

"That makes sense, but why the attack now?"

"This morning the lawn was mowed and raked. We can not smell it, but your sensitive lungs picked it up." As they walked back to the house, he said,

"Thank you Anetta, I'm going to try for the transfer."

It was a touching, romantic wedding. Hope's family was friendly and made him feel right at home. She wore an emerald green dress that showed off her red hair, and slim figure. Abraham removed the bandages from his hands. This way when he danced with her, he could feel her hand in his. Later that evening when he left, she walked out to the car with him to say goodbye.

"Hope, I had a really good time. Thank you for asking me to stay for your mother's wedding. I like your mother and Nathaniel, in fact, all of your family."

"No Abe, it is I who should thank you again for coming to my rescue, if you had not, I may be dead now." Hope reached up and softly kissed his lips. She went to step back, but Abraham put his arm around her and held her tight.

"Hope, you are the most unusual woman I know. I love the way you dress, I love the way you talk, I love the way you . . . the way you . . . oh damn, I love the way you do everything. The curly red hair, those snappy green eyes, even the way you handle yourself. You did some serious damage to those Africans today." As he spoke, Abraham felt her arms circle his neck. Looking down at her, she was smiling her crooked smile with one raised eyebrow. Yep, he liked even this; she was not shy about coming forward.

"I was wondering how long it would take you to speak up. Two months of staring at me through the glass was a bit much. If you had not spoken up, I would have."

"And what would you have said?" He grinned.

"I'd have said Abe; by the way, I'm shortening your name to Abe so it matches my name, I'd have said . . . . take me or leave me."

"I'll take you," and he brought his lips down on hers. Abraham had kissed a few girls before, but they were nothing like Hope. She kissed right back and moved closer to him. They were glued together. Thereafter, Hope and Abraham were always together.

Shannon and Nathaniel had gone away on a honeymoon for a week. During that time Abraham helped Hope and her Aunt Joy, (Shannon's sister) move their household goods from town to Nathaniel's home. Each day after work, they'd take a load out to the Haven. Shannon had given Nathaniel's home its name, because during such a dark period of her life it was a haven for her. For a week the two couples, Hope and Abraham, Joy and Louis, plus his three-year old son, Seun, spent the evenings at the Haven. They gave the cook the week off and cooked for themselves. They ate under the stars and really got to know each other.

Abraham told Hope his family history, his grandfather coming from Russia and about their farm at Four Corners. She said, "Abe, we had heard about your family, we heard about your grandfather having half his face bitten off by a hyena. In fact, because of that, whenever my grandmother, Maureen and Van went camping, they made a circle of fire. He was just about to come to the Larger and Dr. Lukas—that's Anetta's father—was going to operate to help with his breathing, but as you know he died before that happened. She paused, a sad look coming over her face. "You mentioned the burning of Four Corners. The Larger wasn't burned, but my parent's farm was burned with the scorched earth policy. We were taken to the concentration camps. My oldest brother died there, along with my aunt and four of my cousins. It was because of losing that farm that my father moved my mother and younger brother to town."

Hope then explained their history, her grandmother and sisters coming from Scotland, Abraham said, "We heard about the wonderful way the Larger was built. We also heard about the Scottish redheads and how one was captured and she had twin boys. Soooo . . . . that was your uncles, Koos and Keith." Abraham asked Hope, "What happened to your mother's hands?"

Hope explained, she told him that her mother had many other scars from Geret's beatings. "So my mother had a really hard time while married to Geret. You can also see why we did not grieve over his death. It freed her to marry Nathaniel."

"So here I am with one of those Scottish descendents. I can't believe it," said Abraham.

With that Abraham pulled Hope off the chair onto the grass. He lay next to her and said, "Look at that moon; it is the same moon that has shone down on my family history from Russia to now, and your family history from Scotland to now. These two lines are joining up, what do you think is in store for us?"

"I hope as rich and full a life as our families have had."

Lying on the grass brought about an asthma attack for Abraham . . . . Damn . . .

CHAPTER 3

Because of car trouble, Shannon and Nathaniel arrived at the Haven about 1:00 A.M.

They slipped quietly into their bedroom not wanting to wake anyone. The next day was Sunday; they thought they would sleep in before getting back into routine.

Looking out the window, Hope saw Nathaniel's car in the driveway. "Joy, they're home, they're home. The two girls—Shannon's sister, and daughter, burst through the bedroom door and threw themselves on the bed. They wiggled Nathaniel out of the way and settled on either side of Shannon.

"First of all, we want to hear all about your honeymoon," pleaded Joy.

"Oh no, that is private," said Shannon.

"I'll tickle you until you talk," threatened Joy.

Nathaniel closed the bathroom door, smiling to himself. For years his life had been so quiet and lonely, now he had a wife whom he loved beyond words, and he had a family. As he showered, he heard Shannon screaming for help, they were tickling her. When he came out, the three of them were sitting cross-legged in a circle on the bed talking, sometimes all three at once.

"Girls, girls, what's going on?"

"Oh Mr. N., they are both going to get married, Joy to Louis, and Hope to Abraham."

"We want a double wedding, and can we have it here like yours. Please, please Daddy!" It always amused Nathaniel when Hope called him daddy; she did it to tease him.

"Let's discuss it over breakfast, I'm starving," he said.

The two men, Abraham, Louis and Seun (Louis's three year old son) had slept in the barn. It saved them from driving back and forth on a weekend. Smelling the bacon and eggs cooking, they quickly showered in the stables and came through to the kitchen looking slicked down.

Breakfast was a noisy affair, the clanking of dishes as they ate, and the planning of the two marriages. Seun had climbed on Shannon's lap; his father's courting had tired him out; he was sucking his thumb and fell asleep against her breast.

Nathaniel looked at Shannon over all this noise; he pulled his chair closer to her and under the table put his hand on her knee and gave it a squeeze. Suddenly there was silence. Nathaniel looked up and everyone was staring at Shannon. He turned to look at her; she had tears running down her cheeks. In a concerned voice, he said. "Shannon, my darling, what's the matter?"

"Oh, I'm okay everyone; it's just that I am so happy. I can't believe how life can change so much. One minute married to Geret, a very harsh man; we never got together like this." Shannon waved her hand indicating the group at the table. "Now married to a wonderful man and having a real family meal."

Joy and Louis planned on buying the property next to the Haven. It had a cute house, just right for a small family. This way the two doctors, Nathaniel and Louis and both their wives, who worked in the office, would travel into town together. Although Hope would have loved to live out here next to her mother and aunt, it was too far from the mines and the beautiful landscape brought on an asthma attack for Abe. He could not be around on lawn mowing day, or even days that the pollen was high. So for now, they were going to use Shannon's house in town.

The weddings were planned for the following month; there was a lot of work to be done. Again, it was going to be kept small with just family and very close friends. Because Abraham's family from Natal could not take so much time away from the sugar plantation, Abraham and Hope were going to honeymoon down there. Joy and Louis were not going away; they were going to use their week off from work to settle into their new home.

The night before the weddings, Shannon was sitting on the double swing that was attached to the low branch of the huge tree in the back yard, overlooking the hills, her favorite spot. The sun was setting behind the hills and there was a lot of mist, blue, purple and red washed over the mountains. The evening sounds had taken over, birds settling in for the night, crickets wining and frogs croaking. Every now and then a dog barked in the distance. Nathaniel, carrying two glasses of wine came to join her. She snuggled close to him. "Why the sad look?" he asked.

Shannon took a minute to answer, "I know tomorrow is a happy day for the girls, but it closed one part of life and opens the door to another. Did you know Joy was conceived the night before the elephant killed our father? I believe having her saved my mother's life. It was like having the last moments of their lives captured in her, that's why my mother gave her the name Joy. If only our mother and father could have been here for her wedding day. Then there is my baby; Hope is the only child I have left, in spite of having three. I am happy for her marriage, but at the same time it does change things between mother and daughter." There was silence for a while; they were both deep in thought. "But thank goodness for change, because of change we met, we fell in love, we married . . ." Shannon stopped in mid sentence. "What do you think you are doing, Mr. N.?"

"Well, if you don't know by now," he was unbuttoning her dress, "I'll have to explain it to you all over again." He was grinning at her as his hand slipped inside her dress, but he was having trouble with those new fangled type hooks. Shannon leaned forward and did the job for him. "Ah, that's better," as his hand cupped her breast.

"I think we better go inside my love, it would not do to have my daughter find us out here, and at our age too."

"There's nothing wrong with our age; the older you are the better you are. But I agree, let's go inside." Nathaniel picked up Shannon and carried her to the bedroom.

It was a morning wedding, with lunch served afterwards. A morning was chosen because Abe and Hope (everyone now called him Abe) were catching the train in the late afternoon to Natal. Shannon and Nathaniel drove them to the train station. What an adventure. The engine was like a dragon, huffing and puffing, steam coming out of a funnel, around the wheels, there were a lot of strange noises. The train creaked and groaned as it shunted back and forth.

"Talk about change, not too long ago we traveled by wagon, then carriage, and now look at this monster," said Shannon.

"Oh Mom, this is so exciting. I am looking forward to this trip."

They hugged and kissed goodbye as the conductor walked up and down shouting, "All aboard, all aboard."

Once in their compartment, Abe and Hope leaned out the window, and said goodbye again. Slowly the train started to move and build up speed. The clang, clang and chug, chug, just added to the excitement. Abe had traveled by train before, so took great delight in pointing out all the amenities, a little stainless steel washbasin, and the seat bench that folded out into a bed. He explained bedding would be brought in later. He took her down the passage and showed her the dining carriage where they would have their meals. He showed her where the toilet was, one at the end of every carriage. Walking while the train was moving was quite a feat. "I love this; I love this, what a wonderful idea to travel by train." Hope was so excited.

For the next hour, the train stopped at a few more stations before getting set for the nights run. They would be stopping only to refill water and coal. An African dressed in a uniform walked up the passage playing a type of xylophone, announcing supper. Abe and Hope, had a small table to themselves, each table had a window, so you could watch the scenery fly by. Hope hardly noticed the food, between the beautiful scenery; the rocking of the carriage and watching the waiters maneuver to tables while carrying food. They had to stand with their feet apart to brace themselves against the constant movement, but not a drop was spilled.

After supper, they walked back to their compartment. While eating, someone had pulled the bed out and it was made up with starched sheets, pillows and blankets. Having the bed pulled out left them very little space to move about. "Well Abe, looks like its time for bed or are we just going to stand here? I vote for bed," she gave him that crooked smile with raised eyebrow.

"Ahh . . . would you like me to wait outside?" He hesitated.

"Why?"

Hope moved close to him and slipped her arms around his neck. He did not need a second invitation; he lowered his head to kiss her. A kiss that was long and deep. She slipped his jacket off and pulled his tie off. Then she started to unbutton his shirt all while their lips were glued together. While she was doing that, he pulled the clips out of her hair; those red curls fell to her shoulders. Hope was wearing a black suit. The skirt was mid calf length and slightly flared. The jacket was form fitting with buttons down the front. Abe was wondering how they made woman's clothing to fit so perfect around their curves. His shirt was off and she was slowly unbuttoning her jacket. Abe moved her hands and took over the job. When he dropped the jacket on the floor, the skirt quickly followed. Abe's breath was knocked out of him. What ever that was she was wearing was a mess of white lace and see through. This was not the women's underwear he had seen hanging on the wash line at home.

Hope obviously was enjoying the desired reaction. "You like it? It's the latest from France." She slowly turned around; nothing was left to the imagination, her lean back curved out to her rounded buttocks. She also wore the latest stockings that were thigh high and were held in place by a lacy belt specially designed for that. She was facing him again. He was staring at the rise and fall of her breasts as she breathed. She sat on the edge of the bed to unsnap her stocking, but again he moved her hands and unsnapped the four hooks. Slowly peeling off the stockings, her legs were long and shapely.

Abe awoke the next morning to the gentle rocking of the train. Did he dream last night? He quickly turned over. No, there she was still fast asleep, her curls sprayed all over the pillow. They had opened the blinds last night so they could watch the moon as they sped through the night. Now the sunlight was shining down on her. During the night they had thrown the blanket off the bed, a sheet was all they used to cover up later. Now the sheet was only half covering their naked bodies. He ran his eyes over the full length of her body. When he got back to her face, her eyes were open and smiling at him. "You like it? It's the latest from South Africa." Oh yeah, this was his woman; he blessed the day he walked past the store window in Johannesburg.

Late that night they pulled into Durban station in Natal. There to meet them was Abe's mother and father, Jacob and Natasha, his brother, Stoffel and his sister, Tanya. They made Hope feel welcome. Abe looked just like his father. He had warned his family that Hope was different and that she spoke her mind. In spite of the warning they were taken aback when they saw the mass of red curly hair. Seventeen-year-old Tanya jumped right in.

"See Mom, Hope comes from the city; she has her hair cut shorter; it's got to be the latest style. Please, please can't I have mine cut?"

Natasha laughed. "OK, OK if it looks as good, on you as it does on Hope; we may all try the latest style." Natasha put an arm around Hopes waist and the other around Tanya's. I'm so happy to have another girl in the family."

Tanya and Hope immediately became friends. She helped Hope unpack, all the time ooh'ing and aah'ing over the latest fashions—especially the lacy underwear. Hope made a mental note to buy a set for Tanya.

Hope was like a little girl when she saw the ocean for the first time. Running bare foot through the sand, she insisted on swimming every day. Then there were the Indian markets where she bought little treasures for everyone. She was amazed at the size of the ocean liners in Port. She'd get up early every morning to watch the sunrise over the ocean. All too soon they had to leave, but promises were made to visit soon.

During the next few months, Abe had one asthma attack after another. He had applied for a transfer above ground, but so far nothing had happened. He decided to put in a new application after having missed two days of work due to an attack. His doctor wrote a note, mentioning the seriousness of asthma and that he really needed the transfer. Now, because Hope worked on Saturdays, she had a day off during the week. She would do her errands, and grocery shopping. Then she would have lunch with her mother and Joy.

"You are looking pale today Hope, are you okay?"

"Sure Mom, it's just this asthma thing, I think I'm a bit run down. Maybe Nathaniel can give me a tonic." Nathaniel questioned and examined Hope.

"Your tonic young lady is to take out your knitting needles and start making baby clothes."

"I'm going to be a mother!" Shouted Hope, coming out of Nathaniel's office.

"I'm going to be an ouma!" Yelled Shannon, joining Hope in excitement.

"I'm going to be an aunt!" Joy joined the excited group.

"I'm going to be a daddy!" Abraham was overjoyed.

Their daughter Colleen was born the same year they were married. Just ten months later another daughter, Sheree was born.

By now Abe's asthma attacks were getting out of control; he was even losing weight. Finally, the mines offered him a transfer not in Johannesburg, but in Northern Rhodesia. "Northern Rhodesia!—Where was that?" Hope and Abe said together, they spent hours over a map, and reading any information they could find, which wasn't much. It sounded about a generation behind the time; this would be like early pioneers taking part in opening up the land.

Abe got this news Thursday evening. Friday evening, as soon as he came home, they packed the car and drove out to the Haven. Since the babies, Hope had stopped work; the girls were a handful. Shannon loved to help with the girls on the weekend, and they wanted to talk to Shannon and Nathaniel about this offer. It was a cool evening so they were all gathered around the living room fireplace. Shannon had eighteen-month-old Colleen on her lap, busy falling asleep, and Joy was rocking eight-month old Sheree, who had just finished nursing. After hearing about the offer of a transfer to Northern Rhodesia, Shannon and Nathaniel were very quiet. "What do you think Mom, Dad?" asked Abe.

"Hope, Abe, this is a decision you have to make yourselves, because you are the ones who have to live with the consequences, good or bad. I could give you the pro's and con's as I see them." Nathaniel said.

"Yes," said Abe, "I would like to hear them."

"First you applied for a change in jobs because of your health, right?"

"Yes."

"Your heath has been pretty bad lately, and there seems to be no hope of a change in your job here?"

"Yes."

"You're hesitating because of what? It's so far away! You have two babies! There is very little there, and you will be helping establish not only the mine but also the town?"

"Yes, all of the above."

Shannon took Hope's hands in hers and continued the reasoning that Nathaniel had started. "Having babies, starting mines or towns, really should not be an issue. Not with both of your backgrounds. Look what our family; Abe's family, and others like them did for this land. It seems as though the issue is health. So, if you don't go, Abe's health will stay the same or even get worse. If you did go, Abe's health could improve since he will be working above the ground. Now as you have also seen from both family sides, there is a danger in opening new paths. But remember, you will never get to see the view unless you climb the mountain."

"But you will be so far away," whispered Hope.

"If you decide to go, of course we will miss you, and my two grand-daughters. You will come back on visits, and we will travel up to see you. I remember Domine Paul once told me when I was praying about a decision I had to make. 'Your prayers are not always answered exactly as you would like.' You have prayed about a change in jobs, maybe this is the answer."

That night Abe had a very bad asthma attack; it made them decided to go. If it did not work out, they could always come back to South Africa. Arrangements were made. Abe was going to go first—check it out, settle them into their temporary house. Then come back and escort his family to Northern Rhodesia. Hope and the girls would move in with Shannon while Abe was gone.

Hope wanted to take a trip back to the Larger. She did not know how long it would be before she returned to South Africa. Both Shannon and Hope were surprised to see tractors in use. So many changes had taken place, maybe because the original four couples were gone, or maybe because they now lived in town—it was not the same. Arm in arm, Shannon and Hope walked up the hill to visit Maureen and Van's gravesite.

"I need to interrupt here," said Colleen. "So the Larger, is the family farm that the Scottish girls lived on, and Maureen and Van are my great grandmother and grandfather?"

Jacob nodded, while handing his sister the next journal. She continued to read . . .

"Notice the change Hope. The original four Scottish girls are buried under these trees covered in bougainvillea, but look at all the life they left behind, notice too the old covered wagons behind the barns replaced with cars and tractors. That is what life is all about—change—what is here today is gone tomorrow. The point I'm trying to make is: enjoy each day, each phase. One day Colleen and Sheree will be adults visiting their ouma's grave. Things never stay the same. Leave the girls with good memories and remember to tell them how the three sisters came from Scotland. Hope, do you remember the story about this beautiful bracelet I always wear?"

"Yes Mom, but tell me again, I love the story."

"I believe it started with Nicholas. His girlfriend in Russia had given him a rough looking 'Three Cord' strand of twine to wear around his neck. Its symbol was that three cords made for strength . . . something unbreakable. One cord stood for the husband, the other cord for the wife, and most importantly, the third cord represented God. So if a husband and wife kept God foremost in their marriage, they would be able to handle their lives successfully. There was a brief crossing of paths with Nicholas and your grandmother Maureen; it was here she learned about the three cords and its symbol. When she was kidnapped, just before your uncles were born, she made her own three cords out of wire, which she wore to the day she died. It was a bracelet that was a constant reminder to always keep God in her life. It helped her, with her struggles. When my mother died, I took her wire bracelet—I believe it helped me endure the years with Geret and the camp. When Nathaniel and I married, he replaced that wire bracelet with one made of gold, silver and copper."

Shannon now laid a gift on Hope's lap. Slowly Hope opened the box; it was a necklace of gold, silver and copper woven together. Hope was so emotional she couldn't say anything. Tears were running down her face. Shannon clipped the necklace around Hope's neck.

"No matter what you and Abe face in Northern Rhodesia, if you both keep God first in your lives, you will be strong enough to face it."

Anetta had not seen Shannon or Hope since she had come up for their weddings; she was so excited about Hope's babies, and the upcoming adventure of traveling to Northern Rhodesia. She asked Shannon and Hope to stay with her while at the Larger. After settling the babies into bed, Anetta said, "Hope I have made us coffee, come sit by the fire. I would like to talk to you."

The babies were so tired that they fell asleep with no problems; Shannon had lay down with them and also fell asleep. Hope tiptoed out to sit with Anetta; they sipped away at their coffee before Anetta brought up what was on her mind. "Hope, since my mom and dad died last year, I have wanted a change. I was wondering how you would feel if I traveled with you to Rhodesia and checked it out, to see if they need doctors and maybe stay." Hope let out a squeal and hugged Anetta.

"That is a wonderful idea. I am positive you will have work waiting for you. Abe has written to say he was so busy, and he wondered if I would mind taking the journey alone with the girls, but now I'll have you. When could you be ready to leave Anetta?"

"I will check with the clinic. If they need me to stay for a week, I will do that. But maybe I could leave straight away."

The two women stayed up, deciding on what Anetta should pack. She would crate her medical books and have them sent up later. At 2:00 A.M., Shannon came out with Sheree who wanted to be fed. "What's going on—you girls haven't been to bed yet?" When Shannon heard Anetta wanted to go to Northern Rhodesia, she agreed it was a wonderful idea.

Anetta traveled by car with Shannon and Hope back to Johannesburg. Now Hope packed up their final things. She hated to leave her mother and Joy. But she was missing Abe terribly; he had been gone three months.

There were such mixed feelings at the station, sadness because of leaving, but excitement in starting their journey. They hugged and kissed; promising to write each week and visit often. As Shannon held Hope, she whispered in her ear . . . . "Always remember the three cords—you will have the strength if you keep God in your life. Also, remember the reason for your name Hope, no matter what happens, keep hope alive."

Colleen interrupted, "Don't tell me to wait and read the Scottish journals to find out why my mother was called Hope. I want to know now, in light of what you just read."

Maureen explained, "Because your grandmother had such a terrible first marriage, she named her daughter Hope to remind her never to lose hope. Throughout both their lives, it was a constant strength to them."

CHAPTER 4

Northern Rhodesia—1943

Slowly the train pulled out of the station in Johannesburg. Because Hope was crying, Colleen and Sheree thought they should join in. The wail was deafening. Trying to calm them, Anetta said, "Come on girls, we are on the threshold of an adventure. We are traveling in a direction few people have gone. I am sure we are going to see things we have never seen before. The train started picking up speed; curiosity got the better of Colleen and Sheree. They stopped crying and stared out the windows. Both squashed their little noses flat against the glass and watched as they left the city of Johannesburg.

Hope pulled herself together. "Thanks Anetta, I am so glad you joined us. I am going to have quite a time keeping the girls happy for eight days in such a small area." Hope remembered her first trip in a train, how exciting, how romantic. But now she worried about the small area and keeping the two girls busy and happy, gone was the romantic, exciting, adventure. She was now frightened and worried.

Hope explained to Anetta the travel plans. "It will take us a couple of days to get from Johannesburg to the Limpopo River. We will be crossing at a place called Beitbridge; then we will be in a country called Southern Rhodesia. It will take us about three days before we cross the Zambezi River at Victoria Falls into Northern Rhodesia. Now we have to travel almost the length of the country to the north; this is where the copper mines are. It is called the Copper Belt; the mines form a circle, like a man's belt. The town we are headed for is Luanshya."

"I still can not believe the distance we are going to be traveling," said Anetta. We cannot complain though, when you think of the Scottish girls coming from Cape Town to Johannesburg area by wagon, it took months. We will be traveling almost the same distance, and it will take just over a week. We have a dining car, a nice soft bed, with running water."

It did not take Hope and Anetta long to get their compartment organized for the journey. Anetta had brought some medical journals to study. Hope wanted to keep a very detailed account of the trip from South Africa to Northern Rhodesia.

The two girls had a few toys, but the ever-changing scenery from the windows kept them occupied. When they needed to run off some energy, Hope would let them run up and down the passage, much to the disgust of other passengers. When they tried to complain, they got nowhere. Hope put her hands on her hips, eyes flashing. She said, "If you want peace and quiet for the rest of the day or even a quiet night's sleep, I suggest you put up with this noise for an hour in the morning, and an hour in the afternoon. Or Madam, I promise you eight days of hell."

When the train stopped, Africans from nearby villages would run up to them to try and sell a carving, a drum or some local fruits. The African children wore no clothing; the men and women very little. Hope tried her best to keep her children away from then because they always seem to be covered in sores, or had runny noses and eyes. She and Anetta used this time to leave the train; they let the girls run and climb, getting the much-needed exercise.

They quickly settled into a daily routine. Because lines to the toilet could be long, they used a chamber pot for the girls, when they had to go—they had to go, no waiting in line. At first Hope was not happy about taking the children to the dining car three times a day but there were two sittings—families with little children first. Two hours later families with no, or grown, children could dine. It became a diversion from their cramped quarters—a welcome break.

It was both exciting and scary crossing the mighty Limpopo at Beitbridge. The river was in flood; it was a muddy, raging fury. The train slowed to a crawl as it crossed, almost immediately, the scenery changes. This was a high veldt with beautiful and varied landscape. Once in a while they spotted a farm—it was dense bush type shrubs, the trees were shorter than they had seen before. Since it was the rainy season, everything was green and flowering. They noticed some spectacular rock formations. The girls were glued to the window watching the wild life—no matter if it were a herd of elephant, giraffes, zebra, buck, or even lions, they would squeal,—'puppy—puppy'.

One day in the mid afternoon, the train came to a screeching halt; they all fell off the bunks. Of course, Colleen and Sheree let the world know they were unhappy about this. While Hope calmed them down, Anetta tried to find out what had happened. A herd of elephants were on the tracks and refused to move. In fact, they were insisting the train move. This war of will continued for a few hours until hunger made them move on, and then a few rails had to be replaced. They had been flattened out by the weight of so many elephants. The crew on the train was prepared for this; apparently, it happened fairly often, so they always carried spare tracks with them. It was not until after the evening meal that the train was ready to continue.

A few days later during the night, Hope woke to take care of Sheree and noticed the train had stopped. Even the hissing and puffing from the engine had stopped. It was eerily quiet. She sat feeding Sheree in the dark, actually feeling prickles of fear. Anetta whispered from her bunk. "What's wrong, why have we stopped?"

"I don't know, but don't you think it is too quiet? I can not even hear the engine." They waited an hour, still no sound or movement.

"I am going to check on what is happening," said Anetta.

She got dressed and made her way from car to car till she reached the dining car. It was lit up. The engine drivers and conductors were sitting around tables with about six other men. From their dress, they were hunters or farmers. When Anetta walked in, they all stopped talking and stared at her.

"Meneer, why have we stopped, what is happening?"

"Do not worry, miss, we have everything under control."

"By not telling me, I will worry; it is better to explain to people the problems instead of leaving them in the dark." Anetta added, "Walking up to this car, I noticed the train is surrounded by men on horses, looking as though they are protecting us or the train from something."

A man in his late thirties stood up. "You are right young lady; we would have let people know when they woke. We did have problems early tonight with some rebels, who tried to cut down the support beams of the bridge across Victoria Falls. They have been chased off, but we are waiting for daylight to check the damage before allowing the train to cross. Those are my men out there guarding the train in case the rebels return."

"Thank you," Anetta was about to leave but added, "I am a doctor, would you like me to take care of your arm?" The young man had a makeshift bandage around his upper arm; he had been shot while driving off the rebels. Anetta made her way back to her compartment, collected a few medical supplies and told Hope what had happened. Returning to the dining car, Anetta took care of the young man's arm. "Why, Meneer, did rebels try to destroy the bridge?"

"By the way, my name is Desmond, not Meneer, Desmond Landsburg. The train conductor told me your name is Anetta and you are from Johannesburg. Anetta, my men and I try to keep peace between the black and white tribes. Most of the black people are superstitious and look at the train as a snake, something to do with witchcraft; they say it is bringing white people in its belly to take away their land.

They attack some trains, sometimes uproot the tracks, but this is the first time they have tried to destroy the bridge." By now Anetta had finished taking care of Desmond's arm. "Anetta, a few of my men were injured tonight; could I ask you to take a look at them?"

"Of course."

One by one, the wounded men left their posts and Anetta took care of them. A few required stitches and for one of them, she had to dig deep to remove a bullet. The man that had to have a bullet dug out was a minister. As Anetta worked on him he surprised her, with his not-so-minister-like language in a heavy Scottish accent. To take his mind off what she was doing, she asked, "What is a minister doing on violent missions like this?"

"Well, lass, we dina fight unless we have te. Our mission is te keep peace. Sometimes we meet their ministers or witch doctors, it helps if one of our team is a minister, and it helps that I have this Scottish accent, they think I have special powers. I am non-denominational, so that takes care of whatever I run into, by the way, since yer working on me butt, ye should know me name, tis Reverend Shawn Wallace."

Colleen sat bolt upright, "Is that my Shawn, the one whose house this is, the one who is buried on the hill out back—the one whom you named your baby after Maureen?"

"Yes, it is Mom."

By now people were awake and milling around wondering what was wrong. The train driver stopped at each compartment and explained what was happening and that he would keep them informed during the day. At lunchtime, he made an announcement.

"Sorry ladies and gentlemen for the inconvenience. Desmond Landsburg and his men have examined the bridge's supporting beams. The good news is that damage will not bring the bridge down. The bad news is we are not sure how much weight it can take. The good news is we have solved the problem. The bad news is you have to physically walk across the bridge." There was a gasp of disbelief and fear. "What we have decided would be safe," he continued, "is dividing our weight into three. The first third is you, the passenger; you will walk over and then wait on the other side of the bridge in Northern Rhodesia. Then we will unhook half the train cars. The pulling engine will cross with the first half. Once safely over, our second engine, the pushing engine, will push over the second half of the train." There was silence. "We need to start the crossing within the hour, so that it can be completed before dark. Passengers, please carry only your important papers and tickets. Families, please stay together so we can account for everyone. As conductors knock on your door, exit immediately; he will then lock your cabin door. Your possessions will be quite safe."

Some old lady muttered under her breath, "Unless the train ends up in the gorge!"

A very red faced English gentleman said, "I say, old man, is this really necessary? Do we have another choice?"

Desmond was fast losing his patience; rolling his eyes, he stated. "Yes, you do have another choice. We will unload your luggage; you can sit here on the side of the track and wait for the next train in about two weeks. By that time, the beams will have been replaced. Of course, while waiting, rebels could attack you; maybe kill you. Then there are the mosquitoes, they are very bad this time of year."

"Mind your manner, young man. Come along Mildred; let us collect our papers and your jewelry."

Exiting the train went smoothly; people were lined up at the edge of the bridge. Some of Desmond's men formed a protective shield at the beginning of the bridge; others forming the protection party at the other end although there was no sight of the rebels. This was just a precaution.

"George, George, it's not a solid bridge; I can see between the planks." Whined Mildred.

"My God dear man, do you really expect the ladies to cross this?" Sputtered the English man.

Desmond was getting impatient, "Yes—I do! Men, ladies and children will walk across. It is not wide enough for a body to fall through. If you do not look down, you will not get dizzy. Meneer, would you and your wife like to lead the way?" The English couple held back.

"Come on Hope," Anetta picked up Sheree and settled her on her hip, Hope carried Colleen on her hip. As Anetta and Hope led the group, across the bridge, one of Desmond's men shouted.

"Way te go doctor lady, show up the bloody limey. By the way, me butt feels so much better. I'ma thanking ye." Anetta burst out laughing and waved her hand in a salute to the Reverend. Desmond was right. If you did not look down, you were fine. In fact, the view was beautiful. Looking across the gorge at the water thundering over the cliff was not only breathtaking, it was deafening. A fine mist was blown their way. By the time they reached the other side, they were quite wet.

The Africans called Victoria Falls, Mosi-oa-Tunya,—The Smoke That Thunders, it was like listening to the ocean; it never stopped, the noise, the spray, and there was a double rainbow across the gorge. It was beautiful.

"Hope," Anetta had to shout to be heard, above the noise, "We must come back here someday and explore the area."

"Just what I was thinking," shouted back Hope, the water was dripping off their chins and noses. Colleen and Sheree were having fun trying to catch the spray. The last couple over the bridge was the English couple; they were in a panicky state.

Mildred was crying, "My jewelry, my jewelry."

"What happened?" Desmond asked in an irritated voice.

"My wife slipped on those wet boards and the jewelry bag fell, burst open and more than half the pieces fell through the cracks. What dear sir, are you going to do about that?"

Desmond struggled to remain calm. "Nothing; we did ask you to bring only your important papers. If you had left your jewelry in the compartment as others did, it would still be there."

"But—but—it was very expensive; some of it was priceless."

"You are welcome to go diving for it, SIR," said Desmond. Anetta and Hope turned away to hide their smiles.

Everyone held their breath as the first half of the train inched its way across. A cheer went up; then their eyes were on the second half. The bridge creaked and groaned but held fast. Once the train had been connected, passengers were allowed back on. They were wet and hungry; those needs were taken care of.

Later Desmond knocked on their compartment door; he thanked Anetta for taking care of the wounded and asked where she was headed. Anetta was embarrassed to be caught with her hair wrapped in a towel, and could only stammer, "Luanshya."

"Sometimes I travel that far. Would it be okay if I stopped to say hello!"

"Of course, I am not sure where I will be living, but you could check at the hospital. That is where I hope to be working," now she was blushing.

Finally, they continued the journey, the train gently rocked from side to side. As Hope was falling asleep, she whispered to Anetta. "Anetta, do you realize we are in Northern Rhodesia; we are in the same country as Abe. It should only be about two more days. That is if nothing else goes wrong." Anetta grinned; she hoped one day to love someone the way Hope loved Abe.

The day arrived, 4:00 P.M. they were due to pull into the station at Luanshya. After lunch, Hope started to fiddle with packing, trying to clean up the girls, and trying to clean herself up. She was getting worked up. Anetta grabbed Hope's hands and sat her down.

"What is the matter? Just the other day you were saying you could not wait to see Abe again and now you are all weepy and upset."

"Look at us, ten days of coal dust. Since leaving The Haven we have not had a hot bath. Sheree nappies are gray. Look at my hair; it is a wild mess. There is no way we can look beautiful for Abe, he will be so disappointed when he sees us.

"No, he will not. What does he care about coal dust; he will think his three girls are beautiful. Anyway, if it is a hot soapy bath you want, I am sure you can have one tonight. A good hot wash will get these nappies white again. Come on; focus on the important things—you are home, and your family is together again."

"You are right. Help me squash this hair in a hat," they both laughed.

The train started to slow down. Hope could not contain herself. She put her head out of the window to look for the town, the station, Abe, anything. Then as they rounded a corner, there was the small station. Hope, hanging on to her hat, searched the sea of faces and then she saw him. He was waving at her; she waved back shouting, "Cookie, Cookie."

He was shouting "Cookie, Cookie," he pushed his way through the crowd and trotted alongside the train. "Cookie, I can't believe you are here. These months have seemed like years. I missed you so; where are the girls?" Hope was laughing and crying at the same time. As she reached back for Colleen, her hat blew off and her curly red hair had its own way. Hope pulled Colleen and Sheree to the window so Abe could see them.

"Stay where you are, the station is too crowded. I'm coming up there." Abe jumped on the moving train and pushed his way to compartment 302. Anetta got out and stood in the passage so they could say their hello in private. Hope met him at the door and they fell into each other's arms. Finally he pulled back and held her face, looking into her eyes.

"Oh Abe, don't look. We are so dirty from this train ride; I think I have coal dust buried in my body."

"You look wonderful to me," and he picked her up swinging her around. Slowly he put her down and stood staring at the girls.

"They have grown so," he said. He went to pick up Colleen but she scooted behind Hope's skirts. When he turned to Sheree, she started screaming. Abe got a puzzled hurt look on his face.

"Oh! Cookie, it has been almost six months; they have forgotten you a little. Give them time; they will warm up to you again."

"Knock, knock, is it safe to come in?" Asked Anetta.

"Of course" and Abe gave her a big hug. "You were a real life saver, traveling up with my three girls. Eight days is bad enough, but your trip ended up being ten days." Abe turned to Hope again. "I hope we never have to be apart like that again" and he buried his face in her neck. It did not take Abe long to collect their luggage. Anetta sat in the back seat of the car with Colleen. Sheree was on Hope's lap, up front.

"Well, ladies, let's go home." Abe was grinning from ear to ear.

CHAPTER 5

Passing several white washed, yet still very dirty buildings, Abe announced, "This ladies is where you will be doing all your shopping." Hope stared in disbelief; the buildings looked like small homes squashed together, no windows, barn type doors with only the lower half closed. Later she found out that it kept out dogs, pigs and chickens but it helped with snakes. An African sat next to the door using a manual sewing machine while a second African was cooking over an open fire; both men were offering their wears to passersby. They ignored the dust Abe's car kicked up.

"Well," said Hope, "I guess window dressing is out of the question, as is eating at the local fast food," they all laughed.

Abe continued to explain as they drove. "Anetta, on the hill to the right is the hospital, it was recently updated." Unlike the stores, Anetta thought it was beautiful. Again white washed but nestled against a hill with beautiful flowering trees around it. Abe stopped the car before turning, "Straight ahead about three miles down that dirt road is the mine. This area I'm about to drive through is the beginnings of the new town of Luanshya—some of the homes are already inhabited, and about 100 or so in various stages of readiness. This is where we will be living. In the mean time we will be staying in temporary homes that are furnished."

Abe pulled up in front of a house, the last one on the street. He switched the engine off but no one moved or said anything. He cleared his throat and stammered, "It's really not as bad as it looks, remember it was put up in a hurry and it's temporary." As an after thought he said, "It's better than camping."

"Abe, stop making excuses, I think it looks wonderful. Of course, after being on a train for ten days it looks huge. Let's check it out."

The house had a thatch roof and mud brick walls that were whitewashed. The outside walls did not quite meet up with the thatch, so you constantly had a breeze in the house. The inside walls were only about seven feet high and because the thatch had such a high peak, you could toss things over the wall instead of walking around. There was no ceiling, just the open beams. Windowpanes were literally lifted in and out, to open or close, at least the doors were on hinges. The kitchen and bathroom did have running water. The kitchen consisted of a sink attached to the wall, with a long draining board, a wood or coal burning stove and a refrigerator that ran on paraffin. Every morning a lorry would deliver a huge brick of ice to put in the freezer. The bathroom had a sink attached to the wall and a huge oversized cast iron bathtub set on four feet. Outside a huge drum of water balanced on four brick blocks, and by lighting a fire under it, you would end up with hot water for the bathtub. Of course, you would have to pump it into the tub, but that was worth the trouble. Anetta was right; she could have her bath tonight. The toilet was an outhouse in the back yard.

Hope and Anetta walked from room to room. "It's interesting, it's different, it's behind the times but it's ours. I love it," said Hope. Abe looked relieved.

"It will get better," he promised. After bringing in the luggage, he explained that before Hope came, he lived in a place called, 'Single Quarters'. Housing for men whose wives had not arrived yet. The men ate at the mine, 'Mess' (a name used for a dining room). Abe offered that they could eat there tonight, or he could just pick up the meal and bring it home. "I know you're exhausted and may not want to be around people tonight."

"You are right Abe; we really need a good cleaning before meeting people." After Abe left to pick up the meal Hope and Anetta unpacked their few things, while Colleen and Sheree explored every inch of the house.

While they were eating, a messenger arrived to say Abe was needed at the mine. "Sorry Cookie, whenever they have a problem, I have to assign materials they would need. I tried having someone fill in for me once or twice, but they messed up the records. I shouldn't be too long." He kissed her and whispered, "Don't go to bed without me."

Anetta took things in hand, "Hope, and let us get done so you and Abe can be together. I will quickly clean up from supper, while you bath the girls and give Sheree a good feeding. Then let the girls sleep with me tonight, we will close ourselves up in that far bedroom. You take a nice long hot soak and have the evening with Abe."

"Wow! That sounds wonderful."

That's how Abe found her later, soaking in the huge tub of hot water. Since he was late, he tiptoed into the house. Anetta's bedroom door was closed. But he couldn't find the girls or Hope, checking the bathroom he saw the wild mess of red curly hair. She'd obviously been there for some time, because she was dozing and the candle had almost burned down. Anetta must have the girls. He quietly slipped out of his clothes and joined her in the tub.

About two hours later, Hope was awakened out of a deep sleep. Groggy and disoriented, she said, "Really Abe, how could you possibly have the strength to"—she never finished what she started to say. Abe covered her mouth with his hand, really hard and whispered slow and deliberate in her ear.

"Cookie, don't move or make a sound. We have a python in bed with us. He must have smelled your breast milk, and is helping himself to a drink." Hope almost passed out. The very idea of what was happening under the sheets turned her ice cold. She broke out in a sweat and strangled sobs escaped her throat. Abe pushed on her mouth even harder to silence her. "Please Cookie, our—live—are—at—stake."

About five minutes later, the huge python slithered out of the bed and up out of the window hole. When Abe removed his hand, Hope let out a scream that sent chills up his spine. At the same instant, Abe leaped out of bed, grabbed his gun that was leaning against the wall. The snake never knew what hit him after his midnight feast. The gun blasts were deafening, and just to make sure Abe used a panga and chopped off the head. He ran inside to Hope but she was not in the bedroom, again he found her in the bathroom. She was scrubbing her breasts with a brush and crying wrenching sobs that shook her whole body. Only when Anetta came running to see what the commotion was about, did Abe realize they were both naked. He quickly wrapped a towel around himself and together they helped Hope back to bed. She was hysterical. Abe told Anetta what had happened.

"She is in shock. Put on as many lights as you can. I'm going to give her an injection to calm her down." Hope would not lie down, she sat at the head of the bed, her back resting against the wall and the sheet pulled up to her chin. She kept staring at the window. Thank goodness the two girls had slept through all of this.

Some neighbors came over because of the gunshots. One motherly type went and made coffee and brought over milk tart. It wasn't long before the injection took effect, Hope now calm joined her neighbors in her kitchen, "What a way to meet our neighbors," laughed Hope. "Seriously I know you killed it Abe, but what if another snake comes."

"Cookie, it won't. Actually this is my fault, two days ago when the housing committee gave me this house, I found a python curled up in the bedroom. I killed it and knew its mate should be around; I searched and searched for it. Not finding it I mistakenly thought it was dead; but it obviously was not and had come looking for its mate. Pythons do not usually like to live around humans but the house was not inhabited, and it is right on the edge of the bush. In building these temporary homes we have probably taken over their territory."

"Okay, I accept that Abe, but there is something I want you to do. Using some sort of screen or wire, I want it tacked over the window holes, and while you are at it from the outside walls to the thatch. The gap up there can't be good."

Young Mrs. Steyn quietly added, "Bai Dankie, I have been trying to get my man to do the very same thing, but he says I was worried for nothing." Turning to her husband, she said, "Look at that Jan, a python in bed with her, and drinking her milk."

"Okay, okay," the men, agreed. Tomorrow all the homes would be wired up.

Mrs. Steyn volunteered to help Hope and Anetta settle in. First, she took Anetta to the hospital; the personnel could not believe their luck, a doctor walking through their doors. Anetta was signed on immediately. Mrs. Steyn then introduced Hope to the limited stores. There were very few clothing items, some first aid and farming equipment, but mainly only basic foods. Out here, basic meant powdered milk—that took getting used to. You would order meat each day, from the butcher and he would deliver it to your door. You grew your own vegetables, or local farmers would stop at your house each day to sell their vegetables, you could also buy eggs from them. In time, Hope had her own vegetable garden and about a dozen chickens so she always had fresh eggs. Locally they grew mangos, pawpaw, quavers, bananas and avocados. There were different wild berries that Hope had not eaten before.

Abe bought a bicycle, which he rode to work, leaving Hope with the car. The hospital had its own company car that would pick up its employees, so Anetta had transportation. With only two other doctors working at Luansyha Hospital, Anetta was kept very busy. There were the usual pregnant women and babies to take care of, malnutrition, coughs and colds, malaria, snakebites and worms. These Anetta were familiar with, but a few sicknesses she had to study up on were sleeping sickness (caused by the tsetse fly), yellow fever (caused by mosquitoes and monkeys), yaws, leprosy, and tropical ulcers, were also common. Anetta buried herself in her work. Being an important doctor, she qualified for one of the mine houses; it was still being built as was Hope and Abe's. Until then, they all stayed in the temporary thatched house, which was now safer because of the rolls of wire.

It did not take Hope long to settle into this new way of life. There were many lessons she learned the hard way. She was told to iron every piece of clothing because of a fly that laid its eggs on the wet clothing, the eggs would hatch and the larvae burrowed into your skin, and produced an ugly boil. To kill the larvae you rubbed oil on the head of the boil, cutting off the air supply. The larvae would poke its head out, and that's when you'd squeezed it out of your skin. Yuk! Hope thought if she hung the wet nappies and all underwear inside the house, she could eliminate some ironing. Wrong, everyone came down with putzi fly. Ironing then became part of the daily routine.

Mosquito nests were a must, as mosquitoes were very bad. The nets also kept other bugs and creepy crawlies out of your bed. Since there were no ceilings, a beam was laid from one inside wall to another and the nets attached to them. Because the thatch was constantly moving and some disgusting creatures fell in your plate or bath, Hope hung nets over the dining table, kitchen worktable and the bathtub.

Checking your shoes before sliding your feet in was very important. Another lesson Hope learned was, you don't check with your hand. You bang the shoe to get rid of any creatures. Fortunately, the spider that bit Hope was not poisonous. Then you needed to boil every bit of drinking water or you'd end up with parasites in your stomach. Any vegetables had to be soaked in mild bleach water, again for parasites.

"Honest to God Abe, I feel like I'm either digging worms out of the girl's skin or checking their poop for worms. If it wasn't for the fact that your health has improved 100%, I'd say let's go back to Johannesburg."

At last, their house was ready. Many families from the temporary housing had already moved into their new homes. Hope had spent a week helping Anetta move into her home. Her crates of books, linen, and kitchenware had arrived along with a few pieces of furniture. The house was furnished with basic needs from the mine. Anetta's house was across from the hospital. Most of Hope's crates had arrived, but she did not unpack them. They only had a week or two and their home would be ready, she would wait for the new house before unpacking.

Their last night in the temporary house proved to be as eventful as the first night. First Hope had, without thinking, popped an unwashed baby tomato in her mouth. The result, bad diarrhea from a bug she picked up. She was just about ready to exit the outhouse when something huge began sniffing at the bottom of the door. The door was about two inches off the ground, so she could see the huge nose blowing dirt as it sniffed.

"Voetsake," shouted Hope, thinking it was someone's dog. She opened the door and banged it against the dog's head; she was cornered and couldn't get out. At this point she realized it wasn't a dog, the lion roared with only a door separating them, the roar was deafening. In shock and fear, Hope fell back onto the toilet seat. Abe had heard the roar and had come to Hope's rescue. Between the lion's roar, and the gun going off a few feet from her ears, Hope felt like her eardrums would burst. Abe pulled the door open and she fell into his arms sobbing. She saw his mouth move as he spoke to her but all she could hear was a ringing. They were one of the last three families to leave the temporary housing. The other two families came running at the sound of gunshots. The women took care of Hope. Slowly her hearing returned. The men helped Abe skin the lion. He was an old male; most of his teeth were lost so he was on the hunt for easy food. They now had a lion skin to add to their snakeskin.

The girls were already tucked under their mosquito nets, but kept calling out. "Mummy, Mummy, I want my kitty to sleep with me" said Colleen. Sheree copied everything Colleen said, so she added her "Mummy, Mummy, kitty." The day they moved into their temporary house, the neighbors had given the girls a kitten. Hope sighed; it had been a long day.

"No, I've just given kitty a bath; he must sleep by the stove tonight so he can dry out." Hope was the last one into bed and made sure the net was tucked under the mattress. Then she snuggled into Abe's arms, her ears were still ringing.

"Cookie tomorrow is moving day. The last few months haven't been too bad, have they? I mean in the temporary house."

"Of course not Abe, it's been a learning experience but I must say I'm looking forward to having a ceiling and nothing living in the roof of my house. I just hope our neighbors aren't so prim and proper. So many of the ladies from the temporary housing thought I was too loud, outspoken and not the 4:00 tea type. They gave me suggestions of what to do with my hair."

"You leave that hair alone. It was one of the reasons I gave you a second look in the window of the store. Your wild spirit is what I love so. It sets you apart from these frumpy woman."

"I'm a wild spirit, am I?"

"Oh, yes indeed."

With that Hope climbed on top of Abe. Abe ran his hand under her nightdress, but she stopped him. "Wild, remember!" and with that she pulled off her nightgown, she still took his breath away.

"Mummy, my kitty is crying. I think he is dry now."

Hope tried to steady her voice, "No, he is not dry yet. When he is I'll bring him in."

"But he is crying, Mummy."

There was quiet for a while, Hope could not hear the cat because of the ringing in her ears, but she heard both girls giggling. "Colleen and Sheree, what are you up to?"

"I think kitty is trying to climb up the net," said Colleen.

While under the net, both Abe and Hope put on their nightclothes. As soon as their feet touched the floor, they knew they had trouble. Millions of red ants were covering the floor. Some were even on their mosquito nets.

"These are army ants on the march. Let us get the girls out of here," shouted Abe. They ran into the girl's room. Their nets were covered with ants. Hope and Abe's feet were being bitten. Each of them grabbed a girl and ran out of the house.

"Which way, which way," shouted Hope? "Anyway I turn they are there."

"Cookie, make for the road, they must have come from the bush area." The other two families who were caught in this wide swath of moving ants were out in their nightclothes. Once on the road, they started brushing ants off them. Both Abe and Hope's legs were badly bitten. "Oh Abe, we were busy and didn't listen to the girls."

"Yes, we did listen and that's why we're here now. Those ants eat anything in their path; the girls saved our lives by calling out and crying."

"Is there something we can do to stop them?" asked Hope.

"No, nothing stops them. Water or fire, they just climb over the dead in their way. It looks as though this group is three houses wide and we don't know where the end is."

"Mummy, Daddy, where's my kitty?"

Abe looked at Colleen, at Hope, at the house. He made ready to go, but Hope stopped him. "It's too late, I'm sure. Maybe that is why the cat was mewing." Colleen looked from one face to another and started to wail, and then Sheree joined in. She wasn't sure why Colleen was crying but it sounded important. They made their way to Anetta's house and stayed there for three days. When the ants had passed their home, they returned. Kitty was a pile of bones in her box next to the fireplace. So were the chickens in the henhouse. The lion Abe shot earlier was also just bone. Even the skin they had put out to dry was gone—eaten.

The new house was so different. There were three bedrooms, living room, dining room a front and back veranda, and an inside toilet. Most important there were ceilings. The fridge was paraffin with blocks of ice delivered in the morning, and a wood burning stove for cooking. It even had closets and a pantry. The first thing they checked for was a screen on windows; the windows cranked open no lifting panes out. Each house had a garage and outside African quarters, a little place for an African servant to stay if you wanted. There was a large front and back yard.

If Hope had moved to this white village of Luanshya straight from the Larger, she would have been very disappointed. But she had been conditioned for this change by first being in a small house in Johannesburg for a few years. Then a cramped train compartment for what seemed like years and then a temporary house for more than a year. This new home seemed like a palace. She loved it and quickly turned it into a comfortable home. It was not long before the colonial influence took over. Hedges, fences and rose gardens popped up in every yard. Hope planted bougainvillea, as a reminder of the Larger.

Anetta had arranged to change her house from the doctor's quarters to a house next to Hope. Because of Anetta's long hours working, she felt safer with her friends next door. Hope kept an eye on her house and garden while she was working. Anetta really missed being around Colleen and Sheree and now Hope had just given birth to a son—Gordon. As she had no children she wanted to enjoy Hope's.

CHAPTER 6

The following summer they had a heat wave. It was a blistering hot Saturday afternoon; Anetta was off duty. She and Hope were sitting in the backyard with the three little ones. Colleen was five, Sheree, four and Gordon was eighteen months. Hope was due any day with her fourth child. She was huge and feeling the heat. They had the garden sprinkler on to try and cool down.

A knock at the front door brought a groan to Hope's lips.

"I'll go," said Anetta. She wanted to check the mail anyway. "I'll check your mail while I'm at it, and would you like some more ice water?"

"Love it." Anetta returned with iced drinks for them all and two letters, one for Hope and one for her. "Who was at the door, Anetta?"

"It was the mailman, he said he always delivered your Johannesburg letters in person because your face would light up so."

Hope sat bolt upright. "It's from my mother. Oh, how I miss them all. I swear if you weren't here, Anetta, I'd have told Abe we need to go back." She ripped the envelope open and started reading aloud. The first part of the letter was greetings and news about everyone, but then came the bombshell. Nathaniel had suffered a heart attack. He had survived, but the doctors advised him to take some time off from work and rest, rest, rest.

"Hope, my darling, this would be a wonderful time to come and visit you. I'm dying to see my grandchildren and help with the new baby that is due any day. But if you think it would be too much, Nathaniel can do his resting at the Larger." Hope was beside herself, her mother and Nathaniel would be spending an indefinite amount of time with them. She beamed from ear to ear. Hope kept chattering for a while, and then noticed Anetta hadn't opened her letter yet. "Come on, open yours, who's it from?"

It was from Desmond Landsburg, the man that helped them across the Victoria Falls. He had written Anetta a few times over the past years but now, he had a meeting with the mine manager and would be in Luanshya for a few months. Could he visit her? Now it was Anetta's turn to grin from ear to ear. He had been on her mind ever since that rescue on the border of Northern and Southern Rhodesia.

"This is a special day, Anetta—three exciting things happening."

"Three, you mean two!"

"No, three, your letter, my letter and my baby."

Charles was born just after suppertime; he was a huge baby. Abe was beside himself. "Two daughters and two sons; that is a good family."

Hope wrote her mother a long letter, insisting that they come as soon as possible, adding if Joy and the children would like to come too, we have the space. Joy answered she would have loved to come but, with Shannon and Nathaniel away from the office, she would be struggling to keep up with the workload.

The next few weeks Hope spent getting adjusted to a new baby and preparing for the arrival of her mother and Nathaniel. Anetta was preparing for the arrival of Desmond. While she had thought about him these last few years, now she was worried, what if . . . and what if . . .

"Relax Anetta; we can always do a lot of things together. My parents and Desmond know this is a backward little drop.

Shannon and Nathaniel arrived two weeks before Desmond. Anetta kept the children while Hope and Abe met the train. "Oh Hope, I never dreamed it would be so long before we would visit you, time just passes so fast. But you and Abe look good."

"Mom, I've missed you all so much. Nathaniel, I'm sorry you had a heart attack but so glad you can recoup with us. Come; let me show you your grandchildren. Shannon loved each of them especially because of their differences. Colleen was such a take charge, go-getter even at 5 years of age. Sheree was shy and quite, happy to be led by Colleen. Chubby Gordon followed his two sisters no matter what they did. The three of them would not have anything to do with the new baby. He cried all the time.

Desmond arrived two weeks later. He was going to stay with the mine manager, but wanted to spend his free time with Anetta. Arriving at her house the first evening, he handed her a box; not gift wrapped or pretty, just a plain old brown box that looked well used.

"What's this?" She asked.

"Anetta, I want you to read these letters. You will notice they are numbered one through twenty-six. Since I met you on the train a few years back, I've thought about you—a lot—often—okay, daily. Thirty times I started to write to you but twenty-six times I gave up, only sent four. These are the one's I did not send."

"Why did you not send them?"

"I have lived in the bush all my life. I have never courted a girl. I do not know what to say or do. And you being a doctor, you are educated and . . ."

"Desmond, you are still working in the bush, I am still a doctor; nothing has changed, so why now?"

I am tired of just thinking about you. I want to be with you. When I learned I was spending a month or so in Luanshya, I took that as a sign. I said 'Desmond, go for it—she can only say yes, or no.'" Anetta took his hand and led him to the dining room.

"Desmond, let us have dinner and talk, get to know each other. Tonight after you are gone, I will read your letters. Tomorrow we will pick up from there." They both smiled, the ice was broken. When she came home from work the next day, Desmond was sitting on her doorstep.

"I could not wait to see you again, and to see if you had read my silly letters."

"Desmond, your letters are not silly, they were written from your heart, and how you felt at that time. I am glad they were written to me. I would like an opportunity to answer them." After a pause she added, "Tell you what, I am going to answer them one at a time in the order you wrote them. Each morning when I have left for work, you will find a letter addressed to you under the front door mat."

Desmond smiled, "What a great idea."

"I will answer your first letter right now . . . . Yes, I have been thinking about you. I have also wondered what it would feel like to hold your hand." At that point, Anetta held her hand out to him, he took it and they walked inside.

A week later, Anetta had now answered seven of Desmond's letters. Through his letters, and their times talking she discovered there were two sides of him. He was the rugged, good looking white hunter type, being able to handle himself and others in dangerous situations. This they had witnessed at Victoria Falls. The other side was a very loving, gentle man. A little shy but once given the okay, nothing could stop him. The fifth letter brought up the subject of kissing, so that evening when he arrived; Anetta said nothing, just walked into his arms, wrapped her arms around his neck and kissed him. In shock for a few seconds, Desmond just stood there, then slowly following Anetta's lead, his lips parted and his arms encircled her. A few breathless minutes later, he came up for air and let out a loud, "Yahoo!" Grinning from ear to ear, he pulled her back into his arms.

Desmond and Anetta were invited that night to a braaivleis at Hope and Abe's. Anetta breathed a sign of relief when she saw how well Desmond got on with Abe and Nathaniel. When the mosquitoes got too bad, they went inside for dessert. Colleen was sitting on Shannon's lap. "Ouma, why are your hands so red and ugly?" There was an awkward silence for a while.

"Well honey, Ouma fell into a pot of boiling water and that burned my hands. So when Mommy tells you to stay away from the stove, you must listen. Mommy always knows best."

"No, Mommies aren't always right." Everyone's eyes were on Colleen now. "She told me my kitty was getting dry, but he was getting killed."

Hope sucked in her breath and whispered. "That was three years ago and it's still on her mind. With a baby in the house, I don't want a cat but maybe we should think about getting a dog for the children."

To lighten the mood Abe said, "So Desmond, is your mission to Luanshya a secret, or are you allowed to fill us in?" Now everyone's attention was on Desmond, who was sitting very close to Anetta, holding her hand. He was embarrassed at being in the limelight. Clearing his throat, he said, "It's no secret; I met Mr. Retief a few years ago. In fact, he was on the same train you girls were on coming to Rhodesia, when we had all that trouble with the rebels trying to blow up the bridge. He explained how important that trainload was—some very expensive mining equipment was in the baggage compartment. Because of our success in handling the situation, our knowing the language and understanding the local tribes, he approached me with a proposition. The copper mines have important overseas investors. At times they would visit the mines. Mr. Retief would take them on a tour of the mines and show them local areas; but he has a dream of a small hotel, not fancy, but one looking very local and blending into the surroundings. Here he would cater to these important overseas visitors; he is building this hotel close to Victoria Falls. His guests could visit this beauty spot, go on guided safaris with guns or cameras, maybe visit local tribes, and eat local foods. Mr. Retief has several parts to his plan, one the hotel for entertaining overseas guests. Part two is, since Northern Rhodesia is having trouble finding cattle that could survive the conditions, this farm would be a cattle experimental farm, looking for, even cross breeding to find a type that could survive these harsh conditions. A third part of his plan was to grow mealies to help with the food supply in Rhodesia."

"What a great idea" everyone agreed.

"So the proposition—is—what?" asked Abe.

Speaking more to Anetta now than the group, Desmond continued. "He has asked me to be in charge of 'Lagenwa.' That is what he has named this safari camp. He has thousands of acres that need to be secured, and animals he wants protected from poachers. The area has to be known very well in order to guide successful tours. To keep peace one had to know the local language and customs. Then, of course, there would be the running of the hotel. His guests were to be kept happy and entertained both in the bush and the hotel."

"Desmond, that sounds wonderful," Anetta said. Now that she had fallen so deeply in love with him, she worried about his dangerous work, fighting rebels, constantly being out in the bush facing the wild animals. But her heart sank; Victoria Falls was so far away. She quickly lowered her eyes so he would not see the sadness in them, but he had seen the flicker in her eyes. He lifted her chin, so he could look into her eyes.

"Don't you see Anetta my love, I will be living in one place. At last I can ask you to marry me?" Desmond stopped, this was not how he had wanted to ask her, and they had an audience. Four pairs of adult eyes were glued to them. Desmond suddenly froze and his face turned red. He had made a fool of himself in front of all these people. Anetta knew him well enough now to know he had just taken a giant step. She needed to rescue him from his embarrassment. This time she lifted his chin so she could look deep into his eyes.

"Desmond, my darling—yes—I will marry you."

Desmond's face lit up. Forgetting about their audience he pulled Anetta into his arms. They broke apart with everyone clapping and shouting congratulations. Now it was Anetta's turn to blush, but Hope and Shannon were hugging and kissing her. Looking over their heads Anetta's eyes searched for Desmond's. He looked at her winked, and mouthed, "I love you."

Anetta felt as though she was on top of the world. A few months ago when she turned thirty-eight, with no prospects of love and marriage in sight; she thought she was doomed to being the single aunt. She had resigned herself to that, but her heart hurt whenever she saw Hope and Abe together, they were so much in love. Then there was Shannon and Nathaniel—older—both second marriages—but so obviously deeply in love. Now she was in love, her heart sang.

The weeks that passed were busy, both day and night. Nathaniel felt he had rested enough, he wanted to accompany Anetta to the hospital; it was so different from the hospitals and equipment used in Johannesburg. It had been many years since he'd seen and treated such sicknesses as malaria, bilharzias and sleeping sickness. He had never seen leprosy and was totally appalled at the damage done to the human body. The sick usually wait until they could not cope in the villages or they had been outcast, then they would come for help. Most times it was too late.

Each doctor at Luanshya hospital would take one day a week, and drive out to outlying villages to treat any who could not make it into town. Nathaniel and Shannon spent the day with Anetta when it was her turn. Not only did they enjoy the rugged countryside, they helped with any immunizations that were due, or cleaning and stitching wounds. Late that afternoon on their way home, Anetta prewarned them of a stop they had to make.

"This man is in his early forties, he has had Elephantiasis for a number of years. As you know, it is a tropical disease caused by a worm infection. We stop just to check if he has developed ulcers on his limbs and then show his family how to help him."

"To check my memory," said Nathaniel, "it causes massive swelling of the legs, arms and even the scrotum."

"Yes, and in this poor man's case in order to help him in his limited movement, we gave him a wheelbarrow."

"A wheelbarrow! What for?"

"You'll see," laughed Anetta.

What they saw made Nathaniel shake his head in disbelief. This man's arms and legs were swollen but his scrotum was so swollen he would never have been able to walk; but by placing them in the wheelbarrow to supporting them he could move about. Their job today was to check the thickening and darkening of the skin.

That evening as the three couples gathered around the fireplace at Hope and Abe's, Nathaniel told everyone about their different, exciting day.

"Anetta will never be able to say her job is boring," said Shannon.

Later, Desmond walked Anetta home to her house next door. He had some news he wanted to tell her—alone. "Anetta my love, on Monday I will be flying with Mr. Retief in his little plane to inspect Lagenwa. I will be gone for a week."

"A whole week!" She walked into his waiting arms and buried her face in his neck. He felt the wetness of her tears against his neck and he got a lump in his throat.

"Retief thinks he will be ready for me to start in six weeks time. Anetta, we have to be married before that, I can not bear being apart from you." Anetta did not answer him right away. She unbuttoned his shirt and slipped her hand in. Her hand was so soft and warm against his chest it turned his knees week.

"Desmond my darling," she whispered in his ear. "I would like to answer letter number twenty-six in person. Do you remember what you wrote?"

He nodded, and in a husky voice said, "Yes, I wondered what it would be like after making love, to fall asleep in each other's arms, then to wake up and have you right there."

"I'd like to know as well. Let us find out—tonight."

Desmond could not say anything at that moment but he tightened his hold on her so that she had trouble breathing. He started running his hand up her back; he cradled her neck with his hand as he bend to kiss her waiting lips.

Anetta and Desmond sprang apart at the sound of a pounding at the front door and Abe screaming, "Anetta, Anetta, come quick!" Desmond swung the front door open, Abe looked beside himself.

"It's Colleen, she is choking."

They ran back to Abe's house. On her way out, Anetta had grabbed her doctor's bag with emergency equipment in it. Colleen was turning blue. Nathaniel was working on her but whatever it was that was blocking her air passage was deep. Shannon was holding Hope back; she was hysterical. After all, she was watching her baby die. Anetta fell on her knees on the opposite side of Nathaniel.

The two doctors ignored what was going on around them and together worked on Colleen. Each knew what had to be done, if they were to save Colleen's life. Anetta opened her bag and spread out the sterilized cloth and tools on Colleen's chest. Nathaniel was shouting for clean towels, which he spread over and around Colleen. Anetta picked up the scalpel, looked at Nathaniel questioning.

"No, you do it; my hand is shaking too much."

Anetta cut and inserted a tube; she then started to breathe for this little girl she loved so much. Nathaniel was saying "Abe, bring the car around, we must get her to the hospital. Shannon, you need to stay with the babies or follow with Desmond and bring them with you.

Colleen was carried to the car. All the time Anetta was breathing in the tube and pressing Colleen's chest to expel used air. Anetta and Hope sat in the back seat with Colleen lying on their laps. This way Anetta could continue to breathe in the tube. Nathaniel climbed in next to Abe; they broke the speed record getting to the hospital.

At the hospital, the candy that was blocking Colleen's breathing passage was removed. The tiny hole Anetta had made in her throat was closed. She seemed okay but the hospital wanted to keep an eye on her. There was no doubt about it; Anetta and Nathaniel had saved Colleen's life with their quick thinking. She and Nathaniel were sitting next to her bed when the rest of the family tiptoed in. Hope and Abe were thanking Anetta and Nathaniel. Hope had collapsed in Anetta's arms in tears and Abe was crushing Nathaniel in his arms. Then he reached for Anetta and Hope. The four of them formed a mass of bodies. Anetta looked up into Desmond's eyes. He winked, smiled, and mouthed, "I love you."

Anetta was beginning to love that about Desmond—his secret message to her.

Everyone rallied around Colleen when she came home. Abe and Hope had a surprise for her,—a puppy. It was a ridgeback, the color of ripe wheat. Colleen named the puppy Mambo meaning Lord over Shona. No ants would eat Mambo; he would protect them. The dog was really for all four children but Sheree was afraid of animals and the boys were too young. So wherever Colleen was you would find Mambo, wherever Mambo was, you would find Colleen. Hope felt safe with Mambo around the children.

The week Desmond was gone, Abe arranged to take Shannon, Nathaniel and Hope underground.

"Cookie, I am so glad you don't work underground anymore. It makes you feel like a mole scurrying along these dark passages." Shannon felt the same way Hope did, but Nathaniel was really interested in the workings of the mine.

"So these steel rods you work with or rather keep sharp, are what makes the holes to hold the explosives?" They followed the whole process of moving rock to the smoldering of the ore. By the time they resurfaced, they were all happy to be above ground again.

"The air smells so funny, no wonder you'd have asthma attacks while down there!" said Anetta. "Thank goodness, you got transferred above ground."

Maureen looked up at her mother; she was fingering the little scar left on her throat from that incident "You know, I don't remember my cat, but I do remember getting Mambo." Jacob suggested stretching their legs before continuing with the reading of the journals.

CHAPTER 7

Retief's little plane touched down ran the length of the runway and slowly made it back to the Ar-o-drum. Anetta ran into Desmond's arms, he swung her around and around. Mr. Retief just smiled as he walked past this not-so-young couple. "See you in the office tomorrow morning, Des!" Desmond held up his hand in acknowledgement as he continued kissing Anetta over and over again.

"My love, I have some wonderful news for you. God I missed you this past week. How is Colleen? How are you? Did I ever tell you how beautiful you are? You have the most expressive eyes; they are as deep as a lion's." Pulling her close he whispered in her ear, "I have letter number twenty-seven in my pocket, are you free to read it tonight?" Anetta smiled as he slipped his arm around her waist and guided her out to the car.

On the way to Anetta's house, Desmond stopped the car at their favorite spot that overlooked a valley. You could always see some sort of animal walking through the valley. He turned to her, taking both hands in his, he said, "What was the thing you were going to miss most after moving to Lagenwa"?

"My work at the hospital."

"Retief wants to know if you will be Lagenwa's doctor. He will build a clinic and furnish it with whatever you want or need. This way there will be a doctor on hand for the guests, and all his workers, and believe me there are many, in addition, he wants to control outbreaks in the bush area, as they are bound to affect the farm. You will be on his payroll for a lot more than you are getting now."

"My own clinic, oh Desmond, that is wonderful. It is like having a cherry on top of the cake."

"So you will say yes?"

"Yes, yes, yes!"

"Since we are both on his payroll he has offered us the use of his plane to accomplish what we need to. Let us go tell the others as it involves them."

They had no time to themselves. As they pulled up, Colleen, Mambo and the other children ran up to them. Hope and Shannon followed. "Welcome back Desmond, we have all missed you. Like it or not, you're part of this family so you will have to put up with us."

"I love it," said Desmond. He never let go of Anetta's hand. Just then the car pulled up with Abe and Nathaniel. They whisked Desmond away to help with the fire for a braaivleis. He looked over his shoulder at Anetta, winked and smiled, then mouthed, "I love you"—she nodded back.

As they waited for the fire, Abe said, "So tell us, what is Lagenwa like?"

Desmond slipped his arm around Anetta's waist and it was as though he was speaking just to her. "It's unbelievable. I can explain it to you, but will not be doing it justice. I would rather show it to you, like in a couple of weeks!"

They all stared at him. "Sorry, let me back track a little, Mr. Retief has offered Anetta the job of being Lagaenwa's doctor." They all agreed that was wonderful. "Because of that, he has offered us the use of his little plane to accomplish what we need, which is to show you all Lagenwa, to get married, have a honeymoon and get back in time to start work in four weeks." They were all silent in disbelief. Taking a deep breath, Desmond continued. "First of all Abe, can you get time off from work let's say, for about three weeks?"

"I have never taken time off. I am sure it can be arranged. What do you have in mind?" While eating they made plans, everyone was so excited. They all agreed it was possible, even though they did not have much time to put it together.

"Now, if you will excuse Anetta and me, we want to be alone. We have plans to make."

They walked to the house next door. "Anetta, my love," he said as he closed the door, and swung her into his arms. "Last week we were on our way to your bedroom, but had a medical interruption. There is nothing I would like better than to try again . . . but . . . I want our marriage and honeymoon to be memorable on every level. I want us to wait for our wedding day and night. One day we can truthfully tell our daughters and sons it is the best thing to do." After a long kiss, he said, "Now would you take letter number twenty-seven out of my pocket?"

Anetta slowly opened it and read out loud.

> *Every man and woman has said 'I love you', in the past.*
> *And will be said, by men and women in the future.*
> *But none with the feeling I have for you, Anetta my love.*
> *Destiny brought you into my life, that night years ago.*
> *You are the half that makes me whole.*
> *I count the days and hours till we can be one.*

Anetta's eyes were swimming in tears as she looked up at him. He was holding an engagement ring. He slipped it on her finger, and then sealed their promise with a kiss.

Abe was given the vacation he asked for. Anetta's replacement arrived and she handed over her patients, she packed up her belongings and sent them by rail to Lagenwa except for the suitcase she needed till settling in at Lagenwa.

The first leg of the their trip was to fly from Luanshya to Livingstone, Anetta, Desmond, Shannon, Nathaniel, Hope, Abe and the four children, there was even room for Mambo. Three land rovers and three drivers were waiting for them at Livingstone. It only took an hour driving northwest on a rocky dirt road, to reach Lagenwa. The bush country was denser and animals were plentiful. Just riding past in the land rover they saw many different types of buck, giraffe, zebra and even elephants. When they pulled up to Lagenwa they were covered in a fine layer of dust.

The house was a long rambling ranch type. The main entrance was actually the back of the house. That was because the front of the house hung over a cliff. The house was built on this cliff so that it overlooked the valley below. This valley had the main watering hole that animals used. Sitting on the *veranda* with, or without binoculars, you could see all types of animals coming and going. Of course, this was the main idea being that it was built to entertain tourists. The house was in three sections; the middle consisting of a back *veranda* a huge well equipped kitchen and laundry room. There was a living room/dining room combined with two fireplaces and large enough to seat three or four families at a time. Then off of this, hanging over the cliff was another *veranda*. There was a huge wing off either side of the main quarters. One wing was for the guests. Eight bedrooms and four bathrooms, each bedroom had its own different view over the valley. The other wing was for Anetta, Desmond and family, also with *verandas* overlooking the valley. Even though newly built with plumbing, it had a rustic motif, with exposed beams, thatch roof; this thatch was treated so it did not have living creatures in it.

Off to one side, not seen from the main house, were four smaller homes like the mine houses. This is where Desmond's main staff lived. They would do the actual behind the scene running of the farm . . . the growing of food supply for the government. They also kept an eye on the movement of wild animals, so that when Desmond took tourists out, as the great white hunter, they would know where animals were at any given time. In addition, they had to control the poachers. There was an African village even further out of sight that housed the many families of African help.

That evening sitting on the *veranda* watching the animals and drinking a cold *shandy*, Desmond said, "What a wonderful opportunity, we have the best of both worlds here. The clinic is still to be built, waiting for Anetta's requirements and the design she would like."

The foreman, Mr. Tinus Joubert, would take them on a grand tour tomorrow. His wife Lena was in charge of overseeing the cooking of typically South African or local type foods. She was very good at this. They had a son named Michael, who was eight years old. Desmond had met the Jouberts a couple of weeks ago when he flew down with Mr. Retief. He now introduced his family to them, putting his arm around Anetta, he said.

"This is Anetta, my future wife, and the doctor for Lagenwa. These are our friends Shannon, Nathaniel, Hope, Abe and the children. They will be visiting us from time to time."

The next morning, Tinus had the two land rovers ready for the day's tour. Abe drove one with Hope, Shannon and Nathaniel. Tinus, his gun bearer, Desmond and Anetta were in the other. Lean had packed a lunch for them and volunteered to keep the children.

"They will have a lot more fun around here instead of driving all day."

"Thank you, Lena, but there are four of them, are you sure?" Hope, was grateful, as the boys were not good travelers. Lena's son Michael was assigned to show them around. There were a few baby animals that he bottle-fed. Colleen wanted to help but he said,

"No! You're too little." But Colleen felt very grown up at age five, nearly six; after all she helps feed her baby brother.

Tinus made an excellent guide. The growing section of the farm had acres and acres of *mealies* and fields of peanuts, the two main food staples of the local people. Vegetable and fruit areas were smaller, mainly grown for use on Lagenwa. The herds of cattle were still in an experimental stage. They had four different varieties that were kept separate, while trying to find out which was the hardier. Their own veterinarian was due to arrive next week so maybe they could isolate and control the problem of sickness they were experiencing among the cattle.

Lunch was on the banks of the Zambezi, the river that eventually fell away as the Victoria Falls. It was a fast moving clean river. There was the constant chatter of monkeys swinging overhead. Every now and again there would be the bark of hippo, the whine of crickets and the "Y bird" added its call to the hum. Being midday, the heat caused sweat to trickle down their backs.

"Mr. Desmond Sir, we were thinking of building a thatched open *rondaval* here, making it a comfortable stop for the guests you will be escorting."

"This is a beautiful spot, and I think that is a wonderful idea. But Tinus, please don't call me Mr. or Sir, Desmond would be fine."

The afternoon was spent touring the wildlife area. As seen when arriving, game was plentiful. There was a rocky cliff area where lions enjoyed sunning themselves; elephants, rhino and cape buffalo were everywhere. Guinea fowl were plentiful and often made their way to the dinner table. Almost every sort of buck was seen, even the little dick-dick, which was only 14 inches high.

Next they stopped at a hot springs, a rocky area that had its own spring of water, making quite a huge pool. Because of the warm water, early morning and cold days, there would be a mist hanging over the area. They all took their shoes and socks off and sat with their feet in the warm water.

"Desmond, this is another spot we thought of building a *rondaval* for the guests—a change house of sorts—because many people like to lie in the water. In some places it is six feet deep. Not only will it feel good after a long day, but some claim it is therapeutic."

"Excellent idea Tinus," agreed Desmond.

They ended up at the waterhole and could look up at the house on the cliff. As huge as the house was, it did not detract from the scenery; it was designed to fit right into the landscape. The supporting beams of the veranda looked like trees. The thatch roof looked like long dead grass. They started the slow winding climb back to the house, but stopped to shoot two buck.

"We do this twice a week to supply our workers with meat," said Tinus. The carcasses were laid over the hood of the land rovers. When they reached the house, Lena greeted them at the door with a tray of tall cool drinks.

"I am sure you are all tired and dirty. Feel free to take your drinks to your bedroom. You will have time to rest and freshen up. In an hour 6:00 sharp, sundowners will be served on the *veranda*. Try not to miss it; the setting sun is breathtaking. Supper will be at 8:00."

Lena was right, the sunset was beautiful, and the food she prepared was delicious. After supper they moved back to the *veranda*. The three couples were happy just sitting in each other's arms. "Anetta, when we passed through this area a few years ago, who would have thought you would end up living in these perfect surrounding," Hope whispered, almost in tears. While happy for her friend she had an overwhelming feeling of sadness, they would no longer be neighbors.

The next day Mr. Joubert took the three couples on a tour around the falls area. Watching the water thunder over the cliff was breathtaking. Shannon got tears in her eyes. "Hope my darling, do you remember the story your ouma Maureen told, when they had to leave Scotland, about an advertisement she read from Dr. Livingstone?"

"Yes, the advertisement for wanted brides."

"Your ouma never got to see Victoria Falls, but just think; today her daughter, granddaughter and great grandchildren are standing next to these thundering waters. Don't forget to pass these stories on to your children."

Hope was standing behind her mother, she put her arms around her and said, "I will never forget, these stories, they are imbedded in my mind, along with the reason I have an unusual name."

Tinus came over and he whispered something to Desmond; he smiled and thanked him. Turning to the group he said, "Tinus just told me, my assistant has arrived at the farm, he is also a surprise for Anetta."

"For me . . . a surprise . . . what? Tell me, Desmond."

"No, you will see for yourself." When they got back to the house, they had missed sundowners so got ready for supper. When seated at the table they noticed there was an extra place set, Desmond spoke. "As you know, day after tomorrow is Anetta's and my wedding day. She wanted a small wedding with all of you present. The only little uncomfortable spot was having a stranger perform the ceremony. But hopefully my lifetime friend and now fellow worker here at Lagenwa will change that."

Desmond winked and smiled at Anetta—a shadowy outline of a man appeared on the *veranda*. Everyone was silent and stared at the mystery man. Then he spoke.

"Way te go, doctor lady, show up that bloody limey." Anetta knocked over her chair as she jumped up.

"Shawn, Shawn" and she threw her arms around him.

"If ye let me have the honor of doing the wedding, I will promise te use me best language."

"Of course, I want you to marry us, and I am so happy you will be working at Lagenwa with Desmond."

Anetta introduced Shawn to everyone at the table. When he met Abe, he thumped him on the back and said in his Scottish brogue, "What de ye plan on doing, multiplying and afilling the earth yirself. Last time I saw Hope there were two bairns, now itsa four." For a minute Abe was taken aback, and then burst out laughing, he liked this man.

The wedding was arranged for 12:00 noon on the banks of the Victoria Falls. The couple stood with their backs to the water. Knowing there would be wind and a constant mist spraying them, Anetta wore a white lace sheath dress and a matching lace wide brimmed hat. They made a beautiful couple. Shawn was facing them and the rest of the group was behind him. Everything was backwards, but this way they would enjoy the falls. Shawn had no trouble with his loud booming voice being heard over the waterfalls. They hired a photographer to take their pictures. After a late lunch that Lena had prepared, Retief's plan was flying Desmond and Anetta to the Kruger National Park for a short honeymoon. Desmond planned on talking to the game warden there about hints on the best way to control poaching at Lagenwa.

The plane circled the landing strip outside of Kruger National Park; the view was breathtaking. A land rover met the couple, and drove them to a tree house *rondaval*. Anetta held her breath; it was so beautiful. The sun was just beginning to set, and it made the thatched roof look as though it was on fire. They climbed the steps to the tree house; a waiter was standing next to a set table.

"*Jumbo Mfundisi*, this is an evening snack. Tomorrow morning a half an hour after you ring the bell, breakfast will be brought up to you. Bwana Samuel said he would meet you and the madam for lunch in the main dining room. "*Kwaheri*," he bowed and left them.

One wall of their hut was solid. The other three were open windows, so they had a panoramic view of the surrounding bush. The African evening noise was all around them. They both loved the sounds of nature; the roar of lions could be heard in the distance. It was a moment Anetta never wanted to forget. Desmond came up behind her and put his arms around her waist.

"My love today is a day that will live in my mind forever, the wedding at the falls, the plane ride to this beautiful park and now this tree house." He turned her around so that he could look into her eyes as he spoke. "I have letter number thirty-three in my pocket."

Without taking her eyes off his face, Anetta felt in his shirt pocket, after opening it, she lowered her eyes to read it.

> *I am no one special to have this extraordinary thing happen to me . . . you!!*
> *I took a chance and followed my heart.*
> *It led me to yours!!*
> *Today our two hearts became one*
> *Our lives are now one—forever!*
> *I love you,*
> *Yours forever*

"Now, my love, we finally can become one body." The letter fluttered to the ground as Desmond took his wife into his arms.

In the morning Anetta woke to the feeling of Desmond pulling her into his arms. "Now," he said, "we have the long awaited answer to letter number twenty-six, what would it feel like waking up in your arms?"

"And?" teased Anetta.

"I want to experience this every morning of my life," Desmond whispered in her neck. That morning they did not ring the bell for breakfast.

Samuel was able to give Desmond some very helpful hints on controlling poaching. He personally drove them around Kruger Park, and Desmond was able to gather a lot of ideas he planned on incorporating in Lagenwa.

All too soon, it was time to return home. They were eager to start their new life and work. Anetta although missing Hope, became close friends with Lena and her son, Michael. Desmond thought he would miss the open non-structured life he lived before with his band of men, but he had Shawn, and now became close to his foreman Tinus.

CHAPTER 8

Northern Rhodesia—1948

During the next three years Abe transferred from Luansyha to Kitwe mines, it was a promotion that had an extra long vacation period. Abe and Hope had a hard time settling back into routine after Anetta and Desmond's wedding. They marked the months off the calendar, looking forward to their long vacation, when Abe had accumulated three months vacation; they planned on a trip. It would take two days driving to Lagenwa, where they would spend a week visiting Anetta and Desmond. They would then drive three more days to the Haven to visit Shannon and Joy for a week, then on to Durban, Natal, where they would spend six weeks, with Abe's family. The steps would be retraced back to Kitwe. Abe was now the proud owner of a new car, so no train this time, although driving proved to be an adventure of its own.

The roads were either corrugated a cleared area or tar strips. Tar strips were two strips of tar-max placed wide enough for car tires. Once you positioned your tires right, you were fine, but if a car came from the front and you had to pass each other, it meant both cars moving off the tar strips carefully, so the drop down—caused by rain—would not tear up your tires.

Usually there was little traffic on the roads; if a car came up behind you, it never passed. It was safer to ride in convoy, so for the rest of the day you drove together. Since there were hundreds of miles of nothing, the government was not going to invest in good roads. *Petrol* stations could be found only every two or three hundred miles. You always stopped to fill up; and you carried extra petrol in containers. Food and water for the trip had to be carried, at least five days worth.

A week before these trips, Hope always cooked and baked, preparing food for the journey. The *primas* tea, coffee, condensed milk and sugar were packed last for easy unpacking. Unplanned-for stops always required a cup of tea. Drinking water was very important. Besides, the containers strapped to the top of the car, there were water bottles that hung off the front end of the car, the wind, as you traveled kept it cool. Outposts were spaced a days ride apart. You could rent rooms for the night, and after a day on dusty roads a shower was welcome.

Hope carried the prepared food, suitcases, pillows, blanket, and books to the car. Abe was to pack and organize the car. "Cookie, where do you think I'm going to pack all of that? I need the top of the car for petrol and water."

She gave him her crooked smile and raised her eyebrow. "Cookie, you wanted to travel by car with four children. I am sure you will find a spot." As she walked by, she pinched his bottom and said, "Able Abe, (a nickname the mine workers gave him) handle it."

When Hope came out of the house, everything was in the car. She was surprised, although they did have to sit on the blankets and pillows. The children climbed into the back seat, ready for their adventure. Mambo of course, had his spot.

"Yaay, no school for three months."

The first day's journey went well. They traveled as far as Lusaka and were able to spend the night in the lodge. The next morning, Hope and Abe wanted to get an early start, as they would be turning off onto a less used road and wanted to be sure they reached Lagenwa while it was still light. They picked up the children in their pajamas and let them continue sleeping while they drove, three hours later they stopped. Abe started the *primas* and made breakfast; out in the bush like that, it smelled extra good. Hope got the children dressed and the car reorganized. Abe walked with each child and carried his gun, when they left the road area to use the open-air toilet.

A few hours had passed; they hadn't seen another car or even any villages along the way. Rounding a bend, Abe slammed on his brakes.

"Cookie!" yelled Hope. "Where is the bridge?"

Abe got out of the car; there was a steep drop down to the river and a steep climb on the opposite band, but no bridge. "Stay here, I am going to walk down to see what has happened." When Abe got down there, he saw there was a bridge, a concrete slab laid from one bank to the other, but because it had rained the night before, the concrete slab was covered with about six inches of water. Abe walked over and back again to make sure nothing was on the bridge and it was in fact from bank to bank. Getting back into the car, he said, "Okay, let's go." Poised on the edge ready to drive down, you could not see the road; the drop was so steep.

"Stop!" yelled Hope again. "Abe, with all that water and petrol on top of the car, don't you think we will be top heavy and maybe topple head over heels!" Abe stared at her, she was right. He leaned over and grabbed her by the back of the neck and kissed her hard.

"Thank you, I would not want to take the chance. Tell you what; I am going to carry the water and petrol over one container at a time and up the other side of the bank, then drive the car over. How about I take the *primas* and foodstuff over first? You and the kids walk with me. Then while I am carrying the containers and driving the car over, you get lunch, and feed them. I will eat in the car later. This is going to cost us an hour or more in time."

Hope found a spot on the opposite bank and made lunch. The children ran some energy off, but they had to stay on the road. Hope kept her gun ready but with Mambo there she felt safe. He was the best watchdog. By the time Abe brought the car over and repacked, she was ready.

"Let me drive a while," said Hope "you rest and eat your lunch." Abe did not argue. This had been a good workout and he was tired. He had stripped down to his khaki shorts and was covered in perspiration.

They pulled into Lagenwa just as the sun was setting. Anetta was waiting for them and ran out to meet them. It had been three years since she and Hope had been together, they both had a million things to share. Desmond helped Abe unload. "Did you have car trouble, we expected you earlier."

"Not the car, but we were top heavy for the Tonkker Bridge. I had to unpack and then once over, repack."

Anetta and Desmond had had a very busy season and were looking forward to this rest and visit with their friends. It had been a long day for the children; they had their bath and supper early then off to bed. Now the four adults had supper on the front *veranda* by candlelight and quiet. "Oh, this is so nice," said Hope. "Okay Anetta out with it, you have been like a cat that swallowed a mouse since we arrived," Anetta got out of her chair and came and knelt in front of Hope.

"Guess what," she said, smiling from ear to ear. "I am going to have a baby, at last."

The two men moved to one side, shaking their heads. They could not understand why the word baby got women to fall to pieces. Desmond spoke about a well they needed to install, he needed Abe's advice. The well had to fit into the landscape and the water pumped into the animal water hole, so that it was not obvious.

"This year I thought we were going to dry out. If we lose the water hole, we will probably lose the animals, so I need your input Abe." The girls were lost in baby talk and would be for the rest of the week.

Colleen did not see Lena the night before, she had already gone home, but she was in the kitchen now making breakfast. Colleen ran to her and hugged her. "Lena, is Michael around?"

"He is feeding the baby animals; this place is almost like a zoo with all the animals coming and going." said Lena good-naturedly.

"Can I help?"

"Sure, we have moved them from the barn. There is a new building at the bottom of the hill. You will need to take the path behind the house." Colleen ran all the way; she stood at the gate watching Michael, and then called out.

"Michael, can I come in and help?"

He stood up; he was very tall for a twelve year old. "Sure, come on in." They chatted like it was only yesterday he had been assigned to look after them.

"Michael, last time you told me I was too small to help feed the animals, I am almost nine now—big enough to help."

He looked at her, and then nodded. "Yes, you are bigger but let me show you what to do." Position the bottle against your stomach, and use both hands to encircle the bottle, that is because as they drink they nudge, this way you won't drop the bottle." Michael handed her a bottle, and a baby buck, very unsteady on his feet started sucking. He had huge eyes and his nose was shinny, as he drank he made little noises in his throat.

"Oh! Michael, what happened to his mother?"

"She was probably someone's dinner last night." Michael looked up from feeding a lion cub and saw the horror on Colleen's face. Then the tears started to flow. "Hey! Don't ask if you cannot take the truth. This is not someone's back yard—it is wild bush life."

"I am not crying—something flew in my eye." Colleen used the bottom of her shirt to wipe away the tears and her nose. Next she fed a zebra while Michael struggled with a rhino cub. While only a few days old it could still push Michael around.

Walking back to the main house Michael asked her, "Do you want to join my friend Moses and I today?"

"Oh yes! I have to check with my mother but I am sure it would be fine."

Michael waited for the land rovers to disappear down the road. Turning to his mother he said, "Mom, can I take Colleen and introduce her to Moses and our special places please, please." Lena had a nanny who was going to keep the other three children busy playing.

"Yes, but remember Colleen is not used to the bush area, so you are responsible for looking after her."

"Yessss," said Michael jumping up and down.

"But, I want you back by lunch time, do you understand Michael? You can go back out after lunch." Michael grabbed Colleen's hand and off they ran to the African village. As Michael and Colleen approached, a lot of black children joined and followed. It was not often they saw white children especially one like this. They all wanted to touch her hair, and freckles. One little girl wet her finger in her mouth and tried to rub the freckles off of Colleen's nose.

"Michael, some of these children are not wearing clothes!"

"What do you need clothes for? It is too hot, plus they get dirty and you have to wash them. It is easier not to wear them. Only when you start growing hair do you have to wear clothes. This is Moses' hut." Michael stood at a respectful distance and shouted, "*Jumbo*."

Moses' mother came out carrying a baby on her hip. "*Jumbo* Michael, are you looking for Moses?" Michael nodded. "He is milking the goats, he should be back soon. Ah, here he is now." Moses quickly handed his mother the milk.

"Can I go now?" asked Moses, "I have finished my chores."

"Yes, but be sure to behave. You know your father has a responsible position here, he will not tolerate you misbehaving."

Michael turned to Moses' mother. "We plan on a long journey; can we leave our things here?"

"When you go off with Moses, I don't mind. But are you sure the white girl's family won't be upset?"

"Its fine, its fine," insisted Michael.

Inside the hut, Michael and Colleen stripped, folded their clothes in a neat pile and were ready for the morning's adventure. The three children made an unusual picture. Moses was as black as night with the African tight nubby hair. Michael was a tan color with black hair he wore chopped off in a crew cut. Colleen was very white with dark red hair cut short, forming a mass of curls. Off they ran and disappeared into the bush.

They ran single file down a path that led to a stream. It was one of the many streams that fed the mighty Zambesi. This was a clear slow moving rocky—river bed, in dry season there was no water, you had to dig for it, and it was buried deep in the sandy bed. The river was not deep, at places only reaching your knees. Because of the many rocks, it was a favorite sunning place for snakes. Moses and Michael enjoyed sneaking up and catching the snakes. They knew just where to grab them behind the head. If it were a small snake they would let it go right away, it was the thrill of the catch they wanted. But, with the larger snakes, it was the wrestling match that followed they enjoyed most. The trick was to see how long you could hold on while rolling around in the water before you felt you had to let go.

Moses would count for Michael, and then Michael would count for Moses. Both cheated, so that they always seemed to go shorter than the other. The boys showed Colleen how to grab the snake, after she was dunked three or four times, she got pretty good at it. Mambo was always at Colleen's side; he never stopped barking at the snake. Later, sitting on the rocks letting the sun dry them, Michael said, "When I get older, I am going to catch poisonous snakes and milk them. They pay a lot of money for that."

Next they continued through the bush, passing at a safe distance from animals. They reached the tree the boys were heading for and climbed half way up. Each of them picked a branch to sit on. This was a mango tree, not the ordinary small mangos; this was the kidney mango, huge and delicious. Each picked one and peeled it with their teeth, it was very juicy and messy to eat, and the juice ran over their bodies. They used the pits as balls and tossed them to one another. "Time to get cleaned up," shouted Michael. Jumping out of the tree, they ran in single file through the bush. This time they came to a beautiful rocky pool, the same hot springs the adults had visited. After chasing the monkeys away they waded in. It was like a warm bath. Soon they were clean and drying off on the rocks.

"I see what you mean Michael; this is so much easier than worrying about getting your clothes dirty. No mango stains, no mud from the river, and we dry quicker than the clothes."

"Yep, I guess we had better head back, Mom wants us home for lunch."

Back at Moses' hut, they got dressed then headed up to the main house. Lena had lunch ready. "I am glad to see you kids are clean." Michael and Colleen gave each other a secret smile. They ate their sandwiches and drank their milk in record speed. This was fresh milk, none of that powder stuff. Colleen asked for seconds.

"Michael, you know you have to feed the animals before running off again."

"Yes Mom, Colleen is going to help me."

With lunch over, Lena handed Colleen and Michael five feeding bottles of milk. Michael started with two lion cubs that were about three months old, they sat with their legs under them, and the cubs climbed over them while sucking. After feeding, they played with them a while before moving on to the baby zebra and baby buck and finally a baby rhino. He had the super size bottle.

"What happens to these animals, Michael? Are they your pets?"

"I wish they could be, but we are not really allowed to play with them, only feed them. Hopefully my dad says they can be reintroduced to the wild as soon as they can manage by themselves." They took the empty bottles back to Lena.

"Michael, they are going to be dipping and branding cattle. Gordon and Charles are taking a nap, so take Colleen and Sheree to watch."

The cows were funneled down to a single file and were kept moving down a fenced passage, not being able to turn left or right. Farm workers standing on the lower rung of the fence, kept the cattle moving. Michael and the two girls also stood on a rung to watch. The cattle bellowed all the time, not sure what was happening. First, they went through a dip of medicated water completely covered their bodies. It killed ticks and other blood sucking vermin on their bodies. Then while still in this single file, they were branded on their rumps with the initials 'L.R.' for 'Lagenwa Ranch.' When that red-hot iron was pressed against the rump, you could hear and smell the sizzle of burning flesh. This was accompanied by an extra loud bellow. Those with horns had them filed, so they could not do any damage. Then the cattle broke out into a large enclosed area where they were checked one by one for any problems they had.

Back at the house, Lena said, "It is already 4:00; the adults should be back soon. Michael, take the girls to the front *veranda*. You may turn the *wireless* on. I will bring you some *oros*. They lay on their backs listening to a story on the B.B.S.—a British station.

All too soon their week at the farm was over, and they were on their way to the Haven. On the second day of the trip, Hope leaned forward, staring out the window, "Cookie, what is that in the road?" It was huge dark mounds with steam rising off it.

"It is elephant dung and since it is still steaming, they must have just passed this way." As Abe rounded the curve there they were, walking ahead. Abe braked and reversed a few yards. The elephant in the rear turned and walked towards the car. Abe reversed even more. It was no easy task on the tar strips. The elephants decided they liked the road and continued walking on it. Hope suggested it was a good time for a cup of tea. They took out the *primas* and brewed some. Two cars pulled up behind, when they heard elephants were ahead, they joined in the tea break. The elephants were very slow moving and it took three hours before the cars could continue. Elephants do a lot of damage, as they walk through an area. They had knocked a few trees down trying to reach the top leaves and fruit. If the men from the three cars could not pull the tree to the side, it had to be chopped in half, and then pulled off the road.

Because of the three-hour delay, Abe was late reaching the outpost station. There were no *rondavals* vacant; so two tents were set up. Hope and Abe used one, and the children used the other. Stretchers were unfolded and pre-folded bed linens opened out. After a hot bath, everyone enjoyed sliding into his or her beds. They did not feel safe in the tents when they heard the lions roaring, or hyenas barking and laughing. The next morning they were woken up by African workers, walking up and down the path of tents calling "*Lekker warm koffee*" (delicious hot coffee).

The six weeks spent at Durban, Natal was a quiet, lazy holiday. This was the children's introduction to the ocean. The four of them loved it and were quite happy to swim, or rather play in the waves all day. This was a new experience. Because of hippos, crocodiles, malaria, bilharzias and a host of other dangers, swimming was not done in Northern Rhodesia.

All of Abe's relatives were in and around the Durban area. Abe's parents still ran the sugar plantation outside Durban. They could not believe the change in Abe's health. No more asthma attacks, now he had turned into a fit and healthy man. When Abe first married Hope, she was so different they had reservations about her. But now seeing how well their son was, how happy they were together, she was welcomed with open arms.

It was their first visit with their four grandchildren. The children loved to hear stories of The Four Corners, how their Great Grandfather Nicholas had come from Russia, how he had lost half of his face to a hyena. How their grandfather's brother, Abraham, had been eaten by ants and that their father, Abe, had been named after him. Then of course they wanted to hear over and over again how their father's sister died when a crocodile took her to his lair. And the dramatic rescue by their Grandmother, Natasha.

"Dad," said Colleen, "you know how at the Larger we visited the graves of my Great Grandmother Maureen who came from Scotland. Sometime could we stop at Four Corners and visit my Great Grandfather's grave, Nicholas the Russian. I think its pretty cool having people from Europe come here, and eventually their grandchildren, you and Mom meeting and marrying. I am the firstborn of the Russian and Scottish families joining up." All too soon, they were saying goodbye to their new family. Jacob and Natasha hoped to visit the following year. This Northern Rhodesia sounded very interesting.

It was not too far out of the way to stop at Four Corners; Abe enjoyed taking them on a tour. Of course, their homes had all been destroyed in the British Scorched Earth policy, and they had lost three quarters of the farm because of legal matters. He could however, still show them the rocky area where the hot springs were that the family enjoyed so much, and the cave where Stoffel stayed and later, they used to hide equipment. They spent time at the gravesite and found Nick and Marie's graves, their son, Abraham who had been eaten by ants; Alexander, the other Russian and his wife Liz, the English girl, and of course little Anya who had been killed by a crocodile.

Wondering around the site Colleen said, "Dad, there is a grave here that just says, Young Couple and a Baby, why no name?" Abe told Colleen the story of the overturned wagon and finding the bodies of the woman and unborn child in the wagon and the man up on the cliff.

"What about Sam and Sarie?" Their touching love story and violent death brought tears to Hope and Colleens eyes, wiping away tears Colleen asked, "What about Voeljune and four children. How can a whole family get wiped out?" When Abe finished the story Hope and Colleen were crying again. Colleen said, "Is anyone keeping a written record of the Russian and Scottish sagas?"

"I have been writing down a few details but nothing too extensive," said Hope.

"Well, I am going to." That was the trip where Colleen started her writing.

Colleen was walking back and forth behind the couch, she said, "I can see why I wanted to write the journals, the last few paragraphs touch on some interesting facts. Now, I really want to read the early journals so I can fill in the gaps."

Jacob teased his mother saying, "How about the fact that you ran around naked in the bush . . . and . . . played with snakes?"

"Now that was a really stupid thing to do, we could have been killed, I'm sure some of those snakes were poisonous."

CHAPTER 9

Because of spending too much time at Lagenwa, they were running late returning home to Northern Rhodesia. Abe had to report back to work in two days. He decided to drive through the night to make up time. They arrived at the border post at 3:00 A.M. The guards were asleep. Not wanting an argument on their hands, Abe decided to open the gate himself. He drove the car through, and carefully closed the gate again. The guards still did not wake up when he entered the office, so he filled out the re-entrance form himself and left it on the counter. Neither Hope nor Abe saw the huge poster that had been nailed to a stake by the gate. It was not buried deep enough so had fallen over. It read:

SMALLPOX
Quarantine

Northern Rhodesia is under quarantine,
No one is allowed to leave the country.
Only persons with proof of residency will be allowed in.
You do have the choice not to re-enter.
Once in, you cannot leave.

They still had eighteen hours driving before reaching Kitwe. It was way past bedtime when they pulled into their driveway. Leaving the packed car in the garage, everyone collapsed into bed. Abe had to be at work at 5:00 A.M., but no one else got up. About 7:00, Sheree shuffled through to the toilet. Coiled on the lid of the toilet tank was a spitting cobra. It was eye level so when it spat, the poison entered both of Sheree's eyes. Her shrill scream as her eyes started to burn, got everyone up and running. The cobra was swaying back and forth with its head reared. Hope grabbed Sheree, pulled her out of the bathroom and ran to the kitchen. The emergency treatment that everyone knew about was to dilute the poison with milk. Hope had Sheree lay on the kitchen counter, she was trying to pour milk in her eyes, but Sheree was fighting her mother off. It hurt to open her eyes, Hope had to force her.

Sheree was screaming in pain. Hope was shouting at her to open her eyes. Colleen, Gordon and Charles were trying to kill the snake. The boys had a panga that they were wheeling around. Colleen was shouting at them to get out of her way with the panga, she knew how to catch a snake, but the boys were shouting at her to get out of their way. Hope was shouting at all three of them from the kitchen to get away from the snake.

"Just close the door," she yelled.

Hope got the milk in Sheree's eyes, immediately Sheree felt the burning stop. Putting a cloth over her eyes, Hope said, "Don't open your eyes, lie still and I'll be back." Running to the bathroom she had to rescue her other three children from the snake and from each other. That panga was going to do some damage. Hope pulled the three of them out of the bathroom and slammed the door shut.

"Just leave it alone, it's cornered and extra dangerous,—he will leave the same way he came in. Then we need to find the opening and make sure it is sealed." She took a deep breath to calm herself. "Now everyone get dressed pronto, we have to take Sheree to the hospital emergency room."

Hope could not believe the emergency room. For early morning, it was crowded. She carried Sheree up to the nurse's station and explained what had happened. They took Sheree through to a room where a doctor examined her eyes and re-rinsed them, then squeezed some ointment into her eyes. "You did the thing, she really should have no side effects, let her wear dark glasses for a few days and twice a day put these drops in her eyes."

Returning to the waiting room, Hope said to the nurse on duty. "What is going on here? I have never seen so many people in the emergency room and what are they standing in line for?"

"Mrs. Zulewsky, where have you been the last week?"

"Last night we returned from vacationing in South Africa. Why, what is happening?" Hope felt the hair stand up on her neck as the nurse said.

"Rhodesia is under quarantine."

"For what?"

"Smallpox. You should have kept your family safe and stayed in South Africa." The room started to sway. Hope saw the nurse's mouth moving but could not hear anything. Slowly she sunk to the floor. From far away she heard her children calling, "Mommy, Mommy." When she came to, she was lying on the same bed Sheree had a few minutes earlier. When the nurse saw Hope was awake, she helped her sit up.

"Mrs. Zulewsky, did they not tell you at the border that Rhodesia was under quarantine?"

"No!" and then she remembered. "Actually we did not see any guards, they were asleep. We let ourselves through."

"Pity, you had the choice of not re-entering. Once in, you are not allowed to leave, no matter what."

"How bad is it?" Asked Hope.

"So far, only one European in Chingola, he picked it up traveling from Congo through the northern African villages. Out in that area, we have twenty-one cases being treated and ten deaths that we know of. You know, people from the villages do not always come to the clinics."

Hope asked, "Those lines, are they for vaccinations?"

"Yes, while here, you and the children should be done."

It took all morning waiting in line. Hope had a hard time controlling herself. She understood the seriousness of the situation. Her insides were ice cold in fear. Why, oh why had they not wakened the guards? Suddenly she was angry with Abe. He wanted to avoid an argument with the guards, he should have woken them, he should have seen the sign, he should have . . . he should have. But she knew in her heart he was not to blame, she had to lash out at someone.

The children were not helping. They were tired from their long trip, they were hungry, and they had not eaten supper last night and now no breakfast. Sheree was now aware of the fact she was in her pajamas with all these people around her. Her world had come to an end. Left upper arms were first disinfected, and then vaccinated. Hope was given a print out sheet on how to care for the area and what signs to look for as the days passed.

When Abe returned home from work that day, one look at his face and Hope knew, he knew. He had been vaccinated at work. They just stood holding each other. Finally he said, "If only I had woken the guards."

"We did not know." Hope used the word we, instead of you.

"Thank you," he said and buried his face in her neck.

The only movements allowed were men going to work. Schools closed. Groceries were delivered to the top of your driveway. Once the grocer left, you could walk to the top of the driveway and collect your order. Nurses would come to your home if you needed one. You were encouraged to stay in your homes or own yards. You were not allowed to visit your neighbors.

Hope took everyone's temperature twice a day. Every rise in temperature, every ache, every sniffle was a concern. Even during the night, she would walk to each of the child's bed and rest her hand on their foreheads. Weeks went by. To keep herself sane, and the children busy, Hope had them keep up with their schoolwork. Thank goodness, their whole family enjoyed books, because reading helped the time to pass. Sheree's eyes had healed with no side effects. Everyone's scab from the vaccination had fallen off. Just when they thought quarantine would be lifted, there was a fresh outbreak, or maybe just a newly discovered village area that was infected. All in all, it was about six months before things got back to normal, but people now had a heightened concern for everyday health; a closer watch was kept on symptoms.

Rarely did Abe go underground. On the few occasions he did, it would bring on an asthma attack. More and more drills that he daily re-sharpened to use for drilling, and planting explosives were not being returned. He was very protective of his steel rods, so he would take a trip into the tunnels to release those trapped in rock.

This Saturday he had forgotten to mention to Hope that he would be going underground and so would be working all day. The mines had an emergency siren system, which blew when there was trouble, such as an accident, a fire, gas underground, a cave in, a flood. It was at 1:00 in the afternoon, the siren blew six times. Six meant a cave-in.

"Those poor women," thought Hope. Right away she put on a pot of soup; she knew from past accidents that women stayed there until their men were rescued. She, along with other women who were not affected made some food and would later take it down to waiting families.

There was a knock at the door. Standing there with his hard hat in hand was Abe's boss. Hope stared at him. The look on his face caused her heart to flutter. "No, Jack, no, no! Do not tell me Abe is underground."

"I think he is Hope. I know he went down this morning. He was due up at noon because of a meeting we had scheduled, you know he cannot stay down too long because of his asthma. He never showed for our meeting. In checking the logbook, he never signed that he had surfaced. I think he must be down there."

"Oh no, Jack," Hope felt hysteria rising from her stomach.

"Hope, listen to me. Just because he is down there does not mean he is caught in the cave in. He may be working at helping others."

Hope arranged for her neighbor to watch the children and to continue cooking the soup. She joined the other wives, both black and white. They all had the same look on their faces; fear, hope and desperation. For the first time Hope understood what they felt and why they never left the shaft head with its steel cage.

They had to stand behind a roped off area. The noise was deafening from the sirens of ambulances pulling up, different types of sirens from the police, and yet a different type of siren from mine company vehicles. The underground manager had set up a table to one side. He was constantly shouting in his special phone system to different levels underground. There was some confusion as to exactly where the cave in was; the underground cage was constantly taking doctors or mine personnel down, the clanging and whistle blowing added to the noise. The chief ventilation officer arrived, set up his table and unrolled his maps of the mine tunnels.

His voice was rough with fear. "Roger," he shouted at the underground manager. "My men can not put down ventilation shafts if you bloody don't know where the collapse is!" Rodger held up his hand for silence as he listened in his phone and everyone held their breath.

"Its level 100 and 101," he shouted.

The ventilation chief immediately examined his charts. "Rodger, what section of level 100 and 101?"

Rodger was getting more information from his contact underground. He answered. "The stoup collapsed in the middle, section F."

"Okay boys, we need to drill there, there and there. Let's go." They moved into the cage as one carrying their equipment. The steel doors banged shut behind them. Before even leaving daylight, Hope noticed they switched on the headgear lights and the lights hooked on their belts.

Another cage surfaced, clanging to a halt. Men fell out of it, gasping for fresh air. They were covered in mud and dust; you could not tell if they were black or white. Doctors immediately rushed to them, those hurt were put in ambulances and rushed to the hospital. Others were given oxygen, they coughed and coughed, and the dust was so chokingly thick. Mugs of water were handed to them. Some of the men were silently sitting shaking their heads, others were so relieved at being out they couldn't help but sob. The tears washed down their faces leaving streaks. Hope heard one of them say, 'so many are trapped, there are squealers, but we could not do anything to help.'

"What are squealers?" asked Hope to the lady standing next to her.

"Men trapped with no way out, their calling for help sounds like squealing." Tears welled up in Hope's eyes.

Hours had passed; time was of the essence, as fresh air would be running out if not already gone. Abe's asthma added to the problem. One crisis after another was beginning to take its toll. Instead of being what she wanted, a pillar of strength, Hope was trembling and on the verge of hysteria. Her Abe was trapped, or dead underground. She could not bear the thought of being without him. Her mother's voice kept repeating itself to her. 'Keep hope alive in your heart; as long as you have hope, you can keep going.' That is what kept her going now.

With the smallpox crises, and now this mine cave-in, Hope found her hand at her throat, clutching the three-corded necklace. She knew it was her imagination, but it seemed to give her strength. It was a visible reminder that she was not alone, that God would help her no matter what.

Abe had retrieved a few hundred of his drills; it was always safe to collect his drills on a Saturday. It was a day they never blasted; they used it as a clean up day. As the conveyor belts were not being used to carry rock out, Abe would lay his drills on them until he was ready to leave the section or level. He was keeping an eye on the time, knowing there was a meeting scheduled with Jack. He needed to allow enough time to clean himself up after being underground.

Abe worked his way from the bottom up. That way he didn't have to carry the drills so far. When he got to level 101, searching for his rods, he said to his number one lead man. "Don't you think it's wet here today?" Letting his two lights travel over the wall, he noticed the walls had water running off and forming puddles. Abe knew his boss was concerned about a fissure that had traveled into that mining area since last surveyed. That was why they were having a meeting later. Moving up into section 100, the early part of the tunnel seemed fine but as they walked in, Abe felt uncomfortable, the water was first around his ankles, then mid-calf. Looking at the walls, Abe found the new fissure. It was a lot wider than Jack had said, and water was rushing out. "Number One, I don't like the look of this or the sound. Listen . . . it sounds as though the wall is creaking?"

"Yes, Boss Abe."

Abe noticed lights coming from the back of the tunnel. The six men were running and shouting. It was the underground manager for that area. "We need to empty this section" he yelled "maybe even the mine. A wall back there is getting ready to blow. A fissure from many miles below is opening, we need to push the code red button and get . . ." Before he could finish, there was an ear splitting explosion. Rock and water were flying everywhere. The water became a torrent and washed them down the tunnel. Suddenly there was another explosion. Instead of being washed along the tunnel, Abe felt himself falling with the water downwards like he was sucked down a drain. Rock, water and bodies tumbled down. Abe hit something or rather something hit Abe. He let out an agonizing scream before he lost consciousness.

When he came to, he was aware of several sensations. First, he thought his eyes were going to pop out of his head because he was hanging upside down. He was not sure for how long he had been there, but it felt as though every drop of blood was pooling in his head. Then he was freezing, rushing down the river he had lost all but his trousers, even his boots had been ripped off with the force. His leg, felt as though it was on fire, because he had lost his hard hat with a light and, of course, the light around his waist, he was in pitch darkness. He could not see what his leg was jammed in but for sure, it was broken. The pain was unbearable. When he first came to, his two arms hanging past his head were touching the water, now when he let his arms drop, he felt the water almost to his elbow.

"Oh God, I am going to drown hanging upside down" moaned Abe. "Anyone . . . anyone . . ." he shouted. Now he heard moaning, crying and some screaming. "Quiet, quiet, everyone, be quiet! First of all, does anyone have a light?" Slowly lights started flickering on.

"I do," said a voice.

"I do," said another voice. About six people responded.

"Switch them off," said Abe, "we need to conserve our light. Let us identify ourselves and our injuries, and see who needs help first." Abe continued, "My name is Able Abe, the blacksmith for your drills. I am hanging upside down. I believe my leg is jammed into something and is broken. If this water gets any higher, I'm going to drown, as I can't swing myself up. Is anyone mobile?"

There were six of them trapped in this little pocket. Two men were mobile; one of the men was Abe's helper, Number One. "Let us use one lantern at a time, you two mobile men see if you can help us who are trapped."

Number One moved next to Abe, "Boss, I am going to climb up and see what is holding you." Number One and the other mobile man shone their lanterns on Abe's leg. Climbing back down Number One said, "It is not good, Boss. The ceiling came down over your foot. You are wearing a rock shoe; I cannot see where to even put my hands to move anything, it is solid. Your foot must be squashed flat, and your leg bones are sticking out, broken off between your knee and ankle. It looks like you are hanging by the skin of you leg."

Abe was quiet for a while. "Well, you are just going to have to chop me down."

"Excuse me Sir!" This came from the other mobile worker. He looked about twenty years old.

"How long have you been working in the mine, son?" Asked Abe.

"Six months, Sir."

"And what is your name?"

"Trevor, Sir."

"Well, Trevor I've been working almost fifteen years and I have no intention of letting it end like this. Now this is what I want you to do." Abe gave them directions. "First tie a tourniquet above my knee. Good job, now one of you has to chop my leg free at the break. It should be easy since the bone is already broken for you."

"Sir, no, I could not do that," said Trevor horrified.

"Listen to me, dammit. If you do not I am a dead man. At least I will have a chance if you cut me loose." The young boy started to cry and wet his pants. Abe turned to Number One. "Number One, help me."

"I will do it Boss, but afterwards, I will get into big trouble."

"No, I will see to it you do not. First, tell me your name. I have always just called you Number One."

"My name is Samson."

"Well Samson, use your strength and a sharp ax. Don't hesitate. Make the first swing count; I will probably lose consciousness; just make sure I am out of the water. Then you and Trevor help the other men. When I count to . . ." Abe never finished his instructions. He heard the sound of sharp metal hitting rock. He saw sparks fly in the dark, but he felt nothing, he dropped into the water unconscious. Samson knew surprise was good, so had acted before Abe expected it.

When Abe came to, all the men had been helped free and were all settled on a dry area. Someone had wrapped the stump of Abe's leg and at intervals would release the pressure from his tourniquet.

"Samson, why do I still hear people calling?" Asked Abe.

"Boss, they are trapped behind this wall; we can not get to them."

They were all shivering from the cold water, and the dust was beginning to settle from the blast. Now they were having trouble breathing. Dust was one of the deadly enemies of a miner. The dust was a fine mist settling everywhere even in their lungs. Abe knew it would not be long before he had an attack. Everyone was coughing.

They had to get out. Shining one of the lanterns on the water, Abe noticed why it was not getting higher. It was running like a fast flowing river through an opening. How long that tunnel was no one knew, but there was a six-inch headroom of space. Would that space be there for the length of the tunnel?

"Sir." Abe looked towards the voice, it was Trevor.

"I am a good swimmer, let me follow the opening."

"Trevor, we have no idea where it goes, and that air space may give out, then . . ."

"At least I tried Sir, like you said 'this is no way to die.'"

Abe thought awhile. "We have this coil of rope; we will tie it around your waist. If, or rather once you get through, tie it onto something. One by one, we will pull ourselves through. If the rope stops moving and you do not signal you are through, we will pull you back. Trevor made it through the tunnel and one by one; the others pulled themselves through.

Abe started to feel his strength drain. He was shivering, his leg was throbbing and his lungs were closing up. The attack came on with a vengeance. The room they found themselves in was much larger and there were at least fifty men there. One of them was a first aid officer and was able to help Abe. Help had to come soon or the lack of air would claim them all.

Eighteen hours from the first siren blast, the rescue team broke through the pile of rock. Fresh air was pumped in while the hole was enlarged. It took six more hours before the hole was large enough to pass the men through. One by one, the names of the survivors were released; cheers went up from the women, and other mineworkers who had collected waiting for news. One hundred and twenty-nine men had been trapped. Thirty-three were killed, ninety-six survived, twenty-eight of the survivors had serious injuries. Abe was one of them.

Hope rode in the ambulance with Abe, she could not stop the tears; he was alive. The leg was bad enough, but his lungs were closing down. The doctor did not think he would make it. He was put on a breathing machine. To hear the choo, choo, choo sound as the machine breathed for him and flushed his lungs was very hard for Hope. They could not give him anesthetic to neaten off his amputation, so using a local they took care of that before infection set in.

CHAPTER 10

A month later, Abe was released from the hospital with a portable machine that would continue flushing his lungs. He had to use crutches until his leg healed, and his prosthesis arrived from South Africa. He was off work for almost a year. Slowly his lungs cleared, and he learned to use his new artificial leg. During that time, he became good friends with Samson. Samson had saved his life, and helped many of the injured, doing all of this with a broken arm. Abe saw to it that the mines rewarded him for his actions and bravery in helping the other workers. Being friends with Samson opened a view to a different way of life. Abe became aware through Samson, that there was trouble brewing among the black people, black against white, and black against black.

Abe had to give up wrestling, which he loved but Hope was secretly happy about that. It had become too bloody. His nose had been broken a few times and his ears had broken tissue from being rubbed into the mat. Abe went for his final check up before restarting work. The doctor gave him a clean bill of health and added, "Hope, I'm sure you will be glad to get him out of your hair, now that he will be going back to work. He has left you with a souvenir. Your tests have returned, you are not anemic, you are pregnant!"

"What?" Chimed both of them. In time they warmed to the idea, even though their baby Charles was seven years old.

With Abe back at work, life slowly returned to normal, except of course planning for this new baby. The two girls were very happy—a baby for them to fuss over. The boys on the other hand thought it was gross. They made comments like, 'If it's a boy he can't share our room.' Or 'we're not going to baby-sit.' Both boys were full of complaints and seemed to want more of Hope's attention. So when Gordon started complaining that he did not feel well, she brushed it off. She was busy trying to cope with morning sickness. While hanging over the toilet throwing up, Gordon stumbled into the bathroom, complaining that his body was hot and that he hurt all over. Through bouts of heaving, she told him to go back to bed. She would be there in a few minutes, and that he had better not be faking it. Hope made herself a cup a tea, and ate some dry crackers, which helped her stomach to settle down. Taking a glass of water, an aspirin and thermometer, she went to check on Gordon. He was burning up; his temperature was 103 degrees.

"Mom," he cried, "my neck, I can't move my neck."

Now Hope was scared, her neighbor watched the other three children while she rushed Gordon to the emergency ward. When Hope explained his symptoms to the Doctor, he was immediately whisked to another section of the hospital, where several doctors examined him.

"Mrs. Zulewsky, Gordon is the fourth child brought in with these symptoms. I'm sorry to tell you, its polio."

Hope stared at him; hearing over and over the word 'polio,' then everything went black. When she woke, she was in a hospital bed, Abe sitting next to her looking very worried.

"Why am I in a hospital bed? Do I have polio too?" she asked.

"No Cookie, you had a miscarriage and lost a lot of blood."

"Oh Abe," she cried, "I killed them both! Gordon said he was sick and I ignored him, and now our baby!"

Abe could not console her. The doctor explained to Hope, "Even if you had brought Gordon in earlier, it's not as though it would have changed the diagnosis, it would have progressed the same. And as far as the miscarriage, you knew at this age, you stood a chance of not carrying full term. It was nothing you did, or did not do. Even if Gordon did not come down with polio the chances are you would have lost the baby."

Again Rhodesia was thrown into quarantine and everyone was immunized. Gordon was one of two hundred and sixty children that got polio that hot summer. Half of the hospital was devoted to caring for polio victims. It seems new cases arrived daily. No adults were affected, only children.

Hope spent so much time sitting at Gordon's bedside; she read up on polio. It was a disease that affected the central nervous system and is more common in children. This explained why so many children and no adults had been infected. Incubation could run as long as thirty-five days. Hope was beside herself worrying about the other children. Would they come down with it too? There is no cure, just supportive care once you survived. Complications included paralysis of the legs and arms in certain degrees and, or the muscles of respiration and swallowing. Because of that, the Iron Lung was used for many children. Gordon fortunately never had to use the Iron Lung. But he did have the Sister Kenny Treatment. This was hot and cold cloths alternated on his legs while exercised. Even though this was painful for Gordon and to Abe and Hope who watched, it may have been what saved his life.

Gordon was in hospital for almost a year. He had a few other complications. About six months into his polio treatment, he developed rheumatic fever. The hospital became a second home, not only for Gordon, but also for the rest of the family. Gordon's schooling was brought to the hospital. Colleen, Sheree and Charles took turns spending afternoons with him, doing puzzles and reading.

The day he returned home, the family had a little party. Hope sat watching her family; her heart still ached for the baby she had lost, but she was thankful they had survived so many crises. Abe had adjusted to his prosthesis, he was now trying to help Gordon with his leg braces, but they were very heavy and awkward. She heard Abe say, "Gordon, when we travel to South Africa for our vacation, we will get you fitted with lighter and more comfortable leg braces. In the mean time, come on let's try again."

By the time everyone was well enough to travel; it had been four years since their last visit. This was the beginning of the rainy season, and they really should have waited for a safer traveling time, but the family needed the break. As they were deciding what to do, they received news that Jacob, Abe's father, had had a heart attack. Coming so close to death himself—Abe had an overwhelming urge to visit his father in Natal.

Excitement was running high. The day they pulled out of the driveway, the sky was black with heavy rain clouds. They were not stopping at Lagenwa on the way down but planned on a two-week stopover on the way back. So this was a straight five-day journey. The new car tires and tubes that Abe had ordered months ago had not arrived. He would be facing tar strips with worn tires, and not enough tubes. It was either don't go or take a chance. Abe decided to take a chance. They were just six hours out of Lusaka when the first two tires and tubes blew. Using two of his three tubes, Abe fixed them. Just before sunset, one of the other tubes blew and the last spare was used. This time Abe had to work through the rain, the mud made it extra difficult. He had nothing solid to position the jack onto.

They were late getting to the rest camp call Zebra. No amount of *hooter* blowing brought out the camp overseer. Hope did not intent to spend the night in the car. Running through the rain to the first hut, she tried the door. It was unlocked and unoccupied. The hut that contained bathtubs and toilets was right next to them; again none were being used. Normally you stood in line to use the bathtubs. Hope filled four different tubs to the brim; each child was able to play in a tub filled with hot water, or rather the two boys played. The hot water helped the stiffness in Gordon's legs. Colleen was fourteen, Sheree thirteen; they both enjoyed the soak. While the four children were in the tubs, Abe and Hope unpacked the car. Abe wanted to redistribute the weight of the luggage. By now they were soaked to the skin, their hair plastered to their faces and mud splashed up their legs. Walking around the rest camp Abe was able to find a few pieces of wood that he could use to support the jack. He got an uneasy feeling, he saw and heard no people; their hut was the only one that had a lantern lit. "When he got back to the hut, the four children were in bed, the boys and Sheree were asleep. Colleen was working on her diary; Mambo was lying on the bed next to her.

"Colleen, where's Mom?"

"She's taking a bath, says for you to join her, she will be filling a tub for you."

"Colleen, please finish your writing tomorrow. I want to blow out the lanterns. There is something wrong in this camp. I'm going to get Mom; I think we will be leaving." Abe had to shake Hope awake. She had dozed off in the hot water.

"Cookie, I filled a tub for you in the next room. I would say join me in mine, but you are covered in mud." The look on his face made her stop and ask, "Abe, what's the matter? You look concerned." He was on his knees next to the tub.

"Cookie, I am concerned. I have walked through this whole camp and there are no people here. Just the three cars we saw parked outside the office, but no people. I thought we should leave now, but on second thought, we will be safer here with no lights on or sounds to attract attention. If we left, we would be driving at night. The sounds and lights of the car can travel for miles. If I had another flat we would really be struck in the dark, bogged down in the mud and maybe some rebels breathing down our necks."

By now, Hope was out drying herself. While she was doing that, Abe jumped in her water, so they could continue talking while he cleaned up. "You're right, Abe. We will be safer here than out on the road. Let's get back to the kids." Hope picked up the prosthesis while Abe hopped back to their hut. Colleen was waiting for them at the door.

"What are we doing?" She whispered.

Abe put his arm around his daughter, and said, "It will be safer to stay here while it's dark. Let's not make noise or light any lanterns. We will leave as soon as it's light. Hope, you and Colleen get some sleep. I am going to sit watch; but in the morning, Hope you will drive. Colleen and I will be on either side of the car with guns; just in case we have trouble along the road."

It was an hour before sunrise. Abe woke Hope and Colleen and whispered, "You two take over the watch, I want to circle the camp." Abe stripped down to his underwear and rubbed mud over his body then disappeared in the dark.

"Mom."

"Hmm."

"I am afraid; Dad is out there by himself."

"Don't worry my girl; your dad can take care of himself. We just need to know what we are facing or not facing. Remind me to tell you about when your dad and I met. He fought off three Africans single-handed. You may want to add that to your diary."

Abe stuck to the trees and circled the camp. No sign of life, or death was found. He then entered hut by hut, still no sign of people. It was almost time for the sun to rise when Abe got back to their hut. He said, "Not a sign of anything, just an empty camp, something is not right. Get the others up, dress quietly. I am going to wash this mud off, then repack the car. Once we start the car, I want to hit the road running. For the next couple of hours we are not stopping, even for a flat. We will keep riding. Hope, don't stop if anything is across the road, just ride right over it. Put your foot flat on the pedal and go."

Pushing the car into position, Abe filled it with *petrol*. He did not want the noise of starting the car before they were ready to drive. The boys thought this was an adventure. Not Sheree, she whimpered all the time. Gordon was mad because he was not in charge of a gun.

"Son, because of your legs, you can not move fast enough. What happens if you have to change your position? No, your job is to look out for danger that Colleen and I don't see." For the next two hours, Hope drove as fast as she could, half the time she was off the strips. Abe yelled, "Stay off the strips, it's better than trying to get back on."

First one, then another tube blew. Hope kept driving but eventually she called to Abe. "Cookie, my arms are going to break. The car is too difficult to control.—I'm stopping!"

When she stopped, the silence was deafening. Everyone sat still for the longest time. It had been two hours since their mad dash out of the camp; Charles broke the silence. "Hey Dad, I really got to pee."

"Okay, everyone out, but . . . be . . . quiet." Hope started to laugh. Abe glared at her. "And now."

"Abe, you said 'be quiet,' we must have sounded like a herd of elephants barreling down this road, with two flat tires? If we haven't attracted attention by now, Charles peeing against a tree won't do it."

Abe grinned. "You're right, but we do have a problem, two flats and no tubes." Abe paced back and forth running his hands through his hair. After a few minutes, he said. "I've got it. Hope and Colleen, sit on top of the car with the guns. This way you can see over the tall grass. One of you keeps watch to the right and the other watch to the left. Sheree, the boys and I are going to cut this elephant grass and stuff the tubes."

Abe put the two tires that had their tubes stuffed with grass on the back of the car. The two good ones were in front, and off they went. It was rough riding but it worked.

"Like riding a pioneer wagon," said Hope, grinning.

As they approached Camp Hippo that evening, they saw a lot of movement—army and police, all were toting guns. They even had a roadblock before the camp.

The police asked Abe, "How on earth did you people get through? The road has been closed between Camp Rhino and Hippo. The people that were in Camp Zebra were led off by rebels; we don't know what happened to them yet."

Abe explained that they were in Camp Zebra but it must have been hours after everyone had been led off. They suspected something was wrong but thought it safer to stay put at night.

"Good move," said the police. "They would have heard your car and maybe returned. You people were very lucky."

The good news was the police had some tubes to sell Abe. That evening, everyone relaxed with a hot meal and the police helped Abe with the car. Next morning over breakfast, they heard that the army had caught the rebels, but all their captives had been murdered along the way. The police explained, "I think something is brewing in the north. We have had a lot of trouble lately. In the future you should try and travel in convoy, there's safety in numbers."

It was one more day's right to Beightbridge, the border post into South Africa. They went to bed with it raining, in the morning it was still raining. With all the rain, the rivers were in flood. There was no crossing on the concrete slabs. A pontoon system was erected during the rainy season. It was a huge wooden raft, floating on empty forty-four gallon drums. You drove your car onto this floating, wobbling raft and prayed for a safe crossing. Before the rains started, a pulley system from bank to bank on either side of the pontoon was installed. Five men on either side, pulling hand over hand on the pulley system, inch by inch, you'd cross the river. At last they crossed the border at Beightbridge.

Their first couple of weeks stay was at the Haven. Here they had an appointment with a specialist who was going to examine Gordon and get him fitted for his leg braces. The specialist was also going to check on Abe's leg that had been amputated in the mining accident. A minor surgery was done; some bone splinters that had not been shaved away were bothering him.

Shannon was excited with the visit of Hope and her grandchildren. Four years was too long a time not to be able to visit, but with two sets of quarantine, one for smallpox and the other for polio, she was not allowed into the country. She had actually tried, but guards posted at the borders enforced the law, at times even using their guns to turn people away. Colleen used this visit to get as much information from her grandmother, on the Scottish side of the family.

Shannon told Colleen, "I have three items that the girls brought from Scotland which I will give you once you have finished writing your journal. One is a picture of the three girls at ages two, three, and four along with their mother and father. The other is their mother's hairbrush and their father's pocket watch. This was all they had left from the family.

Later, during their visit to Natal at the Lalapansy Farm, Colleen got information from her grandfather Jacob, about the Russian side. She was serious about recording their life adventure. Jacob, had recuperated from the heart attack, and he was doing fine. However, Abe did think both his parents were looking their age. He was glad his brother Stoffel had taken over the running of the sugar plantation.

Before leaving South Africa for the return trip home, Abe bought a box of spare tubes. They were returning via Victoria Falls, they planned on a long visit to Lagenwa.

CHAPTER 11

The last time Colleen had seen Michael, she was nine and he was twelve. Time had made a big difference. Colleen had just turned fourteen and Michael seventeen. She was busy turning into a young lady, and looked just like her mother. Michael, on the other hand, was tall and muscled. The sun had burned him a little darker, and he still wore his hair in a crew cut, he was very handsome. On their first morning there, Michael walked in while they were having breakfast. Removing his hat, he greeted every one. Turning to Colleen, he said, "Hello Colleen, I was wondering if you'd care to horseback ride with me today. I need to check on some projects Desmond is having built." Colleen turned to her mom and dad, who both had strange looks on their faces.

"Please, can I?"

"Michael quickly added, "We'll be back by lunchtime Sir."

"Ahh yes, back by lunch time, right?"

After they left, Abe turned to Anetta. "That was Michael?" Anetta nodded. She understood the strange look on the faces of Hope and Abe.

"Michael has changed a lot these past few years. He had turned into a handsome young man, but at the same time, puberty caused certain features, which were minor as a young boy to become more prominent now.

Hope cleared her throat. "Looking at his mother and father, you'd have a hard time wondering which line his ancestor came from."

"Well, Tinus is not his father. When Lena was growing up, she had fallen in love with a farm worker; he was a colored man. They married, but some local white boys were upset about a colored and a white girl marrying. One day when John did not return from work, a group of farm hands went searching for him. They found him strung up in a tree; the white boys had hung him. Lena left that area; she did not tell anyone she was expecting a baby. Later when she met Tinus, she told him the story. He accepted Michael as his own, and it has never been spoken of since. I am not sure Michael even knows that he is a colored. He has led a pretty sheltered life here on the farm."

Hope looked at Abe. "What are we going to do Cookie? I know they are very young, but they have been friends for so long. What happens if one day it develops into a romantic friendship?"

Abe thought a while, "For now, these two weeks let it go. But once back home we'll think of something."

Michael had a lot of things to show Colleen. Even though four years had passed, they had written each other every month. So they were very much at ease with each other. Michael and Moses had collected poisonous snakes, and were milking them as they had planned many years ago. The money from the venom was being saved. Michael was saving for music school, Moses wasn't sure yet what he was going to do. The collecting and milking was all done professionally. They had built a special house and it was filled with glass cages. At least once a week, a government official would stop and pick up a fresh batch of venom.

"Another thing Moses and I do is we shoot animals."

"Oh Michael, I thought . . .

But he didn't allow her to finish. "Gotcha," he laughed. "No, we use a camera. We are actually pretty good at it. A lot of prominent magazines use our pictures." Michael named a few that Colleen was familiar with. "Now another surprise, because of our picture taking, Moses and I built a secret tree house. No one knows about it, not even our parents. We have to swear you to secrecy if we show it to you. Do you Colleen; swear to tell no one, under any circumstances, about our secret tree house?" Michael grinned as he said this sentence.

"I swear," she grinned back.

The tree house was actually off Lagenwa property, but did overlook it. Unless you knew what you were looking for, it was completely camouflaged. Even thought it had thatched walls and roof, the green vines from the trees concealed it completely. The boys could climb the tree easily, but they had a rope ladder that they could drop down. This was what Colleen used; the ladder was used for hauling their equipment up.

When you first climbed up, it looked as though there were just two huge wooden boxes on the floor. However, these boxes contained their household goods. Everything had to be packed away when they left because of the monkeys. One crate had bedrolls, mosquito netting, some camera equipment, and a bible, which Michael read over and over trying to understand. The other crate had lanterns, and kitchen type utensils. When they spent a day or a weekend here, they would be comfortable; all they had to do was carry up bottles of water.

Michael took great pride in showing Colleen their cameras with telephoto lens. He also showed her some of their work. He and Moses had their own dark room. They developed their pictures, as they did not trust someone else to handle their work. Colleen had to admit they were very good.

That holiday, Michael took a lot of pictures of Colleen; there were two she really loved. One was her sitting on the banks of the Zambesi, the smoke of the falls framing her body as the sun set. The other was at the hot springs; she had been under the water and had just burst forth out of the water. Droplets were caught in the sun's rays; even the ones hanging off her eyelashes glittered like diamonds.

Many evenings Michael would spend playing the piano. As his artistic talent showed in his pictures, so it showed in his piano playing. It was done with such feeling. Listeners could not help but close their eyes and lose themselves in the moment.

After supper one night Desmond said, "Michael, we're having trouble with monkeys in the mealie field again. Would you and Moses handle that tomorrow?" Turning to Hope and Abe, he said, "It's pretty harmless. We shoot the guns in the air to scare them off. Maybe you'd let the children go along. I trust Michael and Moses with the guns."

"Yes please . . . please," pleaded Gordon and Charles.

"Okay, but you all need to listen to the older boys."

Plans were made to meet the adults at the hot springs for a picnic later in the afternoon. Gordon and Charles sat on the roof of the land rover. Sheree did not come she wanted to stay home. Colleen sat on the bonnet of the car; Michael and Moses stood, loaded the guns and handed them to Gordon and Charles to shoot. Between the noise of the shots and the screaming of the monkeys as they ran, no one knew for sure what happened. A female with a baby clinging to her breast was accidentally shot. With her dying breath, she ran straight to the car, jumped up on the *bonnet* next to Colleen. With both hands, she pulled her screaming baby off her breast and handed it to Colleen, then fell over dead. Not one of the five people had moved or made a sound as Colleen took the baby. Charles broke the silence crying. "Did I shoot her, I didn't mean to. I'm sorry." He threw his gun to the ground.

Michael took charge. "It's no ones fault," he said. "Maybe the bullet ricocheted off of something. It was an accident." It was so quiet; the monkeys had left. Charles was sobbing, Colleen was cooing to the baby monkey. Michael and Moses dug a hole to bury the mother, and then they drove to the hot springs.

"That," said Michael "would have made an award winning picture. But of course the camera wasn't being used. It was so unusual the mother pulling the baby off of her and handing it to you Colleen."

The adults all agreed it was unusual. They did not think the baby would survive. It was too young; it hardly had any fur, just pink and ugly, but Michael and Colleen worked with Nagarpy (night monkey), they called him that because his eyes were so big. They found a milk formula he liked. He became a bottle fed monkey and decided Colleen's auburn curly hair was a good place to cling onto. When she wore her hat, he would be under it. You could always see his tail sticking out from under the hat.

Both Colleen and Nagarpy kicked up such a fuss that Hope and Abe agreed it could come home as a pet. As they left, Colleen called out to Michael, "I'll write every week and tell you how he's doing."

Abe and Hope looked at each other. They had to do something before it was too late. The only incident traveling back home was several times they got bogged down in mud. Abe was able to get them out by cutting tons of the elephant grass and pushing it under the tires. They'd have traction and off they'd go.

It was good to get home. Abe's leg was much better after the minor surgery. Gordon, while he did not like his leg braces, did enjoy being able to get around again.

Nagarpy had taken to licking Abe's whiskey glass; this stunted his growth. So although he became an adult, he never grew any bigger in size. He was always able to crawl under Colleen's hat. Nagarpy and Mambo got along very well for a dog and a monkey. Nagarpy would ride on Mambo's back as though he were a horse. No matter how fast Mambo ran Nagarpy would hang on. While Nagarpy was an indoor pet, he did have a little house perched on a pole in the back yard. When the children went outside, he'd be clipped to a light chain and up he'd run into his little house.

Monkeys are deadly afraid of snakes. From his vantage point, Nagarpy would always notify the children when a snake was in the area. One day as a joke, Charles put a dead snake in Nagarpy's little house. When he ran up the pole to settle in his house, he let out a terrible scream, and fell to the ground with a sickening thud, stone dead. They were not sure if the fall killed him or if he died of fright. Poor Charles, again he was in tears because of killing a monkey. Hope said, "One monkey was enough, we're not going to replace him."

Colleen wrote Michael that Nagarpy was dead. But Michael had his own bad news to share with Colleen. The universities in both Johannesburg and Cape Town had rejected him. He was not sure why. His grades were top of the line and anyone that heard his music agreed he was very good. One professor, taking him aside said, "Son, don't even waste your time with these schools. They are not going to take someone like you. If you truly want to play, apply overseas."

Michael asked him, "What do you mean someone like me?" The professor just shook his head. So Michael was going to spend another year or two saving money. From his snakes that he milked, his pictures, and now he was composing music that should make enough for him to attend school overseas. Moses, hadn't decided what he was going to do with his money, he insisted Michael add it to his.

"What is a black man going to do with this money? You use it for your schooling. When you come back and go into business, I'll join you." So that's what the plan was. Michael was going to use the money and then pay Moses back when he returned.

CHAPTER 12

Northern Rhodesia, Africa—1957

The bell was still ringing when Colleen ran out of the school building. What a beautiful day! It had rained for two days, but now the sun was starting to break though the dark clouds. The smell of wet soil was one of the things she loved about storms.

Seventeen-year-old Colleen could not wait for Wednesdays; it was the day she always got a letter from Michael. Not wanting to wait for the school bus, it took too long, she ran home. Colleen cut across an open field, through the back lanes, and then squeezed through a hedge of banana trees. The very same trees her brother had burnt down years ago, she smiled remembering that family crisis. Mambo, her dog barked and jumped around her as she climbed through the trees.

There it was on the entrance table, she snatched it up as she ran to the bedroom she shared with Sheree. Dropping her school bag on the bed, she changed out of her school uniform, being sure to hang it up neatly for the next day. As she passed through the kitchen she picked up a bottle of water and a dishcloth, you always needed that for eating mangos; she also grabbed a soup bone for Mambo. In the back yard she climbed her favorite mango tree and settled in the fork of branches that she considered her own spot. Mambo curled up at the foot of the tree with his bone, he also loved Wednesdays. Colleen had the tree and Michael's letter to herself for at least thirty minutes before the bus arrived with her sister and brothers.

Michael was the boy she loved ever since she could remember. Because they lived at opposite ends of Northern Rhodesia, Colleen and Michael only saw each other every two or three years. But they wrote weekly. Colleen read Michael's short letter twice; Lena, his mother had died. Since they had to wait for family to arrive from the Cape, he wondered if Colleen and her family could come to the funeral. Colleen closed her eyes against the tears, but they squeezed through her eyelids and ran down her cheeks. Leaning back against the branches, Colleen remembered the good times her family had with Michael and his family.

Once when she was nine and he twelve, their family was on their way to South Africa for a vacation, and had stopped at Lagenwa for two weeks. They had arrived late the night before and had gone straight to bed. Colleen woke early and scrambled out from under the mosquito net, making sure not to wake her brothers and sister. She couldn't wait to see and hear the sounds of an African farm. She heard a noise coming from behind the barn, climbing on the fence railing she saw him. He was busy feeding some wild animals they had rescued from certain death. When he saw her hanging over the fence watching, he offered for her to help him feed the lion cubs they had. Without a second thought Colleen jumped off the fence and took one of the milk bottles he handed her.

Michael had shown her how to hold the bottles and brace herself because the animals would nudge her as they drank. He and Moses had shared their secret tree house with her. The beautiful pictures he had taken of her, and she loved listening to him playing the piano, he was busy composing a song just for her. The barking of Mambo jolted her back; she heard the school bus opening its doors. Quickly she wiped away her tears and folded Michael's letter, she never let anyone see her cry.

At first Hope said, 'No, they could not take this unplanned trip to the farm.' Colleen argued, "Mom, that whole family was such a big part of our holidays, our lives, how can we not go to the funeral? Besides, that will give me a chance to see Michael before he leaves for England."

"What about school, Colleen? This is your last year, it is very important to keep your grades up."

"Mom, you know I will keep my grades up."

Hope and Abe reasoned not too much could happen between Colleen and Michael in that short time. He was leaving for England in a few weeks; they hoped his life in England would lead him away from Colleen. So plans were made for Hope and Colleen to attend Lena's funeral.

They all loved Lena; they had spent many holidays together. After the funeral service, they gathered in Langenwa's huge living room. Michael and Colleen were standing to one side talking. He was tall and handsome; he'd grown his hair out from the crew cut he normally wore, it was thick and curly. He had a wide smile, very white teeth and expressive eyes. Hope looked at her daughter; she saw for the first time not a schoolgirl but a young lady. Tall and slim, she had also grown her auburn hair, which today she wore back in a twist. Gone were her childhood freckles across her nose. Colleen's eyes were green and right now they were smiling up at Michael. Hope realized they made a good-looking couple. While talking Michael's hand groped for Colleen's hand. They intertwined their fingers. After a few minutes, Hope heard Colleen say. "Michael, it does not matter to me."

"But it should, it could cause a lot of problems, now I understand why schools in South Africa would not take me."

Hope and her mother exchanged knowing glances. "They both know," whispered Hope.

Just then someone approached Michael, offering condolences. Michael walked over to his father, Tinus. He put his hand on his father's shoulders. A few weeks ago, when Lena first suffered chest pains, she told Michael about his real father who died before he was born, and how Tinus had accepted him as his son. Michael had never suspected anything, so it came as a shock, to find out he was a colored. But his love for his father grew, and right now he wished he could take the pain away that he saw in his father's eyes. He had just lost his wife and in a few days, he'd lose his son, who was going to university in England. Who knows when he'd be back?

The next day, for the last time Michael, Colleen and Moses were spending the day saying goodbye to their special spots at Lagenwa; the river, the snakes, the tree house, the hot springs, even the silly mango tree. After supper, Michael played some music he was working on. He'd told Colleen he had named the song he was composing for her, 'Colleen.'

While playing, they were interrupted when Moses came running up to the house. "The buffalo are in the mealies. The men grabbed their guns and drove off in land rovers. Anetta signed, I just hate it when those Cape buffalo come onto the farm property, and they are so destructive and very dangerous. We are in for a long night; I'll make some fresh coffee."

The men in the land rovers, along with about fifty farm workers would make mock charges at the buffalo getting them to move out of the mealies. One field had already been destroyed. They didn't want them to move to another field. At about five in the morning, they had managed to chase them off. Farm workers jumped into the land rovers, sitting on the roof, the bonnet, hanging off doors, all for a ride home. By the time they got back to the farmhouse, the sun was beginning to rise. Anetta made a huge breakfast for everyone. Desmond, Shawn, Tinus and Michael were busy eating when there was a knock on the kitchen door.

"Come in," shouted Desmond. Leaning back in his chair, he could see it was his foreman Sam. "Pull up a chair and join us," but Sam's eyes were busy searching the room.

"I was hoping Moses was here. He did not return with us. I thought maybe he was with Michael."

Silence fell over the group. Desmond looked around. "Did anyone see Moses return?" They all shook their heads. "Let's go," he shouted. There was a mass evacuation as chairs were scraped back and guns reloaded. Off went two land rovers. They backtracked and covered the ground the buffalo had destroyed. Their fear was that maybe Moses had been trampled on in the *mealie* fields, but no, the field was empty. Just beyond the field was a row of low trees, before the next *mealie* field started.

"There he is, shouted Michael running towards the trees. Michael could see the top part of Moses' body through the leaves. "You fell asleep in the tree making us come all the way back for you. Get down from there so I can give you . . ." By now, Michael had reached the tree. He stopped short and his eyes grew wide. Moses only looked like he was sitting in the tree. He had hooked his arms around some branches, but the lower part of his body was just hanging there. The tree was not high enough for Moses to have pulled his whole body out of the way. It was short enough for the Cape buffalo to stand on its hind legs and reach Moses' legs. The buffalo had licked Moses' legs with its file sharp tongue; he'd licked the skin, then the flesh off. Moses had painfully bled to death. The evidence at the foot of the tree showed two Cape buffalo had surrounded the tree and had worked on Moses at the same time. Finally, the scream escaped Michael's throat. He turned and ran.

By now the rest of the searchers had reached the tree. Moses' father collapsed. No one thought to chase after Michael. They were busy with Sam and getting Moses' body out of the tree. By then they realized Michael wasn't just sitting in the field, but had run off. Tinus went looking for Michael, while Desmond and Sam took Moses' body back. They went straight to the clinic. Anetta examined Moses. She knew he'd suffered before he died. His fingernails were bloody from gripping the rough tree bark and his tongue and lips had been bitten as he screamed in pain.

By mid afternoon Michael still hadn't returned. "I think I know where he is." said Colleen. "I need a horse and I need to go by myself because of a promise I made. This is the boy's secret place." Colleen galloped out to the tree house. It was very quiet and the rope ladder was not down. Of course it wouldn't be. Michael could climb the tree.

"Michael," she called. Silence.

"Michael, drop the ladder for me." There was still no answer.

"Okay, I'm going to try and climb if I fall, it's your fault."

Colleen heard movement, and then the ladder dropped down. She climbed up and pulled the ladder up behind her just in case anyone had followed her.

Michael had moved to the window and was staring out at nothing. Colleen sat next to him. She didn't say anything. She just picked up his hand and held it for the longest time. "Let it out Michael, first you got news you were colored, then your mother died; today you lost your best friend, and in a few days, you leave for England. Suddenly everything in your life is changing." She looked up at him; he had tears running down his cheeks.

"And," he whispered, "I've lost you." He was quiet for a while. "When you were nine years old, freckle faced and running naked through the bush with Moses and me, I decided then that one day we would marry."

"Michael, you haven't lost me. I will be waiting, when you get back from university."

"To live what kind of life, Colleen? Remember I could not even get into school in South Africa. All our lives we can't stay hidden in little bush farms. I've heard how mixed marriages are treated. I can not put you through that."

"Then we will live in England," she said.

"Come with me now, I'll forget about university and get a job."

Colleen put her hand over his mouth. "No Michael, anyone that's heard you play knows this talent must be pursued. You said you could not put me through marrying you and living in Africa. Well, I cannot put you through giving up your dream of music. Go to school as planned, and then we will take the next step.

He cupped her face and tilted it so he could look into her eyes. "But that's such a long ways off."

Colleen slipped her arms around his neck. "It will pass quickly. Just think of it as the times in between holidays. We can write . . ." Colleen never finished her sentence. Michael lowered his mouth on to hers in a long lingering kiss. Then very gently he pulled away and stood up.

"Colleen, it will be dark soon. I think you had better go before . . . before . . . something happens."

"Are you coming back with me?"

"No, I want to spend the night here. Please don't tell anyone where I am."

"Michael, if you are going to spend the night here, I want to spend it with you."

Michael started to say something but Colleen stopped him. "In two days I leave for Kitwe, in four days you leave for England. It will be at least four years before we are together again. This is our only chance of being together."

"Colleen, you do understand, I want to make love with you."

"Yes, and I want to love you."

"Colleen, will you marry me?

She walked into his arms and against his lips said, "Yes."

"Then until we can marry in front of a minister, let us marry in front of God."

"So that your mother does not worry, we will send the horse home with a note tied to the saddle. I'll tell them you are safe, we are together, and that we will be home tomorrow at supper time." Looking at her, he said, "Are you sure, Colleen?"

"Yes Michael, I'm sure."

Michael climbed back up after letting the horse go with the note. Mambo refused to leave with the horse, so Michael used the sling and pulled Mambo up into the tree hours. "First we need to make an alter." Michael opened the crates. On one he lit some candles and placed his bible. Kneeling side by side, Michael took Colleen's hand and rested their hands on the bible. Turning to Colleen, he said

"I love you, Colleen, In front of God; I pledge to you my love and my life. I know, you know, as God knows, we face many problems with this marriage. But a three-cord rope is strong. Together the three of us can cope and handle any problems."

Colleen turned pale and excited at the same time. "Oh my God Michael, it's amazing that you should say that about the three cords. Have you ever noticed my mothers' necklace? Its three cords twisted together; my grandmother Shannon gave it to her, for the same reason you've mentioned. That the three cords make for strength; strength to handle any problem." Colleen stopped; she realized she'd interrupted their marriage vows. "Sorry . . . I'll tell you the story later." Looking into Michaels eyes she said, "Michael, my friend, my love, my husband, I give you my all. I will always love you no matter what."

"The minister would now say, you can kiss the bride," said Michael. They kissed. "Colleen, we have no feast, no wine or champagne, only water."

"We have each other, and that's what is important"

Michael opened the second crate and took out the bedrolls and sheets. He strung up the mosquito net and tucked it under the bedroll. Colleen got their dinner ready, two glasses of water, an apple and a chocolate bar, which they shared. Michael then blew out the candles, took her hand and led her to the mosquito net. They slowly undressed each other. Then crept under the mosquito net, as they kissed, he gently stroked her back. A ripple of excitement overcame them both. Colleen woke in the middle of the night. Michael wasn't there. She quickly climbed out from the mosquito net and wrapped a sheet around her. On one of the crates was a note.

Wife, if you're reading this note, you're awake.
Don't go back to sleep, I'll be back soon.
Husband

Colleen sat by the window; Mambo had curled up next to her. There was a full moon; it was almost as bright as daybreak. Pulling the sheet closer around her she listened to the sounds of Africa she loved so. It was not long before Colleen heard Michael climbing the tree. He had a bag slung over his shoulder. "Colleen my love, you may not be hungry, but making love to you has given me an appetite. I snuck back to the house, helped myself to a lot of goodies and left a note on the kitchen table. Will they ever be surprised in the morning?"

"You left them a note? What did you say? Did you tell them we married ourselves?"

Michael nodded.

The emotional part of the day; burying Lena, the painful death of Moses, Michael collapsing in her arms with grief, their self preformed marriage, now gave way to reality. What had they done, not that she regretted any of it, but they were too young, she and her parents had made plans for her future, now that she'd finished school. She knew she'd have at least four years before Michael returned from England. She knew her parents would be upset, she knew . . . she knew . . . it was going around and around in her head.

"Oh Michael, I know my mother and father are going to be upset, not because of you, but because of our age, your schooling, my secretarial course."

Michael took her in his arms, "My love, I'm still doing my schooling in England, you can still do your secretarial course. In four years when I return, we'll be older, and can have a proper wedding. What I'm worried about is, their reaction when they are told I'm colored. As this is our first and only night together for a long time, let's face that tomorrow, right now—let's eat I'm hungry."

They set out the food and ate left over roast chicken and potatoes; even cold it was good, Michael had brought a bone for Mambo. They ended off with fruit and cheese. Michael had also taken a bottle of wine, which they both enjoyed. "Let's save the bread and milk for tomorrow morning. Now, Mrs. Joubert, let's go back to bed."

They made love again, but instead of falling asleep afterwards, they lay in each other's arm and spoke of the future. Making plans for their life together. Colleen told Michael the story of the three cords. "Michael, we already know we will face problems, let's always keep that motto in mind. If we keep God as an important part of our lives—we will cope." They woke with the sun shining in on them, the birds calling, and the monkeys chattering. "Michael, how far are we from the hot springs?"

"Not far. Shall we go take a bath before people start moving around and find us?"

"Yes." When they returned to the tree house, they had their bread and milk. They only had a few hours together before starting for home. Arm in arm, they walked back to the main house, Mambo running ahead of them.

Hope could not be consoled. After finding the note Michael left on the kitchen table, she had paced up and down the front veranda.

"How could she, how could they! I did not want to do this trip, but she talked me into it. Oh no!! What is Abe going to say?" Hope was beside herself. Shannon grabbed her arms and sat her down.

"Hope, calm down, don't say anything while you're so upset. It's better not to say anything than to utter words you can never take back. It's done; there is nothing you can do about it. Remember you still have four-years; a lot can happen during that time. While you had no control over what happened—you do have a choice on how you re-act; your reaction could have a long-term effect. After lunch, they plan on Moses' funeral. Then, later you and Colleen leave on the train for Northern Rhodesia. Tomorrow I leave for South Africa, and Michael leaves for England. Colleen and Michael just have a few hours left before being separated. Give them that time. When you get home and you have spoken to Abe, then have a serious talk with Colleen."

Hope stood up and hugged her mother, but said nothing. Anetta poked her head around the door, "I see them coming up the hill."

Hope waited on the veranda, Shannon sent Colleen into her mother, but held Michael back. "Give them a few minutes Michael."

"Mom?" Hope slowly turned around and Colleen saw the red swollen eyes. "Oh, Mom! If I've hurt you I'm so sorry, but please don't be mad at me."

Hope took a deep breath. "Colleen, a lot has happened these last few days. A lot is going to happen today, what with a second funeral and us leaving. We also need to consider Tinus and Sam who both lost their loved ones in death. Let's talk about this when we get home."

Coming out of the veranda, they saw Michael and his father talking. Tinus was smiling, he was happy at Michael and Colleen's news. Joining them Tinus asked, "Hope, why the tears?"

"That is what mothers of the bride do." Hope tried to smile while they chatted.

Moses was buried next to Lena. The last few days had been both the happiest and saddest days of Michael's life. He had lost his mother, and best friend in death, but he had also married the girl he had loved for so long. Only now he was leaving for the next four years.

At the train station Colleen tried so hard not to cry—but tears filled her eyes and ran down her face. She held Michael so tight, afraid to let him go. He whispered in her ear, "Remember what you said,—and think of this as time between holidays." He then buried his face in her neck and hummed the music he was composing for her.

During the trip home, Hope and Colleen were deep in thought. Colleen planning on how soon it would be before joining Michael in England—maybe she could do her secretarial course there. Hope was scheming on how to break this relationship up; she wanted to save her daughter the heartache she knew would follow.

Abe was not happy when he heard about the marriage in the tree house, at least they had four years to work on Colleen to change her mind.

Maureen looked up from reading the journal, her mother was crying.

"I can't believe my parents were against Michael, and thought about keeping us apart. But even more shocking is that after all Michael and I went though, obviously we were very much in love—that we got divorced."

"No you didn't Mom, Remember you were not really married. Michal was not the man you divorced. Just wait and listen to what happened. I could not put it any better than you did in your writing."

CHAPTER 13

One evening everyone was already in bed. Lately Abe and Hope had, behind closed bedroom doors, been speaking about a political problem that was raising its ugly head. They had heard of a group called Mau Mau from Kenya, who would take oaths and then attack farms, killing animals and people; people who were back or white. A few incidents like that had taken place in Rhodesia. Since there was this political problem, and since there was the Colleen/Michael problem, the question was should they move? It would be easier to break contact with Michael if they did. They had a Plan A and a Plan B, but there was also Abe's health to think about. Even though it had been years since his last asthma attack, they were not sure if he'd grown out of his asthma? This is what they were trying to work out when there was a knock on their bedroom door. It was Colleen. "Can I talk to you, Mom and Dad?"

Colleen sat on the end of the bed; she had tears running down her cheeks. Hope slipped out of bed and sat next to her. Thinking the tears were because of missing Michael, she said. "Colleen, we do understand that you must be missing Michael terribly. I remember how much I missed your dad when he started working on the mines in Luanshya and we were still in South Africa."

Colleen took her mother's hands, "Yes, I miss him terribly but we knew from the start that we would have this four year wait. No, it's something else . . . I think I am pregnant."

Hope and Abe stared at her. They had a hard time accepting what they had just heard. They had enough problems and decision making on their hands without adding this.

Hope managed to get a doctor's appointment for the same day. Even though they had to wait for some test to return, the doctor said he felt sure Colleen was pregnant. Feeling cornered, not really knowing what to do, wanting only the best for Colleen, they put Plan A into action that very same day. The plan was they would intercept Michael's letters, and make sure Colleen never got them; they also saw to it that Colleen's letters were never sent to England.

The first couple of weeks, they consoled Colleen that maybe he didn't write because of an exam. Then they added to the deception that Michael had been killed in a car accident. Not being used to a big city, he had, they said, stepped into the street without looking. He's forgotten they drove on the opposite side of the road. Hope explained that a telegram had arrived with the news to his father Tinus, who in turn had made a phone call to Abe at the mine office, since they did not have a phone at home. Michael's father, after losing his wife, and with Michael off to England, decided to join the rest of his family in Cape Town. So contact to him was cut off—all the lies and deception seem to be working.

Colleen was devastated; her Michael was dead. She went into months of mourning; she would climb the mango tree in their back yard and lose herself in her grief. She actually felt as though a part of her had died the day she got the news. She did not even care about the baby growing inside her. That's why, at this vulnerable time, she agreed to a plan Hope and Abe came up with. Thinking of Colleen's future, the plan was that first Hope would announce that she was pregnant. As time went by, she would make it look as though she was. Second, as soon as Colleen began to look pregnant she would go to Lagenwa. Anetta would deliver the baby. Hope would travel to Lagenwa at that time and then return with her prematurely born baby and Colleen who had recuperated from Michael's death, supposedly. Shannon, Nathaniel, Anetta and Desmond were the only adults that knew and agreed to help with the deception. Anetta's children were young enough not to figure out what was happening. No one else was to know the truth; even Sheree, Gordon and Charles had no idea.

The three children were surprised that their mother was having a baby at her age. They considered their mother and father way too old to be having sex, let alone bringing a baby into their family. Then there was Colleen's problem, mourning a dead husband that wasn't really her husband. Sheree just buried herself deeper into her books and the boys got a new dog, so they were happy. Because Mambo would not leave Colleen's side, they did not think of him as their dog or as the family dog.

Colleen lived in a fog since the news of Michael's death. That's the reason why she agreed to her parents' plan. Later she hated them for it, but later yet; she saw the sense in it and loved them for changing their lives so she could have one. When she left for Lagenwa, Colleen was not even aware that her parents were worried about political events. She was not aware that Anetta and Desmond were worried about political events. She thought everything was different because of Michael's death. Then, of course, there was Moses, Lena, and Tinus' absence. Things were not the same. She spent hours at her and Michael's favorite haunts. She even learned to climb the tree, to the tree house instead of using the ladder. She was able to do this even with her enlarging tummy.

Colleen knew where Michael and Moses kept the key for the two trunks. She would take out a bedroll and lay there dreaming of Michael. If she closed her eyes, she could even hear him playing the piano. She was tempted to take his bible and keep it as a memento, but decided everything was to stay as it was. This was their home. So instead, she wrote him notes and put them in the pages of the bible. She told him they were going to have a child. She told him about her pain when he died in the car accident, how she did not want to continue living. She told him that Hope and Abe were going to bring up their child, because she was going to devote herself to helping others. She could not give their child a proper life, because she never wanted to marry again. As she wrote, she'd always include the date. Sometimes the only writing on a sheet of paper was the date and "I love you Michael, and I miss you so much."

Hope arrived a week before Colleen was due to have her baby. It had been four months since Colleen left, so mother and daughter were very happy to see each other.

"My, but you have got big," said Hope touching Colleen's tummy.

"My, but you have got big," said Colleen touching Hope's tummy. They both laughed.

"I'm dying to get rid of this pillow," said Hope. "But not as much as you must be dying to have your baby. I remember those last weeks. They seem to go on forever." Hope was shocked when she saw Anetta; she looked so tired and drawn. "I hope our little deception hasn't done that to you, Anetta. You look so tired. Are you not sleeping?"

"Actually not—and don't worry. It's not your secret," she whispered in Hope's ear.

That evening sitting on the veranda, it was just Anetta, Hope and Colleen. Colleen had stretched out on the floor with her head in her mother's lap. Her back had been bothering her and the hard floor seemed to help.

"So Anetta, what's been going on? You look so tired. I noticed Desmond is very edgy, and he keeps his gun close at all times."

"It's this Mau Mau movement. I know it's a Kenyan thing but attacks have been made as far south as here."

"You mean here on your farm?" asked Hope in surprise.

"Yes, it happened after Desmond found a group of men camping out on the farm. He suspected they were responsible for running off some of our cattle. He made them leave, and threatened them with the police."

"Did they leave?"

"Yes." Anetta was looking at them with huge eyes. "Only later in the early hours of the morning, we heard terrible noises coming from the barn area where we had some cattle. These were cows that had just calved during the last week or were due to calf any day. The sounds were inhuman or even inanimal sounds. We thought maybe a lion had got in among the calves . . . but—but." Anetta started to shake and cry. Hope and Colleen moved to her side.

"Anetta, what happened? Was it a lion?"

"No it was the Mau Mau. They had—they had chopped the cows' legs off at the knees, and they had also cut off their udders. Apparently they used the teats for something. Cows that hadn't calved, they disemboweled and pulled out the unborn calf." Anetta lowered her voice almost to a whisper. "You should have seen the cows eyes, their bellowing had changed to a gurgling sound they were in so much pain. There was blood, bowel and unborn calves everywhere. Desmond was slipping in this mess as he moved from cow to cow putting them out of their misery."

The three sat in silence, the hair on Colleen's neck bristled. "How come I didn't know about this?"

"We kept it from you hon . . . what with you expecting a baby yourself . . ." Anetta took a deep breath. "And it's because of this that I've booked you both, along with my two children, on the train tomorrow to South Africa. Colleen, Nathaniel will deliver your baby. Hope, could you ask Joy if she would keep my two children until Desmond and I get there, within a week or two at the most?"

"Of course, Anetta," whispered Hope; this was all so unbelievable.

Anetta continued, "When you arrived this afternoon, I'd hoped you and Colleen could have just continued right then to South Africa, but the train was booked full. The earliest opening is tomorrow at 3:00 p.m."

"Why don't you come with us tomorrow?" asked Colleen.

"Desmond and I will come by car. That way we can pack a few things. It may be the only possessions we end up with."

It was just before sunrise that Colleen woke. Her mother was shaking her, and at the same time she had her hand over her mouth. "Shhh, get up and quickly get dressed," said Hope.

"What's going on?" mumbled Colleen half asleep.

"I think we are under attack. There were gun shots, but now I just hear shouting." Colleen and her mother were sleeping in the guest quarters, the position of the room allowed for more of a breeze, so they were away from the main part of the house. Listening at the door, Hope could hear an African shouting,

"I know you have two pregnant women here. For the last time, where are they?"

"And for the last time," said Desmond, "I told you they left with the milking truck yesterday afternoon."

"My men are going to search this house. If I find you lied to me . . ."

Hope turned to Colleen. "Colleen, you know this place well. Is there somewhere we can hide? I mean really hide. Those Africans are looking for us." As Hope spoke, she made the double bed they shared, and kicked under it anything they had lying around. "This room must look like no one has been here. Quick, Colleen, is there any place?"

"Yes, follow me."

Colleen climbed out the second story window, grabbed hold of the thatch and pulled herself up to the peak of the roof it was an effort with her huge stomach. They could see Africans milling around in the yard, shouting and turning over barrels, looking in and around things. Once Colleen and Hope reached the peak of the roof, which was over the guest bedroom area, it brought them level with the roof of the main section of the house. Colleen lifted a section of the thatch and slipped in, Hope followed. They were actually in the living room/dining room area, at the end of the peak of the open beamed thatched roof. The beams had been placed so that two overlapped each other, making a little boxlike area. Colleen and her mother slipped behind the beam. Hope looked at Colleen questioning.

"Moses, Michael and I used to sit up here and listen to you adults down there. As you can see, we can hear and see everything but because of the beam and darkness up here, we cannot be seen. Mom, what's happening?"

"I'm not sure, but for some reasons those Africans are asking about us. I think they may be—those Mau Mau Anetta was talking about."

It was not long before Anetta, Desmond and the two children were marched into the living room. There were about fifteen very angry Africans with them.

"You said they left with the milking truck yesterday afternoon, but your African servants said they didn't see them leave, after getting that information out of them my men are busy killing them."

Desmond and Anetta could hear the commotion outside, screaming and gunshots. Desmond pulled Anetta and his children close to him; they were standing in a huddle. The leader's tone changed and he screamed. "You are lying to me." He grabbed Anetta's son, Dennis, who was eight years old. Dennis was screaming "Mommyyyyy! Mommyyyyyy!

Anetta was screaming, "Please, please don't hurt him."

Desmond tried to get his son, but one of the guards knocked him down, ten-year-old Letty was sobbing and hanging on to her mother's skirt.

"Listen to me doctor lady; we must have those two unborn white babies. They are for an oathing ceremony today, but since you are hiding them, I'll take second best, your two children."

"No, no," screamed Anetta. "Please leave them be. Okay, I lied . . . they didn't leave on the milk truck but if you haven't found them, I don't know; I truly don't know where they are."

The leader walked over to where Desmond lay after being knocked out. He had regained consciousness but could not stand up, because a guard stood with his foot in the middle of Desmond's back. With one clean sweep, the leader chopped Desmond's hand off with his panga. Desmond's agonizing scream of pain, mixed with Anetta, the two children's and Colleen's screams of horror and terror. The screams intermingled so that no one noticed the extra scream. Hope quickly put her hand over Colleen's mouth and she said between clenched teeth, "Be quiet, do . . . you . . . hear . . . me!"

Colleen pulled her mother's hand off her mouth. "We must go and help them," she whispered back through clenched teeth.

"Help in what way, Colleen?—Do you not understand! They want your unborn baby; they want it for an oathing ceremony. That means they'll cut it out of you. Then cut the baby up, using the parts they want. If we, two women, went down there, what could we do against those fifteen gun and panga wheeling monsters, not to mention the ones outside?"

Hope looked over the beam. They had stripped Anetta and the two children. She wanted to throw up. Her dearest friend and her family were about to die and there was nothing she could do to help. Anetta was screaming, "Please, please let the children go." Letty and Dennis were screaming for their mom and dad to help them. Desmond knew he was about to lose his family in a very cruel way and that he would also be killed. There was not a thing he could do. He was still pinned to the ground. First his daughter, then his son were abused and killed.

The Mau Mau had lifted Anetta onto a table; she was hysterical at what she'd just witnessed. Desmond wanted to get one point over to her.

"Anetta—look at me!" No response. "Anetta—look—at—me!" Slowly she turned her head to look into her husband's eyes. Desmond winked and smiled at her, mouthing, "I love you." It was as though everything stopped for a moment and she got a peaceful look on her face as she mouthed back "I love you,"

Desmond was forced to watch as they abused his wife. The sounds and screams would live with Hope and Colleen for the rest of their lives. Hope realized it was up to her to save her daughter and grandchild. Colleen's eyes were wide with terror. She would have screamed if Hope hadn't covered her mouth.

Hope pushed Colleen down onto her side, her face and stomach squashed into the thatch. Hope half laid on top of her and half behind her. She covered Colleen's mouth with her hand and started talking into her ear. Anetta was screaming in heart wrenching sounds as she struggled with the men holding her down, Hope saw them pluck Desmonds eyes out. She turned back to Colleen.

"Colleen, find a spot in your mind.
Make a room in your mind and go there.
Take your baby there.
Meet Michael there; hear him play the piano.
Listen, he's playing that song he made up just for you."
"Can you see Michael, he is holding his baby
in one arm and his other arm is around you.
You are walking some place in England.
it's beautiful; it's sunny.
Can you hear his music?"

Colleen had closed her eyes and ears. She was with Michael; they were together. Their child had been born, they were happy. They were alive. Every now and again when she drifted out of her mind's room, she would hear the most awful sounds. She ran back and slammed the door. Her mother was always at the door. She was happy, but why was she crying, Michael . . . baby . . . room . . . crying . . . happy . . . terrible sounds.

Her mouth hurt, her tummy hurt, she heard crying . . . Her mother was singing softly in her ear.

Maureen was watching her mother closely, she expecting a reaction, but not like this. Colleen dropped her cup and started screaming.

"Nooooooo, nooooooo, leave them alone!!" This was followed by screams that sent chills up your spine and made your hair stand on end. Both Maureen's babies woke with a start and started screaming too. Jacob looked like a deer caught in a car's headlights.

"Jacob, Jacob, hold her—I have to take the babies outside away from this screaming."

Mary from across the stream had heard the screaming and was running towards the house.

"Mary can you help me?" Maureen's voice was shaking.

"Of'a course I cin lass, what'a tis happening?"

"Can you take the babies—there is nothing wrong with them, they are crying because they woke with a fright. My mother's the one screaming in the house. I believe her memory has come back. I need to calm her down."

Back at the house Maureen gave her mother one of the pills the doctor had given her, for just such an emergency. Then while Jacob still held her down, she phoned the doctor.

Dr. Ferguson said, "Maureen, it will take a few minutes for the full effect of the pill to start working. It should knock her out, just make her comfortable. I'm on my way."

It was an hour before the doctor arrived. Colleen was still sleeping but Maureen was crying, and Jacob was pacing the room.

What if we've pushed her back into that hiding place of her's? What if she doesn't wake up again?" sobbed Maureen.

Taking her hands the Dr. said, "Maureen, sometimes it takes a shock to pull someone out of amnesia. Before you jump to conclusions let's just wait a while and see. How about a cup of tea, and where are those babies of yours? I haven't seen them for a while."

"Oh! My goodness, they're still at Mary's." That snapped Maureen back to reality. Jacob put the kettle on. I'm going over to Mary's for the babies." They just finished their tea when Colleen started to stir. First she looked around in confusion, and then she started sobbing while rocking back and forth.

"I remember . . . I remember everything. It was my fault Anetta, Desmond and their children were killed."

"No Mom, no it wasn't later in your journal you realized that. It was political conditions, time and location that came together, unfortunately when you were there."

Maureen handed her mother a cup of tea. Colleen's hands were shaking as she took it, so as not to spill it she cupped her hands around it. Dr. Ferguson kept a strict eye on Colleen; she was starting to calm down. When he questioned her, her voice was no longer shaking. After an hour, he gave her an examination. Her blood pressure had come down; her breathing was normal. Arrangements were made for Colleen to visit Dr. Ferguson's office the next day. "If you need to Colleen, you can take another one of those pills when you go to bed tonight."

"Mom, do you want to lie down for a while?" Colleen shook her head. "How about a walk outside, for some fresh air?" Prompted Maureen.

"Yes, I'd like to clear my head." Jacob took his mother walking while Maureen saw to the babies and made lunch for them. On their return, Colleen automatically walked up the hill behind the house, and sat down next to the three graves. She put her hand on Shawn's headstone and looked across to Jacob. "Shawn was there, it really tore him up." Colleen lowered her voice. "I know how Shawn died." Jacob held his mothers hands in his as she cried, not hysterically, a soft knowing cry.

After lunch Jacob suggested. "Mom, since your memory has returned there is no need to continue reading the journals. I'll pack them away."

"No . . . no, even though I remember everything, I'd like to see what I wrote." Maureen looked at Jacob, who nodded his agreement.

"Mom, don't you think it would be too upsetting, now at this time?"

"Maybe, but I'd like to get it over with. Since Maureen was nursing the babies, Jacob picked up the journal his mother had dropped earlier that day and started reading, he included the last few lines they had read just before her memory returned . . . .

Coleen closed her eyes and ears. She was with Michael, they were together; their child had been born, they were happy, they were alive . . .

Colleen woke with a start,—what a terrible nightmare. She turned to tell her mother about it, but why couldn't she move? Why was her mother lying on top of her? Why were they lying against the beams and thatch?

"Shhh," whispered her mother . . .

It wasn't a nightmare. "Are they gone? It's so quiet." Colleen's voice caught in her throat.

"Yes, they have been gone for a few hours, but we are staying here to make sure."

"Did it really happen?" Asked Colleen.

Hope did not have to answer. Colleen could see the pain in her mother's eyes. "Oh, Mommy, we didn't save anyone."

"Yes, we did Colleen. We saved your baby, don't you ever forget that. If we had gone down, we could not have prevented what happened. You, I and the baby would have been among those bodies."

Colleen let out a groan and doubled over. "Mom, I think the baby is coming."

Hope looked around in desperation. It had been quiet for hours, but what if the Mau Mau left someone here to keep watch. They knew there were two other women, they knew or thought they were both pregnant. They wanted the babies. What happens if they're just out there waiting? Just when Hope thought she would have to go down and find out if the Mau Mau had gone, she heard land rovers pulling up. She heard voices; and she listened carefully. Yes, it was the police.

When the house was being swarmed, Desmond had used his two-way radio and called for help. He then left the radio turned on, so everything that happened in the living room was heard over the radio. The police stood in silence looking at the remains of the family. Inside were the bodies of Anetta, Desmond and the two children. Outside were nine farm workers, their wives and children. Many of the farm animals had also been killed.

"My God, how can one human being do this to a fellow human being?"

Just then, another police entered the living room. "Sergeant, we can't find the two women Desmond said were visiting. They must have been carried off."

"No, we're up her!" shouted Hope.

All the men's eyes searched the thatch roof, but couldn't see anything. "Where, we can't see you." Only after Hope stood up and waved her hand could they see her.

"We need help getting down. My daughter is in labor."

The police formed a chain on the thatch roof and helped Hope and Colleen down. One of the police had medical training and was able to help Colleen deliver her son Mike. It was a very fast and easy delivery, but shock at what had happened in the early hours of the morning caused Colleen to break down. Once Mike was delivered, she started screaming hysterically. All the early repressed screaming bursting forth. The police gave her some medication to make her sleep for most of the day.

Hope knew this would be on the news so she called Abe, telling him they were okay but that everyone else had been brutally killed. In a strained voice he said, "Cookie, wait for me. Don't even think about coming home by train. I am driving straight through. I am taking you and the children to your mother's until this mess blows over."

It would be at least forty-eight hours before Abe reached Lagenwa. Colleen was sedated but Hope had to walk with the police and identify as many bodies as she could. After identifying Anetta, Desmond and the children, she started to shake realizing how close she and Colleen had come to the same fate.

It was now that Hope realized that Shawn and Mambo were nowhere to be found. They were just making up a search party to look for them when Shawn came galloping up on his horse, followed by Mambo. "Hope lassie, what the hell isa going on here; why all these police?" He dismounted and ran to Hope. She was still shaking and the look of anguish on her face made Shawn stop and look around. Almost in slow motion, he walked to her. "Lassie, please tell me."

"Shawn, the Mau Mau attacked, they're all dead," she whispered. Then again, this time screaming, "They're all dead Shawn, they're dead."

Shawn grabbed her by the shoulders and started shaking her.

"Ye didna mean Des, Anetta and the bairns! Ye didna mean Colleen?"

"Yes, No,—Colleen is safe, but yes Anetta and"—Shawn interrupted Hope.

"Where are they?" His voice had a very controlled pace to it. Hope just pointed. The police tried to stop Shawn but he pushed his way through and ripped the sheets off the bodies. "Nooo! Noooo!" he screamed over and over again.

Hope and Shawn were sitting next to each other on the couch, each lost in their mist of pain. Shawn was sixty years old, but as Hope looked at him he aged ten years, it was as though someone was letting the air out of a balloon. He kept mumbling over and over again. "They were me family, they were me family. I'vea lost another family."

The police gave Shawn and Hope a sedative and suggested they go to bed. The police would continue guarding the ranch so they would be safe. Hope shuffled to the room Colleen was in and she climbed into the bed with her sleeping daughter. Looking up she saw Shawn standing in the doorway looking very lost, very old and his heart in so much pain. She held her hand out to him. "Come, lay with us Shawn." He curled up with them, Mambo at their feet; the four of them slept for hours. The police were in and out, keeping an eye on them and taking care of the new baby.

CHAPTER 14

That's how Abe found them, all still curled up sleeping. He knelt next to the bed and pulled Hope to the end, when she heard his voice, her eyes flew open and she clung to him. Abe was surprised at the strength in her fingers as they dug into him, both of them were crying. Abe held her so tight she had trouble breathing. Finally Colleen awoke and saw her father.

"Daddy, Daddy," and she burst out crying. Abe picked her up into his arms.

"Its okay, my girl, I am taking you away from here."

They could not contact Shannon and Nathaniel to let them know they were okay. The phone lines to South Africa were down. Abe did not want to spend any extra time at Lagenwa. He insisted Shawn come with them, "At least until you know what you're going to do." Shawn had his own Landrover. The two boys and Mambo drove with him, they followed Abe. Sheree sat in front; Hope and Colleen were in the backseat with the baby between them. Besides everything that had happened, they had to keep up the pretense that Mike was Hope's baby. Feeding Mike was solved with a bottle but Colleen had to suffer until nature took its course and dried up her milk. In the backseat, Hope and Colleen would still break out crying every now and then or fall asleep from the results of the sedation they were given earlier. It helped that Mike was a good baby; he just slept and ate.

Shannon was beside herself. She had heard on the news about the attack on Lagenwa she had tried calling, but the lines were down. She knew something was wrong when Anettta had called earlier and said she was putting Hope, Colleen and her two children on the train to them. That was the last she'd heard. Then the radio broadcast the news of the massacre at Lagenwa. No victims' names were released, but of course, Shannon assumed.

When Abe's car and a Landrover pulled into the driveway she collapsed with relief, she had been convinced that she had lost her family. Joy had been with Shannon trying to console her. When she saw what a state Hope and Colleen were in, she took Sheree, the boys and baby Mike to her house next door. Got them settled with her children and the nanny, then returned to see what she could do at Shannon's. Nathaniel had just given Shannon, Hope, Colleen and Shawn something to calm them down—not a tranquilizer, just something to take the edge off. He now carried in a huge pot of tea. Joy poured and sweetened it.

"Let's get this tea down before you talk," she said. Abe was pacing up and down across the room; he couldn't stand seeing Hope and Colleen like this. It must have been bad for even Shawn to be affected. Between sobbing, Hope and Colleen told them what happened. There was not a dry eye in the room when they were done. After what seemed like an eternity they were all jolted back to reality with Colleen's voice, saying over and over again.

"We didn't help them . . . we didn't help them."

Nathaniel was the first one to her side. "But Colleen, there was nothing, nothing, you or your mother could have done. By doing what you did, you saved baby Mike and yourselves, if you had given yourselves up, you would have been three more bodies that had to be identified."

Shawn was like a lost little boy. Desmond, Anetta and the children were like his family, he loved Anetta, she had dug a bullet out of his butt. He had performed their marriage, he was there for each of the births, and the children called him *Oupa*, a title of respect he loved. Not only were they gone, they had been hurt really bad. He blamed himself for not being there. Maybe, just maybe he could have helped.

That night Colleen slept in bed with Hope and Abe. Even in their sleep, the girls would cry out. Abe got up early. He heard voices in the kitchen; it was Joy and Shannon. They had baby Mike with them. Abe realized with all that had happened he hadn't even held his new son, really grandson. Shannon put Mike in his arms then warmed a bottle so Abe could feed him. Baby Mike sucked away hungrily, his little hand held Abe's finger. Abe got tears in his eyes as he thought of what could have happened to Mike. Not looking up from Mike, he said, "Shannon, I must get my family out of Northern Rhodesia. My asthma seems like nothing in comparison to what the girls have just been through."

"Oh thank goodness Abe; I was wondering how to bring it up without sounding like a meddling mother-in-law. You know you are welcome to stay with us for as long as it takes."

"Not to push you in any direction," added Joy. The property next to Shannon and Nathaniel is up for sale."

"Hope would be the happiest person in the world if I could swing that."

"Swing what?" Hope came into the kitchen just in time to hear Abe say she'd be happy if he could swing something. Abe moved over to the couch in the huge family type kitchen.

"Come sit next to me Cookie, I've just been talking to our new son, Mike."

Shannon poured them coffee and they sat talking about the future. It was decided to move back to South Africa. Shawn had joined them; he looked less haggard although still aged. Shannon handed him a mug of coffee.

"Shawn, what do you plan on doing? We want you to consider yourself part of this family crazy as it is sometimes. We were just deciding on our line of action," said Abe.

Colleen had come out in her pajamas and wiggled between her mother and father. They handed her Mike and she continued feeding him. Abe continued. "We'll go back and pack up what we're bringing out. Fortunately, we don't have to worry about furniture. It belongs to the mine. However, I do need to read my contract with the mines. I believe I need to work a six or eight week notice period otherwise I forfeit my saving that was done through the mine."

Abe would buy an enclosed truck in South Africa; Shawn would travel with him and help with the move. An extra man, extra gun was always welcome. While in Rhodesia, Shawn would speak to the mine manager about Lagenwa and collect his personal goods left there. It was decided that Hope and the children would stay, living with Shannon until Abe returned; she would use the family car. "It may be as long as eight weeks, but we really need the money to live on until I find another job and maybe buy the property next to your mother's. If all else fails, remember we do have the little farm at Four Corners."

Colleen sat bolt upright, "Dad, remember *Ouma* Shannon and *Oupa* Jacob gave me important memorabilia from the Scottish and Russian sides of the family. It was entrusted to me because I'm writing the family history. Where is the box?"

"It's in a safe deposit in the bank here in Johannesburg. Why?"

"There were the last two gold nuggets from Russia, how much are they worth?"

"A lot."

"Enough to buy the property next to *Ouma?*"

"Yes, but my father gave it to you."

"Anytime my Great Grandfather Nicholas or Grandfather Jacob used the gold from Russia, it was to buy land . . . right. Great Grandfather Nicholas enlarged 'Four Corners', and the farm halfway to Natal, along with the store Triple S. Grandfather Jacob bought the sugar farm in Natal—Lalapanzy. So let's use the last of it to buy land again." All eyes were on Colleen. "*Oupa* Jacob did say it was to be used for something life saving. This is life saving, besides . . ." Colleen started sobbing again. Hope cradled her as she said between sobbing, "It's my fault the family is in this mess." As everyone started objecting, Colleen held up her hand. "I know the Mau Mau was around, and I could not have prevented that. But . . . if I was not there at Lagenwa pregnant; if you were not there Mom, pretending to be pregnant. They may not have attacked the farm looking for us. That means Aunt Anetta—and—family—."

"Shhh, my girl." Shannon was wiping the tears and hair from Colleen's face. "We can all live our lives with, "what ifs," it doesn't help any. For example, I could say because I married my first husband Geret, it was my fault my children and I ended up in the concentration camp. It was my fault my first-born son died there. It was my fault my second son was influenced by his father and killed in the mines. We can not live our lives with "what if's" and remember, Desmond and Anetta knew there were risks involved in that line of work. Chasing off poachers was sure to have some negative effect."

"But I do feel guilty, many years ago Aunt Anetta saved my life when I was choking on a candy. But . . . but . . . I couldn't save her life . . ." Colleen couldn't continue. "Please use the nuggets for the property. It will be passed down to family anyway, like the other properties.

While Abe and Shawn returned to Northern Rhodesia to tie up business and pack, Hope was going to use the last two gold nuggets and purchase the property next to her mother and buy furniture they needed. She would also get the children settled into the new schools and, of course, there was Mike to take care of. The night before the two men left, Hope was all teary in Abe's arms. "Cookie, I'm so afraid of you going back and for so long.

"Don't worry, remember Shawn is with me. Because of the circumstances, the company may release me from the contract." There was a knock on the door; it was Colleen.

"I need to speak to you both." Colleen sat cross-legged at the foot of the bed. Like she did months ago when she told them, she was pregnant.

"Please hear me out, I know we all have our personal level of pain and mourning. As you said, it takes time to work through." Colleen moved closer to her parents and took their hands. "In the long run, I can see the wisdom in your taking Mike as your son. I will never be able to thank you enough. But, it does hurt to step back, so that everyone else would believe he's yours. My life feels like a mountain of mourning, I lost Michael and now in a way, his son. There is also the feeling of responsibility concerning Aunt Anetta and family." Colleen cleared her throat. "I need to get away for a while. I want to travel with Dad and Shawn back to Northern Rhodesia."

Hope turned pale, "No Colleen, no. If you must get away, we will arrange something here in South Africa, the Larger or Lalapansy in Natal." Colleen stopped her mother.

"No, it must be with Dad and Shawn. At the Larger, or Lalapansy, they would just baby me. Nothing would be worked out. No. There is an ulterior motive for going with Dad and Shawn besides weaning myself from Mike. I want them to train me. I want to know how to protect myself, and others. I don't ever, ever want to be in such a helpless situation again.

Abe, Shawn and Colleen, drove straight through from Johannesburg to Northern Rhodesia. While one was driving, another was always scanning the bush ahead for trouble, the third one would be sleeping. After a few hours they'd switch, this kept them fresh. Mambo, even when sleeping was alert at the slightest movement or sound and he'd be up on all fours.

The house was just as Abe had left it after his mad scramble for Lagenwa. Walking through, Colleen said grinning at her dad, "It's a good job Mom cannot see this mess." As soon as the mine office was open the next morning, Abe was there. Unfortunately, he had to work his two months notice; only because they had to hire a replacement and Abe was to show him the ropes. "Good," said Colleen, "I need that time for training."

Since they did not need a living room, Abe moved the furniture out, used some of his old wrestling mats he lined the floors and walls. Then he hung his old boxing bag from the ceiling. "Colleen, I can teach you what I know and Shawn will teach you what he knows, but girls don't go around kickboxing.

"Neither should girls, like Aunt Anetta, get raped to death, Dad, if I am ever attacked and overwhelmed, I at least want to cause some damage. I want to know not only how to defend myself, but how to cause them hurt."

"Tall order for a young girl, but we will do our best. I could always do with a refresher course myself. I haven't done much since my leg was amputated, so we'll get fit together. Since I work until 3:00 in the afternoon, maybe the morning can be Shawn's teaching time, the afternoons mine. Then on weekends we can sharpen our skills in the bush."

So started Colleen's lessons, the first week Shawn's lessons were mainly verbal. Colleen listened and remembered. All three of them changed their diet; it was not long before their bodies started showing results. Colleen, Shawn and Mambo would run each morning. At first, it was just a couple of miles and they were winded. Gradually their endurance increased. By the end of two months, they could comfortably run ten miles without feeling like collapsing. Shawn would also take Colleen to a quiet deserted area and teach her how to handle a gun. At first, she never even hit the tree, let along the target painted there. In time, she could hit the target while running past it, or rolling over and over. Next, she learned how to handle a knife.

"Remember Lassie, if it's not a killing thrust ye kin make, then it must be a crippling one. Of importance would be first the arms, right one first, then the legs, so he kin not stand."

Colleen made a good student; she had no distractions and had deep hurts she needed to overcome with hard work, then came her father's training in the afternoons. He taught her the right way to throw a punch, and showed her not to overextend her arm.

"But Colleen, my girl, throwing a punch with your bare fist can hurt you as much as your enemy. That's only for extreme emergency use, and when you do, it has to be powerful enough to knock him out because you've now broken bones in your hand. Just as Shawn has given you a knife to carry on your person always, I am welding you a key ring holder, out of light steel. Anyone looking at it would see an ugly unusual key holder, but you can slip your four fingers through it, and holding it in your fist as you punch, it will protect your hand while breaking his bones. Let your keys poke through your fingers as you are hitting, it will feel like steel spikes beating his flesh. Now if you don't have your key ring holder, and for some reason you can't use your feet, as I'll teach you, then use your elbow. That's one of the strongest bones in your body. Aim for the nose, it breaks easy, bleeds easily and will bring tears to his eyes, so momentarily he'll be blinded, giving you time for a second and even third blow."

Colleen practiced and practiced her kicking, until her body was dripping in perspiration and she felt as though every one of her bones were broken. She could run and jump high enough that, had there been a picture on the wall, she could have kicked it off. It was one thing to handle yourself in familiar surroundings, so on weekends, they'd go out to the bush. Colleen would have to run over rough unfamiliar terrain as if her life depended on it. While watching the ground, she'd also have to dodge branches. Shawn would run behind, pretending to chase her. Abe would spring out at her trying to throw her off balance. With Mambo crisscrossing her path, she would have to dodge him too. She enjoyed practicing how to swing herself up into a tree, how to breathe through a reed while lying underwater. However, she did not enjoy learning how to rub animal dung over herself to disguise her smell. "Africans have a keen sense of smell Colleen, if you're trying to hide, especially if it's that time of the month, they will smell you. So rub the shit on you!"

The weekend before they were due to return to South Africa was going to be a true test; It would involve two days and a night out in the bush. Shawn was getting a three-hour head start, she was to track and catch him. Her father would be three hours behind her. She was to avoid him catching her. But Colleen was only an hour into her tracking when Shawn showed himself headed back towards her.

"Hey," she laughed, "you are headed the wrong way."

"Lassy, move, move, let'a us get the hell out of here. There is a renegade group back there. We canna have you running around in these woods now."

Abe hadn't started following Colleen yet so they headed back home. They had packing to finish before leaving on Monday. Shawn took the truck for a short drive, he needed to check on some work he had done on the truck. Abe had some tools he was still sorting through and Colleen had the final things in the house.

From the kitchen window, Colleen saw an African approach her father, they were talking but she couldn't make out what was being said. She noticed her father was getting upset. She started outside just in time to see the African pull a knife on her father. She shouted a warning while running towards them. Her father wasted no time in giving him a kick to the head. His prosthesis made a good hard club. The African was not a fighter and turned to run.

"What was that about," she asked her father who was white with rage.

"He asked me where my yellow Buick and my second-born daughter were. He had won them both in a drawing. They were, His—His—His," Abe kept repeating. "He was going to take Sheree as his wife and our car as his." The more Abe spoke, the angrier he got. When Shawn came back with the truck he gave it an okay, ready for the trip on Monday. "If it wasn't for this petrol rationing, we could leave now. But we don't get our coupons till Monday and we really need them to cross the country."

The next morning, Colleen woke with the sounds of Mambo whimpering. "Come on boy, you can use the doggy door." She felt across the bed, he wasn't there; he was already outside. "If you are waiting for a run you need to give me time to get ready." Colleen used the bathroom and put on her running clothes. Mambo was quiet, probably waiting at the door for her. She opened the front door and froze, before the scream escaped her lips. She dropped to her knees still screaming. Her father and Shawn were at her side, staring at the sight that greeted them . . . They quickly pulled themselves together and weapons in hand; they searched the yard and their neighbor's yard. There was no one, when they returned, only then did they see all the dead chickens that had been disemboweled and tied around the front door. Mambo had been impaled on one of Abe's steel rods that had been pushed about two feet into the ground. He was in mid-air, all four legs kicking. He had stopped whimpering, his eyes had mixture of pain and surprise. They could do nothing to help him. Colleen held her beloved ridgeback, while holding him, she pointed her little gun into his chest and shot.

Colleen did not shed any tears. She retreated into her mind's room, her safe place. Abe and Shawn buried Mambo and cleaned up the mess from the chickens. "Ye know it was a Mau Mau warning," said Shawn.

"Yes, and we are leaving now. I know we don't have petrol coupons, so Shawn; we are going to steal a forty-four gallon drum from the mine storage. We can leave our coupons and money for them."

Being Sunday, there was only one person on guard duty; it was Samson, Abe's Number One worker. Samson moonlighted as a guard on weekends. He was saving money so he and his wife could leave Rhodesia. He was not comfortable with different things that were happening, Samson knew what had happened at Lagenwa and he knew Abe was preparing to leave the country.

"Boss Abe, I saved your life once, please save me and my wife, take us with you to South Africa."

Abe did not have to think twice. "Samson, are you and your wife ready to leave now, within an hour?"

"Yes."

"Shawn and I are here to steal petrol. Go . . . meet us back at my house within an hour. Colleen is there waiting." Abe and Shawn first filled the truck up from the pump, and then rolled a forty-four gallon drum onto the back. "While we are at it, let us take two, this way we are sure we have enough petrol to get out of the country." They returned to the house to pick up Colleen who had taken care of last minute things, she had also cooked and packed food and water for the long run. Samson and his wife were waiting; they had a few items rolled in a blanket.

"You could have brought more, Samson."

"This is all we have Boss Abe, we saved our money for this day."

"Wise man," said Abe. "For your safety and ours, you and Delila need to ride in the back. There will be the usual roadblocks and of course, border post checks. As we are riding, move things around to make a comfortable hiding enclosure."

As they drove, Colleen sat staring ahead; not crying, not saying anything. Shawn put his arms around her. "Lassie, din'a do this. If ye close ye mind down, then they have won; as sure as if they had impaled ye. Remember there are two ways to kill a person, physically and emotionally. You trained for the physical but now ye need to dig deep to save ye emotions. Come on out of that room yer always hiding in." Shawn put his hand under her chin and turned her to face him. She had tears welling up in her eyes and her lips were quivering. "That's me girl, let it out."

Now Colleen burst out sobbing. They let her cry herself to sleep as they rode to Lagenwa. Lagenwa was not back in operation yet. There were guards to stop any looting. They had been notified that Shawn would be stopping to pick up his personal possessions. The mine manager had offered Shawn the job of reopening Lagenwa but he had refused the position. He hoped never to see the farm again.

CHAPTER 15

As Hope watched the truck drive down the road, she had to swallow back her tears. Abe and Colleen were going back into that hellhole. She now hated what was once her beautiful country. She knew the only way she could handle this was to keep busy, very busy. First thing was to put the children into school. Sheree had completed her schooling but was taking a secretarial course. Gordon and Charles were excited about the new school and the different sports they could play. There was even a team for children who had suffered from polio. A lot of children had been affected with that epidemic, so Gordon was happy to play with like children. Mike was a good baby; it was no trouble taking him with her as she first negotiated the sale of two gold nuggets, then the buying of the property next to the Haven. Shannon and Joy took turns in taking time off and showing Hope the best places to buy furniture.

Hope had bought the house and furniture but they were still staying at the Haven. Abe would be bringing all their personal items—sheets, towels, kitchenware, etc. One evening sitting in the back yard watching the sun set over the hills, Hope was busy feeding Mike, but Shannon noticed the usually chatty Hope was very quiet.

"Hope my girl, what's the matter?"

"I was just thinking about the change we have made, it has a good side like finally I can live next door to you and Joy. But it has a side I don't like. Colleen is so emotionally unsettled—imagine wanting to learn how to fight. I just know she is not going to settle down when she returns with Shawn and her dad. Remembering what you said some time ago, whether we interfere or not, our lives are going to change because of Colleen's involvement with Michael. And it has—it bothers me so much seeing her mourn for him, and he is not really dead." After a long pause, Hope said, "Did we do the right thing telling her he'd been killed in a car accident? You know Mom, for the first time I question the strength my three-cord necklace represents. Where was God when Anetta and family were being killed? Where is he now when Colleen is hurting so much? Colleen blames herself for what happened, but maybe it was Abe and I. If we hadn't intervened with Michael and Colleen, who knows, she might be a happily married woman and mother in England."

"Don't do this to yourself Hope, you may not see it, but you are coping and she's coping. It may not be the way, or the answer you want, but years later you will look back, and see how Gods strength helped you through this." After thinking awhile, Shannon continued. "Remember when we were released from the British camp? Dr. Lukas looked after our physical bodies until we recuperated." Hope nodded her head. "Remember Paul took care of us spiritually, we had begun to doubt or blame God because so many ugly things had happened. His answer to our many questions was, 'God is not responsible for these terrible things happening. But, God can and will help you survive, you just need to turn to him.'"

Just then, Sheree ran up to her mother and ouma.

"Seun had asked me to go to the movies with him—its okay, isn't it?"

Joy's adoptive son, Seun, had turned into a very handsome, thoughtful young man. Hope nodded, looking at her mother. She smiled, raising her eyebrows. "Looks like another change in the making!" Sheree was coming out of her shell at last.

They watched as Sheree raced back to the house. Shannon turned to Hope. "I was thinking before Abe starts work, I am sure he would want to visit his family in Natal. Why don't you leave the three children with me since they're in school? Take Colleen and Mike and visit Jacob and Natasha, you could stop at the Larger. That may help Colleen settle down."

"That sounds like a good idea, thanks Mom."

They were just about to sit down to supper when they heard the truck pull into the driveway; Abe blew the hooter till they all came running. He swept Hope up into his arms and covered her face in kisses. She tried to push him off. "Cookie, when last did you shave or bath?" By now, the boys were around their dad.

"Did you remember to pack our bikes?" Hope, in the meantime had Colleen in her arms.

"How are you doing, my girl, you look very thin, in fact you all do."

Shannon walked towards them carrying Mike. Colleen pulled out of Hope's arms and walked to her baby. "Hello Ouma," she took Mike and held him close to her and whispered so only Shannon could hear her. "Hello my baby, my how you've grown in these two months." She kissed his soft cheek, he smelled so good. Looking up at Shannon, her eyes filled with tears. "Ouma, they killed Mambo." Not waiting for an answer or reaction, Colleen walked into the house carrying Mike.

Supper table that night was a noisy affair. Shannon looked at Nathaniel and smiled, she didn't have to say anything. He knew how much she loved having family around her. Gordon and Charles were so excited explaining about school and sports to Abe. They all wanted to know what Colleen had learned. Colleen in turn wanted to know about Sheree and Seun.

They spent a few days unpacking the truck and setting up their new home. Samson and Delila were installed in the house next to the garage. Until Samson got a job, he would help with the yard work, painting, fixing etc. Delila would help with the house and children. Abe agreed they needed to travel to Natal to visit his family before he started looking for work. It was arranged that Shawn would stay in the new house while they were on this trip.

"Shawn, there is a wing to the house that is yours—for as long as you want—remember you are part of this family. Even if you should go wandering around, keep it as your base."

They drove straight down to Natal. It had been some time since Abe had seen his mother and father. Even though they were in their seventies, they looked pretty good. Jacob was still very active in running the sugar farm, along with Stoffel. Years ago he had a heart attack, but after changing a few things in his life he was now doing well. Natasha ran the business end of the farm and was a very busy *Ouma*. Stoffel had four children and Tanya had three.

One evening when Abe was alone with his mother and father he told them about Colleen and Michael, baby Mike and what had happened at Lagenwa. "Colleen is trying very hard to adjust to all these changes, that is one of the reasons we took this trip to visit. If she'd agree to it, could she spend some time here?"

"Of course she can, Abe."

Abe enjoyed riding horseback across the sugar farms. He kept waiting for his asthma to act up, but it didn't. "I remember when we moved here, Dad, standing at this very same spot, looking over the ocean. You were about to start a new chapter of your life. Were you afraid? I am, I'm at that stage now that I'm starting over again and I feel so helpless, not only starting a new job, but one of my children is hurting and I can not help her."

Jacob maneuvered his horse next to Abe. Putting his hand on his son's shoulders, he said, "Abe, speaking from experience, time does heal. Colleen just needs time. You were only five years old when your sister Anya was taken by a crocodile, but I am sure you remember. It took a few years before our family could function properly again. Then we had Four Corners burned out from under us. Fortunately, we were able to buy this land. You have also now been able to buy land, outside of Johannesburg. Let time heal your families' pain. Colleen may not move in a direction that you will be happy with, like I was not happy when you had to leave Natal because of your asthma. You met Hope; you grew in many ways. Just allow Colleen to heal and grow. If she wants to stay here, we would love to have her."

Every morning Abe and Colleen would run on the beach, with his prosthesis, it was more of a slow steady jog. Then he'd hold up his hands while she practiced her kicking moves. She started to look better, not so haggard. *"Oupa* Jacob and *Ouma* Natasha, thank you for the offer to stay here. I am very tempted, but I am still not too sure what I will do, but if after some time I change my mind, could I come back?"

"Of course, Colleen. Your *ouma* and I are so proud of you for writing the Russian/Scottish sagas. You spent the last two gold nuggets in a very wise way; land is one of the things in life that is constant."

A month had passed and while the trip had done Colleen a lot of good, being back with her brothers and sister meant handing Mike back to Hope as his mother, this was hard. They settled into their new house. A week later Abe got a new mining job as a manager so never had to go underground. The boys had become big sports fans. Sheree and Seun were planning their wedding.

Shawn would run with Colleen in the mornings. About two weeks after their return from Natal, Shawn on reaching the bottom of the hill stopped.

"Come on old man, we still have to climb this hill."

"Colleen, stop a while, I need te talk te ye."

"What is it, sounds serious, don't tell me you have finally met a girl. Because remember I am your girl."

"No on kin take yer place, lassy" he kidded. "No, I wante te tell ye I'va joined The Zebra Run, and will be aleaving next week."

"Leaving for where, Shawn? And what's The Zebra Run?"

"Back Te Northern Rhodesia; surrounding countries are having problems with the Mau Mau and other rebels. Refugees are fleeing across the borders. Northern Rhodesia is not equipped te handle so many extra people, especially people with trauma physically and emotionally. Camps are being set up Te help on site, then te help with moving them through Rhodesia, or back te their home country. I'ma going, not only as a minister but as someone who has some knowledge of these attacks. Itsa called The Zebra Run because the organization helps both black and white refugees."

"Oh Shawn, I need you, what will I do without you? You loved them as much as I did." Colleen did not have to say who 'them' was, Shawn knew.

"Sure enough me darling, but these refugees need me too, ye have ye family, and some of those refugees have no one."

"Will you come back when you're done?"

"Yes, I'ma leaving me possessions here."

"Good, come on, race you to the top."

Every chance she had, Colleen would question Shawn about this Zebra Run organization. The following week Shawn put his affairs in order and packed the few belongs he was taking with him. Everyone was focused on Shawn and helping him get ready. No one noticed Colleen was busy getting her possessions packed.

Shawn's plan was to leave at 4:00 A.M. he had a long drive ahead of him. Hope and Abe insisted on getting up early to see him off. They had packed egg sandwiches and a flask of coffee for him to eat later. "Now you take care of yourself Shawn, and come home as soon as you can. Remember this is your home now."

"Sure thing," he hesitated then added, "I'da thought she'da be seeing me off."

"I'll go wake her," said Hope.

"No, no, did'na do that. Tis actually easier this'a away, you take care of that lassie."

As Shawn drove out of the driveway he got tears in his eyes, he had a feeling he would not see them again. About 8:00 he stopped to stretch his legs and take a leak. Good time for those sandwiches and coffee. He opened the passenger door and laid out his breakfast on the front seat. "Are you going to share that with me?"

Shawn jumped back at the sound of Colleen's voice. "Girl, what the double hell are ye doing hiding in me Landrover?" Colleen climbed out, grinning from ear to ear.

"You always told me to check my vehicle before getting in, but you didn't," she was still grinning.

"Colleen, what—what—now I have to backtrack," his voice was showing his anger.

"Relax Shawn, you don't have to backtrack. Here is my I.D. card. I've also joined the Zebra Run. They know I'm traveling with you." Taking a bite out of a sandwich, she said, "No, I did not tell my mom and dad or you for that matter. Because I knew the reaction I would have got—the one I see in your face now."

"Yir parent's are'a going te be so angry and'a upset at me."

"No, I explained in my letter to them you had no idea what I was doing. I begged them to understand why I had to, just as I'm begging you now Shawn." While eating egg sandwiches and drinking coffee, Colleen explained to Shawn her feelings.

"Besides my situation with Michael and Mike, I owe Anetta and Desmond. Their babies lost their lives because of my baby. They lost their lives because of me, and before you say it Shawn, knowing that the Mau Mau would have attacked anyway, does not help the way I feel. I need to work this out of my system; if not around you, then in another camp. At least if we were in the same camp, you can keep an eye on me and I on you. I cannot have anyone else stealing my boyfriend, now can I? Please Shawn."

Shawn put his arms around her shoulders. "Ye do know it is no picnic, ye do now it is dangerous, ye do know ye'll probably see—ugly—again." She nodded. They were quiet as they finished their shared coffee.

They were to meet four other people in Livingstone, then travel together to the new campsite, just outside Fort Jameson. At Livingstone they received a message from the American organizer, Robert. They were delayed a day—'go sightseeing,' he said. Shawn and Colleen looked at each other—they both wanted to, but couldn't say it, finally she asked, "Do you?"

"Yes, do you?" She nodded yes. "Let's go before we change our minds."

Lagenwa had a new owner; they had put up a gate with two guards stationed there to inspect vehicles. Shawn explained to the new owner that they were survivors of the now famous Mau Mau attack. They wondered if they could look around.

"Sure, take your time. If you'd rather use horses, help yourself."

At first, they just looked around the house. Colleen made herself look up at the beams that she and her mother had hid behind. Finally she said, "Shawn, there is one place I need to visit, but I need to go alone."

"Ye mean the tree house?"

"You knew about the tree house?"

"How good a warden would'a I have been if I didn'a know about the tree house. Mind ye, I've not been up in it. I knew it was ye private place."

They used the horses. Colleen had no trouble climbing up without the rope ladder. With her recent training, she was fit. "Since you know about it, you may as well come on up Shawn."

Except for cobwebs and garbage from the monkeys, everthing was just as she left it months ago. Colleen first swept and de-cobwebbed, then sitting down, she unlocked the crate and took out Michael's bible. Sensing she needed to be alone, Shawn sat on a tree branch outside the hut. He settled back and enjoyed the view and animal sounds.

Colleen carefully opened the bible. She reread the notes she had written months before. Even though Michael was dead, she needed to continue writing him notes. This was more of a letter. She told him about the attack, about Anetta, Desmond and family and then, finally that he had a son she'd named Mike, and that her parents were bringing him up and living in South Africa. She told him that she had joined Zebra Run and that she'd stay working with them until she was ready to face life without him or their son. Colleen carefully put her letter in the bible and relocked the crate. Climbing out of the house, she joined Shawn sitting in the branches. She sat next to him; he put his arm around her. "Colleen, me lass, ye know ye'll never heal as long as you do that, tis not good for ye."

"I know Shawn, right now it's all I have, and I'd like to keep it a little longer."

"Okay love."

CHAPTER 16

Arrangements were made to meet the four people they would be working with. Robert was in charge of this group. He was an American, small in size but had a personality that everyone loved. He wore glasses and had curly black hair. Right away Colleen was drawn to his accent and friendly smile. David, also an American was so different. He was tall, blond and very good-looking, but his personality put everyone off. While he was an excellent doctor, he was self-centered; the only person whom he got along with was Robert. Sarel and Ken were both South Africans. Sarel carried about 70 extra pounds. He was an excellent tracker and a crack shot, never missing what he aimed for. His booming laugh could be heard throughout the camp. Ken, a much younger man was skinny, so much so he could not keep his knee high socks up, they kept slipping down. He knew all the African languages in this area. When he had any spare time, you'd find him reading.

Robert was in charge of the camp; he organized the running of everything. David was the camps doctor. Sarel and Ken were in charge of supplying the camp with food and water and protection. Shawn, the minister, and Colleen, the only woman was to console, council and supply whatever help was needed from a woman's perspective.

The camp outside Fort Jameson was still busy being put together. There were rondoval houses, with thatched roofs, to house the staff. Colleen had one to herself, being the only woman in the group. The two South Africans shared a house; the two Americans shared a one, and that left Shawn with one to himself. So they stored extra equipment in Shawn's rondoval.

Tents were erected; they were for refugees that would be passing through. There was a huge tent, with a red cross on the side, and roof. This of course was the make shift hospital. It was used for quick treatment of injuries before the refuges moved on.

There were ten African families taking refuge with them; they intended to go back to their villages across the border as soon as the unrest had quieted. Some local villages would come to their camp for medical treatment. Colleen was appalled at what she saw. For the first time ever, she saw leprosy. Many could barely hobble around because of missing limbs. Noses and ears were one of the first to be eaten by this cruel disease. So many children and adults were blind, caused by flies laying eggs on their eyelids. Flies were so numerous people simply stopped chasing them away. Years ago when they had been quarantined because of the outbreak of polio and smallpox, backward areas like this were badly affected but not helped. This area had been hard hit; many were scarred from smallpox, or deformed from polio. Unlike her brother Gordon, they did not have leg braces to help them. Then there were people with wounds from crocodile or hippo attacks. Each day was a gamble. You had to use the river for water, drinking, bathing or washing of clothes. The crocodiles would lay in wait. Then of course, there was the ever-present malnutrition. People were so thin you wondered how they could walk. Now added to all this misery was the constant threat of attack from rebels.

It was a Sunday afternoon and quiet, all the chores were done. Colleen took her journal and climbed to the top of a hill they used as a lookout station. She had been writing about an hour, when she heard the bushes behind her rustle. She closed her journal, put a rock on top of it for protection and then made her move. She jumped up to a low branch, then swung herself up into the tree and braced herself. As always, she had the knife Shawn had given her and her specially welded key ring holder, from her father. Slipping her hand through it, she was prepared.

The person broke through the bushes. Breathing a sign of relief, Colleen slipped her key ring holder back into her pocket and lightly jumped down next to Robert. "You know you shouldn't be up here by yourself," he said. "Someone could creep up on you like I did."

"I heard you coming" said Colleen, "why do you think you couldn't find me. I was above your head in the trees."

"Can I join you?" He asked.

"Sure." Colleen enjoyed talking with Robert. He was very organized and had the ability to calm people down. She loved hearing about America. As they talked, Robert focused his binoculars to where the road disappeared over a distant rise. Handing the binoculars to Colleen, he said, "Have a look and tell me what you see."

Colleen focused, readjusted the binoculars, and then focused again.

"It's about four to five cars riding fast, kicking up a lot of dust so I can't see if they're being chased."

"Let's go warn the others, I think we have trouble headed our way."

They hurried down and sounded the alarm. Sarel and Ken were already out on their way to see if it was a refugee party or trouble. Every now and then rebels would cross the border for a quick hit and run attack. It was refugees; the first wave brought six carloads. The attack had come without warning. On a hot Sunday afternoon, people relaxing after a morning at church and a lazy lunch. Suddenly, there was a familiar sound of AK47's firing rapidly in the distance. Children stopped playing and ran home; wives looked frantically to their husbands. What? What should they do? Stand and fight for their homes or flee across the border.

"Everyone to their position," yelled the men. In preparation, each block of housing had turned itself into a larger. With ten homes per block it was easy to put fencing between the homes. Backyards formed a huge safe place to house the elderly, children and sick. Everyone else had a pre-assigned spot to stand and defend. Boys and girls aged ten and upwards, would help in the shooting. So the town turned into about twenty largers. The rebels had to ride or run up the street so would face attacks from both sides. Cars were always kept pre-packed with essentials and not only full of petrol, but also always carried an extra drum full of petrol. Within half an hour, the roads were filled with rebels; not only firing their AK47's, but they always carried their dreaded pangas.

As the cars pulled into camp, everyone ran to help. Ken and Sarel were out on the roads making sure the rebels did not cross the border and continue the chase. A woman drove the car Colleen ran up to; she clutched the steering wheel so hard her knuckles were white. She had stopped the car but would not let go of the steering wheel or turn the car off. Colleen reached across and did that. Removing the keys, she spoke to the woman. "What's your name?" No answer. "My name is Colleen, what's yours?" Still there was no answer. In the back seat sat a grandmother and two small children. The grandmother said, "Her name is Helen, I'm Alice and these are two of her four children."

"Alice, are you okay? Can you take yourself and the two children to the big building? There is a doctor that will check you out." Gently Colleen loosened Helen's fingers from the steering wheel. Slowly the woman turned her head to look at Colleen. Her eyes told the all too familiar story. Even though there was blood splattered across her clothing, she was unhurt and allowed herself to be led to the clinic.

Grandmother Alice told the story. The block of homes next to them had been overrun; you could hear and see some of the atrocities that were done. "Helen's husband John; yelled at us to run for the car. John was in charge of bringing two of the children, and Helen in charge of the other two. I had to get myself into the car. I am slower because of a bum knee. Helen, the two children and I reached the car but eight-year old Johnny who was with the father had tripped and fallen. Because of panic or hurt, he wasn't getting up. John put five-year-old Letty down, I heard him yelling to her to run to the car, but she stood frozen and crying for her dad. John ran back to help Johnny but the rebels were climbing the wall. We saw him and the two children overrun. He did have time to yell to Helen to save the other two children." For a while Colleen couldn't speak, and then shaking herself, she said.

"Is the baby breastfed, Alice?"

"Yes."

"Are you sure you're okay?"

"I'm not hurt—but, but," stammered Alice.

"I know love, I know. Lie back on the bed and keep the three-year-old with you. I will be back. Right now I'm taking the baby to his mother to feed. Maybe that will snap her back to reality."

Helen was sitting, staring straight ahead. When Colleen handed her the baby, it brought her back to the present. Automatically she loosened her blouse and started feeding the baby. She started humming to her son, but slowly the humming gave way to sobbing. This is what Colleen wanted to happen. The woman needed to cry. Leading her over to where her mother was with the three-year-old, she settled them on the cots with sweet hot tea. Doctor David would give them a sedative after he checked them out.

Colleen moved on to help someone else. After a quick glance around, she saw Shawn helping a family, Robert was with another family, and the doctor was frantically trying to stop a bleeding limb. Ken and Sarel had returned and were helping with the protection of the camp. At this point, David was the one that needed help. Without saying anything, Colleen scrubbed her hands and stepped up to the table David was working at. Looking at her, he said, "You okay with this?" Colleen just nodded.

"Then put your fingers here and push down. I need to stop the bleeding."

For the next two days, there were still the odd cars that managed to cross over; there were even some walkers. They had managed to stay alive by staying off the roads, and sticking to the bush area. As the refugees were able to, they were moved to the closest towns. There they were helped to make decisions as to what they were going to do, stay for a while in Northern Rhodesia, or go further down to South Africa or fly overseas to family or friends they still had living there.

One morning around the breakfast table Robert said, "I am going into Fort Jameson this morning, we have a list of supplies needed for the clinic and kitchen and we need some spare parts for the cars. Any personal supplies needed just give me a list; I will also take any letters that you would like mailed. Colleen, would you like to travel with me, it would give you a change, plus I'm not comfortable shopping for women's personal needs."

As Robert and Colleen pulled out of camp, Ken and Sarel left to check the border. That left David and Shawn to care for an almost empty camp. Colleen kissed Shawn good-bye on the cheek, and said, "Why don't you catch up on sleep. That cold you had seems to have taken a lot out of you."

"Sounds like a good idea, and be sure our letters go off to ye ma and pa."

They were only an hour's ride out of camp when Robert said, "Damn, the engine is overheating. I was hoping the fan belt would last to Fort Jameson." Being resourceful, he kept a box of unusual backups. Pulling out a lady's nylon stocking, he replaced the fan belt with this. "It will last until we buy a new one," he said with his American drawl.

After picking up the supplies, and money Zebra Run had sent, they shopped for the needed items. Mail was sent off and picked up. There were two letters from her mother and father, one for her and one for Shawn. She would wait to read them at a quiet time. Robert and Colleen had lunch at the Fort Jameson Hotel; sitting on the veranda, they enjoyed an ice-cold coke.

Robert said, "Before we head back, I would like to see if the dentist can refill a tooth for me. Do you want to wait in the reception area, or is there something you wanted to do Colleen?"

"Yes there is. I'll meet you back at the car."

Robert was already sitting in the car, reading some of his mail when Colleen climbed in. "Yikes . . . hey, I like that." he grinned.

"Thank you, you five men could be in and out of the shower and I would still be busy washing my hair and then it would take forever to dry. I figured this was not a ladylike business I'm in, so off with the long hair."

"Well, I think those red curls around your head are becoming, and I agree it's probably easier especially when it's so hot."

That night over supper, everyone was engrossed with their letters. Abe and Hope had forgiven Colleen for going off like that. They encouraged her to be careful. Sheree's wedding was set for the last Saturday of November. Could she and Shawn make it? That was six months away. Their letters were filled with Mike's progress. He was sitting up, or he'd cut his first tooth, or he was crawling. While she loved getting the news, it always made her sad.

Zebra Run asked the six of them to organize and set up a new camp. Just outside of Bancroft, more and more refugees were passing through from the Congo. They were expecting a breakout of trouble. A group arrived to take over their existing camp, releasing them to move on to the new one. They had to start from scratch. A well had to be dug, since they weren't close to a river; the site cleared and enclosures needed to be built. This time the six of them decided to use tents, quicker and easier. Shawn wanted to try something new in this camp, a place he could conduct a service. Instead of an enclosed building since they may not be here too long, it would be out in the open.

Anthills were huge—both in height and dimension. He decided to use one of them. He and his helpers spent days chopping the top half off, then smoothing it out. Mixing cow dung with dirt and water, a paste was made and smeared over the remaining part of the anthill, drying like cement. For seats, in an arch around the one side of the anthill they dug ditches, about two feet deep. The dirt was patted down to sit on, and your feet were in the ditches. It really was quite comfortable. It was such a success; that Shawn's little stadium was used for many projects.

Trouble came in the middle of the day. It was the same day they struck water. Ken and Sarel were out checking the border roads when they heard the distant sound of gunfire. They headed back to camp and put everyone on alert. About an hour later, they heard the roar of cars, trucks and buses traveling in their direction.

The Congolese had attacked in the middle of a weekday—children were at school, men at work, women going about their daily chores. This caused panic and confusion. They could not organize themselves into a fighting force. Parents needed to rescue their children from schools, fathers couldn't find mothers who were maybe grocery shopping, visiting or even at the doctor's office. So there was a lot of confusion with people running around looking for family members.

Something the Congolese was doing was using human barricades. In the past, the first car approaching a human barricade would stop, and then they and all cars behind were overrun. So every driver knew that their life and lives of everyone behind depended on them crashing through the barricade if one was used.

The first wave brought two trucks and six cars. Later that day four cars made it through. In the early hours of the evening, another eight cars came through, then no more. The rest of the town was destroyed. When the leading truck stopped, a middle-aged man jumped out from the driver's seat and ran screaming into the bush. Shawn ran after him. Knocking him down they rolled over several times before the man quieted down. Black women and children had been used as a barricade. He knew if he stopped, he would be signing everyone's death warrant. Putting his foot flat he hoped they would jump out of the way. He heard the screaming and felt the impact as his truck plowed through the walls of bodies. "I killed them," he mumbled to Shawn, "I killed about five children."

David caught up with them. He had an injection with him. Within a few minutes, the man would fall asleep. Later when David was speaking to this lead man, he said, "You need to remember while you may have killed five children, you actually saved sixteen adults and twenty four children, among those your own."

One large family came to the camp in two cars. Only when they got out at the campsite, did they realize one of the children were missing. They had ten-month-old twins. The mother thought the grandmother had one baby; the grandmother thought the mother had both boys; so one baby was left sleeping in his pram on the veranda.

"I have to go back. I have to go back," shouted the father hysterically. David did the only thing he could, slapping him very hard across the face to quiet him down

"Listen, I don't mean to be cruel. That baby is dead by now. You have seven other children here that need you. You can not go back." The man dropped to his knees weeping, his wife and family knelt next to him.

This group had put up a fight so there were a lot of injuries, mostly panga cuts; a few had limbs severed. Two children died. They had lost too much blood before even arriving at the camp. After working through the night, the six of them sat round the fire drinking coffee. Some of the refugees had already moved on down the country.

"Why are people so cruel to each other?" said Robert. Because she was so tired and because bad memories were awakened, Colleen burst out crying. Shawn got up and taking her hand led her to her tent. "Come on Colleen me love, ye need twelve hours sleep, then a lovely hot shower and food in ye stomach." When Shawn returned to the campsite, he told the four men about Colleen's experience with the Mau Mau and why she felt she had to be here.

Colleen slept right through to the following morning. She stood for the longest time under the shower scrubbing every inch of her body as though she could wash away what had happened. In clean clothes and towel-dried hair, she ate a man-sized breakfast.

After each wave of refugees, they had to restock their equipment. Today Robert was going into town. "Want to come, Colleen?"

Robert and Colleen had been spending a lot of time together. He had a calming effect on her. As they drove, he told her that he knew about her experience with the Mau Mau, that her husband was dead, and that her parents were bringing up her baby.

"I did not even know you had been married," he said. "I often wondered what you were running from."

"What made you think I was running from anything?"

"Most people that join Zebra Run or organizations like this are running from something. I knew about Shawn's loss at Lagenwa, Ken's wife left him taking his three children back to England. Sarel's wife and newborn baby were killed in a car crash. David was responsible for a young boy's death, giving him the wrong medication." They were silent for a while.

"So what are you running from, Robert?" He was very quiet.

"Maybe one day I'll tell you."

On their return, they walked into the clinic. Robert made such a sudden stop that Colleen crashed into him, dropping the supplies she was carrying. She bent to pick them up.

"Don't; don't pick up—move back out of here—back to the car."

"What . . . what's happening?"

Robert hurried them back to the Landrover. "Robert, what's the matter?"

"One of David's and my safety precautions is never to move anything. Things have a certain place on a table at a certain angle, etc. If it has been moved, someone else had been in the room. It has saved our lives on several occasions. Almost everything in the clinic has been moved."

"Now that you say that, the camp is very quiet, no dogs barking, no pickininys running around. Shawn and David should have heard the car drive up."

Robert started the car. "Robert, what are you doing? We can't just leave. Ken and Sarel left this morning for border patrol. Let's hope they are okay, but David and Shawn are here."

"Colleen, we're just two people. What happens if the camp has been attacked and the rebels are still here?"

"They're long gone. As you said, we are just two people. They would have overrun us by now."

They made sure their guns were loaded; Colleen's hand automatically ran over her knife. Then she slipped her right hand into her key ring holder. Walking back to back, they searched the camp. Their tents were fine, no sign of trouble. The kitchen area was fine, in fact, no sign of animals or people anywhere.

"No one in the camp, how strange," said Robert. "Now I'm really concerned."

As they walked away from the servant's quarters, Colleen stopped. "Listen." It was a baby crying. They followed the sound into one of the huts. In a basket that was jammed into a corner of the roof thatch was a baby boy. Robert climbed up and handed him down to Colleen. Colleen recognized the baby. It belonged to Feeg, a black woman who worked along with her. They had become friends. Feeg's baby was about the same age as Mike so Colleen felt close to the baby. As he progressed, Colleen could picture Mike doing that very same thing.

"His mother was very brave and smart. She knew sooner or later we'd return and search the camp."

They heard Ken and Sarel's land rover pull up. Running back to their section of the camp, Colleen had the baby on her hip. Robert quickly filled Ken and Sarel in on what they'd found, or rather what they hadn't found.

"We did run across a small band of rebels, they didn't put up much of a fight and quickly slipped back across the border. It looked like a gang of youths, maybe a training mission."

"But if they had no prisoners with them and there are no people here, except for this baby, where is everyone?"

"Robert, Colleen take the baby and wait in the Landrover. If there is any sign of trouble, get the hell out of here. Use the radio in the car to contact the police in Bancroft. We need backup, Ken and I and our two gun bearers are trained for this. We're going to search the camp again. They found nothing.

"Did you get through to the police, Robert?"

"Yes, they had a patrol close by so are headed this way. They figured they'd be here in about thirty minutes."

"Good, we are probably going to move out from here. Why don't you pack your personal goods?"

"We're not going anywhere until we find Shawn and David." Robert's voice had a quiver in it."

Colleen busied herself cleaning and feeding Feeg's baby. Just last week he'd taken his first steps. Right now he was trying his best to walk around Colleen's tent as she packed her few things. She then went to Shawn's tent, figuring she'd help him get packed so they wouldn't waste time. Robert had done the same with David's things. The police arrived and spread out searching.

"Just how many people are we looking for?" asked the police chief. They made a quick count. There were two Europeans, Shawn and David. There were four African families; two of the men were with Ken and Sarel so that left two African men and four African women. Between them they had seven children. Colleen was holding one, so six were missing.

"That's fourteen people, maybe bodies. They can't just disappear like that."

Just then a policeman ran up and whispered in the chief's ear. Slowly the chief turned to them. "We've found them. They are all on that anthill platform thing." Colleen and Robert stood up.

"I wouldn't if I were you," said the chief. "It's pretty nasty. They are all staked out. Some have been disemboweled including women and children." As the chief walked by he put his hand on the baby's head. "You're one lucky pickininy."

From a distance, Colleen heard a terrible noise. She turned around looking for where it came from, but everyone was looking at her. Even the baby she was holding was looking at her and screaming. The sound was coming from her throat, it kept gurgling out. Then she heard this roar that got louder and louder until it swept past her, then blackness. When she came to, she was tied to her cot. Robert was sitting at her bedside.

"Why am I tied down?"

"Colleen, you'd knocked down three police, before two more overpowered you. You were trying to get to Shawn on the anthill." Then she remembered.

"Nooooooo, oh noooooo . . . not Shawn."

Life was filled with too many hurts.

Blankets were collected to wrap bodies in. One by one, they were carried down from the anthill and laid side by side in the clinic. Ken and Sarel's two gun bearers wanted to take their peoples bodies back to their village for burial. Neither surviving black man wanted the baby. It wasn't theirs. Their lives were hard enough without looking after someone else's child. The police suggested dropping him off at the church. "The nuns will take care of him."

"No," said Colleen. "Moses is coming with me."

"His name is not Moses," said one of the gun bearers.

"I know," said Colleen. "But I'm renaming him Moses. His mother saved his life by hiding him in a basket." So the arrangements were made. The two gun bearers were taking twelve bodies back to their village and were taking a two-month vacation. Ken and Sarel were staying here and getting a new set of Zebra Run people established before they left on vacation.

Colleen was surprised; Robert was normally a calm, take-charge person. But now he couldn't seem to make a decision. He kept wandering back to David's body and sitting there crying. She was in pain too over her beloved Shawn, but she realized, as Shawn had so often told her, 'Don't sink into an emotional pit, remember there are two ways to kill a person, the second being the worse.' So she took charge, if she didn't take charge of this situation and the baby Moses, she knew she wouldn't make it.

"Robert, do you want David's body to be flown back to America?"

"No."

"Do you want him buried where he died?"

"No."

"Look, I'm going back to South Africa for my sister's wedding. I'm taking Shawn's body and Moses with me. Why don't you come with, and bring David's body? We can bury him next to Shawn. Then stay with us a few months. Meet my family. You will like them. We have some interesting family history you'll be forced to wade through." Colleen tried to make a joke here but it didn't go over very well, she was in no mood to tell jokes and Robert was in no mood to listen to them.

Ken and Sarel would drive Robert's Zebra Run Landrover down to South Africa when they come. Colleen took Shawn's Landrover; they packed the bodies in the back. They had police zip up bags, but they would need to stop at Chingola to fill the bags with ice. Then again, as they were crossing the border in South Africa, they would have to add ice. They had to drive straight through. Three days driving would have to be done in two days.

Before starting the trip, Colleen used the police phone to call her parents. They could have the arrangements completed; the burial would take place as soon as they arrived, that would be necessary because of time elapsed from the killing. "Mom, Robert is in quite a state, can he stay with us for that two months?"

"Of course, my girl, your friends are welcome."

CHAPTER 17

Because of driving straight through, Colleen and Robert arrived at her parents' house at 5:00 a.m. Pulling into the driveway, Colleen switched off the car's lights thinking everyone would still be sleeping. But Hope and Abe came running out and swooped her up in their arms. Hope couldn't say anything; she was crying happy tears.

"Daddy, you are going to break my ribs!" but Colleen held on just as tight.

"Mom, Dad, this is Robert Miller, the American I told you about." Hope and Abe made Robert feel like one of the family and welcomed him into their home. Colleen picked up the sleeping Moses and they all moved into the family sized kitchen for a welcome cup of coffee.

Abe picked up the phone, while dialing he said, "Because of circumstances the funeral home is on standby. I am to call as soon as you arrive; they will send their crew over to collect the bodies. You and Robert have to fill out some forms. The time arranged is 2:00 this afternoon. Is that okay?" Colleen and Robert nodded.

Moses continued sleeping so Colleen laid him on the couch. Stretching to get rid of the knots in her body from sitting so long, she pulled off her cap. Hope let out a loud gasp, "Colleen! Your hair!!"

"Had to Mom, it was more practical."

Putting the phone down, Abe grabbed a handful of the curls. "Well, I think it looks good. Cookie, when we got married do you remember how shocked my family was because your hair was short?"

"Yes," laughed Hope. "I did cause a stir. So like mother like daughter. But it's so short!"

"Mom, I don't know when last I wore a dress or had a long hot soak in a tub. Sometimes I don't even remember when my last meal was. My hair was the least of my worries."

Taking Colleen in her arms Hope said, "You're right my girl, I didn't mean to sound negative. Which brings up the point, before everyone starts getting up, and Ouma and Oupa come over and the house turning into a circus, would you like a hot shower or a soak in my tub."

Colleen nodded, her eyes filled with tears. She was home, she was safe, she could lay in a tub of water and not worry about wasting water or even making sure her gun was next to the tub, just in case.

Abe helped Robert unpack the car, and then led him to Shawn's wing of the house. "Everything you will need is in the bathroom, Robert, take your time even stretch out if you need to. If you have fallen asleep, I'll wake you for breakfast."

"Thank you, Sir."

"Please call me Abe. Robert, I must thank you for taking Colleen with you to town that day. If she had not gone, she would have been in that camp when the rebels came—and—and, well thank you." Abe gave Robert a bear hug, as he struggled with his emotions.

Colleen stepped into the tub filled with hot water and bubbles. She lay back and enjoyed. Five minutes later, her mom came in with clean underwear (Sheree's), a robe and another cup of coffee. Hope soaped up a huge sponge and started scrubbing Colleen's back.

"Oh, I could get used to this." She lay back or bent over, enjoying the rubdown. Hope shampooed her hair, and then rinsed it off in clear water. Lying back sipping her coffee, she told her mom about that fateful day.

Hope was quiet for a while, and then said, "I think Moses is an appropriate name. Now I know you can not travel with him, so why don't you leave him here with us, he can grow up with Mike."

"I was hoping we could arrange something so he could stay."

"But Colleen my girl, don't go back. This debt you feel the need to repay surely has been paid over and over again."

"We'll see Mom, we'll see."

Now that she was all cleaned up and feeling like a different person, Colleen tiptoed into Mike's room. He was still fast asleep in his *cot* sucking his thumb. He looked fat and healthy compared to all the children she'd been around lately. Colleen put her hand out and touches his warm skin, and then rested her hand on his black curly hair.

"Hello my darling," she whispered.

Hope called her mother, and Joy. "They're here, come over and have breakfast with us." It was not too long before they started filing into the house.

"Nathaniel, could you give Moses a physical? I want to be sure he's not carrying a disease to pass on to my Mike."

When Mike awoke, Hope put him down in front of Colleen, hoping he would walk towards her, but he turned and walked to Shannon holding out his chubby arms. When Colleen picked him up, he pulled away crying and held his arms out to Hope. This really hurt her. Hope saw the hurt in Colleen's eyes. "Oh, Colleen my girl, it's just that he doesn't really know you. You will see he will change after a few days."

Sheree, Gordon, and Charles were full of questions. Colleen felt a twinge of envy seeing Sheree and Seun together. Her sister was so beautiful; her strawberry blond hair was long and shiny. Her skin was so soft and unblemished. Her nails were long and painted. Colleen felt like a frump, chopped off hair, sunburned and her freckles had returned. She sat on her hands to hide her short unpainted nails. Robert always gravitated to her side, he also felt uncomfortable. Moses was always clinging to her leg. Well, she did fit in somewhere.

The funeral service that afternoon was very simple. "We will meet you back at the house Mom. Robert wants to sit here for a while saying his goodbyes to David. I will sit with him so he's not alone." Hope took Moses with them, the two toddlers got along fine.

Colleen sat next to Robert and took his hand in hers. "Robert, you have really been hit hard. Would it help to fly back to America and be with your family?"

"No, no," he squeezed her hand. "It's not America I miss, it's David." Colleen nodded.

"I understand, I really miss Shawn, he was like a second father to me." Robert started to say something but decided against it. They sat in silence for a while, but then she felt that Robert wasn't just letting her hold his hand in comfort, he was entwining his fingers through hers. It was turning from a comforting hand holding to a sensual one. He leaned forward and kissed her lightly on the lips.

"I think you are the only one that would understand."

"I understand Robert, I understand," and she kissed him back. However, Colleen did not understand; only many years later would she really understand what Robert was talking about.

When they got back to the house, the conversation had turned to rugby. Gordon and Charles had games later. They were fifteen and sixteen years old and not yet interested in girls, only sports and movies. Because Robert came from America, they assumed he knew the movie actors, so they had him cornered talking about movies.

Sheree, Seun, Shannon, Joy and Hope were busy with the wedding plans two weeks from today. Abe noticed Colleen was not fully into this planning stuff, so he motioned to her to follow him. Putting his arm around her shoulders, they walked into the garden. Not saying anything, they walked to the garden swing that hung from Shannon's favorite tree and sat swinging in silence.

"Colleen, Mom and I told you that we had forgiven you for running off like that with Shawn, we also need to tell you how proud we are of you. You have helped so many people through their first hours of pain. Even though you're hurting because of Shawn, you are taking care of Robert's hurt. Then there is Moses, do you know you saved his life in more than one way." Colleen just nodded. "When Shawn left for the Zebra Run, you knew he got his affairs in order. Before he left, he gave me an envelope and said, 'If anything happens to me, could you give Colleen this envelope. I hope you don't mind Abe, but I've always looked on Colleen as a daughter.'" That brought tears to Colleen's eyes.

"Oh Dad, I always thought of him as a second father."

Colleen opened the envelope; it was Shawn's will. Together Abe and Colleen read it, and then looked at each other in disbelief. Shawn had left Colleen two pieces of property. One was in Scotland, ten acres with a beautiful thatch cottage (there was a picture). Enough money was left in Scotland to hire a man to keep the land and house in order and to pay taxes for the next fifty years. The other property was in Blouberg Strand, Cape Town. Again ten acres, a beautiful house, and a keeper, all expenses paid for the next fifty years. Shawn had money, but did not trust leaving it in banks, so he bought property, paid cash for it and its upkeep for years to come.

Shawn was born and brought up in Scotland. He had been married and had a daughter named Colleen. Both his wife and daughter had been killed in a fire. That's when he left Scotland for South Africa. With the money he made in South Africa, he bought and recreated his home in Blouberg. When he took vacations, he would visit either property. Now they belonged to Colleen. Colleen not only had the same name as Shawn's daughter but also the same red curly hair; the same fighting spirit, and almost the same age. Shawn wrote at the end of his will.

"Colleen lass, I hope ye don'a mind me always thinking of ye as me own. It gave me joy watching ye grow and turning into such a bonny lass. Use these two homes to recharge yourself. When ye visit Scotland, I believe it's not te far from where ye Great Grandmother Maureen, came from. Back of the property on a hilltop, you will see the graves of me two love, Mary me wife, and our bonny Colleen. Me wish was to be buried next to them. I loved Africa, but they are across the ocean. If ye should make it over there, even though me body such as it is remains in Africa, could ye put a headstone fer me next to me family?" Colleen vowed that she would and soon.

Samson and Delila lived in a cottage on Hope and Abe's property. Samson now worked at the mine with Abe; Delila helped Hope with the running of the house, she was also taking some courses so that she could learn to read and write. They could not have any children, so Delila was only too happy to raise Moses as her own. While Colleen had saved him and brought him to South Africa, they did not want him losing out on his heritage, so even though Colleen would take care of his expenses and see that he was educated, even though he and Mike would grow together, probably be friends, he would live with his own kind and know of his family.

Hope was right. As Mike got to know Colleen, he would walk to her, climb on her lap and hug her. Colleen made it a point to play every day with Mike and Moses. She loved these times. Robert would roll on the grass with them too.

Colleen felt the only person that understood her, was Robert. Her brothers and sister thought that things were important—recreation, movies, eating out, new clothes, not that there is anything wrong with that. However, she and Robert had seen so much suffering, so much death that things weren't important. Simple pleasure, like clean water, quiet, safe sounds of the night, these were important. So they spent more and more time together. It seemed natural to hold hands and kiss occasionally. They were becoming a couple.

CHAPTER 18

Northern Rhodesia—1965

The wedding day was here. Colleen was to be Sheree's only bridesmaid. She endured dress fittings, shoe shopping, even shopping for the right underwear. Now she had to sit at the hairdressers while her hair was trimmed and fluffed, and nails painted a pale pink. Later when Colleen and Sheree were ready to walk down the isle, Colleen said to her sister, "Sheree, you truly make a beautiful bride."

"Thank you, Colleen, and I have to say you clean up pretty good yourself."

The reception was lively and noisy. Robert knew some dance steps from America, and the young ones were eager to learn. Robert was constantly swinging her out of the floor; she was beginning to enjoy it. Once when a slower dance tune played, Colleen found herself in her father's arms dancing. "We like him, Colleen, is it serious?"

"Whom are you talking about, Dad?"

"Robert of course; I guess you have a lot in common, Zebra Run and all. He knows about Michael and Mike, I've seen him play with Mike; he's good with children." Colleen looked over to where Robert was dancing with her mother. He was good looking; they did have a lot in common, maybe her father had something there. Only, she never felt the thrill she had at being with Michael but she knew she would never feel that way again.

One afternoon after the wedding, Robert and Colleen checked in at Zebra Run, to find out what their new assignment would be. They were upset to find out that, they were going to be separated and given different assignments. "Couldn't you assign us to the same camp," asked Robert. "We've been together for over a year, gone through a lot together and would like to stay together if possible."

The captain examined the records. "It would be easier if you were married, but check back with me again in about a month. You still have six week vacation, don't you?"

"Yes." They were both very quiet driving home.

Later, playing with the boys on the lawn Robert said, "You know they are right, about it being easier if we were married." Colleen stared at him. "Let me ask you something Colleen," he sat up and looked into her eyes. "You once said that after losing Michael, you could never love anyone like that again. And even if you did marry, you knew it would not be the same. Right?"

"Yes, I said that."

"I feel the same way after losing someone I loved."

"Oh Robert, I did not know you were married. What happened to her?" Robert stared at Colleen, opened his mouth to say something but didn't. Then tried again, but all he could manage was to shrug his shoulders. Colleen helped by saying,

"Did she die?"

Robert nodded, and then quickly continued, "If you did marry, would you take Mike back?"

"No, it would not be fair to him, he is being brought up as my mom and dad's son; even my brothers and sister doesn't know he's mine."

"Are you ready to settle into this way of life?" Robert gestured towards the house and yard.

"No, not yet. I don't know when, I just know it's not now." Colleen stared off into the horizon as she answered Robert.

"Okay, we've both had and lost our first loves. We both want to continue with Zebra Run. We'd like to stay together, we work well together, we like each other, and maybe in time we'll come to love each other. Let's get married."

Colleen had trouble looking beyond a few years. Right now, she just wanted to continue with Zebra Run. She still needed to distance herself from Mike. Maybe this sister role she played would get easier after some years. But right now, he was too cute, his conception; birth and Michael's death were still too fresh in her mind. Robert was right they did like one another. There were different degrees of love; maybe they'd find one that fit them. She looked up at him; he was still waiting for her answer. "Yes, let's marry that would take care of a lot of problems."

Colleen's parents were not shocked. They had thought of them as a couple anyway. "But you should have said something earlier; we could have made it a double wedding."

"No Mom, Robert and I don't want anything fancy. Just a ceremony with a judge or even a priest here at the house." When Sheree and Seun returned from their short honeymoon the following week, arrangements were made for Colleen and Robert to marry.

"Robert, once we leave on our new Zebra Run mission, we don't know how long we will be gone. What do you think, while we still have four weeks vacation, let's fly over to Scotland and check out the property Shawn left me? Maybe, we could return via the Cape and check that property."

Robert's eyes lit up. "Sounds like a great idea. Since Seun and Sheree still have two weeks vacation, let's invite them to join us?"

The wedding was at 10:00 A.M. and at 2:00 P.M. the four of them boarded the plane for London. "This is so exciting," said Seun. "For us three South Africans this is the first time leaving the country. For you Robert, it's probably just one of many times."

That evening arriving at London airport, they were all exhausted and decided to spend the night in a hotel. As they registered at the hotel, Sheree whispered in Colleen's ear, "I know you get up before the sun, but let's not have too early a start tomorrow. The mornings are very special for Seun and I, plus, sister dear, this is your wedding night, you need to enjoy."

Colleen was not too sure what to expect from Robert after all, they were married. There was a huge bathtub in their hotel suite. She filled it, adding bubbles. "I am going to take a relaxing bath Robert; do you want to join me?" Colleen knew her mother and father enjoyed bathing together.

"Go ahead, I will first see to room service."

Colleen heard room service come and go through the open door, but Robert never joined her in the tub. Her mother had packed a beautiful, cloud blue nightgown; see through with lace trim and little flowers around the neck. Colleen slipped it over her head. Looking in the mirror, she was surprised—she looked good. Her mother knew the color showed off her red curls, and the hot soak had brought a blush to her skin. Robert was already in his pajama bottoms, lying on the bed, and his arms behind head. He never said anything as she walked towards the bed or when she lay down next to him. Turning toward him, she started to say something, but Robert interrupted, saying.

"Do you mind if we wait. I am very tired, plus I feel awkward with your sister and Seun in the next room. Robert gave her a peck on the cheek and turned over. Colleen lay there struggling with her emotions. What had she done wrong? Slowly the tears welled up in her eyes and silently ran over the side of her face, soaking the pillow.

Robert was up before her, and she was an early bird, he'd already had a shower and shaved. He looked really good, like a young bridegroom should look; only there was no twinkle in his eye. He did smile as he said, "Come on; let us have breakfast in the dining room. I am dying to try a typical English breakfast." Breakfast was good; the four of them tried *kippers* and enjoyed it.

Then they spent the day sightseeing in London, and later they caught the night sleeper from London to Inverness. Colleen and Sheree looked forward to the train ride, remembering their childhood experiences on the train between Northern Rhodesia and South Africa. The night spent sleeping on the train brought back memories they loved. Early in the morning, Colleen opened the blinds, lying on her stomach; she watched the magic scenery rush by. They were thundering through forest of spruce and larch. She opened the train window, the air smelled of crisp heather and pine. A farm dog stood barking at the train, while his little master waved to Colleen. She waved back; at an impulse she blew him a kiss, he laughed out loud.

They pulled into Inverness ready for their adventure, breakfast first at a quaint inn. The waitress was very helpful and not only arranged a car rental for them but drew on their map the directions to Colleen's house. Inverness is a town ringed by hills. They headed past neat stone villas to the river Ness. They had to visit the home of the famous Loch Ness Monster. The four of them appreciated the great beauty and wildness they were driving through.

When they arrived at the address, Colleen held her breath. The photo did not do the house justice. It was a beautiful white brick, thatched cottage surrounded by a neatly mowed lawn and flowerbeds. There was a low stonewall that had creepers climbing over it. Mr. Ian KnoxLittle was standing at the front door waiting for them. Colleen walked up to him and held her hand out. "Good afternoon, I'm Colleen."

Ian took her hand, "Mum." Ian had freshened up the house and stocked it with local produce. Downstairs was a huge room that combined the kitchen, eating area and sitting area. There was a huge fireplace that looked like it was well used. The windows had lead criss crossing which added to the charm. The front entrance hall had a coatroom plus a half bath. The back exit also had a little coatroom and a room for stacking wood for the fireplace. Upstairs had two cozy bedrooms and a bathroom between the rooms. The ceilings were low, and the men had to bend slightly. The two double beds were puffy with quilts; it looked very inviting. They unpacked and settled in for the evening. The girls made an early supper for the four of them. The next few days they planned on exploring.

Before settling down for the evening, Colleen walked up the little hill behind the house. Sure enough there were the gravesites of Mary and baby Colleen. Colleen had phoned ahead and a stone had been erected for Shawn. She sat there for a while thinking of Shawn, his younger days here in Scotland with Mary and his baby, and then his mature days spent in Africa. She felt such a tie to these three graves. In her pocket, she pulled out a little box, and dug a hole in front of Shawn's stone. Opening the box, she sprinkled soil from Shawn's grave in South Africa. "Now you're with your loves," she whispered.

They spent their days wandering through the countryside, discovering quaint little stores. Colleen bought some tartan. She knew that Maureen and her sisters had a green and black tartan. Stopping at local pubs late in the afternoon, taught them a lot about local history and family lines. Colleen and Sheree, because of their names and looks (Scottish coloring) were accepted but Robert, an American, and Seun every inch a South African were not treated as kindly.

Colleen spent time with Ian giving him her address and phone number; she also signed some papers giving him a raise. "Thanking ye, Mum," his eyes shone. "Ian, if you ever want to travel, our home in Africa is open to you."

Flying into Cape Town, they flew over Table Mountain, a sight one never tired of. Seun knew this area, so took over. Renting a car, they drove out to Blouberg. It was on the opposite side of the mountain from Cape Town. Still rural, Colleen could see why Shawn chose this spot. In a way it reminded you of Scotland, flat, windy and lots of wild flowers, mountains wherever you looked and the seawater was always cold. Shawn had built the cottage exactly like the one in Scotland. Their housekeeper was also an elderly man. His name was Piet. He had kept the property in good shape. Colleen also arranged for him to get a raise.

In their sight seeing, they climbed to the top of Table Mountain. Watching boats come into the harbor made Colleen think of the arrivals of her Great Grandfather Nicholas and her Great Grandmother Maureen. Suddenly Colleen was homesick to be around her mother, and grandmother. They were links to Maureen; her father was the link to Nicholas. Joy met their plane in Johannesburg.

"Girls, don't panic. Your mom and dad had to fly to Natal, your Grandfather Jacob has suffered another heart attack, but he seems to be pulling out of it." Putting one arm around her son Seun, and the other around Sheree, her new daughter-in-law, she said, "So how are the two married couples?" Sheree blushed, and Seun said, "Couldn't be better," as he pinched Sheree's bottom. Robert looked away and Colleen changed the subject, she had been hurt by her friend, and husband and did not understand why.

Time away had made Mike and Moses look on them as strangers. They only had a week left, so they visited Zebra Run for their new assignment. It was back up to Northern Rhodesia, an outpost they hadn't been to before. Hope and Abe arrived back two days before they were due to leave, giving them a little time together. Colleen so much wanted to pour her heart out to her mother about the strange relationship between her and Robert. However, her parents were so worried about Oupa Jacob that she didn't want to add any burden to them, so instead she chatted about Scotland. "Scotland is beautiful Mom, you and dad should take a vacation there. You'll see the area Maureen came from.

Before leaving on their new assignment, Colleen went to visit Shawn's gravesite. She wanted to tell him she had carried out his wish about the stone next to his wife. She had been there a while before she realized there were fresh flowers on David's grave. Robert must have been here, she thought. Strange, he said he would be busy all day with Zebra Run.

It was hard saying goodbye to everyone, but Colleen was eager to start work. Two months was a long time to vacation. Mike wouldn't come to her; she laid her hand on his black curls and looked at her mother. Because of family around, she couldn't say what she wanted. But Hope read Colleen's eyes and she whispered in Colleen's ear as she hugged her. "Don't worry; he has all of us to love and care for him."

Robert and Colleen were teamed up with another couple, Dennis and Sandra. The Mau Mau days were fading but other groups of rebels were always popping up. The two couples were given the work of keeping all the camps in Northern and Southern Rhodesia, updated, supplied with what they needed and giving advice or help when needed. Colleen enjoyed this; they were constantly on the move. Even though they were now married two years, they still hadn't made love. Colleen accepted that, remembering there were different degrees of love—this was their degree. At least they were friends.

One of the assignments they enjoyed was traveling to Lundazi. After crossing the mountains, the easiest and fastest route, was up the river in a canoe. They had done this several times, so Robert and Dennis thought they didn't need the guides. Rains were late this year and the river lower than normal. This made the hippos uneasy; the boats were too low in the water, bringing it closer to the hippo. The two couples loaded their canoes; they had some heavy equipment this trip. Projectors and generators, as Zebra Run were beginning to teach, and these were learning tools.

They were about two hours into their trip, sticking to the middle of the river; hoping they were clear of the barking hippos. They must have come too close to a mom and her baby, with a bellowing roar, the dad charged Colleen and Robert's canoe, overturning it. Colleen was shouting for Robert, Robert was shouting for Colleen. Robert was not aware of the fact that Colleen could not swim. Her fear was not of drowning but of the crocodiles. As she lost consciousness, her thoughts were on Michael and Mike.

Slowly she came to; she was not in the river. She was not dead. In fact, she was toasty warm. There was a huge fire burning and she was lying next to it. Robert was sitting next to her; he was so relieved that she had regained conscious. Colleen tried to sit up but her head hurt so much she fell back again. "Robert, how did I get here?"

"Dennis aimed his canoe for you. As you surfaced, he grabbed your shirt and headed for shore. I made it with a crocodile right on my tail." Looking around Colleen said,

"Where are Dennis and Sandra?"

"We lost everything, even the canoe. They unpacked their equipment." Robert indicated the boxes, "Then they left to get help. We were not sure if you were badly hurt or not. But regardless we need another canoe and equipment if we are to continue up river." Colleen's head hurt, so she went back to sleep, leaving Robert to make some kind of lean to for shelter. The next morning she felt much better. "If we are going to be here for a few days we had better catch some fish," said Robert.

This was the first time they were totally alone, no one around for miles (except animals). Being away from people or maybe because he had almost lost her, Robert finally took Colleen in his arms. He was very clumsy but very sweet. 'Now, why are you crying' she thought to herself. 'For two years you cried because he did not make love. Now you're crying because he did. You knew it would never be the same as it was with Michael.'

From that day on, their relationship changed. Regularly at least a few times a year, Robert would make love to Colleen. How different people were, she thought. Robert acted like it was a chore, a responsibility. To name some of the men she knew, Michael, Seun, her dad, Desmond, Nathaniel, they were eager lovers. Maybe it was her, it couldn't possibly be Robert. Everyone loved him; he was always helping someone, but Colleen was hard to know. She had always retreated to her mind's 'room,' no one could hurt her there.

Colleen and Robert were combining a vacation and business trip to South Africa. Because they were leaving in two weeks, Colleen did not write her news. She wanted to tell her family in person. She was expecting a baby. She was surprised at Robert's reaction. He loved the idea; he did love children. They were driving back to South Africa via Livingstone. While Robert was in a business meeting, Colleen drove to Lagenwa. She wanted to visit the tree house. The new owner remembered her and gave her permission to wander around the farm. The house looked the same. Borrowing a horse, she slowly trotted to many spots that she and Michael had enjoyed. At the tree house, she climbed up. She kept fit with her work and running, so it wasn't a problem. As usual, she first got rid of cobwebs and damage done by the monkeys. The thatch was beginning to pull apart. It won't last too many more years, thought Colleen.

She opened the trunk, and then sat by the window. The last time she was here, Shawn was with her. She felt the tears fall on the bible. Wiping the tears off, she opened the pages that had her letters and notes. Colleen started to write, telling Michael she still loved him and only him, even though married and now expecting a baby. She was on her way to South Africa and would see their son, Mike. He was now five and a half and would be starting school soon. One of the pictures her mother had sent her of Mike, Colleen slipped in the pages of the bible. She also told Michael about Shawn and that he had left her two properties.

Colleen was tempted to take the bible with her. The tree house was slowly falling apart. No, next time, she thought. As long as the tree house stayed the same, Michael was here. When the tree house was no more, neither was Michael. She wanted to keep Michael there a little longer.

Sitting by the opening they called a window, Colleen thought back on her life. Michael was always there; she was five when they met—almost seventeen when they married. Now their son was as old as she was when they met. She was now twenty-four and Michael would be twenty-seven, what would their life had been like if he had not gone to England—or—if she had gone with him. Colleen surprised herself when she burst out crying; she curled up on the floor and cried herself to sleep.

She woke with a start, the sun was beginning to set—how would she explain this to Robert.

CHAPTER 19

Hope and Abe, were excited at Colleen's news, they never suspected that things weren't normal between Colleen and Robert. They hoped a child could now bring them home to South Africa away from danger. Sheree already had a daughter and was expecting her second baby. Mike was an active little boy, he'd been told his big sister Colleen was coming to visit, and he called her Col. It did not hurt as much being around Mike; maybe because he was not a helpless baby that needed her mothering. He was a happy little boy, busy with puppies, frogs and learning to ride a bike. Moses and Mike were best friends, but now that they would be starting separate schools, it would probably change.

Gordon and Charles were both in university. Gordon, wanted to be a history teacher, and Charles was into rugby. He had received his coat and badge and was playing for South Africa. Two years ago their Grandfather Jacob, had died of a third heart attack. A year later Grandmother Natasha, died in her sleep. Grandfather Nathaniel was not doing too well. He was now seventy-three and had trouble getting around. Grandmother Shannon, said to him, "I love you too much Mr. N., you are not allowed to die." Colleen was envious to see this strong love her grandmother and grandfather had. For the first time Colleen noticed her parents age. Her dad was fifty-two, she though that was old.

While here, Colleen visited Shawn's grave, again she noticed fresh flowers on David's grave, strange. Zebra Run was looking for a safer assignment for them now that they were going to have a child. "Would you accept an assignment outside of Africa?" they asked. Robert agreed, in the meantime they were to continue their present assignment.

"African women travel with babies strapped to their backs, so can I," said Colleen. Dennis and Sandy still traveled with them, so Colleen never had to do heavy lifting. She stopped running, but walked at least five miles every day. She also sat squatting like the African women, getting her pelvis ready. An elderly couple that ran a small outpost for Zebra Run was due their vacation; Robert and Colleen took over their assignment for two months. It was near a small hospital that had midwife.

Colleen had an easy time giving birth to her daughter, who in turn, was a healthy baby. Colleen chose the name Maureen, because she admired her great grandmother so much. Two months later, they rejoined Dennis and Sandra, on their assignment. Colleen had seen a picture of a reed basket the American Indians carried their babies in. She worked and worked on one until it fit her needs, this would not only make it easier for her to carry Maureen, but it would be a lot more comfortable and safer for the baby. Colleen could carry it on her back, swing it to the front, or even let it stand on its own. It worked perfectly.

Maureen was only four months old when Robert got a telegram. His parents in America had been involved in a serious car accident, and may not survive. Zebra Run could not replace them both and since they were so close to getting their overseas assignment, they did not want to jeopardize that. "You must go Robert; you haven't seen them for so many years. If they die, you will never forgive yourself. Maureen and I will be fine with Dennis and Sandra. We are almost done with this circle anyway, and then we will be back at the main office for a month."

Robert left for America and they left for one of their posts that required an overnight camping stay along the river. Years earlier, they had made a rough one-roomed little hut for these overnight stays. It was a very cold night, so instead of letting Maureen sleep in her arms; Colleen wrapped her up and slipped her into her day basket. She would be toasty warm.

Dennis and Sandra were still outside sitting around the fire. Colleen had just finished nursing Maureen and tucked her up in the basket. She heard a scuffle outside the hut, something sounded wrong. Peeping through the grass wall, she saw two Africans had jumped Dennis. As Colleen looked, Dennis was knifed and Sandra knocked down. Swinging around she thought 'Maureen, Maureen, what',—then she remembered Moses. Standing on one of their equipment boxes, she pushed Maureen's basket into the thatch roof.

"Please keep sleeping my baby."

Her knife was always strapped to her leg when on assignment. Picking up her special key ring holder, she first checked through the grass again. Yes, still only two attackers. She was sure Dennis was dead the way he was bleeding. Sandra was pinned to the ground; they had torn her clothing off. Since they hadn't come into the hut looking for her, they must have thought there were just two people on this camping trip. Good, she can surprise them. One African had just climbed on top of Sandra. The other African stood watching, he had his back to Colleen. Colleen was not seeing her daughter hidden in the thatch; she saw her mother; and herself about to give birth to Mike. She did not see Dennis lying bleeding on the ground, she saw Desmond with his hand chopped off. She did not see Sandra being raped, she saw Anetta.

With a roar Colleen burst out of the hut and jump kicked the African standing watching. She knew this would double him over, and give her time to use her knife. She did, and he fell to the ground, dead. Shawn flashed through her mind; she was avenging him, as she used her knife. Turning to face the second man, she though he would be up charging her. But he was still on top of Sandra, looking straight at Colleen he smiled. Sandra was struggling and screaming. Colleen stepped forward but a strong set of arms grabbed her from the back—a third person! She tried to flip him over her shoulder, but couldn't. She tried using her elbow in his ribs, still no effect. This must be a giant of a man.

As she fell to the ground, she prayed that there were only three; she may still be able to handle this. The third man looked angry. He had been washing at the river, now he stood over her naked and dripping wet.

The two Africans were laughing and talking to one another. Sandra was still screaming as she was being raped. Colleen did not want the same fate. As this giant approached her, she pretended to be afraid. She curled up into a ball and started whimpering. He stood in front of her, right where she wanted him. Summoning all her strength, she kicked both feet at his knees. She heard bone and sinue snap as his knees overextended backward. There was a look of surprise on his face, as he fell backwards. His body did a little bounce before it hit the ground for a second time. Colleen was on her feet and slit his throat, before he could collect himself.

Before the startled African could move off of Sandra, Colleen had run and jump kicked with both feet. One foot on his mouth, the other his nose, as he fell backwards off of Sandra, blood and saliva sprayed from his mouth and nose. Colleen was on top of him with her special key ring holder. She felt his jaw break as she hit him. Sandra was up yelling at Colleen.

"Don't kill him, don't kill him." Colleen hit him once more making sure he was knocked out.

"You want to save his life, after what he did to Dennis and you?"

"No, I want him to suffer."

Colleen tied the surviving African up while Sandra dressed. Sandra, could speak his language, so when he came to, she asked him how many more of them were out there. He was now the victim and was quivering.

"Just us three, my father, the big man, my brother and myself."

"Why did you attack us?"

"Because you're white and alone, we thought we'd have some fun with you, and we were hungry."

"We would have been glad to feed you, but that's my husband you killed, and then you raped me. Now I will make sure you never rape anyone again." Sandra had her heavy boots on, they were steel toed and had a steel heel (used for squashing snakes). She now spent several minutes kicking and grinding his equipment into the ground.

"You will never enter a woman again, either for rape or love, and I doubt if you will be able to pee normally again." The man had regained consciousness and was groaning in pain. They did not want to attract attention in case anyone else was out there, so Sandra stuffed his mouth full of grass before gagging him.

"Well," said Colleen, "I've just seen a side of you I never knew existed."

"What about you, Colleen, where did you learn to fight like that?"

"My two fathers, we need to get out of here, just in case," said Colleen ignoring Sandra's questioning look.

They tied the two canoes together, making sure they would not be separated traveling down the dark river. Dennis was rolled in a blanket and put him on top of their luggage in one canoe.

"We'll leave the equipment here; they can send someone else after it." Maureen had slept through all of this. Setting her basket in the middle of the second canoe, Sandra and Colleen, sat at either ends and pushed off down the river. They let the current carry them, using the oars only for steering. That's when Sandra broke down crying, her husband had just been killed and she'd been raped. Colleen was crying too, relief that nothing had happened to Maureen, but she was also crying for the reopened wounds of Shawn, Desmond, Anetta and the two children. She also felt weak in her knees, she had just killed two men and left another badly injured.

They made a strange sight, two crying women, a baby, and a dead body drifting down the river in the dark.

Hours later, they pulled to shore at the African village where they always left their Landrovers. It was the early hours of the morning, and the night watchman heard them paddle to shore. Whispering to them, he told them rebel bands had been coming to the village daily, looking for them. Some may still be in the village; he knew others had gone upstream looking for them. Working fast and quietly, they transferred everything from the canoes to the two Landrovers. "We won't stop until we reach Lusaka."

At Lusaka, it was confirmed that something was happening in the country. Rebel groups were springing up all over. The girls were given the option of staying at the main office in Lusaka, or traveling to South Africa. "Take a small vacation until this blows over," suggested the manager. The girls opted for the vacation.

Now, because of tension between Northern and Southern Rhodesia, planes could not fly across the borders. They would fly to Livingston, and then passengers would actually walk across the bridge carrying their luggage, catch a plane in Southern Rhodesia, and continue on to South Africa. Because of red tape, Sandra could not take her husband's body. They first buried Dennis in Lusaka, packed their few personal items (they'd never collected much) and flew to Livingstone.

"Sandra, I don't know when we will be back here, there is something very important I have to do while here in Livingstone." Sandra, visited friends, while Colleen borrowed their car and drove to Lagenwa; she would not leave Maureen with her friends. Things happened quickly in this country, she only trusted herself to protect her baby. A year ago, the tree house was in bad shape. She was ready to collect the bible and say goodbye to that part of her life.

Lagenwas' owner was happy to see her.

"Colleen, you will never guess what happened about a year ago. A young man drove up. He said he had just arrived from England; he used to live here. While in England his wife had been killed, here on this farm, by the Mau Mau. He wanted to look around. He disappeared in the same direction you have always gone."

Colleen stared at him. Finding her voice, she said, "It can't be Michael, he died years ago."

"He said the same thing to me when I told him you had been here several times. He said 'It can't be Colleen, she died in that attack'. He even made me describe you. Then he galloped off in that direction."

"The tree house," whispered Colleen.

Borrowing a horse, swinging Maureen onto her back, she galloped to the tree. She climbed so fast she stood panting for a few minutes. She searched and searched for signs of Michael. Everything looked the same except the tree house was falling apart. Colleen opened the chest; THE BIBLE WAS GONE! He had taken the bible. He must have read her notes. Why didn't he leave her a note? Where was he? How would she ever find him?

"Michael . . . Michaeeeeeeeel!!!!!!!!! . . . ."

She screamed so loud that the birds flew off; monkeys screeched and ran away. Maureen woke and started screaming. Picking her up out of her basket Colleen comforted her baby as she sank to her knees sobbing. Colleen was much slower climbing down the tree and returning to the house.

The owner invited her in for coffee. "You rode off before I could give you this letter he left for you; he also left a phone number in England." Colleen's hand trembled as she reached for the letter.

"You can call the number from here if you wish." Colleen dialed the number. After going through several exchanges a voice said,

"Sorry, this is no longer a working number."

"Let me and the wife watch this darling baby, you go sit on the front *veranda* and read your letter." In a dreamlike state, Colleen walked through to the *veranda*—the *veranda* where she and Michael, often sat listening to the B.B.C. She could almost feel him there.

Opening the letter, it was only one page, she read.

My darling,

I can't believe you're alive. For years, I walked in a trance.
I buried myself in my studies. I felt I could not live without you.
But time, cruel as it can be, also has the power to soften the blow.
Three years ago, I married, and we have a child, a daughter.
The farm told me you were married and expecting a baby.
I love Alice, but not the same love we shared.
That love lives on in my mind and heart.
Part of me hopes you'll return to Lagenwa and get my note,
the other part of me hopes not.
We're both married with at least a child each.
Nothing can be done about us discovering that each lives. Why?
Why the deception?
I flew back to South Africa to attend my father's funeral,
so he could not give me answers. Who told you I was dead?
This is my phone number.
I can't give you an address as we're moving next month.
Call me.

All my love, my first and only,
Michel

Colleen was not sure how long she sat there, but when she came out of her mist of pain, the sun was setting over the valley. 'I guess some things never change,' she thought. Sunsets were always part of Lagenwas' charm.

The next day, a bus took them to the bridge at Victoria Falls. With Maureen on her back in her basket, a case in each hand, she started walking across the bridge. She remembered her mother telling her how many years ago, she Colleen, was on her mother's hip as she walked across the bridge coming into this country. Now, here she was retracing those steps as she left the country with her daughter being carried over. Armed guards were on either side of the bridge. The question she kept asking herself was, 'Why, why did someone lie about Michael?' Tinus was dead so he could not help her. Maybe her mother and father would know. No. Of course they didn't know they also believed he was dead.

Sheree met the plane at Jan Smuts; she wanted to prepare Colleen that Nathaniel and Shannon, were in hospital. Joy drove straight to the hospital, dropped Colleen off, and then took her luggage and baby Maureen back to her house. Hope was sitting at her mother's side, not saying anything. Colleen pulled up a chair and sat next to her mother, and picked up her hand. Hope slowly explained that while driving home from a doctor's visit, Shannon had suffered a heart attack; she had been driving, as Nathaniel wasn't feeling good. Nathaniel was killed outright and Shannon was on the critical list.

Two days later, they made arrangements to bury Shannon and Nathaniel. Shannon had always said she wanted to be laid to rest at the Larger with her mother, farther, and oldest son who had died in the camps. Nathaniel had never said, but he was laid beside Shannon. Shannon had not seen the next generation, her great granddaughter that had been named after her mother, Maureen. Strange, no matter what, life keeps moving forward.

Days later, Colleen was helping her mother with the dishes; Abe was holding the sleeping Maureen, seven-year-old Mike was playing with his cars at Abe's feet. Watching her children, Colleen decided to ask.

"Mom, Dad, did you know Michael is still alive?"

Hope dropped the dishes she was carrying. That crashing sound seemed to echo over and over again. Colleen knew from the look on their faces.

"Why? Why?" She cried. "Life is hard enough without having to go through it alone. Without the one you love." Colleen was so angry. She had to leave the room before she said something that could never be retracted. She loved her mom and dad, but right now, she had to leave. Without waiting for their answer, Colleen, picked up Maureen, out of her father's arms and walked down the long passage to Shawn's quarters where she was staying.

The next day, Abe and Hope, found Colleen sitting at Shawn's grave. Her eyes were red and swollen. They sat on either side of her; no one said anything for a while. "Colleen, we thought we were doing the right thing, after all, he is a colored. Remember all the things that happened to couples that my dad told us about. We're so, so, so sorry."

"I remember the examples you are talking about Dad, but I also remember those couples were so much in love. Whether they had one year or twenty years together, it was wonderful. Do you know I'm trapped in a loveless marriage, do you know we were married for two years before Robert made love to me? Do you know I can count on one hand, during the years since, how often we've made love? Do you know each day that goes by, I die a little. You thought you were protecting me from hurt, look at all the death and pain I've been around. That could have been avoided. My son cannot even be my son." For the first time, Colleen saw her father cry.

"Oh Colleen, don't hate us."

"Mom, Dad, I don't hate you, but I need to go away and heal."

Colleen and her daughter Maureen went and spent a month at her house in Blouberg—a quiet time. She walked the beaches, reflected on her life; she reached a very low point, even contemplating suicide. Then Robert called, his parents were not doing so well. He was an only child, and he wanted to take care of them. He asked, since they had to make a change, could they spend time in America, and then decide on their next assignment. Yes, this was the change that might make the difference.

Hope and Abe were very upset, "Colleen, please don't go."

"I have to Mom, he's my husband. Remember you followed your husband to Northern Rhodesia? I have to start all over again, dealing with the pain of Michael and Mike. Maybe away from familiar things, it would be easier."

After his father's funeral, Michael flew back to England. During the flight he opened his briefcase to do some work. Right on top of his papers was his bible from the tree house. He picked it up, snapping the elastic band several times. His eyes were closed thinking of Colleen. He never noticed the little sheet of paper sticking out of the pages.

Months later, Michael, was packing some books in a crate. His wife Alice had just died from a long illness, he and his daughter were moving to Italy. He had to decide on which books to take. Picking up his tree house bible, he noticed a piece of paper sticking out. Removing the elastic band, the many notes fell out, notes from Colleen. He started reading them; they spanned a few years.

> She was told he was dead.
> They had a son.
> Even though married with a daughter, she loved him.
> Why didn't he open the bible when he first got it?
> He had to find her.
> He had to find his son.

Michael was on BOAC Flight No. C392 from London, England to Johannesburg, South Africa.

Colleen was on SAA Flight No. Z4YZ from Johannesburg, South Africa to America.

The loudspeaker at Jan Smut's airport announced the departure of S A A Flight No. Z4YZ to America. As the plane's wheel lifted off the tarmac, the same voice announced the arrival of BOAC Flight No. C392 from England.

CHAPTER 20

America—1968

The long flight from Africa to America gave Colleen time to think. Her life was a mess; she made a mental list.

First, she was told the man she loved was killed in a car accident. Then, the morning their son was born she witnessed a terrible massacre. Their close friends were brutally killed. Later, Shawn the man she loved as a second father was killed. Her son Mike was being brought up as her brother, so her mothering instinct was taken away form her. Later, she married but this man did not love her, it was a strange relationship. Shortly after the birth of her daughter, she killed two men. Now, she discovered Michael was alive, and her parents were responsible for the deception. She was at such a low point that while in Blouberg she came within inches of committing suicide. She had gone as far as buying the tube to attach on the cars exhaust system. That same day she received a phone call from Robert, asking her to come to America.

Colleen took that phone call as a sign, maybe Robert had changed, maybe their lives would be better in America, and maybe she could heal her heart and mind and learn to love her husband.—Maybe—.

Because Colleen wanted so much to be loved and comforted, during the flight she convinced herself Robert must have changed and things would be different between them. That she had changed, and somehow her killing rampage had taken away her guilt hurt and anger.

Robert hugged them both and whispered how much he missed them. Taking Colleen's hand he led her over to his parents and introduced her and Maureen to them. It was love at first sight, Maureen gave her grandparents a new lease on life, they dotted over her.

Robert had been staying with his parents as he nursed them back to health after the accident.

"But, now that my girls are here, we will look for our own home," The Millers home was a tiny two bedroom bungalow, not only was their room next to Robert's parents but they shared a bathroom. Maureen's crib was in the room with them squashed up against their bed, there was no privacy. That night Robert whispered, "Let's start looking for our own home tomorrow, not only are my parents well enough now, but I want my girls to myself. Please, understand the wait Colleen."

The days turned into weeks, the weeks into months. But, there were so many new things to see, learn about, and experience. Autumn in America with its beautiful different type trees took Colleen's breath away. She knew it would always be the best time of the year for her. And oh, snow, what a miracle, followed by the bursting forth of spring. Colleen's letters home to her family were filled with all the new experiences. There were accents, customs, money; even the stores took getting used to. This truly was a land of plenty. Unfortunately these letters home gave her family the impression that Colleen's life was wonderful.

The day arrived for them to move into their ranch home. It had a huge yard with an open farmer's field behind. Moving day was so much fun, this was her first home; Colleen could spread out and arrange furniture as she liked.

The Millers neighbors were a young couple, Sandy and John. Their daughter was the same age as Maureen; Sandy befriended Colleen as soon as she arrived from Africa. Colleen was drawn to Sandy, she was friendly and they had a marriage Colleen had hoped to have. Sandy would see love and romance in any situation. So now that Colleen and Robert were moving into their own house, Sandy saw the need for a romantic evening. "Colleen, this is the first time you and Robert have had a chance for privacy since you arrived from Africa. Let Maureen spend the night with us, she and Jill will have a great time." Then with a wicked grin she added, "You and Robert can have a great time too."

The last of the friendly movers said goodnight, it had been a long day. As Sandy kissed Colleen bye she said, "Supper is in the oven, and wear my gift." Supper was chicken pot—pie, and the gift was a beautiful mint green nightgown.

The next day when Sandy brought Maureen home she mistook Colleen's swollen eyes to mean she had enjoyed a long evening of love. Colleen did not have the heart to tell her it was from crying, and that, she had ripped the beautiful green nightgown into tiny pieces, vowing never to wear something so beautiful again. Colleen was so ashamed and humiliated; she had taken the first steps, and yet again suffered rejection. 'What is wrong with me, why do I feel guilty? He is the one who has deceived me; he's broken his promise as a husband.'

There was no one Colleen could confide in, who would believe her anyway. Robert was on his home turf; he was among his family, people he'd grown up around, even old girlfriends. She was too ashamed to tell Sandy there was something wrong with her—enough to make a man constantly reject her. Comments were always made to the affect of how lucky Colleen was to have such a good man.

Robert was a good man, he had no vices, and he was a good provider and as before belonged to an organization that helped people. Colleen too devoted her time in helping people. The things she saw, and the conditions in the world she read about, or remembered, made her problem now seem insignificant. Yet, why was she slowly shutting down, why did she feel as though she was dying inch by inch. She was silently screaming for help but it was as though she was invisible.

More and more Colleen retreated to her minds safe room, the room her mother created for her as a means of escape. Of course, that made her seem unfriendly, that alienated her even more.

Once a week the television news devoted time to a—Call for Help—segment, little new items like, an abused dog needed a home. Or because of a house fire this family needed food. It was always something different. One night a call went out to help abandoned babies. The nurse interviewed explained to the world. "Babies given what they needed, fed, changed, bathed, etc. but kept in their crib with no extra touching, hugging, kissing, did not thrive as well as those who received that extra care." The nurse explained,—"Every human needs to be loved, not only will they thrive, but life, even a hard life will be bearable. Their hearts will sing instead of groan." The nurse looked straight at the camera and said, "Help us, help these groaning hearts."

Colleen burst out crying because she too had a groaning heart. Robert was by her side in a flash. "Colleen, what's the matter?" She mumbled, "I don't know, it's just—it's just—.

Robert patted her hand, (like a grandson would his grandmother). "I know what you need," he said, "A trip home to Africa."

Colleen and four year old Maureen had their noses pressed against the window as the plane landed at Jan Smut's airport in South Africa. She ran into her families' arms hugging and kissing them. By the time, she got to Mike she was crying. Mike, a preteen was embarrassed at his sisters hugging. "Col, everyone is watching you, let me go," and he squirmed out of her arms.

Abe arranged his vacation to match Colleen's trip home. Every person, every experience, even things were special, Colleen drunk it all in. She felt human again. The whole family squashed into her Blouberg house and enjoyed two weeks of doing nothing. The highlight of each day was crowding around the table, talking and eating. Her family had a million questions about America. They thought she was the luckiest person, living in America with none of the political problems of Africa.

Hope, Abe and Mike flew back to England with Colleen to spend alone time with her in the Scottish house. Her parents wanted to give Colleen this time with Mike—away from other family. This way Colleen could walk the Scottish hill with her two children Mike and Maureen. On their last day there Hope had Maureen stand on a chair and help her make supper, "Colleen took Mike's hand and said, "Come walk with me I want to tell you a story."

They did not go far, just up the hill to the graves. Colleen sat and patted the ground next to her, Mike sat waiting for the story. Colleen told Mike the story of Shawn, and how he was there the day he was born. Of course Hope was the mother throughout the story.

At Heathrow airport Colleen waved goodbye to her mother, father and son, she was crying. Maureen tugged at her hand, "Don't cry mommy, I'm still here with you."

"Maureen, these are happy tears because mommy has a plan." Colleen had two days in England before flying back to America. Her plan was while here to find Michael, then back home divorce Robert. Even though that went against her beliefs, and her upbringing, she knew she could not continue living in a vacuum.

Colleen never found Michael; it was as though he had never been. She never left Robert; he must have guessed her trip back to Africa would have given her that thought. He changed for a few months, during that time their son Jacob was conceived.

Colleen could not leave now, not with a baby on the way, once Jacob was born she formulated her new plan. When he was in school full time she'd leave. This way she could work while the children were in school. Colleen took some courses that would allow her to pick her hours of work. She had missed out on Mike's childhood; she did not want to miss out on Maureen and Jacobs's childhood.

Even though Robert reverted back to his old self, and the years could hardly be called happy years, Colleen accepted this because she was working on her plan.

Four years after Jacob was born Robert had to travel to England on a business trip; he would be gone three months and planned on using the Scottish house on weekends. Colleen had named the house 'The Dean' because it was Shawn's surname. Colleen took this time to visit Africa again. The sight of Mike took her breath away, he was now sixteen and the spitting image of his father, he was learning to drive.

This time they not only spent time at the Blouberg house, but also the Larger. Colleen's grandmothers' twin brothers, Koose Keith had turned it into a safari camp. Maureen and Jacob loved the experience of riding in an open Landrover and seeing so many wild animals run free, Mike loved it because they allowed him to drive the Landrover.

Because of a pending air strike, Colleen and the children returned to America a week early, she did not mind because she was going to put her plan into operation.

She did not let Robert know she was coming home early; she wanted him at a disadvantage when she broke the news that she was leaving. Sandy met them at the airport; she had planned to keep Maureen and Jacob so that Colleen could have alone time with Robert.

This time Sandy's plan suited Colleen; it would be better if the children were not around when she broke her news to Robert. What a surprise he would have. Only it was Colleen who would be surprised, shocked and devastated.

She waved goodbye to Sandy and the children. The children were already deep into conversation telling their experiences from the Safari camp, she could see Jacobs hand moving as he explained. It would be at least four or five hours before Robert came home. So before unpacking she was going to make a cup of tea and take a shower. In the bathroom and bedroom there were different, unusual items about. Colleen started taking a closer look.

Someone was living with Robert. Someone was sleeping in their bed with him; there was a picture on the bedside table of them with their arms around each other.

IT WAS A MAN—ROBERT WAS GAY!!

Colleen had pushed down her frustrations for so long that now she felt an explosion coming. She felt disconnected from herself. Her fingers and lips started to tingle, there was a buzzing in her head, and she slipped into darkness.

CHAPTER 21

When Colleen regained her senses she was sitting on the floor in their bedroom; her breathing coming in gasps. She looked around the room, nothing—nothing was any bigger than a shoebox. It looked as though a bomb had exploded; feathers were still drifting through the air.

In horror Colleen looked at the ax in her hand. Where did that come from? She must have gone outside, walked down to the garage, returned with the ax and created this mess, all without realizing what she was doing. The clock chiming downstairs showed that four hours had passed.

Colleen felt and looked like a wild woman. She was covered in blood, and tears. Her hair had pulled loose and was hanging, wet from perspiration in her face. She quickly examined herself and found the blood was just from small nicks while wielding the ax. Just then Colleen heard the car in the driveway; Robert and his lover were home.

Dragging the ax behind her Colleen went downstairs. There was a mixture of surprise, shock, and fear on their faces when they saw Colleen at the foot of the stairs—with an ax—. The lover turned and fled, Robert knew what Colleen was capable of, he moved backwards into the kitchen. Colleen followed him still dragging the ax, but not saying a word.

He held up his hand as if to stop her. "Colleen, listen to me,—I was breaking it off with him. It won't ever happen again, I don't know what—.

Colleen turned and walked back upstairs still dragging the ax; she did not want to hear anymore. She locked herself in the bathroom, and just stood looking in the mirror. She stepped into the shower still dressed, and stood for the longest time sobbing. While still in the shower she stripped and threw the wet bloody clothes out. She washed her hair, then took a nailbrush and scrubbed every inch of her body. Her nicks from the ax re-bled, her skin turned red and every so often she burst out sobbing, even screaming. Stepping out of the shower, she filled the bathtub to the rim and climbed in. Water overflowed covering the bathroom floor but she did not care. She lay back and closed her eyes. A truckload of shame and humiliation swept over her.

"How could I have been so blind?"

"How could I have been so stupid?"

"How could I have ignored all the warning signs?"

The signs were there, the type of—no physical—marriage they had, the closeness with David and the fresh flowers always on his grave, a fresh outburst of crying.

Robert tried for hours to get Colleen to open the door; he begged forgiveness. But Colleen never answered, in time the crying stopped.

In the morning when Colleen still did not open the door or answer, Robert called Sandy. Sandy was completely blown away when she heard from Robert what happened. After calling him a few choice names, she made him break down the bathroom door. Sandy ran to Colleen's side, she was curled up in a fetal position on the bathroom floor, still holding the ax. Colleen had cut her beautiful hair off. It lay thrown over the bathroom floor.

Her mental breakdown was slow to heal. Hope flew out to help and look after the children. Robert had moved out, facing Colleen was bad enough, but to face her mother was another matter. Slowly with the help of her mother, Sandy, the doctor, and a therapist Colleen learned to handle the pain that howled through her.

The therapist warned Colleen that it was going to be a long wrenching struggle. Years earlier Colleen had prepared to defend herself in a physical situation, but nothing could of prepared her for this attack on her emotions. She had to learn how to undo years of brainwashing that made her believe everything was her fault. Michael, Mike, Shawn, Anetta, Desmond, Annette's two children, the two Africans she killed, and of course Robert. These were all physical loses; Colleen also learned how to handle other types of losses, her self esteem, the rejection of her sexuality, trust. She had to learn to wipe out the roar of negative thoughts. The trauma was so profound, that the process of recovery was long and arduous. She spent a lot of time in her special room that her mother had created for her at Lagenwa.

Months later when she was ready to face Robert and talk about their future life, he threatened to keep the children if she divorced him and moved to Africa. Colleen went ahead with the divorce but had to stay in America, at least till the children were eighteen.

It helped to talk to Sandy; finally she spilled her heartache. Sandy made a good listener and never judged Colleen. She knew Colleen needed to talk. "Sandy I felt as though I lost a battle I never even knew I was fighting."

Colleen began her thousand-mile journey of healing, taking one step at a time. While traveling this healing road they made a few trips back to Africa; first for Mikes and Moses' graduation from high school, then years later for Mikes wedding.

Even though Colleen was not living in Africa, she was happy, she was feeling better about herself the weight had been lifted off her shoulders. Maureen was courting. Jacob planning on college, and Mike had just had a son. Colleen was an ouma. Life was good, she felt now, like a young girl who had everything to look forward to.

Maureen's wedding was beautiful; Colleen threw herself into the preparations, probably because her own wedding had been so plain.

Six months after the wedding Jacob was leaving for Scotland as part of his college course. He was planning on staying at Colleen's house. One evening after dinner, Colleen and Maureen were helping Jacob with his plans. They had maps spread over the table.

Maureen straightened up saying, "I'm so jealous, you are going to Scotland, Adam is on an extended overseas trip so I will have nothing to do."

Jacob looked at his sister, then at his mother and grinned. "Why don't you both come with me? I won't have to do my own washing or cooking or . . . ," Jacob never finished his sentence. Maureen shrieked in agreement. A smile slowly spread across Colleen's face as the idea sunk in.

Colleen looked on these future two years in Scotland as a new lease on life, a new home, a new start. They could wonder over the Scottish hillside and enjoy lazy days at the lake. Her heart and mind were well on the way to healing, a long vacation in Scotland might help her body. Colleen had always been a healthy person, but lately she'd been having headaches that sent her to bed.

Two months after they arrived in Scotland the headaches were coming more often and lasting longer.

"Mom, you need a doctor to examine you, I'd like to see one too. Let me make an appointment for both of us."

The good news was Maureen was four months pregnant. The bad news was Colleen had a tumor pressing on her brain that needed removed. Tomorrow she was scheduled for surgery.

Slowly Maureen closed the journal and looked up at her mother. The room was quiet for the longest time. Colleen looked at her children and grandchildren; she got up and walked to the window. Jacob joined her, "Mom, are you okay?"

"Yes, I'm fine Jacob. I want to thank you both for reading the journals to me, and helping my memory to return." Maureen was busy packing the journals away. "Don't put that away yet Maureen, I'd like to read the Scottish and Russian journals."

Late that night the phone ringing woke everyone. It was long distance from Africa. Mike's voice was breaking as he spoke to Colleen. "Col, mom is very sick and dad is beside himself, can you come?"

Colleen called the airport and booked emergency seats for the next day. They did not bother going back to bed, but started packing.

CHAPTER 22

South Africa—1990

At the hospital, Colleen sat at her mother's bedside, her father sat on the opposite side. They had sent the rest of the family home; it was almost midnight. Hope awoke, and Abe was immediately alert at her side. "Cookie, look who's here."

Hope smiled and held up her hand for Colleen to take. "Colleen, your hair!"

Colleen couldn't help but burst out laughing. "Mom, do you remember saying those exact words to me when I arrived home after Shawn was killed?"

"Sorry love, but the white curls are a shock. I'm so glad you woke from your long sleep, Dad and I prayed for you every night." Hope broke out with a wrenching cough.

"Mom, don't talk, just rest."

"Rest I will be doing soon enough Colleen, Dad and I wanted to see you one more time and beg your forgiveness."

"Shhh Mom, years ago I told you I had forgiven you."

"If only—."

"No Mom, let's not think of the past, we can not change that. Something I have learned these passed years is, you can not choose your wounds, but you can choose how you heal, and you choose not to let it hurt the rest of your life. I have healed Mom."

It was some time before Hope spoke again. "Colleen, while your dad and I have managed to accumulate things, and property—which you children will inherit, I want you to have my most prized possession, my three-cord necklace. Cookie, help me take it off and put it on Colleen's neck." While her father was doing this, Hope continued. "I know you remember the story around the three cords—you have recorded it into the journals. Even though our families have had their share of problems, I believe they were able to cope, because of relying on God—as of course these three cords symbolize. Now I'd like for you to wear my necklace." Hope started coughing again. As soon as she stopped, she turned to Abe, "Cookie, ask her."

Abe had tears running down his cheeks, both his hands were wrapped around one of Hope's he brought it to his lips and kissed it. "Colleen, Mom and I have never told anyone about Mike, but we need to know, do you want it left that way or do you want him to know you are his mother?" Before Colleen could answer, there was a loud crash outside the door. She went to see what it was. A nurse was on her hands and knees picking up a tray of medicine. She looked up at Colleen.

"Sorry about that, the man standing at this door turned and ran, knocking me down."

Colleen looked down the passage but saw no one. Mike had stepped into one of the side passages; he was holding his breath but also holding his head. What had he just heard? Col was not his older sister; she was his mother!

When Colleen returned to her mother's room, it was in time to see her father bend forward and kiss her mother's lips. "Goodbye my love, I'll be with you soon." In death her mother looked like she was sleeping.

Colleen spent a few hours helping her father with the paper work. Then, they returned to Hope's room to say their goodbyes for the last time. Colleen, kissed her mother on the forehead, and gave her father his privacy to say goodbye to the woman he had loved so strongly for many years. The kind of love Colleen never had with her marriage—the kind of love she had been on the threshold of having with Michael. It was a few hours later before they drove from the hospital. They got home around 5:00 A.M.

"Shhh, don't wake anyone yet Colleen, I am going to lie down for a while. I am very tired." Her father held her awhile, kissed her forehead, and then limped down the passage to the bedroom. Watching him go, Colleen realized her father was in his mid seventies; her mother had just turned seventy. Both had really aged since she saw them last.

'But, of course, so have you,' she thought. 'You will soon be fifty; you have white hair and walk with a cane. Come on old woman,' she said to herself. 'You need some coffee.' Before she could turn and walk to the kitchen, she heard a thud from her father's room. Hurrying to the room, she found him lying on the floor. In his hands, he held their wedding picture.

"Dad, hold on, I'll call an ambulance."

"No, Colleen, please help me to bed." He lay down, still holding the wedding picture.

"Dad, we must get you to a doctor; I think you are having a heart attack."

"Colleen, my girl, please . . . please let me die here in your mom's and my bed. I need to go to her, she is waiting for me."

"Are you in pain, Dad?"

"No, I am at peace."

Colleen leaned over and kissed her father. She removed his prosthesis, so he would be more comfortable and pulled the blanket up to his chin and sat down next to him. About ten minutes later, she heard him take his last breath. Colleen had been holding her father's hand, now she laid her head on his chest. In less than six hours she had lost her mother and father. Their lives flashed through her mind. What a life they had, what love they had between them, and for their family. Colleen fingered the three cord necklace her father had tied around her neck—what was their secret?

Maureen and Jacob stood on either side of their mother. Colleen would not move until the workers had finished packing the dirt back on the two graves. Then, she walked over to Shawn's grave, she sat a while remembering. Back at the house, they had friends and families offer their condolences.

Finally, it was only family left, Sheree, her husband, children and grandchildren; Gordon, his wife and their children, (no grandchildren yet). Charles and his children; his wife had died a few years back of cancer. He had no grandchildren yet. Mike, his wife and their son; Marnie, Maureen's husband, had flown in from America for the funeral.

The young children were playing outside. The adults were deep in thought, their mother and father were now gone, and things would never be the same.

Colleen looked across the room at Mike, he was staring at her, and their eyes were glued to each other. That's when Colleen realized, he was the man outside the hospital door—he heard—he knew. Mike got up and walking across the room, he stood in front of her not saying a word. Then he put his hand out to her, she put hers in his and he pulled her up, encircling her with his arms.

Colleen at last was holding her oldest son—as a son, not a brother. She held him tight as the tears ran from their eyes. Maureen and Jacob were the only other ones in the room who understood what was happening. They stood up and encircled Mike and their mother with their arms, also crying. Everyone else in the room looked on in puzzlement. What was going on? Gordon, in a very gruff voice, said. "Would someone tell us what the hell is going on?"

Mike looked at his newly found mother. "You tell them."

Colleen looked around the room at her brothers and sister. "Do you remember when I went to live at "Lagenwa" when Mom was expecting a baby—Mike?"

"Yes," they answered, still puzzled.

"Well, Mom was not pregnant, she just pretended to be. I was pregnant. I went to "Lagenwa" and Anetta was going to deliver my baby. Mom pretended to be pregnant so they would bring up my baby since I was not really married." Gordon and Charles stared at her, with a puzzled look still on their faces.

Sheree spoke saying, "What . . . Are you saying that Mike, our brother, is really your son?"

"Yes," nodded Colleen.

"But what . . . I mean when . . . or rather . . ." sputtered her brother.

"Gordon, don't you remember our last visit to "Lagenwa"? Michael and I married ourselves in God's eyes before he left for England. We planned on getting married in church when he came back. But then he was killed or rather I was told he was killed in a car accident."

"Wait a minute, wait a minute," insisted Charles, he was waving his hands, and shaking his head. "Mom was pregnant, I was fourteen and I remember her growing tummy."

"It was a pillow, Charles. Think about this, you were their youngest, their baby and you were fourteen years old. Who starts a family again after so many years?" Gordon was still trying to piece it together.

"So, because you were unmarried, and Michael was killed before you could get married, Mom and Dad raised Mike as their own?"

"Yes."

Sheree, who was a motherly type person, said, "Colleen, is that why you left home. First with Zebra Run, and then to America?"

"Yes, it hurt too much being around Mike, and having to pretend he was my brother and not my son."

Mike, put his arms around his mother, and said, "How you must have suffered?"

The family adjusted to the change. There were a lot of questions, and then trying to work out the relationships of everyone. So you are not my brother, you are my what? So your children are really . . . ? It went on for several hours.

The next morning as was her custom, Colleen was up early. It was still dark outside. She was in the kitchen making coffee when she heard a tap on the kitchen window. It was Mike.

"Good morning Col," he grinned. "I remember you were an early riser. Could we talk?"

"Of course, come let's sit on the couch with our coffee."

"Col, I have so many questions running through my head. Can you tell me about my father?"

Colleen got a far away look in her eyes as she told him about their visits to Lagenwa, growing up with Michael, their falling in love, their marriage, their tree house and then the deception of his death.

"You mean my father is alive!" Mike was wide eyed.

"Yes." Smiled Colleen.

"So you were never able to contact him?"

"No, the phone number he left me when you were about six was no longer a working number. Then I tried tracing him through the university, even calling other music companies. Nothing, he may have left England, so I tried South Africa, still nothing."

"So how do you know he's still alive? He left the note almost thirty years ago."

"About five years ago, I saw a television program of him in concert. He has become a famous pianist and the reason I could not trace him before is, he now has a professional name, and was living in Europe."

"So, now that you know he has changed his name, why don't you contact him?"

Colleen signed, "No point, I saw a picture of him and his family. He has a daughter, and his wife looks very nice. So much time has passed there was no need to upset their world."

"Col, why did someone lie to you and say my father was killed in an accident?"

"Mike, as to who it was, really does not matter now, they had good intentions, as to why, that you do need to know." Colleen turned to face Mike. She took his hands in hers. "You have had a pretty good life, right?"

"Yes," he said puzzled.

"There's no reason for that to change. Before I say anything more, let me just show you a picture of Michael—your father."

Mike took the tape Colleen handed him. "I have two of these, keep this one and listen to your father playing." Mike looked down at the tape. He stared into his father's eyes, they were his eyes, and he had the same lopsided smile. Colleen did not say anything; she waited for Mike to look up at her.

When he did, he said, "He looks colored!" His voice had an edge to it.

"Yes, he is Mike." She told him how Michael never found out until his mother's death.

"History is repeating itself, isn't it? I find out that I'm colored when my mother and father, or rather grandmother and grandfather, died. My father had a best friend, an African named Moses. I have a friend: an African named Moses that you rescued. You saved his life and brought him to live with us, with Samson and Delilah." Mike's voice was rising higher and higher.

"Mike."

"Don't Mike me," he jumped up from the couch. "My whole life has been a deception. First I find out my sister is really my mother. I could live with that, but now I find out my father's a colored, which of course, makes me a colored." Mike was beginning to shout.

"Mike, nothing needs to change."

"Oh, you are so naïve 'MOTH—ER'; I can see you've lived away from Africa a long time. This is not America; this is not Scotland, this is not even Northern

Rhodesia. This is SOUTH AFRICA." Mike was shouting now. Maureen, Adam, and Jacob came running out in their pajamas to see what the noise was about.

"In South Africa, nothing, nothing, do you hear me; NOTH . . . ING stays the same once you discover you are colored!" He spat the word . . . colored. "In a way Moses is your child, you saved him, and he's black. Now I see why you lived in America, to keep your black and colored children separate from your two white American children."

Jacob stepped forward. "Just a minute Mike, that's no way to speak to my . . . our mother." Mike glared at Jacob, and then marched out of the house slamming the door. Colleen had turned very white. She sat down with a thud.

"Oh dear, oh dear," she said over and over again. "My mother and father were right when they said any union between a white and a colored will result in nothing but pain. All my life I've denied that, look; now my son, Michael's son, has turned against me." Maureen was sitting next to her mother, holding her hand.

"Jacob, go after him, he's got to listen to Mom."

"No! No, leave him for a while; he has just received some major shocks to his life. He has found out he is colored, he found out I am his mother, and we have just buried the people he thought were his parents."

A week later Mike still had not come back, but Gordon came over with a message. "Colleen, I don't know what is happening, but Mike sent me over to tell you he is going away for a while. He was due some vacation. They have gone to visit his wife's family. He said he would see you next week."

Two, three, then four weeks passed. Mike never showed, that evening at supper, Colleen spoke to Maureen and Jacob, Adam had already flown back overseas for his work. "I feel I need to sort this mess out. I would very much like to stay in South Africa, at least for a while. My mom and dad left their house to Mike, he was renting "The Haven" from me, and so we will just exchange houses. Sheree and Seun were left the house from Joy. Charles and Gordon own property next to them so the five of us have houses in a row. Of course, I would love it if you two spent time in Africa. You know how big "The Haven" is, there's plenty of room. But, I understand that you have other things going on in your lives."

"Oh, I want to stay," said Maureen. "After the funeral, Adam flew to Paris, he is still there. Let me talk to him Mom. As you know, his business takes him all over the world. He is hardly ever home. So what's the difference if he flies out of Africa or America? Anyway, I can't let you have all the fun sorting this mess out.

"Oh no you don't," said Jacob. "I am also going to stay."

"What about your research?" Asked Colleen.

"The research and groundwork is done. I now have about a year of paperwork, then the writing of my book. That I can do here. I will turn one of those rooms into an office."

"Do you have to be alone in your office or are you willing to share it?" asked Colleen.

"Sharing is good, what did you have in mind Mom?"

"Well, I thought I would use the time and turn my journals into a novel. Do you think it would be worth turning into a fictional story?"

"Yes! Yes!" shouted both Maureen and Jacob.

"So Jacob, let's turn that huge sunny room overlooking the misty hills into an office."

"Great, when are you exchanging houses?"

"We will have to wait until Mike gets home. I just hope it's not too long."

Maureen called Adam, he agreed, saying he'd feel happier when she was around family. Jacob flew back to Scotland to arrange the rental of "The Dean" and collect his notes. Maureen and Colleen had fun shopping for the furniture they needed when moving to "The Haven". Mike still had not returned. He'll come when he's ready, she thought. While waiting, she started working on her novel.

Two months passed before Mike showed up one Saturday morning. He had Marnie, his son with him, but his wife Elizabeth, was not with them. He smiled sheepishly, "Hello Col, can we come in?" Colleen held her arms open and he stepped into them. He hugged her tight.

"I'm so, so sorry, please forgive me," he said.

Sitting around the big kitchen table, overlooking the back garden, they could watch the children play as they talked. Marnie joined his cousins; he hadn't seen them in weeks. Maureen had taken the twins out for some fresh air, so kept an eye on them. Jacob returned to the office and said, "I'm going to leave you two to talk."

Mike took Colleens hands in his. "Col, this acceptance on my part took longer than I thought, but in a way it was a real eye opener." Colleen let Mike talk. "Elizabeth left me. When she found out I had colored blood in me, she went crazy. She could not possibly love a colored or our son, since he is part colored. She would not have anything to do with him. At first I blamed you but the more I thought about it, the more I got to know you."

Mike leaned over and kissed her on the forehead. "You loved my father no matter what after you found out he was a colored. You cared for his child, me even though I caused you great pain. You sacrificed your closeness to the family for me. You had no prejudice; you even took care of everything for Moses. I'm so sorry for all those ugly things I said." Colleen couldn't talk; she just patted his hands that she was holding.

Finally she said, "Welcome home my boy, we will help with Marnie. Believe it or not, life moves on. In times of crisis, you have a choice to either lie down and quit, or stand up and move on. I'm glad to see after you were knocked down, you chose to stand up and move on."

"I've listened to my father's tape over and over again, he's good, he's very good. Did you know Marnie takes piano lessons? I hope that talent is inherited."

The first thing they did was exchange houses. Mike was very excited that he had been left the house. Now he did not have rental expenses.

About a year later, life had settled into a good routine. Colleen enjoyed being around her three children, and her grandchildren. For the first time in her adult life, she was surrounded by all of her family. Her novel was finished, and it had been accepted and was in print. In fact, her agent encouraged her to write another. Life was good.

Colleen was busy washing dinner dishes one night. Jacob was out on a date. Maureen was babysitting for Mike; he was talking a computer class. She had the evening to herself; she put on one of Michael's tapes and worked in the kitchen. She thought she would bake a cake for tomorrow. There was a knock on the kitchen door. Putting the outside light on, so she could see, she let out a shout, "Moses!!!"

Samson and Delila had died some years ago. She was not sure what Moses was doing. But every once in a while, when she took trips back to Africa; he would stop by looking very prosperous. But tonight when she opened the door, he fell in and rolled out of sight.

"Moses, you're hurt, what happened?" He was bent over, holding his side, and he limped when she led him to the bathroom. "Take off your shirt so I can see where this blood is coming from." She was shocked, "Moses, you need a doctor, you have been shot!"

"No . . . no doctor Colleen."

"I'm not a doctor, but since you have a front entry and a back exit, I believe the bullet went straight through the fleshy part of your thigh. But your shoulder, I think it is still inside."

"Colleen, take it out for me, please."

"Moses, why won't you go to the hospital?"

"Because I am a wanted man."

As Colleen worked on him he explained. "I'm with a political party that's banned. Tonight we had a secret meeting only it wasn't so secret. The police swarmed the house; some of our people were killed. I need to make it back to my rendezvous. They will drive me out of the country. I just had to say hello, it's been years and I understand you were pretty sick in Scotland." He put his hand up and touched her white hair. "Is this the result of the surgery?"

"Yes, hold still, will you," she was crying.

"And this," he said touching her tears.

"I'm afraid something is going to happen to you Moses. All this political fighting, I don't quite understand what's happening."

"Colleen, you more so than most people know that Africa has problems. It has changed during the last twenty years. The fight is the same—for freedom—but the fighters have changed, we are now banding together to force a change."

"Where is your rendezvous? I'll drive you there."

"No, if we are stopped by the police, you will be in big trouble, maybe even arrested."

"You cannot walk; you're hurt and you have got to feel weak after losing so much blood. Take my car, tell me where I can find it tomorrow, and leave the keys under the front passenger mat."

Moses hugged her, "You know you saved my life many years ago, and changed my name for a reason."

"What was that?"

"I'm going to lead my people to freedom, just like Moses led the Israelites to freedom."

"The Israelite Moses had some powerful help behind him. You see that you take care of yourself. If I need to contact you, how would I? We don't have an address or phone number."

After thinking a few minutes, Moses said, "Put an advertisement in the local newspaper, I always read it. Code the message something like;—Basket child, call your mother—then just wait, I will contact you."

When Colleen gave him the keys to her car, she hugged him, and whispered, "If you ever need me just come—remember you can count on me."

CHAPTER 23

As Moses drove Colleens car to his rendezvous point, his mind was going over the events of the afternoon and evening. There had to be an informer in their group. Too many facts were known, the exact time, date and even what was to be discussed. As he escaped, he saw his friend and fellow fighter for the cause go down under a hail of bullets. 'Sam, your death will not be in vain my friend.' he thought, 'I will find the person who sold us out.'

Moses had just turned off the N1 onto R553, four blocks west was a car scrap yard—his operative would be waiting to take him to a safe house, since all their other plans were known, what if this escape route was also known. Moses stopped three blocks before the scrap yard, and on foot circled around, approaching from the opposite direction. He saw the Kombie, and the driver sitting behind the wheel, staring in the direction Moses should have been coming from. There was no sign of anyone else, yet Moses stayed hidden and watched. He felt something was wrong, every now and again the waiting driver would wipe his face. Why was he sweating in the cool of the night? Ten, twenty, thirty minutes passed, he was just about to make his way to the Kombie, when an ear splitting explosion and blinding light threw him backwards. He no sooner hit the ground when he was up and running.

Later he found out a hand grenade had been used. The pin was pulled and an elastic band used to hold the trigger in place, the grenade is then dropped into the petrol tank. It takes time for the petrol to eat through the elastic—then it explodes! If he had been in the Kombie, they would have been driving towards Soweto when the explosion occurred.

The painkillers Colleen had given him were beginning to wear off, his thigh throbbed, his shoulder felt as though it was on fire, and now he had some flash burns on his face from the explosion. He was not going to be able to walk to Soweto, and he dare not drive Colleen's car to his home. Slowly Moses drove back to Colleen's house; he turned the lights and engine off before turning into the driveway coasting to a stop next to the garage.

Although it was almost midnight, Colleen had not fallen asleep yet; she was worried about Moses. How could he have become a wanted man? What was he involved with? She stopped tossing and turning and sat bolt upright, she heard the crunching sound from the gravel driveway. Slipping on her dressing gown, she made her way to the kitchen in the dark. Her car was parked next to the garage. Colleen stopped herself, as she was about to open the back door, and run out. Shawn's advice came back to her, 'Always be prepared.' Back in her room, she slipped into a pair of slacks and sweater. Shawn's knife strapped to her calf and her father's key ring hold in her hand. It had been too many years, she was older and unfit, but still she did not want to be caught unprepared.

Moses was still sitting behind the wheel; his head slumped back, he was drifting in and out of consciousness. He was a big man; she would need help. Jacob, had returned from his date hours ago, Maureen was back from babysitting, but they were asleep. Lights were still on at Mike's house; he was probably still busy with computer homework. Not wanting to wake Marnie; Colleen knocked on the window of Mike's office. He looked up from his computer, of course he couldn't see who was outside, so he reached for a baseball bat and walked to the back door. Switching on the outside light he saw Colleen, "Col, what are you doing walking around at this time of the night?"

"Mike, I need your help, its Moses."

"Moses! Where is he? What happened?"

"Shhh . . . don't wake Marnie. Moses has been hurt. I need your help moving him from the car to the house."

Mike switched off the computer and locked his house. He was glad he had a live in house maid, so he didn't have to worry about leaving Marnie. Together they managed to get Moses into the spare room; Mike undressed him and settled him in bed, while Colleen got together some first aid supplies. When she returned, Mike looked at her questioningly.

"He's been shot!" His eyes dropped to her leg, "A knife! Col, what's going on?"

"My knife I'll explain later." As they worked on his wounds, Colleen told Mike what she knew about Moses injuries.

"The fact that he came to you, involving the family, he must really be in trouble," said Mike.

"Mike, do you know what's going on? What Moses is involved in?"

"Col, have you forgotten Moses and I grew up together, he might have gone to a black school while I went to a white one, but we always did our homework and our chores together. We used to have long discussions on South Africa's problems." After a pause Mike continued, "He is a wanted man, not because of drugs, or theft. He is involved with the ANC, and is fighting to do away with apartheid."

"Why didn't he tell us . . . me?"

"Moses deliberately did not get his 'white' family involved. It was to protect you . . . us. Since you have arrived back from Scotland, this is the first time you have seen him, right? I bet you do not know where he lives, that he's married and has a son." Colleen shook her head. Mike continued, "After Samson and Delila died he moved away. He knew he was going to get involved in politics, he knew he would be a wanted man; he knew he would someday be arrested. He wanted to be sure you and yours would not come under question."

Moses stirred and opened his eyes, he blinked for a few minutes not knowing where he was, and then he saw Colleen and Mike. He tried to sit up, "I'm sorry!" He started to get out of bed, but Colleen pushed him back.

"Moses, you are not going anywhere, at least for tonight, or what's left of the night. I have cleaned your wounds again, and those burns on your face. Now that you are awake, take this medicine for pain, and to fight infection. Try to get a restful sleep, then, and only then, can you decide what your next step will be."

Moses laid back, "I am tired, and I can't remember when last I slept in a bed."

Moses awoke to the smell of bacon, eggs and coffee. There was a note next to his bed from Colleen.

> *Your clean, mended clothes are in the bathroom.*
> *Jump in the shower, and then come down to breakfast.*

He stood in the shower for a long time. Ahh, the luxury of hot running water, and as much as you want; he felt like a new man. He swallowed a few more pain pills, and then his nose led him to the food. As he sat down Colleen kissed him on his forehead. "You are looking much better, and according to your forehead, no more fever." Moving to the stove she filled his plate. "Now let's take care of the stomach."

"Where is everyone?" asked Moses

"Mike and Jacob have left for work, and this is the day Maureen has to help out at the children's pre-school." As Moses ate, Colleen continued. "I listened to the news, nothing about you or a political meeting being broken up."

Moses walked over to the kitchen radio, "May I?" Colleen nodded, and he started moving the dial. The radio crackled for a few minutes, and then a voice with a lot of static background could be heard. Moses put his ear closer, looking at Colleen he said, "Now this is the true news—the white radio station is censored, they won't talk about yesterday's raid unless it's to their advantage."

The announcer was talking in Xhosa. Colleen could not understand, but she watched Moses' face. He was very serious as he listened; Moses scribbled a few notes. Going back to the table he explained to Colleen. "We had an informer, many lives were lost, and many like myself are considered missing, not knowing if they are dead. Later I will put a coded message in the newspaper so they will know I'm okay, and in hiding." Seeing the worried look on her face, he said, "Colleen, let me explain. I'm a wanted man because of the politics of this land. Growing up here I did not experience the true problems, I had so many advantages. But in high school, I went home with some of my friends—I saw a different Africa. I saw a suffering not too many people see. It was so unfair, I kept asking . . . why . . . why?"

Moses filed his coffee cup and continued, "I have a good friend Mark, he hit the nail on the head when he said, 'When the Dutch arrived, they had the bible, and we had the land. Now they have the land and we have the bible. Why could we not have shared? Why did they have to take everything from us? When the British came and tried to take it from the Dutch, they were appalled and fought them off. That's what we should have done back then. Now, better late than never, we want to right that wrong. We don't want it all, just a fair share.

"Moses I'm afraid for you, remember it was a similar fight that killed your mother and father."

Moses nodded, "There's not a day that goes by that I don't remember that, I wish I had been old enough to have protected them. That was not to be—but I can protect you. Colleen, I believe things are going to get ugly before getting better. I don't want to involve you or your family. So I won't be coming back. No matter what you hear or see, don't acknowledge me. If I'm arrested and put in prison, don't come to the trial."

"Moses . . ."

"Colleen, promise me, think of your family. They could suffer from this."

Colleen nodded, "It's hard to believe there is so much hatred in this beautiful land."

"The word Apartheid . . . means apartness or separateness—but it should pronounced . . . Apart—Hate, because that's what it breeds—hate." Moses got up, "I must leave, thank you for your help Colleen."

"Wait Moses, you need to phone in your notice to the newspaper."

"Not from here, just in case they trace calls. If I leave now I can catch the bus on the main road. There's a tickey box on the corner, I'll call from there."

Moses hesitated, so Colleen made the move, she hugged him and said, "Look after yourself, and remember if you need me, and you can't come—put an ad in the paper."

Before Moses got off the bus in Soweto, he examined the area, nothing unusual. He did not want to draw attention to himself, so he first stopped at the corner café and bought bread and milk. As an after thought he bought a sweet for his son, they did not allow him to eat too many of them, so this would be a treat. As he approached his house, he gave a birdcall; it would always bring his son running out to greet him. Their house was one of a thousand shanties, but his wife had worked hard to pretty it up. Old klim tin cans were planted with seasonal flowers of many colors. The beginning of each summer she would re-paint the front door. So their little corner of this hellhole was clean and bright. 'To help you find your way home to us,' she would say.

Lulu knew and understood what Moses was involved in. They both wanted a better South Africa for their son. Moses, made his bird call again, by now he was in their walled courtyard, that's when he saw a kilm can knocked over and the flowers spilled; there was a muddy boot print on the freshly pained yellow door. As he stepped through the yellow door, he saw them. The bedroom door was open; they were both lying on the bed, shot between the eyes. His agonizing scream could be heard for several blocks.

"Nooooooooooooooooo . . . . Nooooooooooooooo . . . ." Moses dropped his milk and bread as he raced into the bedroom. He fell to his knees and gathered his family into his arms, still screaming. Nooooooo.

"Yesssssss, Yesssssss . . . *Kaffier*!"

Moses' head was jerked back by the police. "Hey *Kaffier*, this is our lucky day we got three for the price of one. Your woman will never breed more black scum; your son won't grow up to give us trouble, like his old man." Moses felt the first punch in his kidney, as he doubled over a boot caught him in the chin and threw him backwards onto the bed. He saw the two of them pull out their police batons. Later as they dragged him out to the waiting police van, he saw the spilled milk on the floor. 'Lulu's not going to like that,' he thought.

The rough ride and screaming siren, added to the pounding pain in Moses' head. The van pulled into an underground parking; he was dragged out of the car and down several flights of stairs, and then thrown into a holding cell. He heard the door slam shut and the key turn, and then hands helped him into a sitting position. They were fellow members of the ANC; Sam was one of them. Though bruised and swollen lips Moses said, "Sam, I thought you were dead, I saw you shot."

"Shot, but not dead my brother, not yet anyway. How did they manage to get you, when I saw you escape their net on Tuesday, I thought you had managed to make it to the border."

"I was shot too; I made it to a friendly home, where I was helped. But when I got to Soweto, they were waiting for me. Moses closed his eyes, they were beginning to swell shut from his beating, and he also closed down his feelings. He would never let them see how much he hurt. Leaning against the wall he said to Sam, "Do you know who the informer was?"

"No."

"Well, I will not rest till I find out."

"Moses you know we are not leaving this prison alive! One of us is going to jump out of a window several stories up. The other is going on a hunger strike and will starve to death." In spite of his pain Moses had to smile, this is what the newspaper always printed about the death of inmates.

"Well, if I am the one to jump out of a window, I will take one of them with me, that way I can land on him—to soften my fall." Then he got serious, "Sam, no matter what we don't give them any information, agreed."

"Agreed," said Sam.

When Moses woke, he was cold and hot. Cold from sitting on the cement floor for hours there were no beds, chairs, or even blankets in the cell, only the bare floors and a bucket in a corner to use as a toilet. He was hot because of the fever, between his bullet wounds and the sever beating; his body was having a hard time. He wanted water badly, everything felt swollen, and he had a hard time swallowing. Sam's bullet wound was also showing signs of infection.

Daily, Colleen searched the paper for news on the attack. Finally a week later a small piece appeared, tucked away in the back pages.

ARRESTED
Five A.N.C members arrested two prominent leaders; Moses Kharu and Sam Nxumalo Closed trial date set for December 15th

Colleen sucked in her breath, "Oh Moses! What is going to happen to you?"

That night, once the grand children were in bed, Colleen called Mike and asked if he could come over. She told Mike, Jacob, and Maureen about her conversation with Moses and pointed out the newspaper article to them. They were silent for a while, and then Mike said, "You know there is nothing we can do to help him, he emphasized that in his last conversation with you."

"I know, I know, I feel so helpless," said Colleen.

Maureen shook her head, "Wasn't the A.N.C. squashed when Mandela was arrested?"

"Apparently not," said Jacob. "At least Moses had the good sense not to involve us. I hope his wife and son are okay."

A month later the headlines of the 'Sun' newspaper read:

PRISON ABILANCE INVOLVED IN ACCIDENT

While on route from the prison hospital, the ambulance was forced off the road and overturned. The driver, guards and two prisoners were killed on site. Three prisoners are still missing. It is believed they may head for the border. They cannot get far, as two of the prisoners are still suffering from injuries sustained during their arrest.

There a reward of R1, 000, for any information leading to the capture of Moses Kharu and Sam Nxumalo. We are also interested in the return of the third prisoner.

Colleen's emotions did a flip-flop. The good news was Moses had escaped. The bad news was he had been hurt. Things quieted down for a while. Colleen read the newspaper daily, always looking for a message from Moses, but there was none. At least when he was in prison, she knew where he was; now she wasn't even sure if he was alive.

CHAPTER 24

Time moved on, even though Colleen was worried about Moses, they were now swept up in Jacob and Maureen's travel plans. Maureen was traveling to America. Adam would meet her there; they were taking the children to Disney World and Sea World. Then Adam's parents would join them as they traveled in a camper sight seeing.

Jacob had completed his research and the writing of his report on the Scottish castles. Now he was researching the European castles. He had hoped to find out more about the attack in Sestroretsk, which killed his great, great, great grandparents. However, these records were sealed and only for government use. The castles he was assigned to research were in Veliki, Tabor, Bojnice, Bratislava and Trencins.

With her children and grandchildren gone for a few months, the house was going to be very quiet. "I'll start writing my next book," thought Colleen.

In Europe, traveling with fellow students heated political arguments were often engaged in.

"Jacob, you and most white South Africans are ignorant as to what is going on around you, take your blinders off and see what is going on." They pointed out that much had been written about the politics of apartheid. "You have laws that mandate where blacks can live, work, and raise their families, even a law that says where they can be buried. You have a labor system that forces black men to live away from their families eleven months out of the year. They are forced to live in ghetto conditions. They do not have equal or even a fair share of pay, or education—they have no rights."

Someone else picked up from this line of reasoning saying "My God Jacob, there is even an Immorality Act, which dictates who you are allowed to marry, if you are not the same race, you could be imprisoned, because you love each other."

Another voice chimed in. "Have you ever been to one of their compounds?" Jacob had to admit that he hadn't. The voice continued, "Neither have I, but I am willing to bet we know more about the conditions there than you do. For example the name *Soweto*, the government says it comes from, South Western

Township. However, it came from the outcry of pain felt by the people who were forced to move there, '*So where to?*' was their constant cry."

Jacob was embarrassed at his lack of knowledge . . . he knew, but did not know. He had seen, but had not seen. He had heard, but did not hear. He'd done research in Scotland, and many parts of Europe, but knew little about the background of his mother's country. He had been born in America—so was an American. Reeny, while born in Northern Rhodesia, was registered as an American. That's when Jacob knew what his next research project would be—South African History.

In America, Maureen was facing the same accusations that were being heaped on Jacob. However, hers' came from her husband and in-laws. "You have been living with blinders on Maureen; South Africa is getting ready to blow! I want you and my children out of there!"

Maureen could not believe her ears, "What has brought this on Adam? You know I love living in Africa, that's where my mother and brothers are."

"But this is where my parents and I live. It's time to stop your globetrotting and make a home for us. Especially since Laura and Shawn are ready to start school. While you are here, we should look at houses."

"Adam, you still have a year of overseas traveling; give me that year in Africa."

"No, that will make the children a year behind in school; school starts in three months. We will buy the house now; you can go back for three months, while the house is being renovated. You will tie up loose ends and be back by the end of July."

"Adam . . . ."

"No, Maureen. I know the news is censored there; you are not getting the complete truth. Do you know how terrifying it was to watch a necklacing take place? By the look on your face you don't even know what that is."

"No, but . . ." Adam just continued speaking.

"A car tire soaked in gas, or as you call it petrol, is placed around a person neck—hence the word necklace, then Maureen, it is set alight. We saw it on the news, a man burned to death. It wasn't just somewhere in South Africa, it was only two miles from where you live; where my children are sleeping!!"

Maureen neither agreed nor disagreed with Adam. She started looking at him in a different light. What was it, had he changed so much? Or had she changed? Had his years of travel, and them being separated caused her to fall out of love? Now she questioned her feelings for him. She watched him through new eyes, as he dealt with the twins, how he spoke and treated his parents. How he spoke and treated her. She did not know this man.

As soon as she had time to herself, she went to a lawyer. What would be involved in getting a divorce, and leaving the country? She found getting a divorce was easy enough, but she could not leave the country if she wanted custody of the children. She wanted a divorce and she wanted her children, which meant that she would have to live in America. History was repeating itself, that's what her happened to her mother. She had often wondered why her mother did not go back to Africa, to her family. Now she knew, because of her and Jacob.

Reading the newspapers she saw she would have no trouble getting a job, once divorced. Maureen pretended to go along with Adam, but changed a few things that would be to her advantage in the future. Adam could afford, and wanted to buy a large house in an affluent neighborhood. However, Maureen talked him into buying two smaller homes, one in a slightly scaled back neighborhood, which would be their every day home. The other, their vacation home, could be bought along the coast in North Carolina. "Since American schools are closed during the summer we can move to the beach for those three months, the kids would love it." To her surprise he agreed.

So when she was ready to file for divorce, she would have a home—the beach one. Her lawyer had roughly worked out her alimony; it was a good sum. Between having one of their houses, the alimony and part time job, she could manage.

A week after Maureen and Jacob left for America and Europe, there was a knock at Colleen's door. At first she did not recognize the man standing there, it was Mike's father-in-law. "Good morning Mrs. Miller, I was hoping to speak to Mike, is he home?"

"Yes, but he now lives across the road." Colleen pointed out the house. "His car is still in the driveway, so he hasn't left for work yet."

About an hour later the phone rang. "Col, my father-in-law is here with some shocking news, can we come over—this may affect you as well."

"Of course Mike."

Settled at her favorite place at the kitchen table, with the sun shinning in, and birds singing in the yard, Colleen had a sense of doom as she looked at the men's faces. Mike spoke while Peter paced up and down the kitchen.

"Just to give you some background, Col, Peter's family emigrated from England when he was ten years old. Years later he married Sofie, an eighth generation South African. He never did share her strong views on blacks and coloreds. Since it never really affected his life, it was always easier just to go along with her than to make it an issue." Colleen nodded and let them continue.

Peter picked up the explaining. "But of course, we are now affected. Not in my eyes, but Sofie, and Elizabeth feel it's the end of the world. They are the one's that insisted on cutting off Mike and Marnie." Peter signed, "I miss having Mike and Marnie around. Instead I have two women who are constantly whining and complaining about being deceived, and the horror of having a colored husband and child." Peter continued, "Many years ago I almost left Sofie, but again it was easier to let her have her way. I am a man of peace, no match for her fighting and plotting. Another reason I stayed was my daughter, then when she married, there was Mike and in time Marnie." Mike put his hand on his father-in-laws shoulder. "Now I see Elizabeth turning into her mother, where that hate comes from I don't know. They are now plotting to hurt Mike and Marnie—I draw the line at this point." Peter broke down crying.

"Col, they are going to the authorities and reporting the fact that Marnie and I are colored, without passes living in a white neighborhood." After a pause, Mike continued, "Unless I pay them R10, 000."

The only thing that could be heard was Peter's sobs, even the birds weren't singing anymore. Colleen looked at Mike; he had turned pale. Peter collected himself and said, "I just had to warn you Mike, making you move would be bad enough, but maybe you will be arrested. Maybe . . . ." His voice trailed away. Colleen closed her eyes.

"Oh God, what have I done?" She thought. For the first time in many years she thought about the three cords. She felt it had not helped her with her relationship with Mike's father and with her marriage to Robert. Colleen was brought back to the moment with Mike's voice.

"Colleen, are you okay?"

Taking a deep breath she said, "Of course Mike." Looking at Peter, Colleen said, "Do you think they will go through with this threat?"

"No doubt in my mind."

Turning to Mike she said, "You know paying the money would only be the beginning of an endless pit, and when they have bled you dry, they will still hand you over."

"I had thought about that," said Mike. "There is another possibility; Peter has made up his mind to leave them. He has already bought a farm in Zambia, but he has not told them. Peter has invited Marnie and me to join him." Colleen stared at Mike, 'So this is how I'm to be punished for loving your father' she thought.

Peter, hugged Colleen and Mike when he left, "I am so, so, so sorry for what my wife and daughter plan on doing. I leave next week, think it over. If you want more time Mike, you may consider sending Marnie with me. At least he will never have a record that could come back to haunt him one day."

Mike paced the kitchen while Colleen cleaned up, and organized supper for them. "How could she? How could she? I can understand her hating me, but her child—*Her Own Son!!* It's not like you can even see the color strain in him, or me for that matter." Sitting down he said, "What do you think, Col? Should we go? Should I send Marnie? He loves his grandfather so that would not be a problem."

"Mike, think carefully about this, staying and facing the consequences, or going and starting a new life. Whatever you choose, your life will never be the same again." Colleen had a sleepless night, just when she had her family around her politics were going to divide them. Mike and Marnie leaving because of race issue. Maureen phoned to say she had to settle in America because Adam was concerned about politics; Jacob was having a hard time with fellow students, again because of politics.

The next morning Mike came over, "Col, I have decided to let Marnie go with Peter. That will get him out of danger. I will wait to see if Elizabeth is really going to turn us in. If it looks as though she is, then I'll cross the border and join them."

Marnie was a very active eight year old, the idea of living on a farm, and riding horses was a dream come true. He loved his grandfather and really missed him these past months.

"How long before you join us Dad?"

"A month or two at the most." Mike had not told him the reason for this move. Or that maybe they may not return to South Africa.

The day Peter arrived Marnie was ready, of course his dad had packed his clothes and books, but the big surprise was that Mike had bought him a new bike, and a pellet gun, which his grandfather promised to supervise. Of course his dog Rex was going with them, a dog and a farm belonged together.

When it came time to say goodbye, Marnie got weepy. "Think of it as holiday my boy, before you know it I will be there and you will have so much to show me." Mike put his arm over Peter's shoulder, "Look after him, he means the world to me, and thank you so much, not only for the warning, but also for giving us an avenue of escape by letting us join you in Zambia." They walked a few steps from the lorry, "If something should happen and I am delayed . . . ."

Peter did not let Mike finish. "There's no time limit, whenever you get there, we will be fine. Just be safe. It won't be till Tuesday, when they return from visiting relatives in the Cape that they will know I've gone. That may delay them contacting the police about you. They may be too busy trying to find me, of course, that may also make them act right away. So be prepared. They don't have the slightest idea about the farm I bought in Zambia, so Marnie is safe. You will be too, once you get there."

Mike felt a lump in his throat. "One more thing Peter, if for some reason you and I lose contact, Colleen will know everything that's going on."

As the lorry drove down the driveway, Mike put his arm around Colleens shoulder. "We need to talk, how about some coffee." As Colleen waited for the water to boil; her eyes filled with tears.

"Mike, I'm so sorry. This is all my fault."

"No, never, never, you can not take the blame for a system; you are not responsible for how a country chooses to run itself." He added, "But this does give me some idea of how hard it was for you to leave me, when you were with Zebra Run. You did that for my good and protection; I am doing this for Marine's good and protection. Listen to me carefully—I've been thinking about it, you are right our lives will never be the same. I have read stories about people who were exposed because of living in the wrong area. Remember, Elizabeth knows you are my mother, you may be arrested for the Immorality Act."

"Oh Mike!!"

"It's okay Col, really its okay. Now another thing, my house must be taken out of my name, let's put it in your name. You rented the house to me, of course not knowing I was colored. Should anything happen I know you will take care of Marnie. I would also like to move anything of value out of the house, maybe stored here at your house."

They spent the next few days taking care of legal matters concerning the house, and a personal will that Mike insisted on. Mike's valuables were moved to Colleens home. They made sure that Sheree, Gordon and Charles understood what was happening and their role of ignorance. While Sheree's husband Seun had strong feelings about coloreds and blacks, he had never thought of Mike as a colored. Gordon was a typical professor and was too busy with his books and students to pay any attention to current affairs; always just shrugging it off as secondary. Charles though, was concerned; he had played Rugby for South Africa, and now belonged to a club for retired players. He could not afford any scandal.

A week later they were all gathered at Colleen's for supper. They tried to be upbeat, but eventually Gordon voiced their thoughts. "Normally our get togethers are happy occasions; I can not believe what's happening. Mike for many years you were our baby brother, we were always around to protect you. Then the truth came out that you were really our nephew, but that did not change our feelings for you. Now we all feel so helpless, we cannot help you."

Charles added to his brother's comment. "Mike, I think you should leave for Zambia before they come . . . that's if they come."

"Exactly Charles, they may not do anything. Maybe just looking at me they would say it was a false alarm. So I may make this big move for nothing. I do not want to move if I don't have to."

"What do you think is going to happen Mike? Sheree had come and sat beside him, and held his hand, she still thought of him as her baby brother.

"The best case scenario is after seeing me they will wave it off as a prank. The worst-case scenario, they will take me away for processing. Because the color line is so small, it may not show up and they may dismiss the accusation. Then again even the slightest doubt, especially since I cannot produce a mother or father—they may register me, and make me move to a compound. At that point I will disappear from South Africa, and join Marnie and Peter in Zambia."

After her sister and brothers left, Colleen held Mike back saying, "I have a gift for you Mike, it's nothing fancy but it has a lot of meaning for me—maybe later it will mean a lot to you." Colleen gave him an unwrapped box. Mike took out a belt, a normal everyday belt. He looked at his mother and raised one of his eyebrows in question. She laughed, "Your father raises his eyebrows just like that." Then she got serious. Taking the belt from him, she turned it over. The belt had a secret zipped pocket. Opening it Colleen pulled out a very slim knife, it almost looked like a five-inch nail pounded flat. However, on examining it, Mike saw the craftsmanship involved; it had come from a special store selling overseas weapons. "Mike, the knife, little as it is, may save your life one day. The secret pouch can also hold paper money, which may also come in handy. Notice the zipper for the pouch." The clip to pull the zip open or closed had been replaced with a cord so small Mike had to look carefully. It was three different colored cords, no thicker than three ply knitting yard. The cords were woven together just like his mothers necklace. He said in a whisper, "The Three Cords, you've given me the three cords to remind me. I know the story Col. This does mean a lot to me." They held each other in silence.

Wednesday morning when Colleen looked through the kitchen window she saw the police car in Mike's driveway. About an hour later he was led out of the house . . . handcuffed.

CHAPTER 25

At the police station, Mike began to be educated in the system of legalized racism. The white police pushed him into a room that had about twenty desks with men and women working at them. In his very thick Afrikaans accent he announced to all.

"Hey *ke'rel*, look what we found to-day, a *muntu* trying to live like a white in one of the best suburbs *nog al*."

At first everyone thought Sarel the policeman was joking. Mike recognized a school buddy of his, James, who got up and said to Mike, "Who put you up to this joke, nice touch handcuffs and all." Mike started to say something when Sarel swung his *knopkerrie*.

Mike was dragged down three flights of stairs, the same place Moses had been questioned months earlier. He was photographed, and finger printed, all the time being jeered at and slapped around. *"Sies man,* look how white he is—it's got to be paint, let's see if it will wash off." Mike was made to strip, with about ten police watching him. They turned a fire hose on him; Mike thought his skin would peel off.

"*Nee*, no paint—guess he must be a white *Kaffier*. Throw him in the tank for the night." Mike spent the night, as Moses did, on the cold cement floor, no food, no drink. It was two days before they came for him.

"Hey white *Kaffier*, you're going before the judge today."

"Look at me! Could I get cleaned up first?" asked Mike.

The police looked at one another, "Jan, he thinks he's not presentable, what do you think?" They looked at Mike mockingly.

"*Ja*, he's right, he needs cleaned up. How many *Kaffiers* have you hired to scrub your floors and your toilets?" Before Mike could think of an answer, they handed him a dirty bucket of water and a brush. Scrub this cell and empty that shit bucket, then you'll be presentable." They roared with laughter. Mike was never so humiliated in his life. He knew he was filthy, he knew he looked and smelt bad. His teeth felt, as though there was fir on them, he could still taste blood from his beating.

The judge hardly looked at Mike, as he heard his case. He did hold a hankie over his nose when Mike was asked to approach the bench. He looked at Mike over the top of his glasses.

"You have a problem *ke'rel*; you are the worst kind of colored. The whites of course don't want you; the blacks don't want you. You will find even the coloreds will not want you, you're skin it too white, and your hair not kinky enough. On top of that, you don't know who your father or mother was, that makes you a colored bastard." By now Mike had learned not to speak. So he just stood waiting.

The judge thought for a few minutes. "I could sentence you to imprisonment for impersonating the white race, but we will have to feed you. No I'm going to throw you to the wolves. As from this day on you will live in the township of Alexandra. My constables will drop you off there—you will be assigned a sleeping area. You have one week to get all your papers in order. We will be back to check on you; now let me tell you something white *Kaffier*, don't even think of running." Again Mike was handcuffed and half led, half dragged to the waiting police van. To his horror he saw Elizabeth and her mother watching as he was shoved into the van. He was so thankful that Marnie was spared this humiliation. Under his breath he said a prayer of thanks to Peter.

As they approached Alexandra, Mike noticed a larger than life sign staked at the side of the road.

WARNING

This road passes through proclaimed Bantu locations, any person who enters the location without a permit renders himself liable for prosecution for contravening the Bantu Consolidation act of 1945, and the location Regulation act of the city of Johannesburg.

The van stopped at a bus station and they told him to get out. "Hey white *Kaffier*, see that you're at the court house one week from today, with all your papers in order." They were about to ride off, but called out the window, "And make yourself presentable!" they roared at their own joke.

As Mike rubbed his wrists, the handcuffs had left deep indents, he looked around—there were hundreds of people. They were either getting on or off buses. Everyone was carrying packages of some sort. Suddenly he was afraid, he'd heard about gangs in these compounds. He had no idea where his home was. He tried to approach several people, but they quickly turned away at the sight and smell of him. People either did not care or were just too afraid to get involved. It had only been an hour since he was dropped off but it felt like an eternity. He felt so humiliated and inferior, a grown man on the ve0rge of crying with frustration.

"Mr. Zulewsky, is that you Sir?" Mikes head shot up. Standing a few feet from him was Chaka Boma, a black man who worked in the same offices that he did. A few positions were now being given to black persons. Mike had admired Chaka, in spite of having a university degree, the office workers treated him no differently then the black beggar on the street. His work was constantly sabotaged; at rest and lunch breaks he sat by himself. Chaka had to leave the building and walk several blocks to a toilet that blacks could use. The first day he tried to use the office restroom, he was knocked unconscious. Yet he never complained and turned in excellent work.

A few months back, some white office workers had deliberately hidden some files Chaka had prepared for Mr. Ferguson. They were for a very important meeting, and if Chaka did not produce them, he would probably be fired. Chaka got permission to work late into the night, but Mike knew even if he worked all night he would never finish on time. Mike made up his mind to help Chaka. He left the office when everyone else did—if he stayed then, he knew fellow workers would have labeled him 'Kaffier bootie.' As he walked past Chaka's desk he said, 'Vasbeit.'

An hour late Mike returned to the office, carrying a few packages. One of them contained supper. "If we are working through the night we need energy—so let us eat first Chaka." The second parcel contained two new dress shirts, the third held toothbrushes, razors etc.

"Why?" asked Chaka looking dumbfound.

"We are going to work all night, but we don't want to look like it tomorrow. So we need fresh shirts, and some toiletries."

"No, I mean why are you helping me?"

"Chaka, what they did was wrong, hopefully this small act of helping you, will encourage others. Let's get started." That was months ago.

Now, Chaka was looking at Mike in disbelief. "What happened to you? What are you doing here in a compound?"

"Oh Chaka, it's a long story."

Seeing the desperation in Mike's eyes, Chaka did not wait for an answer but said, "Come." Miriam did not question her husband when he brought home a strange white man, and said, "Give him my hot bath water." During the late afternoon while Miriam cooked supper for her and Chaka, she would collect water and boil it in her biggest pot. She kept throwing the boiling hot water in a galvanized tub they had in their bedroom. By the time Chaka came home and had supper, the tub was full of warm water, he would strip and sit in the tub scrubbing, his legs would hang over the edge. Chaka did his best to be clean and neatly dressed for his office job.

Mike realized this was Chaka's warm bath he had been offered. "Oh, I couldn't."

"Oh yes you can, and will Mr. Mike, if I'm going to help you, we first must get rid of this smell."

Mike was given a blanket to wrap around himself, while Miriam washed his clothes in the used water. The clothes were then hung around the stove to dry.

"Sit here Mr. Mike, I apologize for my home and the little we have, but we'd like to share it with you. Now that she's seen you naked and washed your clothes, let me introduce my wife Miriam." Miriam did a little curtsy, and then turned to the stove. It had been three days since Mike ate, he was starved, but he held himself in check when he saw how little they had, but were willing to share with him. It did not take long to eat, while Miriam cleared the table and made coffee; they switched the overhead lights off and lit a candle.

"Mr. Mike, we are among the fortunate ones, we have electricity, but it's so expensive, we only use it for a few hours, and then light the candles. Now, tell us, what has happened and how can we help?"

"First Chaka, drop the Mr. or Sir, plain Mike will do." Mike told them his story from the beginning, his birth in Zambia, to being dropped in Alexandra by the police. Chaka and Miriam were silent for a long time.

"I am not even going to start in on the political system of this land. The question is Mr. Mike, Ahh . . . Mike, what are you going to do?"

"I will make pretence of staying; I will get the papers they want me to. As soon as they stop watching me, I will leave and cross into Zambia."

"Hmmm, in the meantime you plan on living in Alexandra?"

"I have to, it can't be too bad, maybe you can give me some pointers, at least show me the ropes. This is my assigned living quarters." Mike handed Chaka the paper with an address. CSQ 32-164 Chaka interpreted it for him; it was the Colored Single Quarters—Building 32—Bed number 164.

"You'll be sleeping in a long dormitory for single men, not the safest place to be." Chaka stood up, "We have these two rooms, a small bedroom, and this room which serves as a kitchen, dining room and living room. For tonight at least you are welcome to sleep on the couch. Oh! We do not have indoor plumbing." Chaka handed him a big tin can and a role of toilet paper. Just before Chaka closed the bedroom door he said, "Mike, *Vasbeit!*" They smiled at one another knowingly. After three nights on a cement floor in the prison he now had a soft couch, a blanket, he was warm, and had food in his stomach. Mike was asleep within a few minutes. He did not hear Chaka and Miriam talking way into the night.

———

It was still dark when Chaka shook Mike awake, "This is the plan Mike, I am going into work, only to arrange a weeks family emergency time off. Then I will take the bus out to your mothers, deliver a note from you, which you will write now, and bring back anything you think you will need. Do not make it anything valuable, as it will only get stolen. I should be back by three or four o'clock. In the mean time I'll bring in enough water, you can heat it and take another bath. But don't leave the house. I have some books you can read, or paper if you need to plan and work out your next step."

"Chaka, I don't know how to thank you."

"No Mike, It is I who can now thank you for helping me a few months ago." Mike unbuckled his belt and from the zipped pocket took out R100.

"Take this and use a taxi, that way you will be back sooner. Then use the rest to buy food, since I am here for at least another day or so." Mike immediately wrote a note to Colleen, telling her not to worry, things will work out. I'll come as soon as it is safe and explain all. In the meantime, you can trust Chaka; he knows everything. Send back with him two changes of clothes for me."

Because of using a taxi, Chaka was home at one o'clock. Colleen had written a quick note and included four fifty rand notes. In a large OK bazaar bag were two sets of clothing.

"My mother had an OK bazaar bag?"

"Oh no, she had your clothes beautifully packed in a suitcase, but I had to dump the case. Within a few minutes of entering Alexandra I would have been robbed, the case was too flashy. Chaka smiled, "Lesson number one, even if you can afford it, NEVER draw attention to yourself, your clothes, your luggage, your house; even your car if you own one. The way you carry yourself, the way you look at people. You must learn to be a nobody." Chaka smiled and added, "At least this is what people must see. Now it's another story on what people don't see." Chaka then became serious, "Are you ready Mike?"

"Yes."

"Let me just give you an overall picture of your new 'suburb'. Alexandra is a shanty town of mostly shacks and a few decent homes." Chaka waved his hand across the room, "This is considered one of the decent homes." There are a lot of gutters, and unpaved potholed streets. The streets number from First Street to Thirty-Second Street. First Street is the shops, and where the Indians live, they live in homes behind the stores; they are considered the cream of Alexandra's society. Second, Third and Fourth avenues are for the coloreds, that's you, Chaka smiled. The rest are for us blacks. For the most part people here are just burdened with their own survival, but there are gangs that you need to watch out for, one of them being *Tootsies.*" Chaka took out a map of the area, and gave it to Mike. "It's the middle of the day—the safest time to walk around, come I'll give you a tour and we will find your accommodations. I will say you are welcome to stay with Miriam and I, but you will get into trouble for that, still in the wrong area. Remember, South Africa has the right to tell you exactly where you must live."

As they walked, Chaka continued talking; Mike could not believe what he was seeing. Because there were not enough homes to go around, a huge squatter's area had sprung up. The shacks were made of plastic, tin and cardboard. About fifty percent of Alexandra had no running water, the sewage system was few and far between, so sometimes gutters were used as toilets. Malnourished children and old people walked the streets looking for something to eat. The children's bellies were always distended, and the old ones were skin and bone. They were covered with sores, and followed by mangy, painfully thin dogs. As they walked Mike could hear rasping coughs from dark doorways.

This is your building Number 32, going inside they found bed number 164. It was just a steel bed, with a squeaky spring frame; a thin badly stained, smelly mattress was rolled to one end because so many men lived in the building, and would be coming and going at different times of the day and night, there was no door. Looking at Chaka, Mike asked, "What would it take to get me into one of the small houses, at least they have doors."

"You have to be married for that." Chaka stopped and stared at Mike. "There's a possibility," he said slowly, "are you willing to do something unusual, and it won't cost you much."

"Of course."

Looking at his watch Chaka said, "We need to hurry." Mike half ran to keep up with Chaka. Two streets up from the single quarters, Chaka knocked on a door."

A six or seven year old boy opened the door; who broke into a grin when he saw Chaka. "Chaka, Chaka, Mommy . . . its Chaka!"

A petite very pretty girl with the most beautiful almond shaped eyes came out of the bedroom; her hair wrapped in a towel, Mike could still smell the shampoo. "Chaka, how nice to see you . . ." she stopped when she saw Mike. Chaka introduced them; then looking at the boy he winked and said,

"Zack, do you think your mother will let you have a sweet?"

Zack's eyes lit up, "Can I Mom, can I?" She smiled and nodded her head. Chaka counted out six cents, as Zack hopped from foot to foot. As soon as the boy ran out the door, Chaka pointed to the chairs.

"There is no time for small talk, Mike you need Gail, and Gail you need Mike. As briefly as he could Chaka explained to Gail, Mike's situation. She stared at him.

"You don't look colored." She smiled, as she added, "No wonder these living conditions scare the pants off you." Mike just nodded his head, and turned to Chaka to hear why Gail would need him. Chaka continued.

"Gail's husband died two months ago. She is now considered a single woman, and must move out of this house. There are no single quarters for women; she literally has no place to go. Plus, she would have to take her son to her parents to be looked after." Chaka stared at Mike, while Mike stared back. Chaka continued, "Gail can stay in the house if she re-married and if she could afford to pay the back rent, they fell behind when her husband went to hospital."

Mike and Gail were beginning to get the picture, and were looking at one another differently. Chaka continued, "It would be a marriage in name only, while you helped each other out, for however long it takes." Since they were still silent, Chaka prompted, "Zack's life would not be disrupted, and you'll be able to keep him with you Gail." Now Gail's eyes lit up, turning to Mike she said, "Would you be willing? Do you have the back rent?"

"How much are we talking about Gail?"

"One hundred and fifty Rand."

They had to rush, as Mike needed to have Gail's address as his own before he applied for his I.D. card. Time was also running out for Gail, she was to move in two days. Chaka continued, "If you have the local minister marry you now, the papers can be filed before closing time. Of course the law says we have to apply and get permission to marry, but we don't have time for that. We will deal with the authorities and fines later. The rent balance can be paid and Mike, with this address you will be ready for your paperwork starting tomorrow."

Without even changing clothes, Gail's hair still wet Zack's mouth sticky from the sweet, Mike and Gail said their 'I do's.' The marriage went on file, and the back rent was paid. Mike and Gail breathed a sign of relief. It was exactly two hours after meeting each other, that they were married. Gail had a home and could keep Zack with her. Mike did not have to live in the singles quarters, he felt a little safer. At least there was a door that could be locked.

CHAPTER 26

Mike, Gail, and Zack stood in the middle of the kitchen-living room, looking at one another. Zack had no idea what had just happened. Gail sat at the kitchen table and started crying. Mike reached over to touch her shoulder but held back, not sure why she was crying.

"Gail, please don't cry. I promise I won't be any trouble."

"No, Mike, you don't understand. I am happy you are here. Look around. I have had to start packing. In two days, Zack and I would have been out on the street. I would probably have lost my job. You have literally saved us. I'm not worried as to the kind of man you are. Chaka has told me how you helped him at the office."

The office! Mike wondered if he still had a job. Tomorrow after applying for his I.D. card, he would stop and explain his problem to his boss.

At 4:00 A.M. Mike heard Chaka walk up the pathway. Chaka had explained, "This is a time consuming process, so we must get an early start; the bus ride itself is very long, we have to change three times and they will be crowded."

"Let's take a taxi, Chaka."

"What did I tell you about not drawing attention to yourself? Can you imagine how you would be treated arriving in a taxi while some blacks and coloreds could not afford even a bus ticket and had to walk."

They arrived at the post office on Albert Street at 6:00 A.M. The office did not open until 10:00, but there were hundreds and men and women thronged outside the gate, all needing to apply for some sort of paper that would allow them to live their lives, there was fear, desperation and hopelessness in their eyes. When the office opened, the queue moved at a snails pace. As they shuffled along, Chaka explained what would happen.

"There are scores of tables inside; you will have to go through every one of them. Watch your attitude. The men behind the tables are Afrikaners who believe very much in apartheid. They will humiliate you; they will strip you of your dignity. Do not show any anger; remember you need your papers. With a stroke of their pens, they will determine your future."

At the tables every intimate detail of Mike's life was entered on forms, and later fed into computers. The records were kept in Pretoria. After these forms were completed, Mike had to go to another building for a physical. Again Chaka tried to prepare Mike. "Since I am not applying, I have to wait for you outside."

Mike was herded in the room with about fifty men, black and colored. They were ordered to strip and line up facing the wall, waiting for their turn to be x-rayed. While waiting for the line to move, they were fumigated for lice. Next, an orderly smeared his right upper arm with an ointment. As he moved down the line, a man in a white coat jabbed a needle into the prepared spot, next, a chest x-ray. Then, a black man and white man in turn handled and examined their privates. Mike thought they were needlessly rough. Venereal disease disqualified one for a pass. Finally they were allowed to dress.

Mike had been worried about his belt, but here, in this building you had better not steal. Now they moved on to the final room where they were handed their papers. Mike was numb with anger. This was the worst degradation of his life. They were truly treated like animals. The whole procedure reminded him of cattle moving through a dipping and branding line. They were dipped; (Deloused) and they were definitely branded with their I.D. cards. When he found Chaka, they didn't speak, but Chaka understood and just nodded.

By now it was 4:00. While Chaka waited outside, Mike went in to talk to his boss. Although his arrest had appeared in the paper, there were no pictures and the article was small and placed as filler towards the back page. Mike was hoping no one had read it. But he needed to tell his boss the truth, so he closed the door behind him. Mike did not want the rest of the office workers to overhear. As condensed and concise as possible he explained to Mr. Ferguson what happened. "My question, Mr. Ferguson, is will this affect my working here?" Mr. Ferguson was quiet for a long time. "No Mike, you are an excellent worker, as is Chaka. Do not mention it to anyone else, as you know there are some beyond that door that have different attitudes."

Mike looked surprised. "Thank you, sir."

"Mike, as you know I'm out here from England on a renewable contract. My wife who was from Korea was refused an entry visa because we were a 'mixed marriage.' I was allowed in only because they needed my expertise. Before I could cancel my contract with the company, my wife was killed in a motor accident. Even though I was angry with the government for not giving her a visa, I still came out; I needed a change since she died. Your secret is safe with me and if there is any way I can help, let me know."

Before Mike reached the door, he stopped. Turning around he said, "There is something that will help . . ." Mike explained his problem for a few minutes.

"It's yours," said Mr. Ferguson.

As Mike and Chaka walked to the bus stop, Chaka looked at him sideways. "Well, are you going to tell me what you're grinning at?"

"Not only do I still have my job, but something else."

"What?"

"I always wondered why you carried your suit and got dressed here every morning. Now that I've witnessed the travel conditions, the living conditions, the space problem, the *Tootsies* problem, I understand."

Mike looked at Chaka. "That end storage room that's always locked . . . it's ours. We can keep our working clothes there, change there and best of all it has a shower and toilet. No walking down the block for you." Mike grinned. "And I've been given one of the lock up garages, so I can keep my car handy. No one will notice it stay overnight and weekends, because it is a closed garage."

"Yessss," laughed Chaka.

"Let us stop and buy some steak and beer. You and Miriam join us for a braaivleis."

Chaka turned to Mike. "What part don't you understand about—advertising what you have."

"It's a braai, no one needs to know."

"The smell of that meat will travel for blocks, every hungry child will be crying." Mike was very quiet, he kept forgetting. "Now what you can do" added Chaka "is buying some good bread rolls, cheese, cold meats and a cake. No one will smell it and that will be a treat."

While Gail and Miriam fussed over their special treat, Chaka and Mike planned their next day of errands. First to the police station to show his papers—two days early—then a taxi ride out to Colleen's.

Mike knew his mother was worried. After Chaka and Miriam left, Mike helped Gail clean up. "Mike, what you must have spent on tonight's treat, which was very good by the way. I don't remember when last I ate cheese; anyway it could have brought a whole week's worth of food for the three of us." Mike took Gail by the shoulders and gently turned her around.

"Gail, as long as we are helping each other out, you never have to worry about food or rent. Save your money. I don't know what you have in mind for the future, but I will take care of the living expenses for the three of us." Gail could not believe her good fortune.

Colleen was out back sitting on the tree swing that overlooked the valley. She remembered how much her mother and grandmother Shannon loved to sit here. Right now her heart was very heavy, three of her children were in trouble and she could not help. Her mother and grandmother's words came back to haunt her. "Mixed race couples open themselves and their children to heartbreak for generations to come. If your family consists of two races, you live in two worlds, and neither wants you.

Moses involved in politics, arrested, hurt and on the run. Mike's and her secret exposed, she was not sure what was happening to him. It had been a week since the police picked him up, Maureen having to stay in America because her husband thought it unsafe here. Colleen was so deep in thought she did not hear the taxi come and go.

"Hello Col."

Colleen jumped up screaming, "Mike, Mike." She grabbed him and held on tight. "Oh Mike, I have been so worried, the police ride by often, let us go inside." Colleen put her arm around Mike's waist and started towards the house. That's when she saw Chaka. She reached out and put her other arm around his waist and marched them into her kitchen.

A few hours later Colleen had a better understanding of what was happening—not in some third world country—but right here in her backyard, "That is outrageous," she sputtered. "Chaka, you have got to understand not every white person is a racist. But it seems as though we are damn ignorant of what is happening on our own doorstep."

Mike's plan was to come out weekly and gradually empty his house. Boxes packed and put in storage, most other things divided between Gail and Miriam. They could certainly use them. A few things Marnie left behind like books and toys, Mike took for Zack. His work clothes he moved to the storage room at the office; he did not realize he had so much. He gave Chaka some of the suits and dress shirts.

"Once the house is empty Col, you can rent it out. Just deposit the money in my account." As they said their goodbyes, he asked, "Have you heard from Moses? I am so much more aware of what he wants to change in South Africa."

Gail oohed and ahhed over pots, blankets and some knick-knacks. When Mike gave Zack the books and toys, she said, "Mike, you never told us you had a son." Mike stared at her and then sat down heavily and covered his face.

"So much has happened in such a short time. I sent him away with his grandfather and even though I miss him so much, I am glad I did. Imagine putting an eight year old through this." The expression on Gail's face stopped him. "Gail, I did not mean he is beyond living like this. Zack is seven and lives this, but he was born and brought up with it. It has been an unbelievable experience for me—I just thought—for a young boy." Mike never finished. Gail turned and walked out of the room and closed the bedroom door.

Going to and from work was a daily nightmare. First they caught a train to the outskirts to Joburg. It was always so crowded they had to stand, body squashed against body. At times the smell was overbearing, simply from so many bodies in close quarters. Some were unwashed, some were sick. As bad as they felt, they had to report to work or lose their jobs. The buses they caught from the train station were no better. This nightmarish journey had to start at 5:00 A.M. in order to reach the office before anyone else—shower and change—and be at your desk before the other workers arrived. Some of them complained that 9:00 A.M. was too early for office workers to start. Mike had to bite his tongue.

The journey home was even worse. Everyone was carrying a bag of something. Food they couldn't buy in Alexandra or maybe food they had rescued from garbage cans. Secondhand clothes they bought from their madams, even things they may have stolen. Whatever they had was carried in old discarded plastic or paper bags, or wrapped in newspaper. Mike and Chaka joined the throngs of carriers in the evening. The collection of things in the car that he had brought from his 'white' home was gradually carried into Alexandra.

Once they reached Alexandra they had the gauntlet to run. *Tootsies* and other youths would stop, and even attack any they thought looked as though they were carrying something good. Fridays, which were paydays, were hell. The gangs would be out in full force, stealing, even killing men and women for a few Rand, maybe even just for the package of fish and chips they carried, a treat for their children.

Chaka had warned Mike, "If you see them coming, run, run hard and hide. Drop what you're carrying. It will delay them; maybe even stop them. Don't ever run to your house. They will follow you—just hide."

One Friday Chaka was not with Mike. He had gone out of town to a funeral. Colleen forwarded mail for Mike to the office and he was busy thinking about a letter Marnie had written him. It was a few minutes before he became aware of being followed. He dropped his shopping bag and ran. But they caught him before he could even turn the corner. Mike did not consider himself a coward, but he was trembling and looking around in desperation for help.

"We have had our eye on you, 'Mr. Whitey.' We understand you used to live in a white neighborhood. Think you are too good for your own kind." Someone was running his hands over Mike's body, searching for money. They found the R75 in his pocket. Someone else had a knife to his throat forcing him to stand still and not scream. A voice from behind him said to the leader, "That is all the money on him."

The man with the knife to his throat, obviously the leader of the gang, was looking into Mike's eyes. Seeing the fear there, he said, "No, no, he is hiding something, strip him." Rough hands ripped his clothing off. "What, no money strapped to this white body? Hmm, maybe you've hid it inside of you—bend over." Mike thought of his little knife in his belt. A lot of good it was doing him now. They had released his arms when undressing him. He now swung at them. He felt a searing pain in his side. As he blacked out, he heard the police sirens. Apparently the police also raided Alexandra on Friday nights. The *Tootsies* that was standing over him ran, but not before someone ran their knife down the side of his face.

"Our mark," they shouted. When he came to, there was the commotion of sirens, people running and screaming; he was alone. With some effort he pulled on his trousers and picked up his shoes. He left his underwear, socks and shirt. As he started to limp away, he smelled the fish and chips. Mike picked up the newspaper that the fish and chips were rolled in. Before he left for work that morning Zack had said,

"Mike, don't forget the fish and chips."

Gail saw him limping up the walkway and opened the door for him. She did not have the lights on, only one candle burned on the table. Zack started crying when he saw Mike. Gail went to work. She put blankets over the window so that she could switch on the electric lights. She needed to see Mike's injuries. They were both superficial, painful but not life threatening.

Sitting on the chair, Mike leaned over the table. Gail first washed the two wounds, actually three; the knife to his back had exited his side. The cut on his face ran from his temple to his ear. After she washed them in detol she was able to examine them closer." Mike, I think you need stitches. We cannot go out tonight. It would be like walking into a lion's den." She thought for a minute. "I can do the stitching. I have done it before but the scar will be more pronounced." Gail took out her circled upholstery needle and nylon fishing line.

While she sterilized them, Zack sat opposite Mike. He held out both his hands. "You can hold my hands as my mother sews. My dad used to." Mike looked into Zack's eyes, what had this boy witnessed? He and the rest of the children in Alexandra needed to be rescued, but how?

Mike spent a restless Saturday. Between his wounds, and nightmares he was very tired. He was used to waking early for the train and bus ride to work. On weekends he still woke at 4:00 A.M. This Sunday he lay for a while on the couch thinking, "Why not?" He walked into the bedroom that Gail and Zack shared. Zack had the blankets pulled over his head but Gail still had her arms around him. "Come on, sleepyheads, wake up. We're going out for the day. It's time you met my mother."

With her eyes still closed, Gail smiled and said, "I thought you'd never ask." The trains did not run on Sunday so they caught three different buses to get to Mike's office. When Mike opened the garage door, Gail's eyes widened.

Zack said, "Wow."

It was 9:00 A.M. when they pulled into Colleen's driveway; she was not home. "She always takes a long walk in the mornings," said Mike. "Let's wait at my house and pack a few more things in the car. Zack, there is a massive swing set in the backyard. You are welcome to play on it." First Gail and Zack walked through the house.

"You lived here," said Gail and her eyes misted over as she shook her head. While she and Mike put things in the car that during the week would be carried to their homes, Zack played in the fenced backyard. The fence was not for protection but for Marine's dog—right now it kept Zack hidden from any prying eyes. Colleen saw the car as she rounded the corner.

"Mike, Mike," she called excitedly as she ran from her house over to Mike's. She rushed through the front door as Mike rushed down the stairs. Mike swung her around as he hugged her. Only when she pulled back did she notice the stitches down the side of his face. "Oh Mike," and she started crying.

He pulled her close and whispered in her ear, "Please don't cry, please. I have brought Gail and Zack to meet you. She took care of me on Friday. I told her you were strong, so no tears, please."

Colleen looked up as Mike whispered to her. Gail was standing on the top stair looking down at her. Colleen held out her hand and Gail walked down slowly.

No words were needed. Colleen hugged Gail as openly and hard as she had Mike. Looking into Gail's eyes, she said, "There is no way I could possibly thank you for all you have done for my son."

"Believe me, Mrs. Miller; Mike has been a life saver for Zack and I."

"Please, Gail, call me Colleen." After a second she added, "Or Mom, whichever you're comfortable with. Where is Zack?"

The three of them watched Zack through the window for a few minutes. He was having so much fun on the swings. Mike went out to call him, Zack jumped off the swings right into Mike's arms. The two of them romped for a while before Mike said, "Come meet my mother."

Zack turned shy and half stood behind Mike and Gail. Colleen did not press the issue but said to no one in particular. "I have a puppy at my house. I need to feed and play with him."

Zack's eyes grew large and he came out from behind Gail's skirt. "I can help," he said.

Colleen smiled "Okay, Tell you what, while Mike locks up here, you and your mom come with me. You can feed and play with my puppy while your mom and I make some tea and biscuits. Do you like biscuits, Zack?"

"Oh yes, I love them. What's your dog's name?"

They were halfway down the driveway so Mike did not hear his mother answer. Zack was holding Colleens hand and looking up at her as she spoke. He quickly placed the last of the items in the car and locked up the house. As he rounded the corner to the backyard, he stopped and stared. Zack was rolling on the lawn laughing with the puppy, which was climbing over him. The puppy was a Rhodesian Ridgeback the color of wheat. His mother and Gail had just put a tray of tea and biscuits on the picnic table. Gail was laughing at something his mother had said. "This is the other side of the flipped coin," he thought to himself.

"I can not believe you got a dog," he said as he sat down.

"I needed a little company, Mike. Think about it, Moses gone, you are gone, Maureen in America and Jacob in Europe. It is very quiet around here.

"Catch the ball, Mambo," Zack was saying. Mike looked at Colleen with raised eyebrows. He knew the story of Mambo. "What's going on?"

"It's probably just my imagination but several times now when I have come home, I could swear someone had been in the house. You know how I like things in the same spot. Well, I think things have been moved."

"Col, until Jacob and Maureen come home, why don't you stay with Sheree?"

"No Mike, I don't want my life disrupted and I don't want to disrupt their lives. But now I want to hear what happened to you . . ."

Mike made light of it as he told his mother. "Your knife?" she questioned.

"Couldn't reach it, plus if I had opened the zipper on my belt, they would have found the hidden money. Don't worry, I'll figure something out."

While Gail and Colleen made lunch, Mike fixed a few things around the house that needed seeing to, and then did maintenance on his and his mother's cars. Zack and Mambo continued playing. Colleen and Gail got to know each other. Gail felt right at home with Mike's mom, so she felt free to ask.

"Colleen, do I understand correctly, you and Mike's father weren't really married?" Because Colleen didn't answer right away, Gail was mortified thinking she'd offended Colleen.

"Oh Colleen, please forgive me. I don't know what I was thinking of. I didn't mean . . ." But Colleen stopped her.

"Gail, it's okay, really, it's just, I went a hundred years back in time, a teenager running through the African veldt with Michael. I cannot believe so much time has passed and so much has happened, but yes, we weren't married. We planned on it when he was finished with university, but I was told he'd been killed in an accident." Gail came over and put her hand on Colleen's arm.

"The same thing happened to me. I wasn't married to Zack's father. He was killed in a hunting accident even before I knew I was expecting Zack."

"I'm so sorry Gail, but it sounds as though you married a good man later."

"Colleen that was my brother; we pretended to be married so we could have a house. We got away with it as we had the same names on our papers. I have never been married." Gail hesitated then continued. "But if I were to marry I would like it to be someone like Mike. He's not only very considerate and kind; he's good with children. Zack loves him." A sound made both women turn around. Mike was standing in the doorway with an embarrassed look on his face.

At 2:00 P.M., Mike said, "We should start heading back, the car must be locked up in the office garage then we need to catch the buses and we do not want to be out at dark." Colleen made them promise to come and spend Saturdays or Sundays or both days with her. Zack was excited at the idea of coming back and playing with Mambo.

Mike continued to learn tricks to fit in—to disappear, as Chaka said many times, "Learn to be a nobody." He bought a sun lamp and gradually his skin got darker. Coming back from work in the city he tried to look rumpled and unkempt. He even bought an old large brimmed hat to disguise his well-kept hair. Since that first run in with the *Tootsies,* Mike carried his small knife outside his belt. He knew it wasn't a killing knife but it may buy him a few seconds to escape.

You were really asking for trouble and would be singled out if you carried a weapon. Mike remembered seeing a movie where a rolled up magazine could hit as hard as a police baton and it was also a protection of sorts against a knife, plus it wasn't really a weapon, so he always carried a thick magazine under his arm, he was often teased by fellow bus riders. "You waste your money on magazines." Little did they know it was his weapon and his protection.

Life was made a little more tolerable when Sergeant DeKlerk, the police in charge of his arrest and continued verbal harassment, had to serve his six month army renewal term. So it came as a shock when their home was singled out during a 2:00 A.M. police raid of Alexandra. Normally the Indian and colored sections were bypassed, these early morning raids were concentrated on the black and shantytown sections of Alexandra. The point of these raids was to check for illegal residences; those poor souls without pass books.

Winter had turned very cold. On three consecutive days, Mike smuggled in eiderdowns for Zack, Gail and himself. Snuggled down in them at night, you could be very comfortable.

Their door came crashing in, and search lamps bright enough to blind you filled the room. Because of the bright light, Mike never saw the men but he could hear them clearly as they invaded his house. He heard Gail scream from the bedroom, but he was held down and the voice said, "Jan, he must be in the dog box; he's sleeping on the couch." They laughed, and then Jan answered from the bedroom.

"And she's a looker; shall we teach her a lesson for making him sleep on the couch?"

"No man, no time for that. I've got an eiderdown; you get the others and let's go."

"Wait, I want the cuckoo clock." Then, they and their bright searchlights were gone. The raid continued in the black section for several hours and they could hear screaming, running and fighting.

Mike was so stunned he could not move for a second. He heard Gail sobbing; jumping up he ran to the bedroom. She was unhurt but scared. She had backed herself into the corner of the room and was sitting hugging her knees and rocking herself. He swooped her up and put her on the bed. Grabbing the flimsy blanket he wrapped it around her shoulders. "Where's Zack, where's Zack?" He shouted. Zack came crawling out from under the bed. He had been trained that in such an emergency he was to roll out of bed and crawl into an empty cardboard box under the bed. Mike held him tight for a few minutes then put him under the blanket with his mother.

"Where are you going?" They shouted as he left the room.

"I've got to fix the door to stop the icy wind."

While Mike worked on the door hinge, Gail was at the stove, making coffee; she had the blanket wrapped around her, and was hopping from foot to foot in an effort to get warm. "Look at this Mike, the water in the pot has a sheet of ice on it." Not wanting to be alone in the bedroom, Zack burrowed into Mike's bedding on the couch.

The door back on its hinges stopped the icy wind. The coffee Gail made warmed their insides but they were still freezing. "Jump into bed, you two, it's back to newspapers to keep us warm." Covered with one thin blanket, Mike spread layers of newspaper over these two people he'd come to love. Over the newspaper he put the second blanket. Running back to the couch he tried to do the same with his blankets and newspapers.

After a few minutes he called out, "Are you warming up?"

Zack sobbed, "No, why did they take my eiderdown?"

"Curl up against your mother, body warmth will kick in soon."

Between chattering teeth, Zack kept saying, "I'm so cold, I'm so cold."

"Gail." Mike called.

"Yes," her voice quivered.

"A body on either side of him will warm him up quicker."

Without hesitation she said, "Come, and bring your blanket too." Mike laid his blankets on top of theirs and crawled in next to Zack. Gail was lying on her side next to the wall, a lot of newspapers between her and the wall, Zack on his side, squished against his mother. Then Mike on his side, against Zack. In no time, warmth spread through all of them. Zack said, through chattering teeth, "Mike, tell me about your boy Marnie."

Mike recounted Marine's letter to him. The farm was huge; Marnie had built a fort for himself and his dog Rex. Grandpa had taught him to ride a horse and he was quite a sharp shooter with his pellet gun.

"It sounds like heaven," said Zack. "I wish we could go there." Later his breathing told Mike he had fallen asleep. Now that Zack was comfortable and asleep, he turned his attention to Gail.

"You warmed up?"

"Yes, except for my feet, they're like ice blocks."

"Move them this way." Mike rubbed his feet over hers.

"Mike, that feels better." They kept their feet entwined, for warmth, they agreed. Lying facing one another, they looked into each other's eyes.

"Did I ever tell you, Gail, the first thing I noticed about you were your eyes? Not only the color—they are so black they're blue, but the almond shape. It gives you an oriental look." Mike allowed his one hand to move her hair from her face. He left it there cupping the back of her head. Their eyes smiled at each other. Then Gail dropped a bomb,

"Mike, how did they know we had eiderdowns and a cuckoo clock?"

CHAPTER 27

The next day was Saturday; they left early to spend the day with Colleen. She was really expecting them on Sunday but after last night they changed their plans. When the car pulled into the driveway, Colleen and Mambo ran out to meet them. Zack flew to Mambo while Colleen hugged Mike and Gail.

"What a nice surprise. Come on in, it's so cold."

"Wait Col, before we go into the house," Mike and Gail told her what happened last night.

Colleen was appalled. "They can't do that."

"Oh yes, they can. But Col, as Gail pointed out to me, how did they know we had eiderdowns and a cuckoo clock." Colleen stared at the two of them. Mike continued, "We have gone over and over our conversations last weekend when we visited you, we told you about our eiderdowns and clock, kind of laughed at how I got them past the *Tootsies*. Col, I think your house is bugged."

"What?"

"Remember you said you had a feeling someone had been in your house. That prompted you getting a dog."

"My God Mike, you may be right. Well, let's go and find them and destroy them."

"No Col, we will find them, but not destroy them. We don't want them to know we are onto them. From now on we must be very careful what we talk about. Let's always have background noise and write important things down while we talk about daily things. Okay, let's go in now. Do you have the radio on?" Colleen nodded. "Good, leave it on."

Colleen made hot chocolate for them all. They drank it sitting in front of the fireplace. Zack said between sipping his chocolate, "Why don't we have a fireplace like this, then I'll never be cold again." Then as an afterthought he said, eyes all lit up, "Colleen, you live here alone, can't we come live with you?"

"Now Zack," said Gail, "you know that is impossible, just enjoy your weekly visit."

"Since I was not expecting you today, I thought you were coming tomorrow, I have not baked a cake, so while Mike fixes some things in the house for me, and your mom and I bake, why don't you put on your coat and throw the ball for Mambo."

"Yaay" and off they ran. Mike wrote on their conversation pad. "Good thinking, I am going to search the house." So, Colleen and Gail spoke about recipes, movies, and books against the background of music and clattering pots and pans.

Mike moved from room to room and returning to the kitchen, he said, "Hmm, that cake smells good. Did you say you wanted me to adjust the running of your car?" Mike was nodding his head indicating he wanted them to say "yes." He pushed their conversation pad in front of them, and he had written.

One in your bedroom, under bedside table.

Two in the living room, one by lamp the other by phone.

One in fruit bowl, on dining room table.

One in kitchen, over your head on hanging rack with pots.

Colleen could not believe what she was reading. When Mike returned from the garage, he added to the list. One in garage by water heater, and there is also one in your car under the dashboard.

"What is going on?" thought Colleen as she watched Zack play with Mambo.

After lunch, Colleen announced, "It has warmed up a little and the sun is shinning. Let's take a walk down the hill. Mike, maybe you can bring Marine's old bike over to my house. We will let Zack ride down the hill, giving Mambo a good run." Once out of earshot range from the house, Colleen vented her anger. "Mike, what do you think they are up to? For the life of me, I can not see why they would want to bug the house."

"Col, Elizabeth is very cruel; she is probably not happy that her father left her mother. They now have to watch every penny they spend; Elizabeth may have to go to work. She is also mad that Marnie escaped her clutches. She has guessed he is with her father. So I believe the bugs are to find Marnie. If he's in South Africa, they will still go after him. Or maybe to see if my father shows up, so he can be arrested for living in a 'white area.' Remember Elizabeth knows everything. Then again, they could be looking for Moses."

Colleen stopped short, "Mike, oh Mike, what if we have said something. I can't remember what's been said about Moses or even if we have spoken about Moses over the last few weeks."

"From now on, we will be taking long walks. We can not talk about anything important inside the house or in your car."

They always had a hot shower at Colleen's before going home. It beat warming water and sitting in a small tub with your feet hanging over. That night as they got ready for bed Zack said, "Mike, are you going to sleep with us again, and then I'll be a toasty warm hot dog." Mike looked at Gail with raised eyebrows. She nodded 'yes.'

"Yahh," yelled Zack.

Those nights as they all lay entwined for warmth, Gail and Mike exchanged family stories. Gail loved the idea about the three cords. "I've noticed that colored wire on your belt, what a wonderful belief. Maybe that's why you're coping with this mess in your life. Not only do you pray for us at meal times, but I've seen you on your knees at night." Mike had taken to putting his arm under Gail's head. They were slowly falling in love.

Three things happened over the next month that made Mike decide they had to leave the country but he was not sure how. It was a Thursday late afternoon that Mike got a frantic call from Gail. "Zack did not come home from school. Mike, I don't know what to do. I have been to the school. No one remembers seeing him on the bus. Mike, I'm so scared. Can you come home?" She broke down crying.

"Gail, Gail, pull yourself together. Did you check the soccer field? Stop crying, I am on my way home. I will take the car so I don't waste time on the buses. Go and ask Mr. Nidoo if I can park it in one of his garages. When Mike explained his problem to his boss, he and Chaka were allowed to leave early. Mr. Nidoo owned the grocery store in Alexandra. He considered Mike and Gail his best customers so did not hesitate when Gail asked about the garage. Mike was just thanking Mr. Nidoo when Gail and Miriam ran up.

"We've searched all the open fields," Gail sobbed. Her eyes were beginning to swell from all the crying. Mike went to the compound police. They took their time filling in forms, and then appointed two officers to help with the search. By 9:00 P.M., the police called off the search. "The *Tootsies* must have got him; tomorrow we will look for his body." At that Gail collapsed. Mike led her home. While Miriam made something for them all to eat and drink, Mike tried to comfort Gail. Looking over her head at Chaka, he said, "I am going to leave. I don't know how yet, but this has gone too far. I am taking Gail and Zack with me. Think about it, Chaka, do you and Miriam want to go to Zambia."

After Chaka and Miriam left, Mike led Gail to bed and tucked her in. "Try to get some sleep," he said. Mike then tidied up and paced the floor. What could have happened to a seven year old boy? He must leave the country but how? They were watching him. Will Gail and Zack go with him? He was still pacing when Gail came out of the room with one of the blankets wrapped around her.

"Mike, come to bed. I need you to hold me." This was the first time they lay side by side without Zack between them. He held her tight; she clung to him. They were both so upset.

Slowly he became aware of how good she felt in his arms. They relaxed their desperate clinging but stayed close. Without taking their eyes off each other, Mike leaned forward and kissed her. Slowly she responded and kissed him back.

"Gail, did you mean what I heard you say to my mother, that you would like to marry a man like me?" Pulling back, she looked at him.

"With all my heart." Mike opened his mouth to say something but froze. He heard a car slowly pass the house and a heavy thumping sound.

They both jumped up and ran outside. Lying in the path leading to their front door was a bundle. Gail clasped her hands to her mouth and groaned, "No, no, oh God no." Mike picked up the bundle and rushed inside. It was a sack tied up with electrical tape. Mike hesitated but knew he had to unwrap it. Why wasn't he moving? Why wasn't he making a sound? Mike ripped the sack open. At first glance, he thought Zack was dead, but feeling his pulse he knew he was alive. Now Gail couldn't rip the tape off fast enough that covered his mouth, eyes and that tied his hands and feet together. She shook him.

"Zack, Zack, wake up, wake up." He opened his eyes and for a second did not know where he was but once he saw Gail and Mike, he started crying.

"What happened, Zack?"

"Mommy, Mommy, I'm not sure," he sobbed. "Someone pulled a sack over my head and put me in the boot of a car." Gail held him close. "Mommy, I'm sorry. I peed my pants. I kept shouting for them to let me go pee. They stopped the car but instead of letting me pee, they stuck a needle in my arm. When I woke, there was tape over my eyes and mouth and I couldn't move."

"Do you know who did this, Zack?"

"Nooo, why would someone do this?"

"Can you remember anything, voices, sounds?"

"No, except the car did smell funny, like the stuff my mom puts in melkos."

"Cinnamon," said Gail. The look in Mike's eyes stopped Gail. "What?"

"Anytime I was in a police car, it smelled of cinnamon. It's the air freshener they use."

"Mike, are you saying the police did this, but why?"

"Who knows?"

Zack was too upset to eat but Gail boiled water to wash him, he did smell of pee. The three of them crept back to bed. The drug was still working on Zack, he kept saying over and over again as he fell asleep "Mommy, Mommy." Mike positioned Zack next to the wall, Gail in the middle so he could hold her. She willingly melted into his arms.

She was trembling and said, "I was convinced he was dead, that I would never hear my son call me 'Mom' again. For a mother never to hear her child say 'Mommy' is a deep pain in the heart."

"Gail, I'm thinking this is ridiculous. I am going to Zambia, away from this apartheid crap. I love you and Zack; will you marry me and come with?"

"Mike, of course we'll come with you. I do love you each day more and more. But I can't marry you."

"What!"

"Because we're already married, silly."

Mike was quiet for a minute. "I had forgotten," he whispered then added, "It's not that cold anymore, think we could tuck Zack into the couch?" Zack never moved as they made a cozy bed for him on the couch.

The next morning Mike carefully slipped out of bed so as not to wake Gail. He met Chaka as they normally did for work. He told him about Zack's experience and that he wasn't going into work today. "We are going to drive out to my mother's. After last night's experience, I don't think I could concentrate on work, neither could Gail and of course, we have to rethink Zack's schooling. But Chaka, I wanted to tell you I am serious about Zambia. If you and Miriam want to come, you're welcome. I just don't know about the work situation."

"Thank you for thinking about us Mike. But Miriam and I will stay, I do have a good job, Miriam is almost finished with her teacher's course. Maybe later, but right now we need to stay. I've also been approached by the ANC to help; I think I will. But you three seem to be targeted, you need to leave, just be very careful and try and stay in touch."

Mike slipped back into bed and pulled Gail into his arms. She murmured against his chest, "Is it time to get up already."

"No, not yet." Mike scooted down so that he could kiss her neck. He loved to feel her pulse beating there and how it quickened as he ran his hands down her back. Later on as they curled up together he said, "Gail, can you take the day off and we won't send Zack to school. Let's drive out to my mother; we have some serious planning to do."

Colleen was outraged. "Is he okay?" She watched Zack and Mambo playing. They were sitting outside on the lawn. They didn't even trust the lawn furniture in case it was bugged. "Not to add to your worries, Mike, but I also had a police experience this week. On Wednesday when I returned from my walk, they were sitting waiting for me, inside the house, at the kitchen table."

"What," shouted Mike?

"And they had my mail, said they were delivering it to me, Mike, it had all been opened and of course, read."

"Anything from Moses?"

"No, thank goodness. There were letter from Jacob, Maureen, and my agent and of course, bills. They bug the house; they read my mail, what's next?"

The following week, Colleen found out what was next. The police again delivered her mail and handed her an official document.

"Mrs. Miller, you are under house arrest for the next 90 days."

"What! What's the reason," demanded Colleen.

"On suspicion of harboring, or corresponding, or knowing the whereabouts of a political criminal known as Moses the Deliverer, secondly, on suspicion of hiding or knowing the whereabouts of said, Marnie Zulewsky, son of Mike Zulewsky, thirdly, on suspicion of the Immortality Act. You have one colored child, and you may still be involved with his father. The fact that you refuse to give us his name means you're hiding his identity."

Colleen turned pale and had to reach for a chair. As her head cleared, the puzzle fell into place, Elizabeth, who else. It's time to turn the tables on her, thought Colleen.

"Are you saying the fact that my first husband was colored and even though we haven't lived together for many years, I am to be placed under house arrest for the Immorality Act?"

"Ja."

"How did you get all this information?"

"A well meaning concerned woman, Mrs. Elizabeth Cambell, alerted the police department."

'So she's taken back her maiden name.' thought Colleen.

"Sergeant, you really need to do your research on informers. Elizabeth Cambell is really Mrs. Zulewsky. She is married to the colored Mike Zulewsky, the mother of the colored child you seek, Marnie."

The police looked at each other in surprise. Two days later the newspaper headlines read:

TWO WOMEN PLACED UNDER HOUSE ARREST

Mrs. Cambell, and Mrs. Miller were placed under house
arrest on grounds of the Immortality Act instituted in 1940
The two women were found living in white neighborhoods
along with their half-breed children.

Trust the police not to get it 100% right, smiled Colleen. She did not want to use the phone to call Mike. She knew he would come as soon as he read the newspaper. Since they were always early for work, Mike and Chaka read the newspaper over an office cup of coffee.

Mike rushed right over. The police were parked across the driveway. Mike had to park on the street and sign a register allowing him to visit. He was also searched. As Mike hugged his mother, he moved them quickly to the kitchen island where they kept their conversation pad. He wrote, "We need to talk some about this house arrest, or they'll be suspicious. Then say, you don't like to walk alone anymore, will I walk with you." Colleen nodded.

After the obvious remarks and comments Mike said, "So what about visitors or domestic help like the weekly lawn moving?"

"This document lists what I am allowed," said Colleen.

1. In and outgoing mail must be checked.
2. Family members may visit but need to sign the register and agree to be searched.
3. Any persons living in the house at the time of arrest would be allowed to stay but no one may move in after the arrest.

"I have inquired, that includes Jacob, Maureen and the kids since they weren't here at the time of arrest. If it's okay with you Mike, when they return, could they rent your house across the street?"

"Of course," Mike continued searching for something he could use.

4. Groceries would be brought in by family members but checked by police.
5. If a doctor or dentist is needed, a family member may take you, accompanied by a female police officer.
6. Domestic help can still come and go. If needed they can stay in servants quarters behind garage.

That's what Mike was looking for.

Later, while out walking, Mike asked about Sheree, Gordon, and Charles reactions. "I have told them to be low keyed, not to give the police any reason to react to them, but at the same time to stay alert." Colleen added, "Mike, could you put an ad in the paper for Moses. Remember his code name is 'Basket Child.' Say something like, 'Contact through writing must be broken off. Pharo and army still searching for you.'" Colleen never gave up reading the paper looking for some message from Moses. Finally it appeared.

White Mama, Basket Child safe.
While here will visit tree house.
Plan on this vacation for a few months.

Colleen was relieved. Moses was alive and safe. The hint of 'tree house' told her he was in Zambia.

"Col, is there anything I can do for you? Are you okay? I mean really okay, you're looking thin."

"I'm fine, Mike, I have lost a little weight on purpose; even though I'm in my fifties, I want to keep fit."

"Now, I want to ask you something, you and I have a problem here. For many years you lived in America and Europe. Do you want to continue living here in South Africa under these conditions?"

"No, but I can't leave the house to travel. You are watched only because they don't want you to move into a white neighborhood again. Then there are Maureen and Jacob."

"What about your brothers and sister? Would it upset you to leave them?"

"Not really, we would visit. "I'm sure the policy in this land will change and we could come back, if not to stay, to visit."

"This is what I was thinking Col, we need to leave. How, I'm not sure yet. But you are under house arrest and you feel you need a dog for protection. I am banished to Alexandra having to live in terrible conditions, constantly on the run from *Tootsies*. I have seen them kill a man just for a few Rand. Without meaning to, I have involved Gail and Zack. Fortunately it hasn't affected Chaka and Miriam . . . yet. My son Marnie lives in another country. I haven't seen him in months." They walked on in silence for a while.

Then Colleen asked, "What can we do, Mike?"

"Well, I am sure Jacob and Maureen would move. They are really Americans, and have all their connections there. They are here because of you and you are here because of me. They can travel with no problem. You, me, Gail and Zack have no passports. Yours has been taken away; we just don't have any, and we have no travel papers. We won't be able to buy plane tickets to anywhere."

"Gail and Zack are willing to come with us?" Colleen asked in surprise.

"Oh Col, through all this mess, something wonderful has happened. What started out as a marriage of convenience and in name only has turned into a real marriage. I love Gail very much."

"I am so happy for you, Mike. She's a wonderful person. Of course, you do know you're not really married to Gail, you never divorced Elizabeth."

"Yes, I did, or rather she did. Remember when I first found out about my father, got mad at you and left for a few months. That's when she divorced me. I guess I forgot to tell you."

Colleen laughed, "And the police didn't check properly again. Good for them."

"Mom, after Zack's experience, we do not want him to go back to school. Gail can stop work and teach him; he's only in Standard One. But I can't leave them unprotected in Alexandra while I go to work. Since you are allowed to hire a domestic and they can stay in the servant's quarters, could you . . . would you consider . . . ?"

"Say no more, Mike; bring them as soon as possible. But I would feel strange them staying in the servants quarters. They can stay in the house."

"No Mom, the police are watching. Remember Gail has to look as though she is working for you. Believe you me, the servant's quarters with its own toilet and running water is wonderful compared to our house."

"Mike, why don't you stay too?"

"No, the police that kept an eye on me must see me around Alexandra. We don't want to make them suspicious. Things need to look normal."

The next day, a Saturday, Mike brought Gail and Zack to his mother's. Out of prying eyesight, Gail hugged Colleen. "Thank you, thank you so much."

While they were having lunch, there was a phone call from America. Jacob and Maureen would be flying in tomorrow. Mike agreed to pick them up from the airport and on the way home, break the news of the past few months.

Jacob and Maureen knew about Moses. Now they were told about Mike, his experience of living in Alexandra, Marnie in Zambia, his marriage to Gail and his stepson's experience. Their mother's house arrest and accusations against her; Mike also warned them about the bugs so to be very careful as to what was said around the house. He told them they were trying to plan an escape. What were their thoughts on it, but never ever speak about it, in either home.

"By the way, you will be living in my house, when I drop you off Jacob, you and I need to go through it with a fine tooth comb in case they have decided to bug it."

It was a bittersweet reunion; so much had happened on both sides, they had so much news to exchange. Part of the house arrest law was no visitors after 8:00 P.M. As they hugged good night, Maureen clung to Colleen.

"I feel as though our world has fallen apart these past months. I will come over early while the children are still sleeping, we have a lot to talk about and plans to make."

CHAPTER 28

As the police truck rolled over and over down the hill, Moses thought he was going to die. There were no seat belts in the back of the ambulance. Bodies were being thrown against him. He did not know how long he had been unconscious but when he tried to move he couldn't. He was pinned under a very fat police officer. He felt someone beside him move, a voice was calling, "Moses, Moses, are you okay?" It was Sam.

"Get me out from under this fat white pig."

Moses, Sam and Boma were the only ones to survive the accident. Moses and Sam were badly beaten from police brutality. They also had serious gunshot wounds that were infected. While Moses' was bad enough, one in his thigh and one in his shoulder, Sam's was in the stomach. Boma had a broken arm that needed the cast removed. They were on their way to the hospital when the accident occurred. Working fast, they found the keys and unlocked their leg and arm chains. Now they collected the guns and ammunition plus any other weapons found. Taking the guards belts, they tied or hooked weapons on them. It was winter and cold, so they stripped the two guards and driver of their coats. As a last thought, Moses put a two-way radio in his pocket. It would be handy to listen in on the police conversation, knowing if they were being followed.

The accident and moving around had opened Sam's wound. He was in a lot of pain; the yellow and green puss that oozed out had a sickly sweet-sour smell. "We must keep moving, Sam. We must make it to the river before the dogs come." With Sam hanging between the two of them, Moses and Boma supported him. Sometimes his feet moved but mostly they dragged.

Even though it was cold, they plunged into the water. A dead tree trunk floated by. Grabbing it, Moses pulled Sam on it. They walked waist deep up river until dark. The two-way radio crackled again and again with positions of their hunt. As Moses suspected, the police were concentrating their search east on the N4 to Mozambique. They were actually heading north to Blyde River Dam. Cold water from the river had helped Moses' thigh but his shoulder still hurt like hell. After finding a protective rocky area, a small fire was made for warmth, and to dry themselves out, they had the guard's sandwiches from the ambulance to eat. Moses chipped off Boma's arm cast, so he could move easier.

"Moses, you need to check my bullet wound. It's killing me," groaned Sam.

Moses hated the thought of getting too close to that smell. Sam lay back while Moses lifted his shirt. After a few minutes he said, "Sam, it's bad. I think the bullet has pierced your bowel. Besides the infection that's oozing out, there is fecal matter. That means fecal matter is loose inside you. I cannot dig inside for the bullet. I will just do more damage than good. Damn the police to hell, they should have seen to it last week and not waited so long before sending us to the furthest hospital they have."

They were quiet for a while. "Moses, not to worry; I know I am dying. What I am happy about is it's out here in the country I love. Not in their prison or at their hand." After sipping some water, Sam continued, "Moses, let us make a plan. In my death, let me take some of those police bastards with me." Moses had to turn away to hide the pain in his eyes.

"They are not following us Sam," he mumbled.

"This I know old friend, but they will, they will. By tomorrow they will realize their mistake going east. The dogs will point them north." Moses had to agree with Sam. They will come; it's only a matter of time. Their only hope was to get into the canyon. There were many good places to hide.

"Do you plan on using the old animal trail?"

"Yes, I thought I might. Do you have a better idea?"

"No, the animal trail is good. As you know, there are a lot of spots looking back down the trail. The police will be at a disadvantage following us. This is what we need to do." Sam proceeded to lay out his plan for Moses, and Boma.

Way before sunrise, Moses and Boma made a sled for dragging Sam up the side of the mountain. It was rough going, a few times Sam passed out in pain, but he never once complained. Moses and Boma tied a cloth across their noses; the smell of decay coming from Sam was overwhelming. Halfway up, they reached the chosen spot.

"Yes, this is the spot I was thinking of. Now make me comfortable." Sam knew exactly what he wanted to do and organized Moses and Boma in preparing him. Some braches were cut to shade him as he sat between the two boulders. He made Moses tie his wound up very tight, allowing him to move with a little more ease. A bottle of water, one of the guns and ammunition was laid by his side. Turning to them he said, "Go, you must go now. It won't be long before they will come."

"Sam, I can not leave you. Let Boma and me drag you . . ." Sam did not let him finish.

"Don't go weak on me Moses. You will disappoint an old friend on his deathbed and deny him the honor of killing a few of them. You know the rule of war is to leave the mortally wounded behind." Before Moses could say anything he softened his voice and said, "Go friend, and avenge me by finding the traitor." They now heard the dogs in the distance. As Moses and Boma hurried away, he shouted after them.

Umlomto Wa Bantu, (Mouth of the Black Nation). It echoed through the hills.

Moses and Boma had to hurry. They were not climbing up and away; they were running parallel to the path the police would be coming on. It led them to a ravine. The plan was to act as monkeys and at the ravine jump from tree to tree. Not only would it put them on a different mountain, but also since they were crossing the ravine up in the treetops, the dogs would lose their scent.

They had just reached the ravine when they faintly heard the first shot. As the police climbed the singlewide path, Sam was going to pick them off. This would give Moses and Boma at least a two-hour head start and put them on that different mountain. Sam's tribal people lived on the other side of the mountain. His people would hide Moses and Boma. For the police to follow, if they figured it out, going down one mountain, crossing the ravine, then climbing the other mountain would give them at least a twenty-four hour head start. Shots two and three followed in quick succession.

Looking down the ravine, Boma held back. "That's too dangerous, look at all those rocks below."

"Suit yourself," said Moses. "I have no intension of dying in a prison. I am going to jump." Moses walked back to get a run on his jump. As he passed Boma, he grabbed his arm, forcing him to jump with him. They fell downwards a few feet before grabbing a branch, moving to the other side of the tree, they jumped again. Eight trees got them across the ravine. Their last jump brought them to the mountain. As they climbed down the tree, Boma yelled at Moses.

"Why did you do that? You could have killed us."

"I wasn't going to leave you there for the police to question. I am sure you would have told them where I was headed and about Sam's tribal people.

Before moving on, Moses knelt in silent prayer. By now his friend Sam must be dead; he was saving his last bullet for himself. Moses' leg was bleeding a little but actually felt better. Maybe the blood had washed out any infection but his shoulder was still very painful. As he moved his head he would get a whiff of something rotten. Jumping from tree to tree had pulled his wound wide open. He had to reach Sam's tribal village, and he had to dig out whatever was inside his shoulder.

By the time they reached the village, Moses was shivering and sweating. He knew his temperature was high. As soon as the elder of the village heard Sam sent them and they used the password, they were taking into hiding. Moses passed out as they helped him into a hut. When he came to, he was lying naked on a reed mat next to a fire. The wound on his thigh was bound but not his shoulder. The girl in tribal dress kneeling at the fire said in perfect English.

"*Nkosi*, I've treated your leg wound and the burns on your face. I have also sewn the deep cut on your head. The bruises and smaller wounds will take care of themselves. I am afraid your shoulder presents a problem for me. I do not know how to help you."

Moses thought he was delirious, a beautiful black girl in tribal dress a hundred or so miles from the nearest town, speaking perfect English. He tried to sit up but fell back. Through cracked lips he said, "Your name, please."

"My tribal name is Swana, my English name is Susan."

"Swana, my adopted mother removed the bullet from my shoulder, under sterile conditions, and she disinfected it. But, I believe a piece of cloth from my shirt must be stuck inside, and is—you can smell—rotting."

"How do I help you, *Nkosi?*"

"My knife?" he said questioning.

"With all your other equipment."

"Bring it here please, Swana."

This was Moses' prized possession, a survival knife he'd bought in a specialty store in Johannesburg. He unscrewed the handle. There were many small emergency instruments inside. Moses removed a long handled tweezers, a stainless steel rod, a needle and nylon thread, a small bottle of disinfectant.

"This is what you must do Swana, boil water and lay the needle, thread and tweezers in there until you are ready to use them. Put the blade of my knife and the steel rod in the fire. When you use them they must be white hot." Swana laid them in the fire and put the water on to boil. Moses continued, "I hope you have a strong stomach." She nodded.

"First, you need to squeeze as hard as you can to remove the infection, and then use the white hot knife to cut a cross over the bullet hole. That will allow you to pull the flesh back a little. Then, use the tweezers and find the damn problem. Do not stop looking until you find it. With that removed, pours half this disinfectant in the hole. Next take the white-hot steel rod and push it in as deep as it will go. You will smell, and hear flesh burn, leave it in for a few minutes. When you pull it out, put some more disinfectant in. Then you can sew up the hole." Moses had to rest a while, and then added.

"Look at me Swana; do you think you can do it?"

"Yes, but you know it will be painful, *Nkosi.*"

"For that reason you need to bring in some men of the village. They need to stake me out and tie me down." As Moses was being tied down, he looked into Swana's eyes. "Swana remember, rather a moment of physical pain than the pain of a lost dream."

It was several days before Moses woke from his ordeal. He was in pain and very hot, but he did not smell that dreaded smell. As he tried to move, he noticed he was still tied down. Out of nowhere she came and knelt next to him. Pointing to the ropes she said, "You were very restless. I was afraid you'd do damage." She moved to his four quarters and cut him loose. "You were right *Nkosi;* there was a piece of cloth deep into the hole. With it now removed, you will get well."

"Swana, I am very thirsty."

She had prepared a bed for him away from the fire. After drinking, he pulled up the blanket and slept peacefully.

Several days later sitting under a tree, breathing the cold mountain air, Moses was listening to Boma telling young men about their capture and their escape, always Boma was a hero. Moses smiled as he leaned back against the tree but then his smile froze on his lips. Boma was talking about him saying, "Yes, he is a hero, those burns on his face they are from a grenade in the petrol tank of his escape kombi. Yes, even his wife and son were shot as they waited for him; right between their eyes." Moses sat up slowly and stared at Boma. How did Boma know that? Moses had told no one, not even Sam because he couldn't bear to talk about it.

Something Moses had noticed before, but dismissed. Why was Boma without the injuries other prisoners had? Yes, he had a broken arm, but no signs of being beaten. Moses felt a rage start in the pit of his stomach. Here was the informer. Here was the spy. Here was the man responsible for his wife and son's death, his friends' deaths. His best friend Sam died a painful death while saving them. Here is the man that caused him so much physical and emotional pain. Moses did not believe in acting while angry so he waited and watched.

As soon as his shoulder allowed him, Moses started to exercise. He needed to get full mobility back. A homemade boxing bag was used daily, and gradually his shoulder returned too normal. The ugly scar he considered a badge for the cause. One day Moses cut his daily run short. He had spotted a herd of kudu. He needed to return to the village for his gun and Boma. Shooting two or three of them would help feed the village.

Approaching the hut from the back, Moses heard the two-way radio crackle and Boma's voice say, "Sorry Sir, I don't know the exact location. I just know we are close to the Blyde River Dam."

The voice on the other side of the transmitter said, "That's a hell of a lot of territory *Kaffier.*" Before Boma could say anything else, Moses silently slipped into the hut and took the radio out of Boma's hand. He said nothing, just stared at Boma, who was now showing fear, beads of perspiration appeared on his upper lip. Moses picked up his gun and a set of police handcuffs they had taken during their escape.

"We are going hunting for kudu." Grabbing Boma's arm, he half pulled and half dragged him for the next two miles. All the time Boma was begging and pleading for mercy. The sight of Lulu and his son were still fresh in Moses' mind.

Reaching the herd of kudu, Moses stood Boma against a tree, stretching his arms back and around the tree; he handcuffed him there. Without a word, Moses positioned himself and shot three kudu. He dragged them over to the tree and started working on his plan still not talking to the pleading Boma. First, he made a sled to drag—like they had with Sam, and then he positioned two of the kudu on the sled. He planned on dragging it back to the village. The third kudu Moses dragged close to the tree Boma was cuffed to. He slit open the belly, hot steaming entrails slipped out along with a potent smell. Pushing his hand deep into the belly, Moses pulled out a handful and walked toward Boma, dropping some as he walked, making a bloody trail from kudu to Boma.

Moses sat looking at Boma and finally he spoke. "I am not going to ask you why?" Moses started to pace in front of Boma. "You would probably lie to me anyway. Your actions as an informer halted us for a minute in time, like ants we will just keep going ahead with our plan. You are responsible for many deaths—but any revolution, any cause, any war; the men involved know they may die; but not an innocent woman and child. Your actions resulted in them being used as bait." Moses had to take a deep breath. "You are now being used as bait." Walking back to the sled, Moses picked up the end, ready to start back to the village. Taking a last look at Boma, he said, "An informer is a loathsome creature, he deserves to die by other loathsome creatures. Where there are kudu, you will find lions, where there are lions, you'll find hyenas." Waving his hand over the scene of the cut open kudu, its entrails leading to Boma, "I have invited these creatures to eat at your feet."

"Nooo, nooo, please Moses, please."

"Your life for my wife and son." Moses started his long walk back to the village. Before reaching it, he heard the faint roar of lions.

Moses explained to the village why he was leaving; he was a danger to them. Police may come around on routine search. Make sure there are no signs left of our being here." Explaining about Boma, he said, "There will be handcuffs lying at the base of the tree, bury them deep."

Swana asked, "Where will you go?"

"This I cannot tell you."

"Maybe we will meet again one day, *Nkosi.*"

Moses crossed Venda into Zimbabwe then into Zambia. A contact they had there, told him about training camps that not only taught you to use the latest weapons, but also old tried and proven survival techniques.

The first thing Moses did was to send a message to Colleen via the newspaper. Without saying where he was, Moses knew Colleen would know he was in Zambia.

> *"White mama, Basket Child Fine.*
> *While here will visit the tree house."*

His contact, Mr. Jamerson welcomed him with open arms. They knew about his arrest and escape, that he and Sam had fatal wounds. "We grieve for Sam," he said, "but we are happy you made it alive. The last time we saw each other Moses; you were not interested in going through our training camps. What changed your mind?"

"Maybe, if I had this training before, I might have been more aware of an informer in our midst or made sure my wife and son were not so exposed. I want to be the best I can be. I believe spending a few weeks in your camps will help."

The camp Moses was sent to was on the border of Zambia and the Congo, "This site was established many years ago by a group called 'Zebra Run.' They dug this well, they built those lookout towers, and something that has come in very handy; they chopped down this huge anthill and made a platform. Don't know what they used it for, but we use it for our verbal classes."

Moses did not hear another word Dr. Jamerson said. As he got older, he had asked Colleen about his parents and that fateful day. Now it was if he was seeing her stories come alive. He broke out in goose bumps and his hair stood on end. He walked past Dr. Jamerson and climbed the steps of the anthill. He knew he was standing on the spot where his parents were massacred. He knew somewhere down there among those brick huts there used to be a grass hut where his mother hid him in a basket saving his life. He knew this was where Colleen, his white mother worked out her pain. This is where he would work out his pain. Moses kept things to himself. He never told Dr. Jamerson what this campsite meant to him.

The training was divided into two types of lessons. One, sharpening your mental and verbal skills; the other, was fieldwork, sharpening your physical skills. Some did not understand the need of mental and verbal skills until they listened to the speaker. He asked the question, "What is the best weapon we have?" Of course, hands shot up and some of the answers were guns, knives, grenades, etc.

"Those are good weapons and necessary sometimes. You will receive training on the best way to use them. But words, money, power, influence are also weapons," he continued. "It's useful to know not only a man's strength but also his weakness. Knowing his weakness can act like a leash and hold him back, or it can act like a lever and move him to act. So how do you get to know a man? How do you get into his mind? You learn his language. We are going to learn to read, and speak English and Afrikaans."

There was a hush before the murmurs started, someone shouted, "Why don't we just shoot all the whites, then we don't have to learn their language." A roar of laughter followed. The speaker held up his hand. "The people in Africa are mostly black and white, like a zebra, right?" Everyone agreed. "Now if you shot a zebra in all his white stripes, will the black stripes continue living?" There was silence. "Of course not, the whole zebra dies. So it is, my brothers, kill all the whites and you'll end up killing the blacks. We need each other. We are also going to learn history—we will learn from their mistakes and not repeat them."

Another voice shouted, "How can history help us, that's old outdated stuff, we have new, different, and unique problems." For a while the speaker was quiet, thinking of a good answer.

"Not so new, not so different, not so unique. I won't teach history if you can answer this question for me. Why is giving different tribes their own homeland not working?" No one could come up with a good if not right reason. No one knew if this had ever happened before.

"The answer is this, learned from history. Europe, hundreds of years ago, was divided into little homelands. The difference, the reason they succeeded, is that these homelands would trade and cooperate with each other. Our homelands while often the worst sections are not given or allowed the investments needed. Even private sector white industrialists are forbidden to invest in homelands. With no one putting money into the homelands, how can they generate income, how can they grow?" They now saw the need for history to be taught.

Then came the physical training. They were introduced and trained in the latest guns, explosives, and taught how to read maps and how to plan battles. This course also taught them how to survive while being hunted in the bush, jungle, or even cities. "Remember, guns do run out of ammunition, explosives can fail or go off at the wrong time. Maps can be lost." Waving his hand over all the equipment a soldier carries, the teacher said, "This can be too heavy to wear or carry if you need speed. Out there your prized possession should be your knife. It should always be strapped to your body. Your knife can be used to make other weapons."

They were then taken into the bush with only their knives and shown how to make sharp spears, how to make traps, how to immobilize a man without killing him or how to kill a man quickly and silently with only your hands. They learned how to camouflage themselves with whatever was handy. "Lastly, if you are being tracked by dogs, don't try and outrun them, you won't succeed, face them and kill them."

It had been many months since Moses left South Africa. He was eager to return home. He had a renewed vigor and felt better equipped to help his people and country. The picture that was forever in his mind, of his wife and son moved him forward. With no family, and no home, it would be easier for him to travel around the country. He wanted to see Colleen before reporting to the ANC headquarters. He couldn't wait to tell her where he'd spent the last few months.

CHAPTER 29

Something was very wrong. Moses had spent five days watching Colleen's house. Why were the police there twenty-four hours? She must be under house arrest. Why? Was he responsible somehow? He did not approach Colleen's sister or brothers; they may turn him in; and Mike, why wasn't he living in his house? Why were Jacob and Maureen living there? Moses took note of everyone's comings and goings. He decided the next time Mike visited; he would wait alongside the road.

Mike slammed on the brakes when he saw Moses standing in the road. Leaning over he opened the door. "Get in, get in. I am so glad to see you. Don't go to Col's . . ." Mike never finished.

"I know, house arrest. I have been watching the house for five days now. Mike, what happened? And why aren't you living in your house?"

"Let's ride and I will tell you everything that's happened. You are not going to believe this."

After talking for an hour, Moses said, "You are right, I can't believe this. The only good thing is Elizabeth got what was coming to her. Sorry Mike, I know she was your wife."

"No, I agree," said Mike.

"Talking about your wife and son . . . Mike, they killed my wife and son."

"Oh, no," and Mike dropped his head onto the steering wheel. They sat in silence for a while.

Moses broke the silence, "Mike, how can I get to Colleen? I must speak to her."

"I don't think that's possible. Everyone has to sign a register . . . wait a minute, she walks every day." Moses interrupted, "But the police walk with her."

"Yes, but not all the way. You know that stretch of road that first goes down a long hill, then climbs steeply." Moses nodded. "Well, the police don't like that steep climb. He sits and waits for her at the bottom of the hill. The view is so beautiful that she usually sits on the wall for about ten minutes before starting back. Remember there is a brick wall running parallel with the road. Now, if you were waiting behind that wall as she sat to admire the view, you two can talk and the police would not see you."

"Good, I notice she goes about 4:00 every day. Tell her I will be waiting for her today." As Mike dropped Moses off he said, "Where are you staying?"

"Here, there, everywhere, as you know I don't have a home in Soweto anymore."

"Come crash at my place. We must talk. Pick you up at the end of the road at 5:00."

Mike's face could not hide the good news he had for Colleen. She had been worried about Moses. As soon as he said hello to Colleen, Gail and Zack, he wrote on the pad for Gail. "You and Zack, keep the chatter going. I am taking Col to the bathroom." The bathroom was the only safe place to talk. As soon as he shut the door, Mike said, "Moses is here."

"What . . . where? Is he okay? Did you warn him to stay away?"

"Calm down, calm down, he has been watching the house for days. He realized you are under house arrest. I filled him in on all that has happened over the past few months and he told me his news. Col, the police shot and killed his wife and son."

Colleen sat very still; the only movement was her lips quivering. "I never got to meet them," she said softly.

Mike told her how Moses was going to wait behind the wall so they could speak. "Remember you must act naturally, don't do anything out of the norm, sit slightly sideways so the police can not see you talk."

Normally, Colleen hated when it was time for her family to leave. But today time seemed to drag waiting for 4:00. That was when her afternoon visitors left and she would go walking. For Mike, the time flew. Now he was not only visiting his mother but it was also the only time he had with Gail and Zack. They had to be careful not to be overheard or seen together. They did not want the police to suspect Gail was his wife and not the maid. But between Jacob, Maureen and her twins, Zack and the dog, there was enough noise to cover anything Mike and Gail would let slip.

Colleen had to hold herself back and walk her normal speed. At the top of the hill she stood for a minute, and then walked over to the wall. She heard a rustling of leaves as Moses moved into position under where she sat. After the greeting and making sure everyone was okay, Moses said, "I must ask, is this house arrest anything to do with me?"

"No, no, well not completely, it is also because of Mike and Marnie. It's an unbelievable mess, Moses." Then sounding like an angry mother, she said, "You just make sure you never get caught again." Moses then told her where he had done his training, and that he actually stood on the chopped down anthill Colleen had told him about. The spot his parents were killed.

'And the spot Shawn was killed,' she thought. Colleen found she was very tearful as they spoke. The last few months were beginning to take its toll of her. As she got ready to walk back, Moses said, "I am going home with Mike. After making plans tonight I will be back here tomorrow."

Moses was waiting for Mike at the prearranged spot. They were both very quiet the first few miles. "Moses," said Mike. "I need to apologize to you. I never really understood what was happening around me. I was among the privileged. Since I was not affected, I never really saw, I was looking but not seeing. If I had maybe I could have helped you more, maybe I could . . ."

Moses never let him finish. "Mike, don't worry about the past. What is your plan for the future? Colleen said you wanted to make a run for Zambia, you and who? How are you going to do it?"

"I don't know. I was going to ask for some suggestions. You might have some ideas." Because of all the emergencies they had lately, Mike had permanently rented the garage from Mr. Nidoo. He needed to have his car close. They locked up the garage and walked the three blocks to Mike's house.

As Mike unlocked the front door, a colored teenage boy hobbled from around the corner. Moses pulled out his knife looking around, but the boy was alone and hurt. He was clutching his arm to his side and blood was running down his pants leg and pooled at his feet.

"Good Sir, I have been waiting for you to come home. Please allow me to talk with you."

Mike pushed the door open and helped the young boy in. "Let me take care of your wound."

"No, I don't have much time, please, just a little water." He only took a sip then turned to Mike. "I know the kind of man you are." Mike looked puzzled. "From Zack, at school, he would say what a wonderful new father he got, he also told us you must be rich because you lived with the whites and you have a house—out there. I have also seen your car, and noticed you have taken Zack and his mother away to protect them from life in Alexandra."

Moses was standing watch at the door. This was a strange situation. Mike had seen the young boy's wound and knew he was dying. Kneeling next to him, he said, "Let me take you to the hospital, a knife stab like this needs a doctor."

"No, you don't understand Sir. I don't mind dying. It will get me away from this. At last I will have peace." When he stopped coughing he said, "I don't want help for myself, but can you see it in your heart to help my brother. He is only five years old, and once I die tonight, he will be alone." The teenager put his head on the table for a few minutes, and whispered, "You cannot be five years old and be alone in Alexandra."

Mike lifted his head and asked, "Where is your brother; why are you and he alone?"

"Three years ago my father was taken to prison because his pass was out of order. It was not long after that we were told by the police that he had died. Six months ago, the *Tootsies* attacked my mother. I tried to nurse her as well as I could but she died that night. My brother Daniel and I were thrown out of the house because of not being a family and not paying rent. The authorities said they would try and fine a home for us. They didn't"

"How have you managed since then?" asked Mike.

"Not very well Sir, not very well," he gave a sad sign. "The garbage dumpster behind the store near your garage is both our home and food source." The teenager was quiet for some time just staring, straight ahead. It was as though he willed himself to come back from the threshold.

"That's where Daniel . . ."

The nameless teenager laid his head on the table and breathed his last breath. Moses and Mike stared at each other for the longest time. Then Mike brought his fist down on the table so hard, the boy's head jumped.

"I am going to find Daniel," said Mike.

"Wait, I don't want to sound heartless but what about this boy's body. You don't want Daniel to see it, and you do not want to get involved with a dead body and the police." Mike looked like a lost dog. Moses continued, "Let's take him home. While you take Daniel out of the dumpster from one side, I will put his brother in from the opposite side." Mike wrapped the wasted body of the teenager in a blanket. He was so angry, so sad that anyone had to endure such tragedy, especially a child.

"I promise you, young man, whatever is in my power, I will use to make your brother's life better."

Mike lifted the dumpster lid and called, "Daniel." No sound or movement, he called again, "Daniel." Still nothing. "Daniel, your brother came to the house and asked me to take care of you." Still no sound, Mike added, "He said you knew my son Zack." Now there was a sound and movement. Daniel had burrowed deep into the garbage for safety and to keep warm. Mike groaned when he saw the boy. He was so thin and dirty. His eyes were too big for his face; they were filled with tears, fear and hunger. Mike lifted him out of the dumpster while Moses put his brother in on the opposite side.

Mike broke a few slices of bread in a bowl, sprinkled it with sugar and poured heated milk over it. Daniel wolfed it down and used his finger to pick up any milk left in the bowl. He never asked for more but looked pleadingly at Mike.

"Daniel, we don't want to make your tummy sick with too much at one time. You are going to have a bath and be put to bed. When you wake up, you can have more." Daniel had not spoken yet but looking around he asked, "My brother?" Before Mike could say anything he continued, "Has he joined my mother?" Mike nodded. "Will I join them too?"

"Not yet Daniel, not yet, not for many years if I can help it." Daniel was asleep sucking his thumb before Mike left the room. While Mike saw to Daniel, Moses had made supper for them and boiled water so he could take a bath. The five days of watching Colleen's house and sleeping in the bushes made him feel as unkempt as Daniel looked. They ate in silence.

After Moses bathed his body in the washtub, he took a cup of coffee, sat at the table and said, "What's your plan, Mike, and how can I help?"

"I don't have a plan, Moses, only that I know we must leave here. We will need advice and help from you."

"How many people are you talking about?"

Mike thought a while. "Well, we know Maureen and the children are flying back to America. Jacob is going to stay to complete his book on the Europe castles. Then he is planning on South African research so he will not be coming. It's Colleen, Gail, the two boys and myself, five of us with no passports, no travel papers."

"Well, let's get to work Mike."

Moses looked at Mike and said, "You, Gail, and the two boys, will not be missed or chased by the police; it is just that you do not have travel documents. Colleen, on the other hand, will be hunted down. Her house arrest has just been extended for another 90 days. We know that can continue indefinitely. While she did own a passport and necessary papers, they are being held by the police." Moses paused then added, "Money for you and Colleen should be no trouble, but liquidating it may be."

Mike checked on Daniel before he continued. "For now, Colleen and I don't want to sell our homes; we are hoping if the government changes hands and apartheid is done away with, we will be able to return. Since I have been exposed and moved to Alexandra, I have not deposited my wages. So I have a fair amount of cash." Taking out a sheet of paper, Mike worked out the amount he had in a safe hiding place. Moses nodded his approval. "We may have to pay some bribe money along the way and we will need some guns."

Mike continued, "Mom's book deals have always come through an American publisher. Her money is deposited in an American bank."

"So financially you are both fine. Now, where do you want to go? You cannot fly anywhere—no papers. So we have to cross a border into one of the African states."

"That will be Zambia. My son Marnie is living there with his grandfather Peter, who has opened his home to us. Zambia should be a safe place for us. Once there, we can decide if any other move is necessary."

Moses opened the map. "They will expect us to head one of three ways. Mmabatho and cross into Botswana or Moamba crossing into Mozambique or Messina to cross into Zimbabwe. But we will fool them and stay in South Africa for a month or so until the search quiets down. Then we will cross the border. Daniel was whimpering, so Mike went to comfort him. When he fell back to sleep, Mike joined Moses again.

"This is what I thought," said Moses. "We will take your car and drive the 400 or so kilometers to Nelspruit, where we will get out and continue on foot. A man that will be traveling with us will drive the car down to Transkei and abandon it in some back farm road to eventually become a chicken roost. Of course, you know that's the end of your car." Mike nodded his okay.

"We are walking—where to?"

"One of the most beautiful spots in Africa; I know the area very well. There are some villages there that will hide us if necessary. Then, after a safe time we will make our way into Zimbabwe, then cross into Zambia. At that point, I need to return to Africa and help save the black and white races from each other." Moses grinned at that joke.

"That sounds good. But how do we get everyone in the car especially my mother, and drive past the police that are always outside her house?"

"Here's what we'll do."

Moses laid out the plan. "The five days I spent watching Colleen's house, I noticed that when visitors left at 8:00 PM, she sat at her desk writing until about 10:00. The police can see her silhouette against the light. Gail and Zack are down in the servant's quarters. The only sounds are the radio and the dog." Mike nodded.

"We need to make a 'Colleen dummy' to sit in her chair so the police think it is her. This dummy needs to sit on a battery cushion so it moves once in a while. We will also need an electronic timing device to switch lights on and off, switch the radio and television on and off. Arrangements need to be made for the two houses and Colleen's car, maybe handed over to Sheree or her brothers. Not Jacob, because he travels a lot; and not Maureen since she's going back to America. By the way, arrange for Maureen to join Colleen on one of her walks. I would like to talk to her."

After writing a few things down, Moses continued. "The day before our planned escape, Colleen will ask you to take Mambo to the vet the next day. So the police won't be suspicious when you leave with Mambo. Since you can't talk freely at Colleen's or your old house, you need to have a family get together at Sheree's explaining what's going to happen, handing over signed papers etc. Now, there's not much the five of you can pack because of space in the car and later you will have to carry it. I suggest you make it backpacks. Wear durable clothes and only pack one change. You need to understand you will be leaving everything behind. You may want to leave instructions for Sheree to crate and store your things in case you come back. While you start on this, I need to check in with the ANC."

Colleen and Gail were sitting on the swing in the back yard overlooking the valley, which was very misty today. Zack was busy playing with Mambo. They did not hear Mike pull into the driveway or walk across the lawn to them. So Colleen and Gail were surprised when he stepped out in front of them and knelt down. Sitting on his shoulder was a painfully thin little boy. He had on one of Mike's caps that fell over his eyes and ears. Every now and then he had to lift it up. Mike took one of his mother's hands and one of his wife's hands.

"This is Daniel, who not only needs a home and protection. He needs someone to love him. Do we have enough room in our hearts to take him into our family?" Before either woman could answer, Daniel spotted Zack.

"Zack, Zack," he called and ran down to join him. Daniel threw his arms around Zack's neck. The two boys went down with Mambo on top of them.

Mike told them Daniel's story. Both Colleen and Gail wept as they heard how Daniel and his family had lived. Gail accepted him saying, "We now have three sons. Let's hope the next child is a girl," and she patted her belly while smiling. Mike got a comical look on his face, and as always raised his one eyebrow. Watching the two boys play, they heard Daniel say to Zack.

"I'm going to be your brother."

Zack answered him saying, "Cool, did you know we also have an older brother named Marnie?"

Mike made the arrangements for Maureen to walk with her mother. While taking the rest on the wall, Moses spoke to her.

"Maureen, since you and Jacob grew up in America and have only been out here a few years, you may not have formed an opinion on the South African policy of apartheid. But I would like to ask you what you feel, especially now that your mother and brother have felt the sting?"

"I'm outraged, of course," whispered back Maureen. "Up to now, I have somehow managed to keep myself busy being a daughter, wife and mother. But I am certainly going to educate myself on the history of Africa and its policies."

"I understand you are returning to America and getting a divorce."

"Yes, but what better place to do my research. No censorship there."

"Well, I wish you well in your new situation. If I need to contact you in America, maybe need your help in some way, would that contact be welcome?"

"Of course Moses, I will do whatever I can." Then she added, "Since Mom got sick in Scotland, I have always felt the need to take care of her. Now that I have to leave, see that you, Mike and Jacob look after her." Maureen was close to tears, but she giggled and said, "Or I'll be contacting you."

Colleen and Maureen walked back slowly realizing this might be the only time they have alone. "Maureen, our paths are going to separate for a little while. Right now I have to go to Zambia. Once there I will apply for a new passport and travel papers. I am not sure what Mike's long-range plans are but I know in time, I will return to America. I am getting a little too old for this political back and forth pull. I'm also way overdue on my tumor checkup." Sliding her arm around Maureen's waist, she said, "I know my journals of the Russian and Scottish side have been published but I'd like to send the handwritten manuscripts with you for safe keeping. Maureen, from this point on, you take over the family saga. Keep adding to Nicholas' original words. Do this for your children and their children. The story must continue and always weave the three cords through people's lives."

They had almost reached the bottom of the hill when Colleen stopped and faced Maureen. "Talking about the three cords, my necklace which my mother gave me on her death bed, I want you to take it and keep it safe for me."

"Oh Mom, I couldn't, you always wear it."

"Maureen, one day it will be yours, but right now I want it kept safe. It would not be wise to wear jewelry like that while marching through the bush; anyway you will need it. I remember how emotional my divorce was. There may not be the three cords in your life as it hasn't in mine, the husband part was always missing, but the motto of relying on God will see you through."

Everyone agreed it was a good escape plan. Colleen and Mike set to work with legal papers, sorting their property, packing, etc. Gail made the 'Colleen dummy'. Moses bought, with Mike's money, the electronics and some weapons he thought they needed while making their way to Zambia. Colleen had her knife and key holder from her younger days, but Moses thought the four adults needed guns. To make a dangerous time seem like fun and adventure for the boys, Moses bought them each a toy cap gun.

Everyone was ready; they had even had a dry run using the dummy and electronic equipment. Colleen had called and made the appointment for Mambo, knowing of course that her phone was tapped. The police were now aware of the vet's appointment.

CHAPTER 30

On Thursday evening for the sake of the police listening through the bugs, Colleen said, "Mike, remember when you leave tomorrow evening, you need to take Mambo with you. His veterinarian appointment is first thing Saturday morning."

"Sure, I also need to pull my car into your garage. I must rotate the tires, drain old oil etc."

Friday during the late afternoon, Mike worked on the car—the garage door was left open. If they wanted to, the police could watch. But as expected, they got bored and returned to their car talking, and listening to their radio. Wiping grease from his hands, Mike walked up to the police and asked what station they were listening to. He liked the music and wanted to turn his radio to the same station. With his radio turned a little louder than needed, Colleen and Gail were able to pack the car. Any noise they made would be hid under the sounds of the radio and Mike's working on the car. They never spoke while in the garage. They did not want to be picked up on the bug hidden next to the water heater. Their voices, pre-taped, were playing in the kitchen, getting supper ready.

A roll away mattress had been cut to fit the *boot* of the car. This is where Gail and the two boys and their backpacks were going to hide until the outskirts of Johannesburg. Colleen was going to curl up on the floor of the front passenger seat, covered with a blanket that would extend over the front seat. That's where Mambo would be sitting going to his supposed vet appointment the next day. Sleeping pills had been added to the boys' milk. They could not take a chance of them making noise. At 7:30 Mike carried the two sleeping boys and laid them in the *boot*. Gail climbed in and lay beside them. Mike covered them with a blanket. Kissing Gail, he said, "Are you going to be all right?"

She nodded. "Just a little nervous."

Colleen folded herself on the floor in the front while Mike covered her. "Sure you'll be all right, Col?"

"Of course, I've been in tighter spots before."

Mike pulled his car out into the driveway and closed up the garage. He went back into the house, supposedly to say goodbye.

For the bug's sake, he said, "Well, I'm off. The work on my car took longer than I thought. Earlier today I moved your car to Sheree's driveway while I worked on mine. I did not want the sap from the trees marking the paint. I will move it back tomorrow and work on it."

The plan was to leave it at Sheree's. The following week it would be taken to a garage. The engine was going to be given more power, changing it from a granny car to a souped-up getaway car. Then it would be taken to a body shop, not to beautify, but to be partly destroyed. Paint roughed up, scratched, tail lights broken, seats cut and duct taped, windows cracked, the inside ceiling cut and left to hang down. It had to look like a junk car. Colleen had given it to Moses. So it had to look like a black man's car, but act like a well maintained racer. Mike switched on the prerecorded taped answers.

"That's fine Mike, don't forget to take Mambo. Let me just get his papers. They are in my desk." Mike switched on the light. The 'Colleen dummy' was already seated. Everything was set.

"Come on, Mambo, let's go."

Mambo jumped into the front seat. As the police walked towards the car to check which they always did, Mambo lunged for the window barking and growling, getting saliva all over the window. The police waved Mike on. "*Tootsies,*" they called to one another.

At the prearranged street, Mike stopped and picked up Moses and Eli. They sat in the back while still in the town area. After a safe distance, they turned off of N. 12 onto a side farm road and everyone changed places. Colleen, Gail and Mike sat in the back, the two sleeping boys made comfortable on their laps. Moses drove with Eli as the passenger. Mambo was demoted to the spot Colleen had before. They knew they had maybe sixteen to eighteen hours before the police would suspect something was wrong. Moses wanted to reach Nelspruit before that, so they could start north on foot while the car traveled south taking the police on a wild goose chase.

The trip took them through the night and half of the next day. Once they reached the spot Moses was looking for they finally stopped. It was good to stretch your legs after such a long drive. They watched as Eli disappeared heading south. Mike knew he would never own such a good car again. They had been dropped off at a very isolated spot at the foothills of the Drakensberg Mountains and quickly disappeared into the dense growth. Moses did not want anyone to see them. The two boys and Mambo could not be held back. Being confined for so long, they had pent up energy to run off. Each adult had a backpack and Colleen had her walking stick. At times she still had problems with her left leg.

"We're only going to walk for two hours today," Moses said. "As we drove through the night and half of today, we are sleep deprived and sleep deprived people make bad decisions."

The campsite that Moses chose was one he had used many times before and was ideal for protection from the elements, and it had a watering place. They carried food for tonight and all tomorrow. Then, they planned on living off the land. Sitting around the fire, Moses laid out the plan for the next section of their trip.

"I have used these mountains many times before. Like this campsite, I have many sites spread around. Some up the mountain, some down the mountain, even a few inside the mountains. This is how we will be moving around while listening in on the police radios. Once we know they are not trailing us, we can be a little more comfortable in a village that has hidden me before. I know the people. This duffel bag I am carrying has equipment that we must all be familiar with using." Unzipping it, Moses explained, "These two small guns are for Colleen and Gail."

"I don't know how to use a gun," said Gail.

"Don't worry; our days won't be just moving from campsite to campsite. As we move, you will all be trained to use your weapons." Moving next to Colleen, Moses put his hand on her leg just above her ankle. Feeling the knife strapped there, he said, "Good, now I know many years ago you received training in the use of this knife, guns and radio operating; yours will be a refresher course, but one thing I've added for you Colleen, is this," and Moses took a walking stick out of the duffel bag. "This will replace your old stick." The curved top screwed off. Inside was a compass and miniature first air kit. The bottom of the stick could unscrew, exposing a very sharp point, turning the walking stick into a spear or lance. Everyone was given his or her weapons. Zack and Daniel sat wide-eyed. This was exciting, this wasn't play-acting; this was the real thing. Moses fiddled in the duffel bag and brought out two belts with holsters and two realistic looking cap guns.

"And this is for you boys. From now on remember, not too much noise as we travel and don't use your caps until we tell you its okay." As the boys played with their cap guns; Moses showed the three adults how to use the two-way radios.

Lying around the embers of the dying fire, Colleen thought, how strange, she was a fairly wealthy woman. She owned three homes and had many comforts in these homes. Now, here she was on the run, sleeping in the open on the ground, smelling the dying fire, listening to the sounds of Africa; the insects, the night birds, the hunting bats, the yip of jackal, the grunt of a badger. In the distance she even heard the bark of hippo. She realized how much she missed this. So while they were fleeing the ugly part of Africa—the beauty of nature and the animals—the best part of Africa surrounded them.

As the days passed, they all got efficient at using their weapons and the radio. Any extra weight they had was melting off as they walked and climbed. Colleen was so glad she kept up her walking over the years. Mike was concerned for Gail and their unborn baby.

"Don't be silly Mike; this is good for both the baby and me. Have you noticed how much stronger little Daniel is and Zack, he's just glowing."

The radio confirmed what Moses had hoped for. The police had no idea. After three weeks the trail was getting cold. "I think it would be safe to go to the village now," said Moses. "You'll be a little more comfortable."

"Moses, if the police aren't anywhere near us, why don't we just head for our first border?"

"I would like to wait until New Years Eve," said Moses. "The guards will be drunk and ready to take a bribe."

"You want to cross at Beitbridge?" Colleen asked, surprised. "I thought we would cross the river a few miles away from the border post."

"I am a little hesitant with that Colleen. If, and that's a big if, we can find and steal a canoe, there's the crossing of the mighty Limpopo. In that canoe will be a big dog, two little boys, everyone's backpacks and weapons, a pregnant woman, and excuse me, Colleen, a grandmother. Only two men to do any rescuing and saving if needed; No, it's too risky."

"You're right. Well it's only three weeks to New Year."

Making their way to the village, they passed magnificent scenery in the Blyde River Canyon. It was still thickly forested and full of animals. As they approached the village, Moses asked everyone to be quiet, while he crawled on his belly to check. He crawled backwards to them. "It is too quiet and it just does not smell right."

"Smell!" laughed Mike. "You mean you can smell something in that village at the bottom of the hill?"

"Yes, it's a—, a—mixture of unwashed European smell, someone who smokes and drinks hard liquor and the smell of death."

As Moses was thinking, Gail said, "Let's just skirt the village."

"No, I can not just leave. These people helped me more than once. I need to check this out. There is a cave back the way we came. I will take you there and then return to see what's going on." In the cave, Moses removed his backpack.

"Colleen, you and Gail stay here with the boys and Mambo. Mike and I won't be long."

"Moses, wait. I know you think of me as a grandmother, but I can still help." Moses hesitated, so she added, "That is why you bought me a gun and this fancy walking stick, isn't it?"

"Colleen, I know your skills and that is exactly why you are the one to protect these four lives." Moses looked in the direction of the pregnant Gail and the two boys. "I feel strongly about this, Colleen. Remember my wife and boy, were taken from me. We can not let the same happen to Mike's wife and boys."

Colleen agreed to be the protector. Turning to Mike, Moses said, "I need your help to lift a lid on a trap. All these campsites had been and still are hiding spots. Most have booby traps. This cave has, at it's opening a deep 9 x 6 foot hole with pointed stakes."

Mike and Colleen saw what Moses meant when they lifted the lid, which looked like earth. The lid was placed in the cave and a screen was fitted over the hole then covered with branches and dead twigs, looking quite natural.

"This is the plan," said Moses. "We will make our way to the waters edge, the women should be coming down to collect the evening water for cooking." They did not have long to wait before the women started coming down in pairs. That was strange since they usually all came together. Swana and her sister were the last to come.

"Swana, don't look up. This is Moses. I am behind the tree, to your left. I've been watching your village for hours. Something is wrong."

"I am pleased to hear your voice again, *Nkosi*. Your wound, it is well?"

"Yes, it is well." Moses had forgotten that she'd stick to manners and inquire about his health before talking business.

"You are wise, *Nkosi*. All is not well. Hiding in our village are poachers. They have kept the village elder tied up, threatening his life if we go for help, or if we don't keep them hidden."

"How many are there?"

"There are six white men and eight black men."

"The white men I could smell. But why do I also smell death?"

"When they arrived last week *Nkosi*, two of our men and a child were killed in the battle. They have not allowed us to buy them, saying it must be left as a reminder to us." As Swana placed her pail on her head, she said, "You will help us?"

"Yes."

"How?"

"I'm going to pass you a handful of bullets. Go back to the village and wait for my birdcall. Then walk past the fire in the center of the village and drop those bullets in the fire, as you do this you must fall to the ground. Don't worry, they are only blanks but will sound like the real thing. Tell your people to shout and run around. I am hoping it will cause confusion and the poachers will run in all directions."

Moses crawled through the grass and laid a handful of bullets on the pathway. As Swana passed, she picked them up and placed them in her pocket. She never looked in their direction. Mike and Moses retreated to a safe distance.

"We're badly outnumbered, twelve of them and two of us." Moses thought a while. "When the bullets explode, I am hoping they will scatter. Now I don't think they will go toward the river or the left side of the village because of the cliff. So we need to concentrate on the half circle from cliff to river."

Moses and Mike started work. They sharpened branches into daggers, spikes and spears. Then circling the village, Moses set traps; traps that would come up from the ground or down from a tree, traps that would throw them into the air or squash them under rocks. Mike was impressed. "Where did you learn this?" Moses just grinned.

"So that you don't run into these traps, I want you up that tree. Get comfortable, take my gun as well, and load up. You will be the sniper and will pick them off one by one."

"But you will need your gun. Moses."

"No, I'll be too close to them. This is what I'll use," and he held up his knife. They were ready. Mike climbed the tree; it was a good spot. He turned to give Moses a thumbs-up sign but he was gone. A few minutes later in the opposite direction Mike heard the bird call. He counted to himself. Before he reached ten, Swana dropped the bullets. As Moses predicted, there was total confusion, the villagers were screaming and running in all directions.

It was easy for Mike to pick out the poachers as they ran about in confusion looking for the enemy. Every now and again, he would hear a scream, as a poacher would set off a deadly trap. Two men were running towards the tree he was in. Mike shot one but the other poacher looked up and took aim at Mike. Out of nowhere Moses' knife flashed through the air. In a blink of an eye, Moses ran past; pulling his knife out of the man's back and disappeared in the undergrowth. Slowly Mike and Moses picked them off. Mike had shot four, Moses and his traps had killed five. "We're missing three." Just then they heard a shot from the area of the cave. They dropped everything and ran. Someone did climb the cliff.

Colleen had made herself comfortable at the mouth of the cave. Mambo lay at her side sleeping. Toward the back of the cave, Gail was keeping the boys busy playing. "Let's build a fort with these rocks." Zack and Daniel were running around picking up rocks and stacking them on top of each other. Every now and again Gail would look towards Colleen. Just a few months ago, she was living in Alexandra with her son under terrible conditions. No husband, and soon to lose her home, which in turn, would lead to her losing her job. She remembered praying to God to help her; she wanted her life to change. Now she was married to a wonderful man, had not one but three sons and was expecting a baby. She was on the run to a better life. Her mother-in-law, a white woman, certainly did not act like a mother-in-law or a grandmother. There she was sitting on guard at the cave opening. Yes, he answered her prayers all right. Life had changed. Both women jumped when they heard the screaming and shooting.

"Come on boys; let us hide behind your fort wall." Colleen and Mambo were on the alert. Mambo heard them before Colleen did. He was growling. Three of them were running straight towards the cave. "They must know about the cave," thought Colleen.

The first man fell through the wire onto the stakes below, his scream lost in the shooting from the village. The other two men caught themselves at the edge. There was not a thing could do to help their friend. Looking up, they saw Colleen behind a boulder in the cave mouth. She had her small handgun aimed at them. They drew their guns. Mambo, seeing Colleen threatened, ran towards the men. As he passed too close to Colleen, he bumped the gun out of her hand. It clattered down toward the hole.

"No, Nooo," screamed Colleen. She could picture Mambo falling on the stakes, impaled like her first Mambo. He made the jump only to have one of the men hit him with his revolver as he landed. He fell backward and slid into the hole.

"Nooo," screamed Colleen. "Not again, not again." Both men backed up to get a running start to jump the hole. Colleen picked up her walking stick exposing the point, she shouted, "Gail, boys, use your guns."

As the men jumped, Colleen heard Gail's gun and the two cap guns. The two men landed in the cave; one dropped from Gail's shot. The other man dove for Colleen. She held up her new walking stick, the man impaled himself and fell heavily on top of her.

Moses and Mike got to the cave as Gail and the boys were trying to pull the man off of Colleen. They jumped the hole with no trouble. Mike could see Gail and the boys were unhurt, but his mother, she was lying at a funny angle and a man was on top of her. Sticking out of the man's back was Colleen's new walking stick with its spearhead. Mike and Moses dragged the man off Colleen, but she didn't move. When Mike tried to lift her, her head rolled to the side and her arm hung limp, like a rag doll.

"Oh no! No, no Mother . . ." Moses, Gail and the two boys stood watching, "Is she dead?" Asked Daniel.

"No!" shouted Mike, "My mother is not dead." Clutching Colleen to his chest, Mike said, "Mom, Mom, wake up . . . wake up."

Colleen had the wind knocked out of her when this giant of a man fell on her. Slowly she came to, she heard Mike calling her, calling her Mom, and not Col. Colleen struggled out of Mikes crushing hold,

"Mike, you called me Mom, that's the first time you called me Mom." Mike was laughing and crying at the same time.

"I thought you were dead, and then realized you had never heard the words Mom from me. I could not help but remember something Gail said some time ago when we thought Zack was dead. She said, she would miss hearing his voice call her Mom. It hit me that you had never heard me call you Mom, and I did not want you to die without hearing the word—Mom."

This time Colleen crushed Mike to her. "Mom, you are crushing my ribs!" Everyone laughed.

But then Colleen remembered and screamed, "Mambo, Mambo is in the hole."

Moses climbed down and lifted Mambo up to Mike. The gun had knocked him out and he had slid down the side of the hole, not falling backwards onto the stakes. Colleen was crying and holding him. He was whimpering and licking her face.

Moses and Mike collected the twelve bodies. "What should we do with them? If we contact the police, and then leave before they get here, they will question the villagers. They may put two and two together and know it was us."

"Let's just bury them," said Gail.

One of the villagers had just cleared a field to plant corn. A huge grave was dug in the field and the twelve men buried. Then the corn was planted over the grave. Identifications had been removed and in time would be sent to authorities. The three bodies that had been killed when the poachers arrived were buried according to the village customs.

The villagers welcomed this small group of people who had saved them. Moses and Mike helped repair the damage that was done while the poachers were there. They would hunt together, so each night they had plenty of meat. Colleen and Gail learned skills from the village women. In turn, the village women were able to learn from them. The boys had a wonderful time playing. Daily Daniel got stronger but Gail noticed he was quite backward in some abilities.

In the evenings, the boys were asleep early. All the outdoor playing and work tired them out. The adults enjoyed conversations around the fire. Swana and her sister Kwna always sat with them. Colleen became the great storyteller. Mike and Moses had so many gaps in their lives; only Colleen could fill them in.

"Start at the beginning Mom—from the time of Nicholas, the Russian and Maureen the Scot." Gail, Kwna, and Swana sat on the edge of the rocks as Colleen spoke.

They're last night in the village, Colleen wanted to enjoy the outside, so she dragged her bedding outside next to the fire. She lay there enjoying the African sounds. They reminded her of Michael and their youth, time spent in the tree house or running across the velt. Mambo alerted her with his tail wagging that someone was coming. It was Moses. "Can I join you, my white mother?"

"Of course."

"Tomorrow we leave on the last leg of our journey. We may not have time alone again. There is so much I want to thank you for. I do not think I ever thanked you for saving my life." Colleen tried to say something but Moses stopped her. "When I visited the old Zebra Run camp and saw the anthill, it was driven home to me how lucky I was. So for my life, my upbringing and all the advantages I had, I thank you. I do not know how I can ever repay you."

Colleen took his hand. "There was no need Moses. Think of this, by taking Mike, Gail, their two boys and unborn baby out of Alexandra, you've given them a new life. You have saved their lives." Moses nodded, and then Colleen continued. "I know the work you are doing is very dangerous, please take care of yourself. One more thing Moses, you kept your wife and son from us, for their and our protection. When your pain heals and you are ready to take a new wife and have more children, don't keep them from us. Moses nodded his agreement.

They reached Messina late afternoon of the 31st of December. Celebrations were well underway and many people were drunk. This tiny group was hungry for something different to eat, but being the mixed bunch they were, they could not go to a restaurant. Colleen was elected to go food shopping. Moses and Mike were going to look for a car to steal. To keep Gail and the boys' safe, they were taken to the edge of town and a little off the main road.

"How about that car?" Said Mike pointing to a very nice looking red Chevy.

"No, too good; we'll stick out in that car. Look for something a little beat up."

"Well, how about that one?" This time Mike pointed to a car that must have been in an accident it looked so bad.

"No, too bad, it will also be remembered. We must not stand out. We must blend in. We must be a "nobody" in the crowd." Moses settled for a pale yellow Kombi, well used but not memorable.

"Mike, check on Colleen and the two of you head out to where we left Gail and the boys. Be ready to fly when I come with our yellow bird."

The five of them were ready when Moses drove up. They jumped in and enjoyed traveling by car instead of walking. They drove to within a mile of Beightbridge, and then slipped down a side road. The smell of Cornish pastries, sausage rolls, and fish and chips was driving them all mad. They sat quietly enjoying every bite of this supper. Colleen had bought the two men beer, and she and Gail and the boys enjoyed an ice cold Coke. Mike had bought each boy a sweet. They nibbled away at it trying to make it last. Moses turned away; he remembered the sweet he had bought for his boy so many months ago.

At 11:45, they drove up to the first border post on the South African side. Again as Moses predicted, the black and white officers were quite drunk. Colleen and Mike were the ones to enter the building. Mike carried a beer for everyone and wished them all a happy New Year. Colleen picked up the immigration papers and filled them out with false information. The officer stamped them and moved on to the next person. No one noticed that Mike had left an envelope on the counter containing the identification of the poachers. In a day or two when things got back to normal, someone would fine the envelope and hand it over to the police who in turn would notify the families.

As Colleen and Mike came out of the building, their hearts stopped. Two white police were pulling Moses from the car while shining their torches at Gail. A thousand thoughts ran through Mike's mind. Is it the stolen car? Is it Moses because—he's wanted by the South African police? Or was it because of Colleen, an escapee? Mike took a deep breath so he would be calm.

"Happy New Year" and he gave them each a slap on the back. "Have a beer on me," and he handed them each a Castle Lager. "Hey, what are you *kerels* doing with my *Kaffier?*"

"Sorry man, we just saw a *Kaffier* and a colored woman sitting in this car. Just didn't look right if you know what I mean."

While Mike was boiling with rage, he calmly said. "That's my muntu; he always goes with us when we travel. Hell man, I don't do my own work. And that woman is a nanny. If you look closer, you'll see my children sleeping on the floor."

"Sorry man, thanks for the beers."

They drove in silence over the bridge to the other border post. The border guard waved them on with no incidence. As they drove, Mike said, "Moses, Gail, sorry about that. I had to play along with them."

CHAPTER 31

They crossed Zimbabwe without incidence. The border into Zambia, especially this one at the Victoria Falls, brought back a lot of memories for Colleen. "We only have a days ride to Broken Hill, where Peter has his farm," said Colleen. "I'd like to make a suggestion and a request. So that we don't look completely unkempt, let's spend a night in the motel (Zambia allowed different races in public building). I have inches of dirt to scrape off as, I'm sure you do."

"That sounds like a good suggestion," said Mike. "Now what's the request?"

"Do you want to see where your father grew up and where you were born?"

Mike's eyes grew wide. "This is the area where 'Lagenwa' is?" Colleen nodded. "Of course, I want to see it; I want to see everything."

"Can we come too?" shouted the boys. But Gail stepped in saying, "No, this is a special moment for your dad and Colleen."

Mike waited in the car while Colleen climbed the steps to the house. She couldn't believe it was the same manager that took over so many years ago. They welcomed Colleen and Mike. They were made to drink coffee and eat fresh milk tart. The house hadn't changed much. They had added more rooms, so the guest quarters were larger. It was still a popular tourist spot. Colleen pointed out to Mike the rafters she and her mother hid behind, showed him the bedroom he was born in, the veranda where she and Michael would listen to the BBC. The spot where a piano stood that he played. They then used horses and trotted around the farm, the house Michael lived in, the house where Moses lived; the tree where Moses was killed, the mango tree, the hot springs. Lastly they stopped at a huge tree. "The tree house is no longer there, Mike, but you can see the marks we made as we climbed up."

"Well, come on, the house may not be there but we can still climb it." Sitting on the branches and looking down at the view, she had to bite her lips—looking at Mike sitting there she saw Michael. She also remembered Shawn sitting there.

Colleen signed, "That was a lifetime ago. When we left, you were not even two days old, strange that you'll be living not too far from here."

At breakfast the next morning, Moses announced, "I am not coming with you to Peter Cambell's farm." Mike was surprised, "Why not Moses, you will be made welcome."

"Oh, I'm not worried about that. I just do not want anyone at the farm to see us together, if Mr. Cambell and Marnie should be traced. If Colleen should be traced, I don't want the situation made worse because I was with them. What farmhands don't see, they can't talk about."

"What are you going to do?" asked Colleen.

"I have some contacts to make. In fact, one is picking me up in an hour. Six days from now, tie a white cloth on the farm's gate. That will tell me all is well. If the cloth is red, I will know you need me. Wait, and I'll contact you."

As they said goodbye, Colleen said, "Moses, please promise to keep in touch."

"I will."

"Another thing, take this money and the next time you are in Swana's village, use it to have a well dug. That way they do not have to carry water so far."

It was a long driveway from the main road to the farmhouse. They passed mealie fields and sweet potato fields. Being a Saturday Mike knew Marnie would be home. Stopping between the house and the barn, Mike slowly opened the door. He was both nervous and excited at seeing Marnie again. Mike started towards the house but stopped, he'd heard voices from the barn. Turning he walked to the barn. Coming out was Marnie, leading a horse and his dog Rex at his heels. Marnie stopped when he saw Mike and stared for a few minutes. Dropping the reins, he ran. "Dad, Dad," he yelled then threw himself into Mike's arms. Mike was not expecting that and fell backward with Marnie on top of him. They rolled around laughing. Rex ran and jumped on top of them. Peter came out of the barn to see what the commotion was. He grinned from ear to ear watching father, son and dog roll in the dust.

Mambo was scratching at the car door to get out. Colleen let him out, and she walked over to Peter, Mambo at her heels. Gail and the two boys got out of the car but stood waiting. Mike held Marnie at arms' length. "You've grown so tall and look how brown you are." Marnie stopped laughing and looked at his dad.

"But you've got so thin, Dad."

Mike looked down at himself. "Not thin, my boy, I am in tip top shape. No more love handles. Hey Marnie, do you remember what you prayed for the night before you left?"

Marnie thought a while. "Yes, the same thing I pray for every day. That you come and live with Grandpa and me, that I can have a mother and brothers and sisters. That way I won't be so lonely."

"Well, your prayer has come true."

That night after the children were tucked into bed, Peter heard the whole story. Mike's arrest, his experience in Alexandra, Moses' arrest and escape, Gail helping Mike, the threat on Zack, Daniel's experience and, of course, Colleen's house arrest. The months they'd spent in the bush while waiting to cross the border.

"It's hard to believe that the actions taken by one woman could cause so much damage and hurt. I apologize for what my wife and daughter did to ruin our lives."

A few days after arriving at Peter's farm, the neighbor came over. He was from England and wanted to return, he wondered would Mike be interested in the farm. It was very reasonable and it backed on to Peter's farm so they could work the land together. It had a very large house, big enough for four children or more. After a lot of discussing and planning Mike and Gail decided to buy the farm, it was too good a deal to pass up. If they should later decide to return to South Africa or move to America, the farm could be sold or left in Peter's hands.

On the sixth day, Mike tied a white cloth on the farm gate. He also left the yellow Kombie by the gate. Maybe Moses would need transportation back to South Africa. That evening when he checked, the white cloth and Kombie were gone.

Life settled into a comfortable routine. Mike's farm had a guest cottage with a beautiful view; Colleen used this as her writer's cottage. She would walk from her cottage to the main house. Peter would come from his bachelor's cottage to the main house and they all had breakfast together. Then the men left for the day, dividing the farm work. The two huge farms kept them very busy. Colleen would drive the boys to school, check the mail and do the grocery shopping for all three homes. Once home, she'd spend the day writing. Then back into town to pick up the boys. The school bus did not drive out for the farm children. Gail would take care of the home, cooking and preparing for the new baby. Mike bought a computer and Gail would also keep the farm records.

Colleen always listened to the South African news. They had given up on catching her. The last she heard they thought she'd returned to America. In time Elizabeth's house ban was lifted. A week later while she and her mother were driving along the coast, their car mysteriously went over the cliff into the ocean. Colleen wondered if it was the work of Jacob or Moses. Both had threatened the woman.

Moses often had his name in the news. So far he had always escaped the traps they set for him. One morning coming back from dropping the boys off at school, there was a white cloth tied to the gate. She looked around but saw no one. Untying the cloth, there was a short note and a picture of Moses and Swana.

All is well. As promised, a picture of my wife.
The Village thanks you for the well.

Moses kept in touch, always by means of the white cloth. He had enemies everywhere so, for his and Colleen's protection, he was a shadow that passed by every now and then. He now had a daughter.

Mike, and Gail, made a wonderful loving couple. They were brought together by some very sad events and endured a lot together. Because Mike had empathy for different races and tribes, the men that worked his farmland gave him their best. The result was the farm was productive, making a good income for him and his workers.

Marnie and Zack were joined at the hip. You'd have thought they were born brothers. Mike beamed with pride when the three of them worked together, road horses together or went hunting together. Daniel was dealing with some health issues. Too many years of hunger and eating garbage left their mark on him. Gail was patient and taught him to use the computer. This not only helped him with his schoolwork, he even began to help her with the farm records. Then, of course, there was their daughter, Meggie. She was the apple of Mike's eye.

Jacob had completed his papers on the Europe castles. While doing research on Africa's history, before and after the arrival of the white man, he worked at the university. It was at the university he met and fell in love with Rachel. They were getting married in six weeks time. But since his immediate family could not come, he was having two weddings, one in Johannesburg, for the sake of Rachel's family and his aunt and uncles, the other service in America for his family. Colleen, Mike and family, were flying from Zambia to America. Jacob and Rachel were flying from South Africa via Scotland they would arrive two weeks before their second wedding date.

Maureen was living in North Carolina. She had divorced Adam and was granted custody of her twins. Laura and Shawn were now ten and doing well at school. Adam had remarried, but he and Maureen remained friends. Maureen's home was a big rambling beach house there was enough room for everyone. Maureen had offered to have the wedding and little family reception at her home. The setting would make for beautiful pictures.

What a wonderful family reunion, it had been years since Colleen's three children, and many grandchildren were all in the same house, for that matter even the same country. She curled up in a chair and enjoyed the moment. Maureen, Jacob and Mike were telling each other what had happened over the last few years.

Jacob said, "Mom, I understand you gave Maureen the journals from the 1800's for safekeeping. I have a package that needs to be kept with it for safety." Colleen looked at him questioningly. "When this trouble started, Mike arrested and sent to Alexandra, and you put under house arrest, all because of the race issue, I decided to do some investigating on my own. I wondered how many people could claim to have a pure line. You will be surprised."

Jacob spread out his chart. "As you know, in the 1600's, when the white people arrived at the Cape, it was a boatload of men. They were to establish a trading post that would supply ships from Europe with fresh food on their journey to the east. Well, nine months later the so-called 'colored' race started appearing. In time, white women arrived from Europe. But quite a few men kept their black mistresses in the background. It took quite a number of years for the so-called 'white' race to grow. In the meantime, black and colored wives were kept on the side. Look at this, Mom." With his finger Jacob traced backward quite a few prominent names.

Colleen could not believe what she was looking at. "Are you sure about this, Jacob?"

"Mom, that's what I do, research. I had to dig deep; many records were even sealed. This is accurate."

"If this information ever came to light a lot of lives would be destroyed. Some of these families could be hiding their skeletons but others may be unaware," said Colleen.

"I know. This is the only copy I made. I was thinking it could go into safekeeping with your journals. The information being used only if really needed."

"It could ruin so many lives of the so-called upper class," said Colleen. "But on the other hand it could stop thousands of middle class and poor people's lives from being destroyed." A thought struck Colleen. "Jacob, you had better be very careful with this information. Your life maybe on the line, talking about life on the line, do you know anything about Elizabeth's accident?"

"Don't ask, Mom."

Maureen then added her bombshell. "I could not write or call about my secret. But I have not been a pampered housewife these past years. I am also leading a double life."

"What?" All eyes were focused on her.

"I am Moses' contact in America. I do his record keeping. I raise money for his cause. I have even arranged some weapon transactions. So in a way, I do undercover work." Maureen laughed at the look on her mother and brother's faces.

"You two better be careful. Just remember, Mike and I are no longer in danger."

"It's no longer just about what they did to Moses, Mike, and you Mom; it's the whole concept of apartheid. It needs to be abolished."

CHAPTER 32

America—1995

Alice Ross was the New York agent that represented Colleen. She was busy editing Colleen's, fourth novel when her secretary knocked at her door and walked in. Without even looking up, Alice held up her hand. "Not now, Penny, I am almost done here."

"Sorry Alice, but he insists it's important."

Alice looked up annoyed. "What?" She was obviously irritated at this interruption.

The man was in his late fifties with distinguished gray hair, very tall and lean. He had a lopsided grin. "My name is Joubert; I just flew in from Paris. I know from this book cover that you are the agent for Colleen Miller. Where can I find her?"

"Excuse me, that is not the kind of information an agent gives out."

"It is important that I find her," said the man.

Alice's phone rang, picking it up she said, "Penny, show the gentleman out." Someone else came in with a load of papers and put them on Alice's desk. Another phone rang; she was on two lines at the same time.

Joubert gently loosened his arm from Penny. He closed the office door and pulled the phone jacks out of the wall. Standing in front of the desk, leaning towards Alice, he said, "I will not be a gentleman for much longer if you don't tell me where to find Colleen."

"Really, Mr. Joubert, do you want me to call security?"

"Alice, you have read Colleen's books haven't you?"

"Of course, but . . ."

"Alice, I am Michael!"

It took a few minutes to sink in; she was still holding the two phones she had been talking into, now they dropped to the floor as she fell back in her chair.

"Michael!"

He nodded, there was that grin again.

"Michael!"

He nodded again. "You okay, Alice?" he asked.

"Yes, yes, of course. Oh my God, what news this is." Alice was really confused; she started pacing. "You cannot just walk in there; it might be too much for her. She, she, she, uh, she's . . ." Michael took Alice's hand. "Sit down, do you want some tea?"

"Yes, please."

Michael turned to Penny who was also smiling. "Could you get us some tea Penny?"

Alice collected herself as she sipped her tea. "Let me call her daughter and see what would be best."

Maureen answered the phone. It was late afternoon and Colleen had spent the day working on Jacob's and Rachel's wedding; she had just left for her usual long walk down the beach. Jacob and Rachel were stretched out making their final travel arrangements; the wedding was on Saturday. Mike was installing a new computer in the office. Colleen was going to type instead of hand writing her next book. The room Maureen had turned into an office for her mother overlooked the beach. She would be able to see the sunrise every morning.

Maureen was very quiet as she listened to Alice. "Oh my God," her hand flew to her mouth. Jacob and Mike looked up.

"What—, what—, you look like you've seen a ghost."

"No, Jacob—Mike, its—its—Michael." There was a long silence.

"Michael is at the agency; he has asked Alice for Mom's address. She wants to know if it's okay to give him my address." Turning back to the phone, Maureen said, "Of course it is Alice—Mom is not going to believe this."

"Maureen, I'll call you back with his flight arrangements, just a minute he's indicating something to me." After a pause Alice continued, "Michael said, not to tell Colleen, he wants to surprise her." About an hour later the phone rang, answering it Maureen expected Alice, but a deep rich voice said,

"Hello Maureen, this is Michael speaking," Maureen got goose bumps; this was the phantom man. "I have called all the airlines that fly into Wilmington; the earliest flight I can get is the 'red eye' at 4:00 AM tomorrow morning. That should bring me into Wilmington about 5:30; I will take a taxi from there."

"No, no, Michael, we will pick you up."

"Thanks Maureen, how will we know each other?"

"We will know you, from a picture on your CD cover, and you will recognize the person waiting at the airport."

Michael had collected his bag and was waiting at the front entrance of the airport. He was tired and excited, but at the same time he was nervous. What if it was just a dream he had held onto these past forty years? What if she did not feel the same about him? He got up and started to pace, a voice behind him said, "Hello Dad."

Slowly Michael turned around, that was his voice he had just heard. He was looking at himself, about thirty years ago. This man even had the same lopsided grin.

"Mike," he whispered. Then again louder, "Mike!" Mike nodded grinning. Michael pulled Mike into his arms. It was a very emotional time for them both. Eventually Michael pulled back and held Mike at arms length, laughing through tears he said, "Son, are you going to take me to her?"

Mike, and Michael, could not stop talking as they drove to Maureen's house. Mike told his father that he had a picture of him, his wife and daughter. Michael laughed. "That wasn't my wife; it was my wife's sister who helped me raise my daughter. My wife died twenty-five years ago."

Maureen opened the front door to this man that was always, yet never in their lives. "I am Maureen and I have to tell you, at about six months old, I was in your tree house." Michael pulled her into his arms; it was like looking at Colleen. He stood holding her for a while.

Jacob walked up, "I'm her other son, Jacob." Jacob put out his hand to shake but Michael pulled him into his arms for a bear hug.

"Where is she?" he asked hoarsely.

"Every morning and evening she goes for a walk down the beach. She's due back any minute. She will be coming up over those dunes."

Michael looked around. "Good, you have a piano. I would like to play it. Many years ago when your mom and I were still teenagers, I composed a song for her. I never finished it before leaving for London. Years later when I did, I refused for it to be released. It was her song; it was just for Colleen. As she comes over those dunes, I would like to play it. I wonder if she will remember."

Jacob went out to look down the beach. "She's coming!"

Mike, Gail, Maureen, Jacob and Rachel moved to the gazebo outside. They wanted to watch but be out of the way. Michael settled himself at the piano, closed his eyes, and took a deep breath.

He was a hundred miles away; it was a hundred years ago.

His fingers flew over the piano and worked magic on the keys. The music drifted down the beach. Colleen smiled. Maureen must have put on one of her tapes. She slowly strolled over the dunes, and then stopped. That wasn't one of her tapes. That was her song. Michael had started composing a song for her called 'Colleen' but he never finished it before he left. She was hearing parts she hadn't heard before. The song was completed—Who?

The music stopped. She stopped.

Michael got up form the piano and slowly walked down the deck steps and across the sand.

He never took his eyes off her. He stopped inches from her.

Reaching out he touched her hair. He then ran his fingers over her lips.

Looking into her eyes Michael knew she still felt the same.

He slipped a ring on her finger; it was three cords woven together of copper, gold and silver.

He had remembered.

Inside was inscribed the words; Love never fails.

They stepped into each other's arms,

Their lips met as though it was yesterday.

All her pain was washed away.

THE MAIN CHARACTERS FROM BOOK TWO

Journey of Courage

Abraham Zulewsky—married—Hope Van Vuren

Their Children

Colleen
Sheree
Gordon
Charles

Colleen Zulewsky—married—1ˢᵗ Marriage Michael Joubert.

Their Child

Mike

2ⁿᵈ Marriage Robert Miller

Their Children

Maureen
Jacob

The story of Mike, Maureen, Jacob & Moses
will continue in a third book

GLOSSARY

Ar-o-drum—Airport
Bonnet—Hood of car
Boot—Trunk of car
Boom—Tree
Baie Dankie—Thank you
Braaivleis—Cook out
Bwana—Master
Biltong—Dried Meat
Cot 1—Folding camp bed
Cot 2—Baby bed—crib
Cornish Pastries—Meat Pie
Dominee—Priest
Dorp—Town
Eiderdown—Comforters
Hooter—Car horn
Jumbo Mfundisi—Greeting
Kaffier—Degrading term for black people
Kaffier boetie—Brother to a black man
Ke'rel—Boy
Kippers—Dried fish
Klim—Brand of powdered milk
Knopkerrie—Baton
Koeksisters—Braided sweet doughnut
Koffee—Coffee
Konfyt—Rind of watermelon boiled and sweetened.
Kudu—Deer
Kwaheri—Goodbye
Limy—English man
Lorry—Truck
Lekker—Delicious
Larger—Circle of wagons—defensive camp
Meneer—Mister

Mealies—Corn
Muntu—Black man
Melkos—Milk soup
Nappies—Diapers
Nog-al—Even though
Nkosi—Title of respect
Ouma—Grandmother
Oupa—Grandfather
Oros—Fruit flavored drink mixed with water.
Petrol—Gas
Padkos—Food for the road
Primas—Camping stove
Pram—Push chair
Rondoval—Round mud house
Rusks—Dried bread
Shandy—Beer mixed with 7 up
Sundowners—Drinks served at sundown
Squealers—Men trapped in a mine cave in
Sies—For shame
Tickey—English coin worth three cents
Totsiens—Goodbye
Voetsek—Get away
Veranda—Deck porch
Vasbeit—Hold on
Wireless—Radio

ABOUT THE AUTHOR

Shirley was born in South Africa in 1941. Her schooling was done in Northern Rhodesia. After working in the Copper Mines for a number of years, she became a teacher. She now lives with her children and grandchildren in North Carolina, USA.